Zombie Hae

Part 1 of A British Zombie Apocalypse

By Iain C.M. Gray

Copyright

Amazon Self-Publishing

This book first published in Great Britain by
Amazon 2021
© Iain C.M. Gray 2021

Iain C.M. Gray asserts his moral right to be
identified as the author of this work

No part of this text may be reproduced,
transmitted, down-loaded, decompiled, reverse
engineered, or stored in or introduced into any
information storage and retrieval system, in any
form or by any means, whether electronic or
mechanical, now known or hereinafter invented,
without the express written permission of Iain
C.M. Gray

ISBN: 9798766193524

This is a work of fiction. All names, characters, places, and incidents either are products of the author's imagination or are used fictitiously. Any resemblance to actual events or locales or persons, living or dead, is entirely coincidental.

Information about the author and details of other work by Iain C.M. Gray can be found at iaincmgray.com

This book is dedicated to John (Ian) Gray, (1842 – 2020), my father; he never got to read any of my stuff, but I know he would be proud.

Prologue

The sun slid slowly off to sleep, as night rose to cloak Scotland in its deep grey shroud. The fading light shimmered over a thin slick of oil that mirrored in the softly undulating waters of loch Brimmington. The oil spread its incongruous rainbows over the surface of the small loch.

Fireflies and midges buzzed around in pretty patterns of random happenstance, spinning like electrons around an invisible nucleus. Squawks and chirps, and the trilling of various birds, spoke of their last communications before retiring for the night. Darkness was coming to the land. Nocturnal animals stretched out their bodies and limbs getting ready for their nightly exertions.

A soft mist rose from the loch as cooling air interacted with waters warmed by an unusually balmy Scottish day. The wispy mist twirled and flirted with the brooding twilight.

Baring brook trickled its meagre contribution into the waters of the loch. The little brook wound down from a hilltop, past the neglected remains of farmyard buildings, pooling in various places before joining the deeper waters of the loch. At one of the pools a little vole scurried to the side for a drink. He sniffed at the water, wrinkled his nose, and then scampered away, disturbed, his thirst unquenched.

The water was no good.

A neglected farm loomed in the nook of a valley between two treeless hills. Broken down barbed wire fencing surrounding the farm told of a past where security measures were once considered necessary. Plants spray their seeds effortlessly over the fence. Voles and other small rodents plop through the gaps in the fencing, while larger animals burrow under the fence without any due impediment. Curious human beings had bent and broken the rusty wires in various places to gain access; empty cans and various other detritus evidenced their social presence.

In one of the farmyard barns an old, rusting, barrel stood emptied of its contents. The noxious liquid, once safely contained in the metal vessel, had leaked out and oozed its way through the ground, and into Baring brook.

The clear oily liquid had flowed down with the brook and saturated loch Brimmington. At a molecular and microscopic level within the liquid a pernicious, malignant, virus proliferated. The virus desperately sought a suitable host to enter into, with the express purpose of complete organism mutation, it desperately craved heat, blood, protein, brains, oxygen, sentience. The virus required life in order to destroy life.

In the loch, billions of needy parasitical molecules searched frenetically for the perfect host to achieve the pinnacle of its evolutionary quest. The fish in the loch were cold bloodied, they would not do. The insects and larvae in and around the loch were too small, and insignificant, they would also not do.

Animals. Warm bloodied, mobile, oxygenated, conscious animals were required. The virus innately knew what it needed, wanted, craved, and nothing would prevent it from achieving this supreme objective.

The animals around loch Brimmington wouldn't drink, or even touch, the water. By instinct, one sniff of the water was enough to alert them to the contamination contained within. The virus had investigated the loch in its entirety; there was no obvious way out to continue its fervent quest.

Near the bottom of Brimmington there was an ever so slight drip, drip, dripping sound of water seeping slowly out of a valve, into a large pipe leading away from the loch. The pipe led to loch Mintern, which sat further down the hill.

Mintern was much larger than Brimmington. At the bottom end of Mintern there was a collection of buildings interconnected with pipes and pools. The buildings intimated of the potential for life. A sign on the gates enclosing the buildings provided the information that this was 'Greenock Water Refinery'.

Underground pipes led from the water refinery to Greenock, Gourock and Port Glasgow, a collection of

Scottish towns sprawling along the banks of the river Clyde. The area was a hive of activity. Human beings shopped, drank, and visited friends; children noisily played outside in the unusually warm Scottish evening. Life was busy, obliviously, happening.

The virus waited, hungrily.

Part 1

Chapter 1

The activities inside signalled a change of shift at Greenock Water Refinery. The back shift was clocking off, giving way for the night shift to take over. Weary men and women rummaged about in their lockers. Track suits and jeans replaced blue, functional overalls; training shoes replaced steel toe capped boots. The night shift reversed this process.

Idle banter pinged between the changing workers in the mens' locker room.

Sitting on one of the old worn-out benches lining the walls of the locker room, tying his shoes, John Deacon raised his head to address Innes McDonald, who was nearly changed and ready to leave. "So, where you off to the now then, Inny?"

Innes's body language communicated belligerent defiance. "I'm off to the boozer, obviously. The missus is away at her sisters wi the weans, so I get a couple of free nights. First off, I'm away to the Hole in the Wall to neck a few gills." This proclamation was accompanied by the gesture of a raised arm twisting a wrist to empty an imaginary glass into Innes's thirsty mouth. "Then it's probably off to the curry hoose for a cheeky wee vindaloo." Innes stood boldly with hands on his hips, defiance writ large in his watery bloodshot eyes. "At least that's the plans anyways. Probably need to play it by ear. Once the old vino collapso starts to flow plans often go awry, eh John? You know what I mean?"

"Och you're an awful man for the bevvy, so ye are Inny."

"Aye, that's as maybe Johnny boy, that's as maybe. However, must get on, eh?"

The ritualistic process of changing shift continued in momentary silence, the air was thick with judgements emitted from John, and denial run deep from Innes. Innes chewed vigorously on gum; the taste of his sneaky sup, consumed in the toilets a couple of hours ago, had all but faded, his need to get to the next one was growing exponentially.

"Do you reckon McGregor has slept in again then, Inny?"

Innes snorted a laugh, relieved that the subject had moved on from his penchant for alcohol. "He's the only lad I have ever heard off that can actually sleep in for the night shift."

"Aye, sometimes I just don't know what is going on for that boy, I really don't," John was probing for gossip.

"He's a good lad though. And not a bad wee grafter when he sets his mind to it." Innes was in no mood to indulge John in his desire for defamation.

"I just don't know where his mind is at most of the time, Inny. He looks like he's miles away sometimes."

"Aye, I don't fuckin' blame him for that mind. Being miles away from this fuckin' place sounds awright to me."

John laughed, "We'll soon be miles away ourselves, Inny. You off to the boozer and me off to my old dear."

"Aye, unless she's changed the locks while you were here, Johnny boy. She might still have the hump about your new chainsaw."

"Aye, Inny, that she might. I'm still well in the dog hoose for that one. But she is a beauty of a chainsaw. Well worth the money, all mod cons on her, small and light too. Well worth a couple of nights in the old dog hoose." John's wrinkled features exuded pure, unadulterated joy.

"See you laters, Johnny boy. Same time same place tomorrow, eh?"

"Aye, Inny, same time same place."

Reflecting on his life; married with children and grandchildren, John Deacon left the Greenock Water Refinery, his place of employment for the last 20 years. He strolled to his car, an old Volvo: safe as houses, and as solid as a rock.

Innes finished getting ready, before heading out the door. He was motivated by an escalating need to satiate his craving for more alcohol. "See you later Jean. See you Stella," Innes nodded to the ladies in the gatehouse on his way out.

"Aye; see you later Innes" responded Jean. "Now, you be a good boy tonight, won't you? I ken well your Mary is off at her sisters, and I know what they say about when the cat's away. But you play too hard, Mr McDonald. We don't want you getting into any trouble." Jean faced Innes with a fierce look on her face.

Adopting an air of obvious saintliness, Innes exaggerated offence. "Jean Gourley, I cannot believe you are doubting my honour. On this fair evening, I shall be going straight home. After visiting church of course."

"Aye, if your church is called the Hole in the Wall, Inny," overhearing the conversation, Stella pitched in.

"Stella, not you as well. Do you ladies have no faith?"

"I don't know anything about faith. But what I do know is, that you are officially a reprobate. It's just as well you're a grafter, or you would have to be classed as a complete and absolute waste of space."

"The only waste of space around here is the space around you Stella my love; I would come and fill that space with my warm, eager body any time. I am, forever, all yours."

Stella blushed bright red, "Oi you, I know your Mary, and I think she'd have something to say about you cosying up to me."

"Aye, you could be right Stella. I wouldn't want to upset your John either I suppose. Perhaps I best just bugger off to the Hole in the Wall after all." Innes puffed out his chest and shrugged off imaginary chains binding him to the drudgery of work.

"Aye, Inny, accept the inevitable I suppose. Just don't do anything *really* daft. And try and stay out the cells for once, eh?"

"Aye, will do Stella, see you tomorrow sweetheart. See you later Jean, eh?"

"Bye Inny," they both shouted as Innes ambled onto the bus that would take him nearer to his regular hostelry.

The hustle and bustle of the shift change at Greenock Water Refinery settled down as last few stragglers from the back shift headed onto the bus. Night shift staff filled the vacated posts at various machines and computer terminals.

Just as the bus pulled out, and away from the refinery, a taxi sped into the parking lot, a light stirring of dust swirling up and away from its tyres. The taxi disgorged a dishevelled and panicked looking occupant. Flattening down his unruly and disobedient hair, the occupant flew through the gatehouse and into the factory. "Awright Jean, awright Stella," he hollered as he scooted past.

"Good evening, Kenny," they shouted at Kenny's receding back as he disappeared into the changing rooms. His clothes were rapidly removed, to be replaced by a pair of dishevelled looking overalls and tatty steel toe cap boots.

"Did you clock in, McGregor?"

The dishevelled figure imperceptibly shivered and tried to appear as calm and composed as possible.

"Not as of yet Jim. I'm just on my way to do exactly that now."

"Late again then, eh?"

"Aye Jim, just a wee bit I suppose. I had a bit of trouble starting the car this morning, so I had to get a taxi."

"It's the night shift McGregor. It's not fucking morning. And that car of yours seems to have a lot of trouble starting. And it's not the only one, its owner seems to have a lot of trouble starting too."

Kenny pulled a sheepish a smile, "Sorry Jim, I'll get the car looked at, I promise. I'll just go clock on. What am I on tonight?" Kenny tried to get the topic of conversation away from the personal and as close to work related as he could.

Jim Mackenzie (known colloquially, and secretly, as Mac the Sack) sighed, the inevitable intervention to address Kenny McGregor's timekeeping, and general lackadaisical attitude, would have to wait for another time. "You're on the pipes and monitors. And tonight, you might actually have to do some work. Due to all the hot days, and lack of rain, Mintern is running low. It's looking like we'll have to pull some water down from Brimmington."

Kenny was pleased to be not talking about his timekeeping. "Just you let me know when you need more of the old H_2O eh." Kenny feigned an air of efficiency both of them knew was false.

"Aye, McGregor. We will indeed keep you in the loop and up to speed regarding any further work-related communications. Now fuck off out of my sight. You really are a just a fucking waste of space." Jim marched off to his office.

Kenny, accustomed to getting away with things, flounced off in the direction of his allocated workstation, the pipes. It was a simple job and meant that he would have ample opportunity to indulge in his full-time hobby of consuming mind-altering chemicals. Hashish and temazepam were on his menu for tonight.

As he breezed across the refinery floor towards his workplace, Kenny was blissfully unaware of the number of eyes that followed his every move. Eyes that spoke of the same subject but from divergent perspectives. Eyes that communicated concern and worry, "*What kind of state would Kenny be in tonight.*" "*Will we get him through the shift without him being sacked?*" And eyes that spoke of disgust and virtuous judgement. "*That boy needs a good slap.*" "*It would serve him right if he were to get the sack*". "*He's a liability, a health and safety nightmare, a danger to all of us.*"

Settling in at his workstation, Kenny checked the gauges and connections, tapping the meter faces to make sure the dials were not stuck. He ran through a diagnostic check on his computer to ensure the readings were all as they should be. He base-lined all the measurements and satisfied himself that he didn't need to do anything, then allowed his eyes to wander round the refinery floor.

Danny Henry was there, Kenny noted. He nodded over. Danny nodded back, scrutinising Kenny to establish what kind of state he was in, Danny subconsciously tapped his back pocket, feeling the hard shape of the half bottle of wine nestling there. He knew, as everyone else did, that Kenny was being watched, closely, and that management were looking for an excuse to get rid of him. Danny correctly concluded that with the focus of attention being on Kenny, it protected himself somewhat from any unwanted scrutiny. Danny was free to quietly indulge in his own interests.

Long-time refinery staffers, and allies of Kenny, Joe and Bobby were assessing the situation, they glanced at Danny. Eyebrows were raised in question. Shoulders were shrugged in response. It all looked ok so far, but that could all spin on a six-pence. Joe and Bobby were going through in their minds what kind of interventions would need to be made to get Kenny through another night without killing himself or others. The threat of him being sacked was forever present, employment in Greenock was scarce and being fired was akin to receiving a death sentence.

A more in-depth assessment of Kenny was required. Joe grabbed his trolley and casually started a tour of the factory floor, stopping at various workstations, exchanging pleasantries, and making general enquiries about what tools or supplies people needed.

He made his way round to Kenny. "Awright, Kenny boy?"

"How do, Joe?"

I'm awright, how are you?" Joe tried to put as much significance into his question as he could.

"Fine and Dandy, Joe, fine and dandy." Kenny either missed, or ignored the subtext of the question.

Joe studied Kenny closely, weighing up his words, checking his eyes and body language. He glanced round the room at Kenny's allies, who were waiting for a hint as to what kind of night Kenny, and by default, they, would be having. Joe gave a non-committal but overall positive shrug. Kenny's intoxication levels looked reasonable for the time being.

"Awright then. I'll be off on my rounds then. Make sure you let me know if there is anything you need." Emphasising the *anything,* Joe hoped he got the message through that there were people in the factory looking out for him, if only he could clear his head for long enough to realise it.

"Aye, will do Joe, no worries, no hurries dude." Kenny returned to pottering around at his workstation.

Joe returned to his trolley and carried on with his rounds, leaving Kenny to his own, somewhat dangerous, devices. Kenny had not slept in for the night shift this time. The reason for his tardiness tonight had been a visit to the notorious McDonald brothers, top dog local drug dealers, prior to starting his shift. Kenny's hand rummaged in his overall pocket as he sought out his tobacco tin, just to reassure himself that the tin, and its precious contents still existed. He was relying on these contents to get him through another very dull nightshift.

Twenty minutes into his shift, Kenny knew it was early to start consuming his stash, but it was so incredibly dull for him being on the pipes. He had done his initial checks, and now all he had to do was monitor the dials and computer screen from time to time, to keep an eye on the diagnostic information. The only authorised form of entertainment was the refinery radio, which piped middle of the road music, at just about audible levels, around the refinery.

Kenny tapped the dials and checked the computer screens again. All was as it should be, so he decided he might as well start with his own un-authorised evening's entertainment. He took a deep breath and scanned the room. There was no sign of Mac the Sack, so, with exaggerated nonchalance, he ambled down to the disabled toilets.

Once he was inside the toilets, Kenny morphed from being a somewhat shambling and inept individual to being a focused, efficient, well-oiled machine. Everything he undertook from here on in was performed with practised precision. First, he popped a temazepam jelly into his mouth. Next, he carefully prepared a pipe with enough hash for just one big lungful of cannabis. Lighting the cannabis with a clapped out lighter, he watched as the hash first glowed bright red, then turned to ash white as it released its intoxicants. Holding his breath for as long as he could, to prevent the recognisable musky odour from pervading the toilet, he snorted slightly and blew out what little unabsorbed smoke there was, straight into the air vent.

The effects from the quick blast of cannabis were instant, the receptors in his brain fired and sparked, sending signals all over Kenny's body and mind, his arms and legs tingled, and a warm calm filled his stomach. The effects from the temazepam jelly would start to make themselves known in about 10 to 15 minutes. Kenny popped some eyedrops in his eyes to combat redness.

He looked at himself in the mirror; he was 22 years old, but already had a few grey hairs poking through his mop of dark brown tousled hair. He had a couple of small scars on his face from various scrapes with other people, and other unremembered incidents. He was thin to the point of skinny, largely due to his liquid and pill diet.

Kenny licked his finger and ran it over each eyebrow. That would do. Through the distorting lens of mind-altering chemicals, he was convinced he looked like the coolest person on the planet. Other eyes saw him as he truly was; someone who was deeply troubled and descending inexorably into increasingly harmful behaviour.

Taking a deep breath, Kenny centred himself and unlocked the bathroom door. He sauntered casually out to resume the pretence of gainful employment. His stomach was just starting to tingle with warmth from the effects of the temazepam jelly. Walking across the refinery floor to his workstation, Kenny was blissfully unaware of the resentful, judgemental glares he was receiving from his co-workers.

Two of his colleagues discussed their malcontentment, "Been to the bogs already, eh?" Most of Kenny's workmates had realised that his numerous visits to the toilets and subsequent degeneration into intoxicated uselessness were connected.

"Aye, and the shift husnae even hardly started yet. It's gonnie be a long night."

"Did you see the state he was in yesterday when he left? He wisnie even there. Look into the eyes and he's vacant. The lights are on, but there's naybody home."

"Aye, I know. If Mac the Sack had seen him his arse woulnae have touched the ground. He would have been Joe le Toff there and then."

"I know. He'd be long gone if it wisnie for Joe Dunlop and Bobby Thompson."

"I don't know why they bother; they'll get no thanks for it in the long run. Trust me, they are just putting off the inevitable. That boy is getting worse. Some nights he cannie even see by the end of the shift. It's fucking disgusting, I'm telling you."

"I'm not gonnie argue with you on that one, Conn my old China. Whatever happens it is not going to end well, let me tell you that."

Conn O'Mara and Peter Clarke parted, stimulated, and warmed by their aired judgements. They anticipated that they would soon be getting ring side seats for a particularly spectacular fall from grace starring one Kenny McGregor. Neither Conn nor Peter had any desire whatsoever to consume drugs; drugs scared them. But there was no doubt that Kenny had embraced the drug taking lifestyle, and the fact that this seemed to make work more enjoyable for him caused anger, resentment, and fear. They knew Kenny was consuming some form of drug, repeatedly, during his shifts. And presumably he was doing this because he enjoyed it. The question that plagued Conn and Peter was: why should Kenny be enjoying his work when, for them it was nought but a pointless grind, to be endured only by adopting an attitude of magnanimous stoicism?

But they could never bring themselves to report him; that would violate the worker's unwritten code, that you never 'clipe' to management about anyone. The concept of 'us and them' superseded their obsessive desire to see Kenny caught, publicly shamed, and punished. It was unfortunate, but workers stuck together, even when one of them was patently a twat.

Conn and Peter returned to their respective workstations to observe the events of the evening from a safe distance. Their desire to witness the public shaming of an obviously flawed human being remained, for the time being, unsated.

Jim McKenzie strode back onto the refinery floor. His gaze sprayed the floor like laser beams shooting out from under his wrinkled brow. His massive forehead was furrowed by the heavy burden of middle management, and one too many life lessons. Just by noticeably staring over the refinery floor he would increase vigilance and compliance with company policies and procedures, the purpose of these policies more often than not completely lost in their slavish implementation.

"McGregor", Jim shouted across the refinery. The tension on the floor escalated, was this the moment everyone had been either waiting for or dreading? Had there been an unseen disciplinary indiscretion? "Before the end of the shift you need to let out 100 units from Brimmington. Make sure you don't forget or there'll be some dry mouths down in Greenock soon. And don't forget to make sure the valves are shut off and re-calibrated afterwards. Alright?"

"Aye, aye, Mac", Kenny responded, a small section of his brain was already acknowledging that the chances of him remembering this 6 hours later were somewhat slim.

Jim bristled. Though Kenny had not uttered his full nickname, he was well aware that the workers called him Mac the Sack. This had a conflicting effect on him. The nickname cemented his tough reputation, which was necessary and useful, but it also reminded him of the disdain and disrespect conferred upon middle management by the workers. Jim had served his time on the refinery floor and had experienced and expressed the same disdain towards previous middle managers. Now the boot was indeed on the other foot, it was him that was in charge now, and there would be hell to pay if people didn't acknowledge and respect him as the boss. Jim bristled with resentment as he marched back to his office. "I'll get that little fucker one of these days. His arse is not going to touch the floor when I get him," he muttered, not-so-under his breath.

"Did you hear that Joe; we need to keep an eye on Kenny the night, Mac the Sack is gunning for him."

"Aye Bobby, I heard. It's gonnie be a long night, Bobby son."

Joe had been working with Kenny since he started at the water refinery. Joe liked a drink the same as the next man, but he couldn't for the life of him understand the drive to obliterate yourself with drugs. Having two teenage children he greatly feared the world that they were growing up in. Life seemed filled with many more dangers than when he was growing up, and drugs were one of the most feared lifestyle pursuits in this part of Scotland.

Joe was hard wired to look after people; he desperately wanted to make sure Kenny was given a chance. Bobby was Joe's long-time workmate; they had developed a friendship that continued out of work. They both liked a round of golf at the weekend, and a small bet on the horses from time to time. They both lived near each other on the Stones estate in Greenock. Bobby supported Joe in all of his ventures, therefore he also looked out for Kenny.

Bobby had teenage grandchildren and had even less of an understanding about what drugs were than Joe. What effects they had and why people took them was a mystery he had no interest in probing. He just wanted to keep his head down until he could retire, so it was with some measure of reluctance that he involved himself with Kenny and his like.

Bobby remembered an extra risk factor in the increasingly complicated issue of keeping Kenny McGregor from getting fired. Daniel Henry. Danny was in his late 20s and had slid down the slope from being an attractive and sought-after party animal in his late teens, to becoming just another raddled Scottish alcoholic.

"We need to keep him away from Danny as well, Joe, he'll no help any situation."

"Aye, I know. Danny is on the tanks though Bobby, you know that means they'll need to work together."

"Shit and corruption, I just hope Danny doesnae have any of the "who you looking at" in with him."

"He will; he always does."

"It just messes Kenny up worse when he adds the bevvy on top of all that other stuff."

"I know. Gonnie be a long night Bobby son."

Joe and Bobby gazed with worry at an increasingly detached looking Kenny.

The effects of his first temazepam capsule had made themselves fully at home in Kenny's central nervous system. The sober, straight Kenny floated away on a sleepy, green, river. He completely zoned out. His anxiety, and undiagnosed borderline personality disorder, were quelled and subdued. He became quite at ease with himself, watching the dials on his computer screen flicker and twitch as they measured the water levels in lochs Brimmington and Mintern.

The figure of Danny Henry swayed and rocked into Kenny's ever-decreasing peripheral vision. "Danny boy, me old China. How's your arse for love bites?"

"No bad, Kenny, not bad at all bud." Danny studied Kenny for reactions, "Did old Mac the Sack give you any gip for being late the night?"

"Aye…well…kind of…I dunno…I get the feeling he don't really like me much!"

"And I guess that feeling is mutual."

"I don't mind him really; he can be a bit of an arse sometimes I suppose. He really needs to just chill out, you know, let his hair down a bit."

"He's not got any hair left to let down, that's the problem right there, Kenny-boy." Jim McKenzie's hairline had unfortunately receded rapidly from a young age. "You been letting your own hair down yet Kenny boy?" Danny puffed out his chest and made his move, "You been to the bogs yet, Kenny?"

"I might very well indeed have paid a wee visit to the little boy's room, Danny. I do have my evening's entertainment sorted." Kenny gave his tobacco tin a little pat. "How about you fella, you got your usual?"

"Aye, a cheeky wee bottle of *"who you looking at"* is nestling most comfortably in my hip pocket right now. You up for a little chaser for your *'entertainment'*?"

"Do you know what, Danny boy? A little snifter of the old LD would go down nicely right now. Shall I go first?"

"Aye; traps 4 and 5 Kenny boy. The usual." With the evening's collusions sorted, Danny felt more secure with his own self-indulgent plans. He had established his connection with Kenny and had been given reassurance that Kenny would be joining him in his journey into oblivion. This provided Danny with the safeguard that, no matter what state he ended up in, Kenny would be in a much worse one. This would deflect any heat away from him onto Kenny.

With an overtly nonchalant air, Kenny ambled off towards the communal toilets. At this stage of the shift the toilets were quiet. Everyone was busy getting the evening's operations moving, doing obligatory tests, and sorting out the various tools and supplies required to ensure the shift kept functioning.

Kenny ensconced himself in the fourth cubicle from the entrance. He knew Danny wouldn't come straight away, as it would draw attention, so he occupied himself by having another hash pipe. Just as he gently exhaled, he heard Danny enter the toilets, singing gently to inform Kenny it was him. They had performed this undertaking many times, so the operation was like a finely tuned military manoeuvre.

Kenny heard the door to cubicle 5 close. Bending down to peer through the gap he could see Danny's steel toe cap boots planted firmly by the toilet bowl. Danny unleashed a mighty fart. Kenny couldn't help but splutter muffled laughter.

After a couple of minutes wait a small, flat, green bottle came poking through the gap in the cubicle wall. There was a sizeable amount of the liquid missing, nearly half of the half bottle. Kenny undid the cap and swallowed about a quarter of the remaining contents. His taste buds were fully sensitised by his cannabis consumption. Considering the taste of the wine, this was not a good thing. He barfed, but didn't throw up. He passed the bottle back and exited his cubicle.

"There's no one here dude," he gently called out to Danny.

Danny stepped out of his cubicle, smacking his lips theatrically. "That's me ready for another shift methinks, Kenny boy."

"You wanting any jellies, Danny? Or a wee toot of hash?"

"Naw, I don't think so. Them jellies just knock me out, and hash just makes me para. I'll stick to the LD I reckon. I've got another wee half decker stashed in my locker for after dinner This one isnae gonnie last."

"Aye looks like you've been caning it a bit, Danny. Mac the Sack was on me again this morning, old cunt."

"That's why you should take it easy on the old jellies, my son; they fuck with your head, Kenny boy. You were in a hell of a nick with them the other night. And it's not morning Kenny, it's a night shift."

"Aye, I know; it's my morning though." Kenny couldn't take advice from anyone, least of all from someone who drank as heavily as Danny did. Kenny popped the lid of his tobacco tin and flicked out another slick, green temazepam capsule, which went straight down his throat.

"And you know Mac is gunning for you tonight, Kenny boy. Your jacket is on a proper shaky nail son. You'd better watch out, seriously."

"Aye, Danny, whatever mate." Somewhere deep in his subconscious these words had an effect. The greater mass of his consciousness was drifting and floating away. Most of his thought processes were slowing down and clouding over, distorting under the effect of the various chemicals he had consumed. But there was a small voice that was just able to exert some modicum of control. The small voice was a moderating influence, promoting a logic-based survival strategy. To further pursue his ongoing chemical experiments access to funding was required, ergo work, hence the need not to get sacked. Also fighting to be heard above the morass of chemical oblivion was the image of what it would be like to have to inform his mother that he had been sacked from his job. Jobs were hard to come by in

Greenock, and if you had the privilege of having one you were supposed to not wreck it by being a fuck up. Kenny needed not to get sacked, but he also needed to not feel, to not be Kenny. Unfortunately, Kenny needed drugs.

He took a deep breath; "Hey ho, Danny boy, I'll go first eh?"

"Aye, Kenny boy. I'll give you a couple of minutes then I'll follow you out."

Left alone in the toilets, Danny took out his half bottle and assessed the amount. He took a quick peek at the toilet door, listening for the sound of doors opening. All was quiet; he drained the bottle. Popping a couple of Polo mints into his mouth Danny also took a deep breath and bounced back to the refinery floor.

Chapter 2

Innes McDonald rounded the corner of Copper Street and Bagshot Road at a brisk, determined march. Approaching the Hole in the Wall public house he heard the familiar grumble a room full of Greenockians makes after an evening spent systematically imbibing alcohol. The general ebb and flow of indistinct chatter and laughter was punctuated by the occasional screech of a drunken woman, or the incensed howl of a slighted, confused, drunk man.

Pausing at the door Innes began to discern distinct voices. The ubiquitous bark of Robert McKillvany could be heard over the general hum. "Utterly preposterous," he heard Robert shouting, "Utterly, absolutely preee… poss… ter… oooose." This was Robert's universal war cry.

Innes sighed with anticipatory contentment and pushed open the door. He could taste the smell of alcohol in the atmosphere. The pub was busy, as were most public houses in Greenock on a Friday night. All the regulars were present, with Robert holding court at a tall round table next to the fruit machine. "So, then he says to me, '*Rab sometimes I just doubt your commitment*'. Commitment? Me? Committed to fucking Plaster, Optics and Electronics? I don't fucking think so McClumpha. The only fucking thing I am committed to is wine, women and song. Utterly fucking preposterous."

"Aye, so when was the last time you pressed the flesh of a maiden then Vanie?" Innes said as he whacked Robert on the shoulder to announce his presence.

"Innes fucking McDonald, you old reprobate, how's it hanging?"

"No bad Rab, no bad. I'm fairly gagging for a bevvy though." Innes looked round at the various assembled drinkers, there were many familiar faces dotted around. Innes noted the presence of Dave Anderson and Ian 'Fergie' Ferguson who were buzzing around playing pool.

"Are we doing rounds, or have you got a kitty going?" Innes was keen to continue appeasing the untameable beast of his latent alcoholism.

Unsteady on his feet, Robert sidled over to Innes, mumbling drunkenly he pulled at Innes's arm to bring his ear closer to his mouth. Although discomfited by the proximity of Robert, and the spray coming from his mouth, Innes knew that he had to attend to Robert before he could start some serious drinking. "It's currently every man for himself, Inny my old son. Fergie is here; and he is being a cunt as usual, he's probably on the Billy Whiz. But I've had a wee result on the old gee gees. So on the QT I shall treat you to a half and a half. That sound cool Inn?"

"Sounds good to me matey. A half and a half would indeed be just what the Doctor ordered."

"Utterly preposterous Inny," Robert shouted, "Utterly preposterous." Weaving like a helicopter in a hurricane, Robert returned to his drunken whispering. "I'll be back in a tick with some refreshments. Make sure Fergie doesnae clock me though. He's such a cunt."

Innes propped himself on the edge of a bar stool and surveyed the room. This was a man's pub, though there were indeed a few couples dotted here and there. The wives talked among themselves, and the husbands sat quietly looking out enviously at the unfettered single men drinking raucously.

Robert came weaving back from the bar, balancing perfectly in both hands two half pints of lager and two large glasses of fortified wine. Although very unsteady on his feet, Robert spilled not one drop of alcohol. "Get that down your neck Inny me old China," he said placing the glasses on the table.

Opting to go straight for the wine Innes drained the whole glass in one satisfying gulp. The strong alcohol hit his throat and caused conflicting experiences. His taste buds sent the message to his brain that this tasted disgusting, causing a mild retch. The absorption occurring on his tongue told him that alcohol was now coursing through his bloodstream, sending flashes of dopamine across the receptors in his brain. Innes felt nice.

Somewhat suddenly, the atmosphere in the room altered dramatically. The sounds in the pub dropped in volume and the mood changing noticeably from carefree jollity to awkward, nervous, anticipation. There was a charge of electricity in the air that wasn't present a moment ago. Two very drunk lads, wearing Celtic tops, had just staggered into the pub. They were obviously not local, if they were, they would have known that the Hole in the Wall was a diehard Rangers pub.

They should still have noticed the sporadic Rangers memorabilia dotted about the bar. They should have noticed the charged reaction of the denizens to their entrance. They should have noticed the exasperated, silent, entreaty from the bartender to leave, thus preventing his pub from being wrecked. They should have noticed the number of eyes flicking incredulously in their direction. There were a lot of things they should have noticed. They didn't.

"Do you fancy a wee wine Billy." The speaker was short but stocky with badly bleached blond hair.

"Aye Bobby get us an LD....... Get us a pint as well but."

The barman's eyes pleaded, begged, and threatened, "Are you sure boys? Really?" The not so coded message was completely missed by Billy and Bobby. They had both consumed enough alcohol to blunt any instincts they would normally have possessed.

"Sure am my good man," Bobby slurred, his bleary eyes blinking hard in an attempt to achieve a level of focus that would ensure he was permitted to continue drinking. "Two wines and two pints of your finest lager please mine host."

The bartender surveyed the pub in front of him. He saw Ian Ferguson glowering over at the two newcomers, menace burgeoning behind his eyes. He noted that Ian and Dave had paused playing pool with their game remaining unfinished. "Oh fuck," the bartender muttered under his breath. '*It was all going so well too,"* he mused ruefully, *"Why my pub? Why Friday night of all nights? The politically correct brigade would have a field day if I refused to serve them. I can just see the headlines now, 'Sectarian barman refuses service to nice Catholic boys', och well, on their own heads be it.'* "There you go then gentlemen, two pints and two wines, that'll be £7:20 please." *'Best get their money before it goes tits up.'* "Enjoy your refreshments lads." *'While you can, better drink quick.'*

Bobby handed over a pile of coins and some crumpled notes that he estimated would cover the cost of the round. "Just keep the change my good man," he said feigning a posh accent. "Billy, I like the cut of that man's jib, what do you say?" he continued.

"What?"

"I am just saying that this looks like a fine hostelry to continue our merry making."

"Eh?"

"Och, you really are just a useless cunt, aren't you?" At the top of his voice Bobby looked to the roof and shouted, "Lord help me, could you not have provided me with a more intelligent and sophisticated companion." Bobby compounded his multiple errors by crossing himself theatrically.

Just at that moment, as fate would have it, the money ran out on the jukebox and the music stopped. The murmur of voices dropped dramatically, some of the older couples hastily donned their coats and left. In the vacuum of silence that was left the Celtic boys heard something that broke through their alcohol induced denial systems. The message that they had just, unwittingly, committed a fairly grievous error was rammed menacingly, and lyrically, home.

"*For it was old and it was beautiful, and its colours they are fine.*" In the conveniently timed silence Ian Ferguson launched into a gleefully malevolent version of The Sash. Arrogant faith in his violent capabilities was communicated in his every move.

The obvious danger of their situation broke through Bobby and Billy's drunken denial system like a hammer smashing a blancmange. They reacted instinctively; adrenaline coursed through their systems. The advancing loon singing The Sash, and twirling a pool cue like a baton, cut them off from their only opportunity for flight. Fight was therefore, unfortunately for them, their only option.

Bobby grabbed a half empty bottle of Newcastle brown ale from a nearby table. The only person in the place too drunk to notice what was happening reacted angrily to the disappearance of his beloved Geordie beverage, "Oi whose nicked ma bottle of dog?" He stared around with woozy eyes, then shrank as best he could once it dawned on him what was going on.

Being high on amphetamines Fergie did not feel the full effects of all the alcohol he had drunk; amphetamines plus adrenaline heightened his senses and caused his time perception to play tricks; everything seemed to freeze frame in slow motion. He saw the Celtic boy pick up and smash the bottle of Newcastle Brown, the brown foamy liquid cascaded in an explosive stramash around the old boy rueing the disappearance of his booze and doing his best to reduce his size.

Fergie saw, read, and relished the desperation writ large on the face of the Celtic boy as he wielded his broken bottle. Bobby knew he was beaten already, but he was not prepared to go down without a fight. Deep in Fergie's subconscious he acknowledged and admired the foolish bravery of the bottle wielding thug.

Fergie swung the pool cue in an arc aiming for where he knew the Celtic boy, by instinct, would bring the hand containing the broken bottle. Pool cue and bottle met in the briefest of violent unions, causing both to break. The pool cue split down the middle to be left hanging at a 90-degree angle. The bottle broke further to leave only the narrow throat. Bobby threw it away, he now only had fists and ferocity in his armoury.

Fergie discarded the broken pool cue, its job was done, it had nullified the threat from the broken bottle. Bobby flew at Fergie snarling, "Come ahead ya proddy cunt." He swung his fists desperately and without proper aim, the only possible purpose being the vain hope of achieving a lucky connection. Bobby prayed it would be enough to prevent the speed fuelled nutcase from battering his brains in. Fergie easily evaded the flailing fists and lurching, drunken body of Bobby. Bobby slid on the wet floor and crashed into a table, spilling more alcohol, and knocking over a couple of chairs. He bounced off the side of the pool table and ended up sprawled in a thin pool of booze snaking its way lazily across the floor.

Fergie grabbed him by the back of his Celtic top and dragged him to standing. "Come here ya fenian bastard." Bobby was dazed, petrified, and aware that his one chance to avoid a beating had spectacularly failed. Fergie propped him on the side of the pool table in one swift movement and followed up with a massive head butt, BANG, right on the bridge of Bobby's nose. Bobby's head bounced back, and his busted nose sprayed a shower of blood over the pool table and floor.

Fergie grabbed Bobby by the scruff of the neck and hammered repeatedly at his mashed-up face with a tightly clenched fist. Bobby's eyes had glazed over with the power of the head butt; now they gradually closed as unconsciousness intervened to save him from further trauma. Fergie let him go. Bobby slid to the floor to flop face down in a pool of blood speckled booze.

With a sinking feeling settling in his gut Bobby's friend Billy looked on in dismay. Bobby was by far the better fighter out of the two of them, and he was beaten easily. Billy was acutely aware that an equally grisly fate awaited him if he didn't do something about it quickly. Dave worked as a labourer on the building sites. He was short but built like a brick shit house. Dave was not as dedicated to fighting as Fergie was, (who considered fighting as his hobby), but he was equally as effective, and just as clinically brutal. "Where do you think you're going?" Dave growled, as Billy desperately began to sidle towards the exit. Dave was not about to let this particular fish off the hook, "You're going nowhere ya wee cunt, except the infirmary."

Resigned, Billy reluctantly accepted his fate, there was no way for him to escape, so he decided to embrace his demise with as much dignity as he could manage. Mustering as much bluster as possible he stood up to Dave Anderson. "Come ahead ye wee orange prick," he growled.

Dave's left arm shot out and he grabbed Billy by the throat, he wasn't expecting this, he froze. Then Dave's right arm flew with a swift, scything motion; round to smash a balled-up fist hard into Billy's jaw. Billy's jaw snapped; two teeth flew out his mouth in parallel arcs, riding high on a spray of drool and blood.

Billy went down poleaxed, searing pain cut through the adrenaline of the fight. He spat blood and bits of teeth onto the floor. Dave wasn't finished. As Billy squatted on the floor staring at his molars Dave ran and swung his booted foot into Billy's already broken jaw. Everyone in the pub flinched and averted their eyes. It was disgustingly violent. This was why no-one argued with either Ian Ferguson or Dave Anderson.

Unsurprisingly, Billy joined his friend in unconsciousness. Dave and Fergie admired each other's handy work. The pub was silent. The bartender breathed deeply, his eyes flicking between the prone bodies of Bobby and Billy and the door. He was concerned that the fracas might have attracted some unwanted attention. The Police and the ambulance service needed not to be involved, or there could be implications for his licence. The Police needed not to be called by him, or there could be repercussions from Fergie and Dave, and he most definitely did not want that. This was not the first time he had seen them in action, he knew what he had to do.

"You two fuck off now please," he said quietly, but firmly, to Fergie and Dave.

"We barred Jim?" said Fergie, the vulnerability of this comment was in stark contrast to the brutality of his violence. But this was Fergie's regular drinking den and general all-purpose hang out venue, he needed this place. The bartender knew that having Fergie both attracted, and repelled people in equal measure. He also knew that having Fergie on his side in a town like Greenock afforded him a certain measure of valuable protection.

"Naw, yir not barred. Just don't come back for a couple of weeks, eh? Lay low for a bit lads."

"Aye, awright Jim. See you in a couple of weeks then, eh?" Fergie was gleefully relieved.

"Aye, see you later Fergie, Dave."

"We off for a Ruby then Dave?"

"Sounds good." Dave dusted his hands and wiped them clean on his jeans.

Without a glance at the devastation left behind them Fergie and Dave grabbed their jackets and headed out the door.

Jim slouched over towards the devastation, assessing the damage done to his pub. Sylvia, his long-time barmaid, was a step or two behind him. "Best get the mop Syl," Jim directed her. Sylvia scuttled off into the back room, returning with a worn mop and a clanking metal bucket, from which emanated an overpowering smell of pine scented disinfectant. Jim righted knocked over chairs and picked up a couple of unbroken glasses. "Get the brush and shovel too Sylvia, there's broken glass as well."

Bobby and Billy were lying apart, united only in oblivion. But the pain from Bobby's broken nose was demanding attention. He made throaty, gurgling moaning noise as he gradually started to surface towards consciousness. He spat blood from his mouth. Jim got a pint tumbler full of water and threw it over his blood covered face. Bobby was jarred further into full consciousness. "Get yir mate up to the hospital pal," Jim told him. Bobby's bulging eyes scoured the pub for the head-case with the pool cue, he was immensely relieved that there was no sign of him.

Bobby dragged himself to his feet and winced as he saw the wreckage of his friend's mouth. Bobby was now acutely aware that he had gotten off lightly. "Billy, wake up pal. You'll be alright, I'll just take you up the hospital." Bobby gingerly shook his friend gently awake.

"Be careful what you tell them up there. You two wurney here, ok? And you most definitely don't want to be describing your attackers, awright? Cause if them two hear that you have been blabbing to the Hospital staff or the Police, they *will* come looking for you. You understand?"

Bobby was fully cognisant about what was expected of him. He helped his friend to his feet and they both supported each other out the door.

The remaining denizens of the pub looked on as the remnants of the carnage was quickly and efficiently cleared up. Jim and Sylvia had, by necessity, performed this operation many times. Jim scrubbed at the blood-stained pool table, there would be a permanent stain. The pub was quiet, no one said a word. People were grappling with how to respond to the brutality of the situation. Sylvia and Jim returned to the bar.

"Utterly preposterous", shouted Robert McKillvany, and the ice was duly broken. The sound of muted chatter resumed, and individuals returned to the bar to quietly, and without complaint, replace spilled drinks. The juke box resumed its musical accompaniment to complete the return to normality.

"Them two are complete bampots," Innes said to Robert.

"Aye, I know Inny, but they are *our* bampots; which means we tolerate their lunacy. Especially as this tolerance prevents the aforementioned lunacy from being unleashed in our direction."

"Aye Vanie, I suppose you're right. Drink up bud, it's my shout. A half and a half do you alright?"

Utterly preposterous Inny. Aye, a half and a half will do nicely," slurred a very drunk Robert.

Chapter 3

Jim called time. It had not been an evening without incident, but the takings still looked good. Seeing such extreme violence close up always seemed to make people drink more. Perhaps this was to erase graphic images of people being pulverised from flowing through their minds.

No matter what the profit margins were, Jim would have much preferred not to have seen the horrific brutality of Fergie and Dave. Plus, there would be the costs associated with replacing the broken chairs and glasses, and there was also the now permanently stained pool table to consider. His pub was never going to be classy, but blood stains on the pool table? That was a bit much even for the Hole in the Wall.

The blame for the contretemps though was being laid unanimously and firmly at the door of the victims: "*Them lads had it coming to them, imagine them thinking they could come in here wi Celtic taps on.*" "*They should have known.*" "*They should have just drunk up and scarpered instead of coming in here giving it large.*" In an all too familiar instance of self-serving collusion, no one blamed Fergie or Dave.

"TIME LADIES AND GENTLEMEN PLEASE," Jim called a close to the evening.

Innes and Robert were exceptionally drunk.

"We heading for a curry then Vanie?" Innes slurred.

"Aye, Inny. Whatever." Robert could hardly see, never mind eat.

"Them two heid-the-baw's will have gone to the Taste of India so let's go to Patel's instead, I don't really want to get involved wi them."

"Whatever you say my good man, whatever you say. Utterly preposterous." Robert swayed gently like a pendulum. His alcohol hungry eyes scanned the table ensuring all the glasses were empty now it was time to leave.

Weaving his way to the door, with his friend in tow, Innes called over to the barman, "See you laters then, Jim."

"Aye, see you later lads." Jim focused on tidying up his pub. Him and his barmaid slipped into their nightly ritual, a routine they knew well. They needed to get everyone out, get the door closed, and off home as quickly as possible. "TIME TO GO HOME, NOW!" Jim let it be known this was non-negotiable.

There were just a few drunk and determined hangers-on left as Innes and Robert bundled themselves out of the door. Jim and Sylvia were ready to start physically picking up the most reluctant drunkards in order to eject them from the premises.

The warm weather meant that no one was in a rush to get home, the streets were active with various Friday night revellers, content to be out and about, mixing with each other, though a certain level of violent tension was always present in Greenock. Innes was very drunk; his eyelids were making their way down eyes that could only have been described as rheumy. The pair staggered in silence through the town narrowly avoiding puddles of vomit or urine, and the occasional splattering of fresh blood.

They reached Patel's Curry House. Though it was late in the evening Patel's was still brightly lit and busy with drunkards. Patel's was not the place to be for a romantic dinner at the weekend. "Table for two please?" Innes asked the waiter.

"Not a problem sir. I shall be with you right away." The waiter was always well mannered regardless of the behaviour of his clientele. Innes and Robert were regulars, and their behaviour was regarded as reluctantly acceptable by the waiter, that particular bar was, by necessity, set low.

"Excuse me sir," the waiter asked of a customer, who was weaving his way round the restaurant. The customer had strategically bitten various holes in a naan bread and was wearing it as a mask. The waiter didn't bat an eyelid, his courteous manner remained intact.

"Naan Bread Man." Innes nodded acknowledgement to the man with food on his face. "Not seen you for ages. How you been?"

"Been busy out fighting crime, Inny. My mission knows no end."

"He's a fuckin' nut," muttered Robert. "Don't encourage him."

Naan Bread Man either ignored or didn't hear this proclamation regarding his sanity.

"Anyone require the assistance of a bread powered superhero?" Naan Bread Man hollered across the restaurant.

The diners at Patel's were accustomed to his performances, and Naan Bread Man was uniformly ignored.

"This way please gentlemen." The waiter escorted Innes and Robert to their table.

The waiter knew his customers well. "Can I get you gentlemen something to drink before I take your orders?"

"Two pints of lager please sir," Innes ordered. Robert was deeply ensconced in trying to un-button his jacket and was wondering when all his fingers were replaced with sausages. The waiter nodded, bowed, and clicked his heels together in one fluid, graceful movement.

Innes sat back and sighed; Naan Bread Man was still running around the restaurant pestering people. The first time he had donned the naan it was genuinely funny, and he got the plaudits and attention he craved. But that was many years ago and, despite the occasional flurry of amusement from new patrons foolish enough to eat at Patel's, his act now only earned him contemptuous derision.

Looking sideways at Robert sitting beside him almost completely incapacitated, Innes had a moment where his existentialist angst almost conquered the effects of all the alcohol in his system, the voice of his soul almost got through to his consciousness to ask the question: "*Is this it? Is this all there is to life?*" Innes was in danger of slipping into maudlin self-pity.

"Oi Raj, gie us another bowl of them spicy onions will you," Naan Bread Man shouted across the restaurant.

With a barely perceptible grimace the waiter turned, nodded, and clicked his heels again. "Right away sir".

Sitting alongside his existentialist voice, fighting equally hard to be heard over the thick swamp of sated alcoholism, the voice of Innes's righteous moralism raised an objection in his head. Thinly veiled racism was another reason to disdain and despise Naan Bread Man.

The waiter returned to Innes's and Robert's table with two pints of lager. As semi-respected clientele, serving Innes and Robert their alcohol was prioritised over spicy onions for Naan Bread Man. "Are you gentlemen ready to order?" the waiter enquired, with a fake smile curling on his face.

"I reckon we are my good man. Can we have a few poppadums with spicy onions and I'll huv chicken vindaloo with pilau rice please," said Innes.

"And gie me a lamb boona, please," slurred Robert.

"Certainly, gentlemen. I'll be right back." The waiter, with a seamless graceful movement, swanned past the food hatch, picked up a pre-prepared bowl of spicy onions, and placed them unnoticed on Naan Bread Man's table.

Innes set about draining his pint as Robert slouched beside him. Robert's head bobbed closer and closer to the table, his head jarring occasionally in a futile but determined effort to remain conscious. The waiter returned with a plate of warm freshly cooked poppadums and spicy onions. Innes glanced at Robert. "Bring us two wee whiskies 'n'all would you?"

"Of course, sir," the waiter replied.

Innes set about delivering poppadums and spicy onions to his face. Robert didn't.

The whiskies were delivered with the waiters' accustomed efficiency.

Innes drained one glass, straight off. Robert remained unaware of his surroundings. Innes drained the other glass.

The waiter returned with steaming plates of curry. The smell of food provided Robert with the motivation he required to drag his consciousness from the edge of the abyss. He glanced at the drained whiskey glasses, his face registered suspicious confusion. He gripped a spoon in an unsteady hand and dropped a few spoons of pilau rice in the approximate direction of the plate in front of him. "Is that ma curry?" he asked Innes pointing at a plate.

"Aye, Vanie, that's yours," said Innes helping himself to his own curry. With the first mouthful Innes could feel the bite of strong chilies; he washed it down with a large draught of lager and carried on shovelling curry mostly into his mouth.

Robert made the same effort to get as much of his curry into his mouth as possible. He again eyed the empty whiskey glasses, his brain grappling with conflicting messages, his memory fighting to achieve certainty. "Hey waiter, gonnie bring us two more wee whiskeys please," he ended up shouting.

"Of course, sir." The waiter clicked his heels, nodded, and obliged Robert with his request.

To the sound of raucous banter, and the occasional shout of "*Naan Bread Man to the rescue*," Robert and

Innes finished their curries while they poured as much lager as they could into their bloated bellies.

"Bring us the bill please?" Innes slurred at the waiter as he floated past.

"Right away sir," he clicked and nodded.

"I'm fucked Vanie. I'm off home. You getting a cab with me?"

"Utterly preposterous Innes. Utterly preposterous," Robert managed only an automatic response.

Innes acknowledged this probably meant Robert would be compliant with anything he suggested, due to him being dimly aware that it would be in his best interests to do so. Innes grabbed their denim jackets. "Give us 35 quid Vanie, we need to pay the bill."

"He who pays the piper calls the tune Innes my lad." Robert lifted his eyelids as much as he could, gazed vacantly out and said, "I cannie count. Can you do it for me?" He wrestled a bunched-up wad of notes out of his pocket, and with intermingled coins dropping everywhere, he dumped it all on the table.

Innes scrupulously counted out Robert's share of the bill and, adding his own contribution, placed it all on the silver dish laid on the table by the waiter. He left a generous tip for the waiter, guilt money for the tidying up job that would need doing to their table. Innes winced again as he looked back at their table on the way out, it looked like a war zone. There was rice everywhere and splattered smears of curry sauce sludging across the tablecloth like pungent slugs. Innes and Robert left Patel's satiated.

"We'll get a cab at the boxing booth then, Vanie."

"Whatever you say Inny, whatever you say."

Making sure his friend remained in his near orbit, Innes lurched off towards the town centre and taxi rank. The taxi rank sat nearby a fast-food van that served up pot noodles and hamburgers to drunken, hungry Greenockians. The van was colloquially known as the boxing booth due to the large number of drunken brawls that regularly occurred there.

The scene that met Innes and Robert as they approached the taxi rank was fairly typical of the boxing booth. There were about three or four small groups, mainly young people, chatting and laughing amongst themselves, and four or five older lone drunkards weaving around in random orbits of the van. Leading up to the serving hatch of the van there was a remote resemblance of a queue, and other groups were hanging around in the environs of the van, consuming their purchases. The pavements in the immediate vicinity of the boxing booth were decorated with a smattering of spilled noodles, burnt fried onions, crushed Coke cans, discarded greasy hamburger wrappings, and the occasional dollop of foul, festering meat.

There were no fights underway when Innes and Robert arrived, but one of the lone drunkards was scowling and muttering under his breath about some inexplicable, perceived slight. The object of this persons simmering resentment was standing nearby, ignorant regarding his evident transgression. He was happily immersed in the process of consuming a pot noodle, chatting obliviously to his friends.

There were groups, couples, and lone drunkards waiting, more or less orderly, in the queue for a taxi. Some watched the boxing booth taking in the atmosphere, gauging the dynamics for a potential fracas. Others contemplated their own navels, lost in the thought that there might very well be more to life than their own present reality.

The resentful drunk's incoherent mumblings got louder, and angrier, as Innes and Robert joined the back of the taxi rank. "UTTERLY PREPOSTEROUS", Robert announced their arrival.

"I fucking hate him," the resentful drunk changed the focus of his ire. "I've always fucking hated him." Innes sobered up just a little bit. This particular resentful drunk just happened to be one John McClelland. John was old and well past his fighting prime, but he had a reputation and, though his ego was well dented by previous failures, he was still driven to prove himself. And he could still do a lot of damage. Robert was, at this moment in time, an easy target.

"Just take it easy John, eh?" Innes entreated the approaching drunk, weaving his way menacingly towards them.

"I've nothing against you Inny. But he is a cunt," John said, flecks of foam spraying from his mouth. "And I'm fucking sick of him." Hatred sprayed from John's eyes. "He's getting a fucking dooin'," John said, head down, fists clenched, adrenaline pumping.

Innes on his own could have managed a quick getaway. But a cursory assessment of Robert was enough to inform him that there was no chance of the two of them getting away, not with Robert in the state he was in. Robert couldn't even see the troubled wave of drunken misfortune that was rolling towards him, never mind escape from it.

Innes had always relied more on charm and humour, than fists and ferocity, and at this moment in time, he really didn't fancy taking on John McClelland, even if he was as drunk as a lord, and well past his prime. Innes had seen John brutally dismantle many a man before, and he didn't want to take the chance that he and Robert would be joining that particular list.

Providence intervened. Just as John McClelland was weaving his way past the group of people where the previous object of his hate was; the object of his loathing was shoved in the chest by one of his friends, as a joke. This unfortunate individual fell back, straight into John McClelland, and, as if this were not an excuse enough, the remaining contents of his pot noodle cup was pebble dashed all over John's once white T-shirt.

John roared, "Ya wee fucking prick," and grabbed the unlucky teenager by the scruff of his neck. The teenager had no chance. John was older, drunker, and much less fit, but he had many more years' experience of fighting, and he also had his reputation and ego to protect. John butted the poor teenager on the bridge of his nose, which exploded in a spray of blood. The teenager went down only to be pummelled further by John's fists and feet. The damage done was mostly superficial, but the teenager was no fighter, and he had pretty much given up at the first blow.

"Don't fuck wi me ya wee shite," John crowed, his fierce face spraying spit into the bloodied mug of his victim. John straightened, just a little bit taller than before, and with his need to prove himself sated, he swagger staggered off into the Greenock night. John felt his pride was restored.

"He's a fucking nut," Robert slurred as John weaved merrily down the road. "UTTERLY PREPOSTEROUS," he shouted at the top of his voice. John stopped, his ego was bloated, his pride was flush. Tonight, he decided, he would sort out Robert McKillvany once and for all. As John turned to return, Innes hurriedly ushered Robert into a waiting taxi.

"Opal Road, first please my good man," Innes spoke hurriedly to the taxi driver as he climbed into the back seat beside the crumpled figure of his friend. "It's on the Stones estate. We'll drop of my esteemed friend first. Then it's round the corner to Emerald Crescent please."

"Sure thing pal. You boys had a good night?" the taxi driver asked as he drove past the irate figure of John McClelland waving a clenched fist in the direction of the taxi.

"I'll fucking have you yet, ya wee fucking gob-shite," John McClelland shouted at the receding head of Robert McKillvany as it floated past in the taxi.

"Aye, the usual pal. Quiet night really," Innes replied to the taxi driver as he slumped back into the seat. Innes felt finally free to let his alcohol-soaked mind transport his troubles into complete oblivion.

Chapter 4

The gatehouse shift change happened later than the rest of the refinery, gatehouse staff had to oversee the shift changes. Jean and Stella busied themselves making the office presentable for the next shift to take over. Pride dictated that all the used cups were cleaned, dried, and tidied. Desks and surfaces had to be properly wiped down, and all the shift paperwork had to be logged and filed.

Jean and Stella knew that the slightest discrepancy would be seized upon by the incoming shift to prove them negligent and lazy. They knew this because the search for slovenliness is precisely what they did when they took over from the previous shift.

"Who's on the night?" Stella asked.

"Reckon it is Billy and John," Jean replied.

"Hrumph, the whole place will go to shite then eh? Pity the next shift coming on after them two have been on a nightshift."

"Aye hen, the place will be a proper two and eight."

"Evening Jean darlin, evening Stella, how's my favourite ladies?" Billy Coleman came striding into the Gatehouse. Jean's face and neck flushed red, and Stella raised her eyebrows in question, "*How much did he just hear?*"

"Err not bad Billy, not bad," Jean replied, the blush fading slightly as her composure reasserted itself.

Stella tried to steer the conversation round to work related topics to give Jean time to recover. "It's been a long, hot, and very dry summer Billy ain't it. Mintern must be drying right out, eh?"

"Aye, probably going to be a busy wee shift. I really don't know where you girls get the time to keep this place so clean," Billy said swinging off his bag and removing his jacket.

"Evening Jean. Evening Stella". Billy's colleague John Howie announced his arrival.

"Evening John," Stella replied.

"You two ready for the handover then?" Stella asked. As she spoke, she closed the hatch that faced the refinery floor and picked up a well-worn clipboard from a hook by the hatch. Stella sat down at the desk.

"Aye, we'll be ready once we get our teas, eh?" Billy said as Jean raised her eyebrows and placed two cups of tea in front of the two lads, Jean was always well prepared.

"Fire away then Stella, then we can finally get out of here, and get off home," said Jean, heading towards the door that led out onto the main refinery floor. Jean opened the door and checked all was quiet; she was just in time to see Kenny disappearing into the toilets, followed conspicuously by Danny. Jean sighed and flicked the wooden sign on the gatehouse door from 'Open' to 'Closed'.

"If you are all sitting comfortably then I shall begin," announced Stella. "There was a delivery of Chlorine and desalination kits earlier. The desalination kits are due to be sent out next week, they're in the storeroom now."

John and Billy sipped their tea. Stella continued, "Management have decided that, due to the weather forecast, and the increased demand for water, we're going to boost Mintern levels tonight with an uptake from Brimmington. Management will be coordinating this."

Stella glanced up from the clipboard to make sure John and Billy were listening. "All staff for the nightshift have turned up for work so there has been no need to arrange any short notice cover. There's nothing to follow up about staffing."

"Are they all sober?" asked Billy, he knew the staff well.

"They all looked pretty sober when they came in," said Jean. "But I've just seen Danny and Kenny hit the toilets. Kenny's starting to looked spaced out again. Stupid boy," Jean said shaking her head. "He's such a bright boy too. I just don't know why he's on such a mission to destroy himself?" Jean looked impotently angry.

"Is Mac the Sack on tonight?" Billy asked. "Them two are fucked if he is."

"Aye, it's Jim on tonight." said Stella pausing with the tick box handover and continuing with the un-official handover. "He's crossed swords with Kenny already 'cause he was late for work, again."

"I really don't give a fuck if he destroys himself," said John. "Just as long as he doesn't take anybody else down with him. He's a health and safety nightmare that boy. I reckon he's on the smack!" Jean and Stella bristled at this comment.

"No, he's not John," said Jean jumping to Kenny's defence. "He's stupid, yes. But he's not that stupid".

Stella backed Jean up, "I know his mum well John Howie, so don't you dare start spreading any rumours like that around. Poor Mary would have a heart attack if she heard that her boy was on the smack."

"That's his responsibility then Stella?" said Billy. "It's him being such a fuck up that'll upset his mam. John is just calling it as he sees it, and he's calling it right if you ask me."

Silence descended in the Gatehouse, and, like a cheap blanket, it caused deep and irritating discomfort. Stella took a deep breath and returned to business. "Remember environmental health are coming the morrow, so everything needs to be ship shape. We've made sure all the files are up to date." Stella looked round the gatehouse, "All you boys need to do is just not fuck anything up."

With John and Billy taken down a peg by her final comment Stella flicked closed the handover sheets and handed the clipboard to Billy. "Over to you boys," Stella said as she stood to leave. Jean rose with her and nodded a silent goodnight to John and Billy.

"See you later ladies, and thanks for the tea, eh?" Billy said by way of making peace.

"Aye, see you later boys. You have a good shift, eh?" said Jean as she followed Stella out of the door.

The night was fresh and pleasant, the heat from the day still remembered in the plants and tarmac. They could hear a gentle thrum coming from the various Friday night activities happening in the town below.

"I wonder if Innes has managed to stay out the jail?" said Stella gazing towards the lights of Greenock sparkling amber below them.

"He's not as mad or as bad as he likes to make out that one Stella. He'll be alright. It's Kenny I'm more worried about. Do you think he really is on the smack?"

Stella took a deep breath, "I really don't know Jean. I don't know what he's on. But I know for sure he is on something. I see him at the McDonalds all the time. They sell all sorts of stuff, and I know they sell smack. But who knows?"

"I don't get why the Polis don't do something about them McDonalds. Everyone in Greenock knows they're drug dealers. So why don't the Police?"

"Beats me, Jean, but there's probably quite a few of them have got backhanders from them."

"Bastards," the expletive spat out by Jean was aimed generically at everybody involved in self-centred gain. "They need a good clip round the ear the lot of them."

Stella just smiled. "See you Monday then, Jean," she said as they both veered off to their respective cars.

"Aye, see you then, if not before Stella. You look after yourself love," shouted Jean as she reached her car.

After gently persuading her car to start, Jean drove slowly past Stella, peeping her a short goodbye as she headed out of the car park and onto the road home. Stella stood for a moment beside her car, lost in her own thoughts and feelings. Was he going to be in when she got home? It was a Friday night so that pretty much meant that he would surely be out and about and drinking heavily. Stella looked round at the refinery. She gazed at the disappearing red lights of Jean's car as it turned the corner of the road out of sight.

It wasn't much, but Stella loved her job, she enjoyed working with Jean. She was a solid, dependable, woman. No one messed with Jean Gourley. Stella often wished that some of Jean's defiant personality would rub off on her. The night was still, warm, and calm, but Stella shivered as she unlocked her car to drive home. She followed the same route that Jean had taken, but veered off at the first junction she came to. This road headed into the Homerton Estate where she lived.

The Homerton was probably the most notorious estate in Greenock. It was ruled by the McDonalds. Driving onto the estate Stella spotted the McDonald's 'eyes', little Danny Cameron who was standing on a street corner at the entrance to the estate. Danny was scanning the cars, and the people walking into the estate. Stella knew that should there be suspicious looking people or cars entering the estate, Danny would ensure the McDonalds knew about it, instantly. It was his 'job', and he would be 'paid' with drugs. He was 14. Danny knew Stella and her car, so she passed unreported and unacknowledged.

Passing by Danny Stella's subconscious prickled with a continual concern. There are many things a 14-year-old boy could, and should, be doing with his childhood, rather than hanging about on a street corner on the Homerton Estate working for drugs. The culturally driven impotence to do anything about it reasserted its dominance again and once again her moral indignance faded in yet another powerless internal scream.

Stella drove past the inevitable gathering of people hanging about at the local shops drinking. Bobby McDonald was there, which meant that drugs were being sold. Bobby's audience were laughing sycophantically at his oration, hoping that the light of his subsequent benevolence would provide them with some future favour.

Stella parked outside her house as usual. No one paid her any attention, she was harmless and unconnected; she was no threat, and she posed no opportunity for gain. As she turned the key in the door, she knew her cat, Fluffy, would be sitting waiting patiently for her. No matter what was going on in her life Fluffy was always there. "Hello, my little Fluff," she quietly welcomed the small, long haired tabby cat as it rubbed itself around her legs. She gave her cat a little scratch behind the ear. Fluffy responded by giving her a purring "Brrrrrmmp".

"Let's get you something to eat then my wee love."

As she walked through the hall Stella noted the missing jacket from the coat hanger and the missing keys from the key holder fitted to the wall in happier times. On the living room table lay the detritus from a Chinese takeaway, the smeared plate, and mostly empty tin containers were left discarded on the table. Stella set about tidying up. Fluffy followed continuing to communicate her request for food and joy at Stella's return. These were now the only happy times Stella enjoyed in her house.

After putting the dirty plates in the sink and the empty containers in the bin Stella focused all her attention on her cat. With the familiar sound of a tin of cat food being opened Fluffy redoubled her efforts to persuade Stella to deposit the food in her bowl post-haste.

"There you go my wee love, tuck in." Fluffy needed no second invitation and buried her head in a full bowl of noxious smelling food.

Stella returned to the sink, putting the kettle on to boil she filled the sink with hot water and washing up liquid. After washing the plates and wiping down the worktops she returned to the living room. With a damp cloth she wiped down the living room table and rounded up the stray bits of rice that had made a bid to escape the mouth of John Reid, Stella's partner.

Returning to the kitchen Stella poured herself a cup of sweetened tea to bring back to the living room. Switching on the telly she grabbed the remote control. Plopping a plump cushion on her lap she flopped on the sofa. Stella checked the time, 11:45 pm; she might have another 45 minutes, perhaps an hour. Anxiety was already creeping out from her stomach and prickling her taught nerves.

Hot sweet tea helped calm her jangling nerves. She turned her attention to the telly and encouraged her mind to zone out to the inane babbling of a bunch of celebrities on a late-night chat show. Sipping her tea and allowing the celebrities mindless chatter to soothe her conscious being, Stella's subconscious was provided with the space required to contemplate the main concern of her life. *"Why can I not just leave him?"* Stella's thoughts spiralled inexorably into all too familiar territory; *'No one knows about it. I have no-where else to live. I still love him. Do I still love him? How can I? He needs me. He hates me. He loves me. We have great sex. He rapes me. Sometimes you just need to tough things out. This is your lot, deal with it'.*

The sound of keys rattling, being dropped, and being fumbled into the lock dragged Stella back from her sub-conscious self-flagellation. Her breath shortened, and her anxiety flared. Adrenaline pumped into her system causing her skin to prickle; she removed the cushion from her lap and put her unfinished tea on the table. He was earlier than expected. Straightening her legs out Stella sat rigidly upright on the sofa. She turned the telly off, no matter what she was watching he wouldn't approve of her choice.

John Reid stumbled unsteady into the room. He was a short, stocky man with cropped hair, he had love and hate tattoos on his knuckles. Stella looked at him with a passive expression, but her detached mind recoiled from how truly repulsive he was.

"You just fucking sitting there in silence then?" John said blearily looking around the room for what Stella was occupying herself with.

"Aye John. I've not long finished my shift at work, and I was just sitting having a wee cup of tea with Fluff." Stella fruitlessly looked round for her cat. Even before the sound of the keys being dropped were perceived by Stella, Fluffy had hidden herself in her usual hiding spot behind the sofa. Fluffy had heard John coming from far, far away. She was inordinately alert to any sign regarding his appearance.

John grunted and stumble staggered into the kitchen. "Fucking hate that cat".

Stella heard the squeaking of a tap being turned and the subsequent torrent of water. "Don't drink from the taps John, there's bottles of boiled water in the fridge." Stella, like many who worked at the water refinery, had a phobic distrust of the water coming out of the taps. She had heard too many stories about various bodily fluids being discharged into the tanks.

"Fuck yir water, and fuck yir water refinery. They're all a bunch of fucking jokers if you ask me."

Stella sighed, resigned. Mysteriously her anxiety lifted; there was now no doubt about what kind of night she was going to have. Bad nights were regularly predictable anyway. Stella's mood shifted from one of uncertain anxiety to cavalier acceptance. "At least they know how to laugh up there," Stella muttered loudly under her breath.

"What did you say?" John said from the doorway of the kitchen, water dripping from the tip of his unshaven chin.

"Nothing John." Stella rose from the sofa, excused herself, and squeezed past him into the kitchen. "Do you want me to make you something to eat?" Stella was hungry after her shift.

Eyes swimming drunkenly in his head, mouth hanging unconsciously open with flecks of foam gathered at the sides, John tried to process thoughts too complicated for his brain at the best of times, and this was not the best of times. "Aye make us some chips eh," he ended up saying as he slumped on the sofa. "Pass us the remote," John demanded.

Stella distractedly threw the remote control vaguely in his direction. The large device spun through the air, they both watched it rapt as it seemingly twirled in slow motion. It bounced off a cushion, spiralled up, and whacked John full on the chin.

"YOU FUCKING BITCH." The flashpoint had sparked his already short fuse and set the inevitable explosion in motion.

John sprang off the sofa, adrenalin moderating his drunkenness.

"I didnae, mean it John," Stella stammered. "Honest love, it was an accident." With John bearing ominously down on her, Stella's emboldened attitude melted in fear.

John was an experienced perpetrator of domestic violence. He knew that feelings caused more significant damage than physical violence. He liked to prolong the inevitable attack to enhance the psychological fear. He also knew that he had to keep it secret. His total lack of self-esteem meant he had to protect what little standing he had left in the community. This meant he had to hurt her where the physical evidence of his violence could easily be obscured.

"You've been asking for this ever since I got home you fucking cow," he snarled. He kicked out at Stella, aiming a brutal kick between her legs. Stella buckled. John followed this with a punch to her shoulder, right at the point where it would cause most pain, resulting in a dead arm.

He grabbed her by the arm, twisting it up to force Stella's face up towards his own. Snarling with flecks of foam and spit flying from his twisted mouth, John forced her to face his bloodshot, bulging eyes. "You want to fuck with me bitch? Eh? You think you're fucking better than me just cause you're working? Well, you're fucking not. You're just a piece of shite and you need to mind your fucking place. I am fucking John Reid you cunt. And no one, but no one, fucks with me, ok?" John was shouting.

"Ok, John, ok. I'm sorry John, I'm really, really sorry." Stella would say anything at this point to get him to calm down and to allow them both to move on to the next scene of this most dysfunctional play.

His spike of adrenaline spent in one violent outburst John was left feeling confused. The copious amounts of alcohol he had consumed earlier did not help. Shame and regret fought to make their presence felt, alcohol demanded these feelings not be allowed to flourish. Blame as always came to the rescue. "This is all your own fault Stella love. You need to be more careful. And stop going on about your fucking work, eh? It's not my fault I'm not working. You know my back is too fucked for work." Neediness took over from blame, and the tragic, pitiful play moved on.

Rubbing his back and moving with an exaggerated creaky gait, John sought to reassert his control over the situation. "Any chance of those chips now Stella love, I really am quite hungry now."

With her head bowed and her heart numbed, Stella played her part. She nodded subserviently and scuttled speedily away into the kitchen.

Working on automatic pilot Stella prepared potatoes to make chips. The repetitive action of peeling and chopping potatoes allowed her subconscious mind freedom to process this latest round of behaviour that confused, agitated, and exasperated her.

"I just don't get it! Why don't I leave him? There is nothing I like about him! We have no children like the others I know. Why don't I leave him? Do I still love him? Did I ever love him? What is love anyway? He needs me. He would collapse without me. He would kill me if I left him. Why don't I leave him? I can't."

Lowering perfectly cut chips into the deep fat fryer Stella enjoyed the agitated crackle they made meeting the hot oil. With the lid on the fryer, she was left with no actions to take her away from the intrusive thoughts passing from her subconscious mind into conscious awareness.

"This is it Stella love. This is your life, this is your future, and it is never going to get any better, ever."

Stella's stomach sank, and her mind shut down. In automatic pilot she finished cooking the chips. In a final act of defiance, she spat on his chips before taking both plates, along with a bottle of tomato sauce, and the salt cellar, into the living room to present to her partner and bain of her existence.

Chapter 5

Kenny stood staring vacantly at the mirror in the disabled toilet. He blinked his eyes many times, squeezing them shut and opening them wide to the point of bulging. He tried so extremely hard to focus, but every-time he looked in the mirror all he could see were multiple Kenny's swimming around a main Kenny who just, frankly, looked confused.

The buzz and hum of the air conditioning unit peaked and flowed and transformed into a multi-layered oppressive, industrial concerto in Kenny's mind. Kenny was dimly aware that he was in bad shape, again. Dropping more eyedrops in the approximate direction of his eyes he licked his fingers and ran them across both eyebrows. That would have to do he thought. Taking a few deep breaths, he unlocked the door and tentatively ventured out onto the refinery floor.

Joe was, at that point, traveling down the corridor, he was returning to the refinery floor from a trip to the storeroom. He saw Kenny emerge from the toilet and start to weave his way unsteadily down the corridor, jogging Joe caught up with him.

"You alright Kenny?" he asked, though the answer to that question was patently obvious.

"Rippling, Joe Bob. Rippling my old china," Kenny slurred, his eyes spinning.

"Kenny, you are so *not* alright son. What the fuck are you doing? You've had fair warning from that fuckwit Mac already." Joe was beyond exasperated. "He's fucking after you son. What were you thinking?"

Joe sucked in large breath to help abate his anger, "You're nothing but a fucking eejit sometimes Kenny, you really are. Could you not just take one night off from fucking yourself up?"

Half-way through Joe's lecture Kenny had noticed the patterns the motes of dust were making in the bright refinery light; he had zoned out. Kenny remained stupidly silent, pulling a sheepish, stoned smile. He wasn't quite sure what Joe was saying but he thought it didn't sound good, so he didn't listen.

"Me and Bobby will get you through this Kenny. You just need to do exactly what we tell you alright?"

Kenny remained mesmerised by the dust motes dancing just for him, but he had heard Joe asking him something and he knew that, even though he might be a bit annoying sometimes, Joe generally did have his best interests at heart. "Aye, Joe no worries," Kenny replied. "Anything you say Joe. Anything you say dude."

Furrowing his brow, Joe remained unconvinced that Kenny knew what was going on, or the gravity of his situation.

Jim Mackenzie had the handy habit of being a whistler. You could always hear him coming. Joe heard the refrain of a barely recognisable Elvis song, coming whistling towards them.

"Quick Kenny, into the loading bay." Joe pulled Kenny through the opaque plastic flaps of the curtain door leading into the loading bay. The loading bay was about 5 degrees colder than the refinery. Joe shivered with the cold combined with the fear that Mac the Sack would head into the loading bay for some reason. How could he explain randomly standing about in an empty loading bay with a stoned Kenny McGregor? Joe sent his hope projector into overdrive. "Just please don't be coming to the loading bay," he mumbled quietly to an unnamed God.

The whistling peaked and ebbed as Jim headed past and off further down the corridor.

"He must be heading to the storeroom," Joe whispered.

"Huh?" Kenny asked.

"Mac the Sack. He must be heading to the storeroom," Joe replied, convinced now that Kenny was completely oblivious of reality.

Kenny struggled to understand the relevance of the whereabouts of Mac the Sack. He thought maybe Joe needed him for something. "Shall I go get him?" Kenny asked.

"Fuck," Joe said. His stomach sank as he realised just how out of it Kenny was. Joe looked round the loading bay, searching for inspiration, or divine intervention.

The loading bay was semi-lit by low level emergency lighting. In the corner was a desk, chair, and computer, partially enclosed from the rest of the loading bay by semi-permanent partitioning. The partition was transparent from waist high, but it was better than nothing. And for Joe, it seemed a better plan than allowing a very stoned Kenny McGregor to flounce around the refinery floor.

Joe grabbed Kenny by the shoulders, and forced him to look directly at him, "Right you. Listen up and listen good." The directness of the comment grabbed Kenny's short attention span. "You sit there and don't move," Joe pointed to the desk and chair. In order that there was no confusion he walked him over to the chair. Kenny's brain struggled to digest the information being imparted in this fast-moving situation. Joe gently placed Kenny in the chair.

"You hear me now Kenny? Don't move. And if Mac the Sack, for whatever reason, comes into the loading bay get your head down under that partition and hide. If that doesn't work, you'll just need to style it out. OK? Tell him you are ordering parts or something."

Kenny was aware that some response was needed so he nodded dumbly. Kenny had also noticed that there were calendar pictures plastered around the partitioning. Pretty blond ladies, naked from the waist up, were pictured in a variety of unnatural poses designed to better show off their naked breasts. Kenny was entranced.

"I'm going to go get Bobby. We'll get you through this Kenny boy, I promise." Joe took one last look at Kenny drooling over the calendar pictures, then he grabbed his trolley and left the loading bay to enlist some support.

Kenny sat for a while ogling the pictures of nice breasts, then he began to take in his surroundings. The loading bay was not a place he was in often. He poked his head above the partition. The bay was dark and airy, there were draughts swirling around from the large, roller shutter doors. No-one could see him where he was sitting, and the place was full of breeze. It was, Kenny realised, the perfect place for a sneaky pipe.

With a little less precision than usual, Kenny prepared and smoked a large hash pipe. His attention to conspicuous precaution had gone and he blew a large cloud of hash smoke out into the atmosphere. Kenny slumped back on the battered chair, his head lolling backwards at a 90-degree angle. The inside of Kenny's head had turned into a blob of throbbing mush. The rhythmic sound of bleeping electronics, harmonising with the whistling wind blowing through the loading bay doors, was hypnotising him. Kenny's conscious thought was now completely subverted, he slid gently into a deep, drug fuelled trance.

Walking quickly down the corridor Joe checked his watch, 5:45. There was just over an hour left until the shift was over. He stepped out onto the refinery floor and sussed out who was where. Danny Henry was attending to his pipes, preparing them for the impending inspection. There was no sign of Billy Coleman or John Howie, Joe suspected they were probably sleeping in the gatehouse. Bobby was standing in the doorway of the breakout area finishing off a cup of tea. And there was still no sign of Mac the Sack. Joe worried that if Mac had gone to the storeroom, he might just pop into the loading bay on the way back. If he did Kenny's end would indeed be as sticky as pot of glue.

Emitting a discrete cough, Joe parked his trolley, and sauntered nonchalantly over to stand beside Bobby.

Looking over at Danny, Joe spoke softly to Bobby, "We have a problem."

Bobby sighed, "Don't we always Joe? Where abouts exactly is our problem?"

"I've left him in the loading bay. I bumped into him as he was coming out the disabled bogs. He's completely fucking wrecked. Mac the Sack is on the move too." Joe scanned the refinery floor again. "I think he's gone to the storeroom but I cannie be sure. If he sees Kenny, he's gone this time, his arse won't touch the ground." Joe pleaded for a plan, "What are we going to do?"

Bobby puffed out his cheeks, "Loading bays are probably the best place for him. No one ever goes there on a night shift." Bobby looked at his watch, "Fuck, we've got a long way to go Joe, he'll be missed at his workplace. And we've got to get him clocked out at the end of the shift. What do you think about papping him in a taxi out the back? Just get him to hell out of here?"

"No, I think you were right. We need to get him seen and clocked out at the end of the shift. We've got the inspection tomorrow so Mac will be all over the place checking everything's all right. And frankly Kenny McGregor is anything *but* alright."

"How bad is he?" Bobby asked hopefully.

"Totally fucked Bobby. Completely mashed up. I don't reckon he knows where he is, what the time is, or even what planet he is currently on. He's fucked."

"What a fucking twat." Bobby puffed his cheeks, exasperated, "Tonight of all nights, eh?"

"I reckon we just try to keep him in the loading bay for as long as we can. Then drag him out near the end of the shift. We can check in on him from time to time, just to make sure he is still breathing."

Bobby and Joe paused, and stared into space, ruminating on the creeping fact that the world had moved in a direction that they completely failed to understand. It was dawning on them that they were only ever going to get older, and more out of touch with the activities and interests of the younger generation.

"Fuck it," said Joe. "I'll go see if Mac is still in the storeroom. We need to keep tabs on him."

"Right," replied Bobby. "I'll go check on Kenny."

"Nice one Bobby. See you back on the floor in a bit and we'll see where we are at then eh?"

"Sounds like a plan Joe!"

The world was changing too fast for Joe and Bobby. The traditional industries they grew up with had closed. Computers were now commonplace at work, though they didn't have much involvement with them. Jobs involving computers tended to be given to the younger generation, like Danny and Kenny. The likes of Joe and Bobby were given the more physical jobs, like maintenance or portering. They didn't understand the music people listened to, and some of the programmes on TV now were incomprehensible to them.

Bobby reached his destination. He took a deep breath and stepped into the dimly lit loading bay. Drugs and drug users were way out of his comfort zone. Living all his life in Greenock, Bobby had gotten used to dealing with drunkenness and general misbehaviour. There were even a few times where he had to admit he had drunk more than he should have, but drugs? He had read about them in the Daily Express. They were unpredictable, they made people mug old grannies and steal from their families. Bobby knew a few of the McGregor family, they were all good people. He knew that, at heart, Kenny was also a good person, which was why Bobby tried to help, but drugs and drug users made him nervous.

The loading bay was darker than the refinery floor. Shadows populated the room with suggested surprises. The loading bay doors rattled sporadically responding to invitations from the breeze outside. "Kenny?" Bobby ventured hesitantly. He took his glasses out, perched them on the end of his nose, and squinted round the loading bay. There was simply no sign of him anywhere. It was a warm evening, but the loading bay was cool, Bobby shivered. He didn't like this one bit. Where was Kenny?

Joe passed by the loading bay on his way to the storeroom just as Bobby was scratching his head wondering where the hell Kenny was. He didn't really want to see Kenny for a bit, Bobby could deal with him. Joe was also confused about drugs and drug users. He saw the results of drugs and he couldn't for the life of him fathom why people would do that to themselves. Joe had also read the stories about mad, desperate junkies, and he knew a few people who had been robbed by the local addicts. But Joe knew Kenny desperately needed protection, and he was going to provide it.

Therefore, he was about to deliberately put himself in the blame frame by intentionally seeking out and engaging with Mac the Sack. He strolled nervously down the corridor towards the storeroom. The door to the storeroom was closed. Trepidation about having to attempt to influence a man he considered a vile enemy resulted in massive hesitancy. He quietly and gently opened the storeroom door.

Creeping cautiously into the storeroom Joe was in no way shape or form prepared for the sight that confronted him there. Jim McKenzie was standing at the back of the storeroom at a chest high table with his trousers down, bundled around his knees. On the table in front of him was a pornographic magazine, and he was furiously wanking his semi-erect cock.

Joe coughed loudly.

Panic stricken beyond embarrassment Jim swiftly pulled up his pants and trousers, his cock shrinking further from the shame now coursing through his system. Jim hastily stuffed the magazine into the nearest available hiding place. He turned to face Joe, shame crawling over his skin, his face crimson with humiliation.

His pride could never permit him to admit being caught *in flagrante delicto*. So blatant attack was his only option for defence, though he was quite aware that this was going to be futile. "What are you doing in here? You should be on the refinery floor," Jim said with exaggerated bluster. His body language carried a desperate, unspoken appeal to Joe to not mention the unmentionable. He silently begged, and entreated, Joe to please just collude with him this once.

Joe met Jim's eyes fleetingly and he remained silent while the seismic shift in power was fully established. "I was just looking for Kenny, Mac." The solution to his little *'what to do about Kenny'* issue had just presented itself in a most unexpected and fortuitous manner. "I can't seem to find him anywhere. Have you seen him?"

Jim just spluttered some garbled nonsense while his brain sought to grapple with what Joe was about to do. Joe strolled over to stand beside him. He reached forward to retrieve the magazine from its hurriedly sourced hiding place and started to flick slowly through it. "Thing is Jim. It appears that Kenny is a little bit 'tired' tonight. Do you understand me?"

Mac's already crimson face reddened further towards exploding. He was a little boy again. He just nodded and bowed his head, eyes studiously avoiding Joe's exultant face.

"So, Kenny just needs everybody to take it really, really easy on him. Do we understand each other, Mac?" Joe continued to flick through the magazine, making sure to linger over the pages displaying the most graphic images. "Interesting," Joe commented.

Jim was beyond vocalisation; he gulped down the shame rising like gobbets of bile in his throat, he nodded mutely.

"I knew you would understand Jim. I always knew you were a reasonable man." Joe couldn't help but turn the knife. "Everybody else says you are a complete cunt. But no, I always say, 'say what you like about old Mac the Sack, but he is nothing but a reasonable man when all is said and done.'" Joe placed the magazine back on the table, opened at a suitably lurid place. He turned to leave Jim alone with his humiliation. "Enjoy the rest of your shift Jim." Joe closed the door to the storeroom triumphantly.

This was a gem; a complete game-changer. Joe now had something serious on Mac the Sack. He was bursting to tell someone, anyone. Joe needed to find Kenny and Bobby. Strolling victoriously down the corridor he stopped off at the loading bay, it was empty. His triumphant mood was short lived, worry took control again. The incredibly loose cannon that was Kenny McGregor seemed to be very loose and very lost. He needed to find Bobby quick. He headed for the refinery floor.

The refinery floor was a hive of activity. Time was travelling towards the end of the shift, and everyone was bustling about cleaning, checking, and double checking their responsibilities. The workers all knew they needed to meet management expectations regarding the impending inspection or there would indeed be hell to pay. Billy and John, from the Gatehouse, were out and about on the floor supervising the ongoing efforts. Weaving slightly at his machine Danny was doing a final diagnostic check on the pipes. Bobby was checking various bolts and joints that connected the pipes all around the refinery.

Joe headed over to Bobby. "Where is he?" he asked, rising panic obvious in his voice.

"I don't know Joe, he wasn't in the loading bay," Bobby replied, cowed. "I had my own checks I need to get done. I was hoping you might've bumped into him on your travels. Did you find Mac the Sack?"

Joe smiled slightly through his anxiety. "Aye, I'll tell you all about that later Bobby. And trust me, it's worth waiting for. All we need to do now is find that twat McGregor and we'll be fine and dandy." Joe's triumphant mood returned, "I reckon I've got it all sorted Bobby. Where do you reckon he's gone?"

"Fuck knows Joe. Maybe check out the back of the loading bay? I *think* the doors were closed, but he could have nipped out the side door."

"I'll be back in a tick. But if he shows up, could you just keep him out of the way?"

"Keep who out of the way?" Billy Coleman had seen the somewhat intense discussion going on between Joe and Bobby, and just happened to noticed there were some pipes nearby that looked like they might need a little clean.

Joe bristled, "You just mind your own business, Billy. This has nothing to do with you."

Billy was used to, and thrived on, confrontation. "Joe, you know very well as gatehouse staff *everything* that goes on in this refinery *is* my business. Now who needs kept out of the way of who, as if we didn't already know. And more to the point *why* does he need to be kept out of the way?"

Now was the time for Joe to take control, and he knew just how. "Listen Billy, you know how much of a pain Mac is, yeah? Well, I've only just gone and caught him having a fucking wank in the storeroom. He's got a stash of scuddy mags in there. He's probably in there knocking one out every night."

As if on cue Jim McKenzie emerged gingerly onto the refinery floor. He looked over at Joe, Bobby, and Billy Coleman. Their topic of conversation was written all over their faces. The combination of a major piece of juicy gossip, and the appearance of a very embarrassed looking Mac the Sack, was too much for Billy, he couldn't contain his glee. He exploded into very loud, relentless laughter. "No fucking way," Billy bellowed loudly between snorting guffaws.

With his worst fears duly confirmed, Jim scuttled off the floor as swiftly as possible. He sought sanctuary in his office, pulling closed the blinds as quickly as he could.

"No fucking way," Billy repeated. "The dirty old fucking pervert. Joe this is fucking gold dust mate. John-John, wait till you hear this one", Billy shouted over to his gatehouse colleague.

Always keen to be included in any refinery gossip, John hurried over. "What's happening Billy?" he said eagerly.

"Joe's only gone and caught Mac the fucking Sack having a ham shank in the storeroom with some scuddy mags." Billy was exorbitantly triumphant; this news was the best event in the refinery since Danny Henry had followed through on a fart due to an excess of vindaloo curry and cheap wine.

John joined in with the unbridled joy, "Well, I'll be hornswoggled and dipped in fucking pig-shit, no fucking way. I could do with knocking one out myself! Where are the scuddy mags Joe?"

"Fuck off John-John. You cannie use them after Mac the Sack has been at them. Think about all them pages stuck together. Yuck. You must be desperate son," Billy berated his friend.

With the powder-keg of his news delivered, and exploding all-round the refinery floor, Joe parked up his trolley and set off on a mission find Kenny.

Kenny had come around from his drug fuelled reverie still in the loading bay. Focusing his eyes with great difficulty he took in his surroundings, he had no idea where he was, but one thought permeated through his drug addled brain, and gained dominance over all else. The voice of Mac the Sack reverberated through Kenny's fried brains: *"Pull some water down from the Brimmington."* Kenny was determined that he would get this right. *"I'll just pay a wee visit the little boy's room first,"* he thought.

Finding his way to the familiar disabled toilet he slumped down on the toilet seat. Kenny felt himself drifting away again, but with a gargantuan effort he focused his thoughts; he thought having more temazepam followed by another pipe would help to clear his mind. It didn't.

After his pipe he drifted further away from reality. The voice of Mac in his head roused him again: *"Before the end of the shift you need to let out 100 units from Brimmington."*

"I'm on it Mac, I'm on it", Kenny thought to himself as he roused himself once more in a massive effort not to get sacked. He weaved out of the toilet and

crashed straight into the arms of Joe who had come looking for him.

"Fucking hell Kenny. Where have you been? Me and Bobby were looking everywhere for you."

"I just needed a pish Joe, had to visit the little boys' room."

Joe knew exactly what that meant. "You are such a fucking twat McGregor. Thank fuck Mac is a bigger twat."

Kenny had no idea what Joe was talking about, "Aye Joe, but he's still the boss, and I need to do his bidding."

Joe had no idea what Kenny was talking about. "You just need to keep your head down son. Get your arse back to them pipes, and look busy eh Kenny?"

"Aye Joe, I can do that." Kenny's eyes were drowning in his foggy brain.

Joe gently guided Kenny back to the refinery floor. With a triumphant smile directed towards Bobby, Joe deposited Kenny at his workstation.

"*Right, 100 units Mac said.*" With a superhuman effort Kenny focused on his computer screen. Little green flashing symbols whirled and twirled randomly over the screen.

Busying himself with his own duties, while keeping a watchful eye on Kenny, Joe was content that the shift would now end well. He felt like, finally, he had everything under control. He was pleased Kenny had seemed to listen to his advice about making himself look busy.

Tapping out the number 100 on his computer, Kenny pushed the button that would execute the action. In the distant depth of the darkness in loch Brimmington a valve sprang to life, as commanded to by technology. The valve slowly began to open, and the water, and its contents, flowed freely.

Part 2

Chapter 6

The sun rose resplendent, bathing the blooming heather and verdant bushes in its restorative heat. Nocturnal animals made final preparations for their day of rest. Owls gently hooted, and voles nervously sniffed out secure routes to scamper safely home to their nests.

Conversely, the daytime animals woke and stretched, sniffed, squawked, and squeaked their way into a new day. Wild rabbits investigated potential dangers and hopped off to find food. Flowers bloomed to absorb the sun's replenishing rays, inviting the busy bees to partake of their fresh nectar. Long, gently swaying grasses emitted a reedy scent as they started to dry out from their light coating of dew.

In the depth of loch Brimmington a profusion of bubbles heralded a profound change to life as it had been known. The virus that inhabited the loch detected an alteration in water pressure. This was the opportunity it sought, the possibility of escape. Rushing with the flowing water, through wire mesh filters, the virus sought out new surroundings, and more fruitful prospects. Through the pipes the virus travelled; and out into the comparatively more massive waters of loch Mintern.

The virus was efficient, hungry, and desperate; it analysed the fauna of Mintern probing for suitable hosts. The fish in Mintern were bigger than in Brimmington, but they were still fish, they were not what the virus required.

Near the bottom of Mintern there was a flat stone slab with various pipes leading out, and away from the loch. The virus travelled down these pipes, which led to numerous, massive, outdoor tanks. From these tanks more pipes led the virus onward. The virus followed the path of the pipes.

The pipes eventually led into Greenock Water Refinery. Inside the refinery the virus progressed with the water into smaller tanks and more pipes. The virus sensed movement inside the refinery. Mammals. Sentient mammals. This was what the virus strove for; this was its reason for being.

There was no obvious infection route from the tanks, the people in the refinery all wore rubber gloves, and the tanks inside the refinery were closed. There was no way for virus to infect the mammals it sensed nearby. The chemicals the water was rinsed with in the refinery were ineffectual to the virility of the virus. The virus persisted in its quest.

The virus abandoned the refinery and journeyed with the water flowing out of more pipes. The pipes leading out of the refinery were longer, thinner, and branched off many, many times. The virus travelled along these pipes to their ultimate destination. These pipes eventually disgorged the virus, along with the water, into various receptacles in Greenock town. Tanks and toilets all over Greenock, and its environs, were slowly, but surely, filled with toxic, noxious water.

The virus floated expectantly in a plethora of tanks and toilets and waited until it could continue its journey and fulfil its ultimate purpose.

Chapter 7

Jim McKenzie sighed a depressed, self-absorbed sigh. Leaving work early to avoid any potentially embarrassing encounters, he drifted slowly in automatic pilot, towards his car. His mind was preoccupied. He had completely lost the power and dominance that he had systematically built up over many years. It was fait accompli that everyone in the refinery would now know he got caught masturbating in the storeroom.

His mind grappled to find a way that he could again regain control. He desired nothing more than to just march straight in and wipe the floor with them all. But this would now result in Joe Dunlop heading straight in to inform senior management about his sexual peccadillos. However, it would still be Joe's word against his. Senior management would listen to him surely, wouldn't they?

The trouble was Jim was an extremely ambitious man. There had been many occasions where he had taken certain tactical swipes at various senior managers. This was done to curry favour with other managers, those who seemed to be in the ascendency. The trouble with this tactic was that ascendency, and influence, were very much fluid and mysterious beasts. The tides of favour ebbed and flowed in very unpredictable ways.

Jim couldn't be sure that Joe wouldn't, by accident or design, manage to gain an audience with one of the managers whom he had himself upset somewhat. Any assertion of his clout could backfire on him mightily. He turned back to gaze at the refinery, in his mind's eye, emblazoned there forever, he painfully recalled the smug look of triumph on Joe Dunlop's face.

Shame crept up from his stomach to crawl about his neck and face. Resentment and rage rode to his rescue. *"Just who the fuck does he think he is anyway. Mr fucking high and mighty, holier than fucking thou. This is not over yet. Fuck that wee shite McGregor as well, I'll deal with him too. Either that or he'll deal with himself and fucking die. I'm going after Saint Joe fucking Dunlop with all guns blazing, him and all his fuckwit mates."*

With his mind hardened on hate, his step became more strident, and he finally reached his car. It was a brand-new top of the range BMW, and it was not yet paid for. Jim needed his job; in fact, he was counting on promotion. He was living way beyond his means. This scandal would be extremely detrimental to his prospects. *"That wee cunt McGregor, Dunlop, and all their fucking cronies, are only going to go one way. Down the fucking toilet like the shite they are".*

Jim popped the lock on his car and climbed into the padded leather front seat, he fired up the engine. Jim decided he didn't want to go straight home. Driving at speed he passed the work minibus as it entered the car park to deposit the early shift. The bus would then wait to pick up and drop off the night shift in town.

Instead of taking the back roads straight home, he drove down the hill towards the town. Underneath the ground, flowing along the pipes, the virus mirrored his journey from refinery to town.

Driving through town Jim observed with great disdain the human detritus left over from yet another rowdy Friday night in Greenock. He drove past Billy and Bobby, still wearing their blood-soaked Celtic tops, on their way to the train station after spending the night in the local hospital.

Further on he passed Ian Ferguson and Dave Anderson, still up after indulging in a frenzied night of alcohol and amphetamine fuelled violence. Fergie was stalking the town, desperately looking for another victim, so he could flood his system with more violence fuelled adrenaline. The pickings were thin. Dave just looked lost, and as if all he really wanted to do was go home to bed.

Jim drove through the town and out towards the coast. Driving along the coast road he ruminated on his life, reflecting on the circumstances that had led him to be where he was today. He had always sought conformity. He was married by the time he was 23, though he was never what anyone would ever have called a catch. Even at 23 his hair was thinning dramatically. He was never popular at school, and indeed had always been a target for bullies. Initially he had endeavoured to be liked at school, and perhaps he had tried too hard.

Jim remembered the defining moment of his life when he decided to stop trying. He remembered every second, every feeling, and every face that taunted him then. These historic thoughts mirrored his recent, shameful experience.

He had always been a nervous child, he was petrified of the teachers at school, and therefore always desperately sought to avoid attention. This worked most of the time, but it didn't work when he had needs that required attending to. The moment that had shaped the rest of his life was a time when he had an extremely urgent need to go to the toilet in the middle of a lesson.

He was nine years old at the time and was too scared to put up his hand to ask to go to the bathroom. He knew the teachers wanted them to go during break time, they really didn't take kindly to their lessons being disturbed. On this particular occasion the teacher was in an especially foul mood, she had demanded complete and absolute silence from the class, and unmitigated dedication to their work. She had already belted someone for disrupting the class by muffling a giggle.

Jim desperately needed to go to the toilet, he could feel the building excrement urgently demanding immediate release. His stomach gurgled and he felt queasy. He desperately desired the absolute relief of being able to let it all go, but he just could not bring himself to put up his hand. The silence in the class was oppressive, and he knew he would never be capable of breaking such a studious peace with his quivering, nervous voice. Sweat beaded and dripped down his flustered face.

He knew that break time was near, and he prayed frantically that he could just hold on until the bell. Unfortunately for him he started to feel an insistent tickle starting at the back of his throat. He tried to quell it, but the need to cough was irrepressible. The first cough was the thin end of the wedge, once he started, he couldn't stop. Children started to mumble and look at him, the teacher looked over at him and frowned. This made it worse, and his coughing fit established itself, becoming completely irrepressible.

Jim coughed and coughed and coughed, he was mortally embarrassed at breaking such serene silence. Panic started to set it. The pressure on his stomach from his coughing was just the trigger his sphincter needed to give up the ghost and relax its hold on his burgeoning need to excrete.

A visible mark of his internal shame crawled up his neck and over his face. Jim turned bright crimson. Distracted by this new reason for fear, his cough faded away. The smell took some time to seep through the fabric of his trousers, but when it did it was horrendously potent.

Jim was sitting beside 'Spindly' Finley Marwood. He was the nearest thing he had to a friend. Finley was obviously the first in the class to detect the offensive odour, his nostrils dilated, and he turned to locate the cause. Finley saw the shade of Jim's face and the anguish writ in his eyes. Finley's eyes locked with his. The communication transmitted between them was complicated and multi-faceted.

Jim's eyes pleaded for understanding and compassion. Finley's eyes communicated incredulity and disbelief. Finley's eyes communicated that this time there was no way he could support him. Finley knew that to preserve what little status he had, he would have to cut his ties with Jim completely, his eyes expressed inevitability and apologetic regret.

Regretfully, Finley finally broke eye contact. As the rest of the class slowly became aware of the emerging situation Finley took the only strategic option he could. Finley knew that only desperate measures would prevent him becoming drawn into the shame storm that was soon going to engulf poor Jim McKenzie. As soon as a murmur of dawning started to rise from the rest of the class, Finley broke the impending news, "Miss! Miss! Jim has shat himself," he shouted out, pointing at Jim with one hand while holding his nose theatrically with the other. Finley's face was contorted with mock disgust, though deep down he felt great pity for Jim. He also felt deeply disappointed in himself for lacking the courage to support his friend.

For Jim time did bizarre things, it seemed to contract and expand at the same time. Some events seemed to happen in slow motion, while an instant seismic shift occurred in his psyche, which would set him on a behavioural course that would map out the rest of his life. He interpreted betrayal in Finley's actions, he learned in an instant that he could trust no one. He read rage in the eyes of the teacher, he knew now, that authority was both to be hated and coveted. Jim felt the overwhelming power of scorn from his peers. No one would laugh at him again. Common people deserved to be dominated and destroyed.

Finley's outburst ignited an uncontrollable explosion of untrammelled childish derision. Jim's classmates were always on the lookout for every opportunity to pour scorn on any unfortunate individuals. A chant went up, loud and relentless. *"Jim McKenzie is a jobby pants,"* over, and over, and over, again, and again, and again. The teacher was completely powerless to quell such an unremitting tide of childish contempt, though she almost burst a blood vessel trying.

"Would you lot just be quiet this instant. Silence. Class. NOW!" The teacher tried hard to be heard over the unrelenting chant. Her face flushed red, and veins throbbed on the side of her head as if about to burst and spray the room with hot, angry blood.

"Jim McKenzie; you need to leave the class right now," she pointed a quivering finger in the direction of the door. "Go straight to the main office and tell them exactly what has happened." Her eyes burned shame into his soul. "The rest of you BE QUIET NOW," she shouted to absolutely no avail.

The children continued to chant with rampant glee. To the refrain of "*Jim McKenzie is a jobby pants*," he slunk away from the classroom. The chant rung in his ears and imprinted itself on his consciousness forever. His long, lonely walk along the corridor to the main office was accompanied by the smell of his own excrement exuding from his trousers. Slimy bits of cooling ordure slid down the back of his legs. Resentment, low self-esteem, shame, and a thirst for revenge took up a complicated, interwoven residence in Jim McKenzie's core that day, and never left.

Driving down the coast road in Greenock, after his recent experience, his mind sang with this now familiar discordant quartet: resentment, shame, low self-worth, and a thirst for revenge. Jim muttered and mumbled angrily to himself; he was utterly oblivious to the glorious beauty of the Clyde estuary, bathed in the sun's early rays, as he drove by.

Jim completed the natural circuit of the coast road and headed back towards the town. Turning off the main road on the outskirts of town he took a winding road that would take him up the hill to his childhood home. Since his divorce Jim had moved back in with his mother. Jim's wife had employed the services of a particularly good lawyer, and Jim had lost the house and a sizable chunk of his wages to her in court.

Parking his, as of yet, unpaid for car outside his mother's council house his resentment darkened further, and settled in to indulge in some toxic, soul-destroying, bitterness. The house was in semi-darkness as he entered. In the kitchen was a glass of milk, and a cheese and pickle sandwich laid out for him by his mother. She did the same thing every time when he was on a night or back shift.

Pouring the milk away and throwing the sandwich in the bin Jim opened the fridge and reached in for a can of Tenants lager. There was a half-eaten bag of salted peanuts on the kitchen counter. Grabbing the nuts, along with his lager, Jim stomped into the living room.

Sitting down on the worn-out old sofa he flicked on the television. All that was on that he could feasibly watch was a repeat of a moronic chat show which had been on the night before, everything else was aimed at children. Jim watched the celebrities indulging in their usual ego driven self-promotion. He watched scornfully as they chatted with self-importance, discoursing about their latest senseless ventures, as if it were high-brow art. Jim stared vacantly at them with their sharp suits and expensive dresses. He both despised them, and desired to be like them. How could his life be so shit? Did he not deserve better?

The toxic resentment simmering away in his core made him thirsty.

Jim needed water.

As he poured the water out of the tap Jim paused to acknowledge his part in delivering this fresh clean water into this, and all other houses in Greenock. He refused to believe there was anything wrong with water straight from the tap. Jim refused to believe the nonsense other workers spouted about various bodily fluids being ejected into the tanks. He raised the glass to his lips and poured the water, and virus, straight down his throat.

The virus hit his stomach. It had now achieved its initial goal. It had sourced the perfect host, and now it went to work. Travelling quickly through his stomach lining, the virus passed into his liver. The liver tried and failed to neutralise the toxin, so it continued unhindered into his bloodstream. The virus was calibrated to go directly to the control centre. Riding through his blood vessels, the virus entered Jim's brain.

Jim finished his can of Tenants. Munching on some more peanuts he went back into the kitchen to get another can. The peanuts tasted different, off, he didn't like the taste. Going back into the living room he cracked open another can and flopped once again into the sofa. The virus started to take control. It assessed his brain, locating motor functioning, vital organs, desire, hunger, the dopamine reward systems, the adrenal glands, the virus knew what it was doing. It was ready. The virus started to shut Jim McKenzie down.

He felt heavy, fatigued, tired beyond tired. He supped at his newly opened can, he gulped as much of it as he could, he didn't like the taste of it either, he couldn't finish it. He had to get to bed. He couldn't ever remember feeling as tired as this, but it had been a difficult night. A vision of Joe Dunlop's triumphantly smug face flashed through his mind, followed by a vision of Kenny McGregor's stoned, arrogantly patronising face. *"Bastards,"* he thought, *"I'll fucking have the pair of them cunts".*

Tiredness overcame him completely, and he had no option but to lurch up the stairs as quickly as he could. He fought the lassitude gripping him determinedly. He made it into his bedroom and just managed to flop on top of his bed. This time the old saying was true, and he was indeed truly unconscious before his head hit the pillow.

It would take some time, the virus had a lot to do in the first flush of infection, there was a lot to learn, but the virus systematically went to work in order to complete its objective.

Chapter 8

The cool morning air hit Kenny's face like a wet fish as he and his colleagues left the refinery after their night shift. The invigorating freshness caused his eyes to flicker behind hooded lids, he took a big, deep breath. The large intake of oxygen battled to bring some semblance of coherency to his drug addled brain.

Joe walked steadily beside Kenny. He positioned himself close enough to Kenny to act as an anchoring guide for him to follow. Joe headed, and herded Kenny, towards the minibus that would take them all home. The wealthier workers headed to their cars, and the poorer workers headed to the minibus. Some of the early shift staff were hanging about outside the refinery, enjoying the morning sunshine while finishing off last minute cigarettes. Joe sought to shield Kenny from their quizzical eyes.

"You alright Kenny boy?" Joe asked quietly.

Kenny's eyes pointed themselves vaguely in direction of Joe's voice. He coughed, "Aye Joe, I'm alright." Kenny's voice was thick and rasping.

Climbing in behind him, Joe guided Kenny to the back seats of the bus. The bus filled up quickly with quietly tired workers keen to be heading home for breakfast and bed.

Bobby headed towards his car, turning to give Joe a triumphant wave before he climbed in. Bobby was relieved that a significant victory had been achieved that night, he was hopeful that now that the eternal war between them and Mac would finally be over. He drove home content in the knowledge that tonight had indeed been a good night.

The bus, once loaded with workers, was the last vehicle to leave the refinery car park. The route into the town centre, and the surrounding estates, took the bus past the Homerton estate. Driven by deep-rooted instincts, Kenny looked round and realised where they were. "You know? I think I might just get off here, Joe," he said nonchalantly.

"What?" Joe exploded. "Are you fucking kidding me Kenny? Look I know fine what you are getting off here for," Joe hiss whispered to Kenny. He was dumbfounded that someone, who was in such a wholly intoxicated state as Kenny was, would seek to bombard their brains further with more substances.

"No, no, no Joe," Kenny protested. "It's not what you are thinking mate, honest." Kenny's drug impaired brain scrambled for a plausible lie to justify getting off the bus in a part of town infamously awash with drugs. "My mam wanted me to run an errand for her, Joe. That's all." Kenny latched onto the first thing that came to his mind. "I need to go get her some bread before I go home, see?" Even in Kenny's extremely altered state he winced at the lameness of his lie.

"Are you fucking kidding?" Joe's face registered his absolute incredulity. "There's a shop right next door to your mam's. Why don't you just go there?"

"Aye, I normally would, but it's a special kind of bread she wants pal. You can only get it from the corner shop on the Homerton Road." Kenny knew his lie was awful, but as he began to embellish it, he became more comfortable with it. "What are wummin like Joe, eh?" He tutted and twitched his head upwards in feigned exasperation.

Joe raised his eyebrows, "Do you really expect me to wear that one Kenny?"

"I cannie turn up to my mams without that bread, Joe. She would go mental so she would." Kenny had started to believe his own lie.

Joe knew he was up against a powerful enemy; he knew when he was beaten. He looked straight into Kenny's swimming eyes. "Kenny son, I know I can't stop you doing what you're going to do. But just promise me you're going to be careful eh son?" Joe's paternal instincts were alive and humming. "I dunno, just stick to what you know Kenny. Don't get involved with any of the hard stuff, eh?"

The bus turned a corner and the Homerton estate, clinging like a manky limpet to the side of the hill, came into view. "This is me then Joe." Kenny tried to assuage Joe's concern. "Don't you worry about me Joe, I'll be tickety boo pal, tickety boo."

Reluctantly, Joe shifted aside in order to let Kenny pass. Joe's face revealed only resigned, passive stoicism.

Kenny lurch walked down the aisle of the bus as it bumped down the uneven, pot-holed road. Acknowledging Kenny walking down the aisle the bus driver signalled that he was stopping and pulled over at the nearest bus stop. Kenny stepped off the bus and back into the fresh morning air. He was reviving and ready for more chemical indulgencies. He waved at the stoical figure of Joe Dunlop as the bus continued on its way to deposit weary night shift workers in the vicinity of their respective homes.

Kenny turned off the main road into town and entered the bowels of the Homerton estate. He nodded at little Danny Cameron hanging around as usual at the entrance to the estate. The Homerton estate didn't accord the same respect for time as other places did; things happened when they happened. Generally the Homerton did not follow societal norms. Turning up for drugs early in the morning was not unusual.

Kenny headed straight for Lennie Wilson's house, at pace.

Lennie lived in a semi-detached council house. Detritus of various descriptions was in the process of being enveloped by overgrown grasses, bushes, and weeds in his front garden. Empty cans and bottles were being inexorably consumed by the overgrowing flora. Lennie's garden had its own peculiar furniture, a weather-beaten fridge and a tatty old chair nestled among the weeds. Empty bottles and cans grew their own fungal decorations.

Lennie's door had been kicked in so many times, by raiding Police and impatient addicts, that he had given up reporting it to be fixed. The council had pretty much given up repairing it anyway, and an inevitable acceptance that the door would remain broken was tacitly agreed on by both concerned parties.

Kenny did, as everyone else did, and just pushed the door open shouting, "Lennie, you in? It's me, as he entered." This served to inform everyone in the house that the entrant was friend, not foe.

Lennie's house smelled bad. The odour was a mix of dust, stale alcohol, sweat, old socks, dirty clothes, and rotting food. Lennie's house smelled like death. All the internal doors had all been removed, someone had tried to sell them to the local sawmill. After a curt rejection by the sawmill management the doors now lived propped up against a wall in his back garden. The back garden was in an even worse state than the front. It was home to an extremely battered old, stinky sofa, a huge pile of empty beer cans, wine bottles and a collection of takeaway cartons. In places the rubbish in the back garden reached such a height that it threatened to spill over the fence into next door's garden.

Lennie's long-suffering neighbours had been informed many times, by various dubious people, that retribution would be swift and effective should they ever consider reporting him to Environmental Health. This of course did not prevent the neighbours from grousing in vain periodically, both about the emanating smell and the creeping mass of stuff from both garden and house.

Kenny poked his head into the living room. Lennie was rummaging in one of the remaining recognisable items of furniture left in his house; an old, battered tallboy, devoid of doors but crammed full of valueless, broken knick-knackery. Similar to the tallboy, Lennie had also seen better days, his deeply lined face told of a tale that would probably qualify as a horror movie. There were three other people ensconced in the living room. Picking intently at a scab on his arm was Angus Gaffney. Crashed out side by side on the sofa were Jenny McAdam and Jack Curry.

"How do, Lennie?" Kenny ventured.

Lennie ignored him. Kenny was relatively new to the heroin scene in Greenock and had not really been accepted yet into this most distrusting community.

"Gaff! You alright?" Kenny tried getting some kind of response from Angus Gaffney.

"Hrumph," he replied.

Kenny pursued his quest for recognition. "Is there anyone else around?" he hopefully addressed the room in general. Lennie continued, with intense focus, to delve into the contents of his tallboy, Angus continued to pick at his scab, Jenny and Jack remained, to all intents and purposes, unconscious.

"You holding?" Lennie asked Kenny.

"Naw mate, I'm looking," Kenny replied, trying not to sound too intoxicated.

Remaining rooted to his allocated spot of living room floor, Kenny listened hard for any sign that there might be a more responsive life form anywhere else in Lennie's house. There was nothing. The living room was always the most likely place to find anyone, although the kitchen at the back of the house was also used frequently. Kenny decided to inspect the kitchen in the hope of finding someone, anyone.

He started moving towards the kitchen. "Where do you fucking think you're going?" Lennie barked, breaking off brusquely from his obsessive hunt in his tallboy.

"I was just going to see if anyone was in the kitchen Lennie. Is there anyone around?" Kenny's query was laced with implicit meaning. The precise identification of the "anyone" was left deliberately vague, but the insinuation about who that might be was crystal clear.

Lennie returned to his quest; bits of debris fell from the tallboy as he resumed rooting around. "Ed's coming round later," was all he said.

The mention of Ed McDonalds name caused Angus to desist from his scab picking. "What time's he coming?" he asked. The question was futile and the answer pointless.

"Said he was coming at nine," answered Lennie playing his part in the game of 'When is the dealer going to arrive'. Jenny and Jack even seemed to rouse slightly from their drug fuelled slump in response to the discussion about Ed McDonald just in case he miraculously appeared.

"Cool," said Kenny. "You mind if I wait here for him?" Kenny had good manners drummed into him from an early age, and it was a habit he found hard to break, even though manners were largely viewed as pointless and weak in the present company.

"Couldn't give a fuck," replied Lennie as more debris drifted away from the tallboy.

Kenny sat in the vicinity of Angus, close enough to be interpreted as joining him but far enough away that he wouldn't really have to take much to do with him. Angus was a long-time heroin addict and was known to be hard but fair, almost decent, but he was still an addict. "You alright, Gaff?" Kenny asked.

Angus sniffed. "I'm strung oot. You holding?" he asked, getting straight to the point.

"Naw mate, I'm looking," Kenny reiterated his reason for being there. The remaining temazepam jellies and hash from his nightshift 'entertainment' weighed heavily, and comfortably in his pocket. He knew that at least he had something if Ed McDonald failed to show up, which he frequently did.

Kenny was paranoid about being in possession of drugs. "I'm a bit strung oot myself, Gaff. I'm hanging out fir a boot," Kenny laboured the point somewhat.

Angus broke off from picking at his scabs and rubbed the back of his hand across his dripping nose. He looked at Kenny and took in his heavily lidded bloodshot eyes. Kenny broke off eye contact. "You're no strung oot ya shite. You're holding ya prick? Don't fucking hold out on me, eh!" Angus found renewed energy for the world beyond the scabs on his arms.

Kenny's paranoia scaled new heights. "My mate at work had a few jellies, Gaff. I had a couple earlier, and a wee bit hash. But I don't have shite mate, honest. If I had I'd sort you out, you know that." Kenny's face expressed honest, open concern and comradeship.

Angus sneered, grunted grumpily, and returned to picking his scabby arm.

Kenny opted for silence as the safest strategy.

The chemical composition of Kenny's bloodstream caused him to drift off, his eyelids drooped, and his head lolled.

Slowly but surely Lennie's house filled up with heroin addicts in various states of desperation. The noise subtly permeated Kenny's semi-conscious condition. Sporadic arguments broke out about who was holding out from whom, and who owed what to who. Slumped bodies in Lennie's house tended not to attract too much attention. Occasional bouts of envy were projected towards them verbally, but mostly unconsciousness was honoured as the desired objective of all.

Kenny opted to remain in an unconscious pose, and to await Ed McDonald's potential arrival. "What time's Ed coming?" was an oft repeated question aimed usually at Lennie. "I don't fucking know. He said nine," was inevitably the only forthcoming response. Both questioner and questioned knew they were performing an ubiquitous ritual and all parties duly honoured the part they played.

Increasingly the collective desperation level in Lennie's living room grew. Every rattle of the door signifying a new arrival was greeted at first with pregnant expectation, only to be followed by howls of anguish when the arrival announced themselves to be only yet another desperate, questing addict.

Eventually the man arrived.

The reposing addicts roused themselves with great alacrity. All the drug den denizens desperately tried to compose themselves in order to feign an insouciant attitude of indifference.

"Awright my people," Ed McDonald announced his arrival, scanning the room with his penetrating cold blue eyes. He took in who was there, which ones would have money, which ones owed him money already, and which ones would only attempt blatant manipulation.

"No fucking tick today people, by the way. Cash transactions only," Ed announced, diving straight into business, inviting the procurement to proceed.

A huddle of addicts promptly formed around him. Grubby hands delved swiftly into seedy pockets, grasping for their ill-gotten, hard-earned cash. Kenny joined the huddle. Angus, through well practiced superior menace, was the first to get his supply. He returned to his previous slouching spot and produced a small pouch. From his pouch he pulled out a well-used syringe, a spoon, a half-used packet of Abdine, and a battered bic lighter.

Angus prepared his injection with accomplished proficiency and set about finding a useable vein. He knew both his arms would prove fruitless, and his left hand was already puffed up from a previously botched attempt. So he dedicated himself to digging about in his right hand with the hypodermic needle, searching for a suitable vessel to transport heroin to his opiate deprived brain. A little flower of blood sprayed its way into the syringe, darkening the clear brown heroin. He was in. Angus's dry tongue nervously licked his lips, he pulled back the plunger, more blood burst into the syringe. Angus didn't wait for a second invitation; he slowly and very carefully deposited the contents of the syringe into his bloodstream. The effect on him was instant, his eyes rolled back in his head as the heroin hit his brain in one massive flood. He emitted a long, drawn-out moan of pleasure, and relief.

Kenny had money so he was also served quickly. Kenny was relatively new to the heroin scene, but he had learned quickly to keep his cards close to his chest. Once he was served he removed himself silently from the huddle and went on a search for tinfoil and solitude. He headed into the kitchen, this time no one paid him any heed, not even Lennie, they were all otherwise occupied.

Lennie's kitchen stunk of grease and neglect; it was grimy. Kenny rooted gingerly around the cupboards. As he expected there were many rolls of tinfoil in various levels of use. He pulled a pen from his back pocket and fashioned a smoking tube. Once the tube was ready, he emptied half the contents of his heroin package onto the tinfoil. Lighting the heroin from beneath Kenny inhaled a large plume of heroin smoke. Kenny chased the dragon all the way to his brain.

The effects of smoking heroin took slightly longer to manifest themselves than they would if he injected, but Kenny had made a solemn vow to himself that he would never, ever inject. Though he did recall at one point making a solemn promise to himself that he would never, ever take heroin. Kenny was learning that sometimes the promises he made to himself contained certain degrees of flexibility.

The taste of the heroin smoke was the first thing to hit him, sweet, almost milky, like warm brown sugar. The taste was slightly sickly but satisfying. The heroin made its way to his brain to join the rest of the chemicals currently dancing in his mind. An extreme sense of well-being settled in his core. The ever present, but unacknowledged, anxiety he lived with subsided in a warm, welcoming, opiate fog. Kenny had another long chase, then he folded the tinfoil carefully to keep the rest for later. The tinfoil and tube were placed carefully in his tobacco tin, a welcome addition to his ever-growing substance collection.

Kenny went back into the living room; Jack Curry was in the middle of a protracted and complex negotiation with Ed McDonald. Ed was impassive, "No fucking tick, Jack. I already fucking told you all".

Jack desperately studied Ed's face and body language, looking for the slightest chink of acquiescence. He just needed to detect the slightest sign of weakness in Ed, and he would pounce like a hyena. "You know I am good for it Ed," he whined. "I just need one wee hit before I go grafting," he pleaded. "I wouldnae fuck about with you Ed, you know that."

Jack did have a reputation for being an exceptionally good shoplifter. Ed knew this, but he also knew that even the best shoplifters eventually become too well known, thereby becoming bad shoplifters. Ed knew that Jack was heading inexorably in that particular direction.

Ed assessed the rest of the addicts, who were keenly waiting to see the result of Jack's negotiations. In his heart Ed knew that Jack was probably right, and that he probably was good for it, they had known each other a long time. But, unfortunately for him, Ed knew that Jack would be the thin end of the wedge. He was well aware that should he show any sign of weakness, and give in, there would be a cascade of addicts flooding in behind him, a precedent would be set, and it would cost him dearly.

Ed knew that the heart was not a good place make a business decision, especially when it concerned selling heroin to drug hungry addicts. His cold eyes narrowed, and his voice became quiet, tight, and hard. "I fucking told you Jack, no fuckin tick." Ed ensured that it was understood by all that this statement was to be taken as the final word.

Jack's stomach sank. Jenny McAdam, sitting on the battered sofa had been intensely following every nuance of the negotiation between them. At the conclusion she hung her head, as usual their day would not have an easy start. They needed a plan B. Jenny always had a plan B.

Ed had drained what little cash there was in the room. Guilt was beyond his capacity, but a need to be liked was not. "I tell you what," he announced to the room in general, catching the eyes of Jenny and Jack in particular. "There's a free bag of smack for anyone who brings me in that wee shite Kerr McClean. I don't give a fuck what nick he's in when he's brung, but I *really* want to see him."

It was generally known that Kerr had transgressed in his relationship with the McDonalds. The precise nature of his wrongdoing was unknown, though it was of course the subject of intense speculation. "Free bag of smack for the first person to bring me

Kerr McClean." With this tantalising offer left hanging in the air Ed McDonald exited Lennie's house.

Kenny felt the full force of the heroin hit his system as he staggered back to sit beside the slumped form of Angus Gaffney. This time Kenny didn't care about maintaining any distance from Angus and he sank in directly beside him. They sagged together and drifted off to join Morpheus in the underworld.

Jenny clocked the condition of Angus and Kenny, and she subtly sought her partners attention. Jenny was aware of how Kenny operated, and what stage of his addiction he was in. Unspoken, charged communications ensued. Jenny looked hard at Jack and then pointedly at Kenny. Jack grasped what she was implying and realised that there might be an opportunity for some free drugs after all. Plan B was initiated.

Jack had undertaken this kind of manoeuvre many times. Jenny knew what to do to assist, a distraction was needed. Lennie Wilson had distraction written all over him. Jenny made her move. Lennie was busy chasing the pitiful amount of heroin Ed had given him for the use of his premises to deal from.

"Gie us a wee hit Lennie would ye? I'm fucking hanging oot Len." Jenny's voice was gratingly pathetic, nasal and whining.

Lennie looked suitably incredulous. "Are you fucking kidding? Fuck off ya fucking shite-bag."

Jenny erupted with indignation," I fucking sorted you out last week Lennie you fucking prick." Jenny was loud and self-righteous. "You're aw the fucking same," she shouted round the room. "Yir aw just take, take, take. Yir aw just so fucking self-centred."

All open eyes in the room turned to her. The thinking going on behind the eyes ran along similar lines. Most were thinking that this was the biggest case of the pot calling the kettle black that they had ever seen, but they all enjoyed the prospects of some free theatre.

Lennie's eyebrows just about reached his rapidly receding hair line. Lennie spluttered his incredulity, his ire refused to allow coherent words to come out, and he ended up just mumbling an expletive laced stream of nonsense.

Meanwhile Jack's practiced hands had quickly located Kenny's tobacco tin. Jack had seen the receptacle for Kenny's stash before, and he strongly suspected there would be some tasty treats there for him and Jenny to consume. By the time Jenny had concluded her rant, Kenny's tobacco tin was nestled in his pocket. He caught Jenny's eyes and indicated it was time for them to leave. Jenny's righteous anger abated dramatically. "I'm not hanging about here with you fucking wastes of space." With her head held as high as she could Jenny marched towards the door with an exaggerated display of dignity. "Come on Jack, lets us go and find some better company to be with."

Jack quietly admired Jenny's acting skills and joined her in her march towards the exit. They would now investigate and digest their liberated chemicals. If they came across Kerr McClean in their future travels, then all well and good, but Plan B had borne fruit, and that was pretty much all they cared about.

The remaining occupants of Lennie's house breathed a collective sigh of relief that the commotion was over, and they returned to their own self-obsessed activities. Jenny and Jack were forgotten, instantly.

Chapter 9

As she finished doing the dishes Rosie Deacon gazed out at her husband as he pottered about in his beloved garden. The pleasure he was experiencing with his new chainsaw was plain to see. Rosie flicked the switch to boil the kettle, she would make him a cup of tea to demonstrate her forgiveness for his unauthorised extravagance. Another spasm of pain shot out from her stomach to echo through her body. Since breakfast she had become increasingly aware that there was something deeply wrong with her. She had returned to bed countless times, slept, and had been woken repeatedly by sharp explosions of pain. This was the longest she had managed to remain upright all day.

Rosie rapped the window and made a 'T' sign with her hands, John smiled, nodded, tidied away his chainsaw and sauntered his way into the kitchen.

"Make sure you take your muddy boots off before you set foot in this kitchen." Rosie kept her standards even though her head was screaming.

John studied his wife, she looked awful, her face was grey and dry looking, and her eyes were fiery bloodshot. "Are you sure you don't want me to stay behind dear. I really don't mind. I could look after you."

Greenock Morton were playing Queens Park Rangers in the quarter finals of the Scottish Cup. John had been following Morton his whole life, and the game this afternoon was one of the biggest in his lifetime. John was torn between two callings: his wife or his football team.

Presenting him with a hot sweet tea, Rosie avoided eye contact. "No, John you go to the match. You'd just get under my feet. I'll have another wee nap and I'll be right as rain in no time."

"Well, as long as you're sure love." Relieved at having his decision made for him, John took his tea upstairs to get ready for the match.

Relieved to be alone again Rosie flopped on the sofa and closed her eyes, again. She fought the nausea bubbling up in her gut and all she wanted was for John to go so she could just go back to bed, let go, and sleep. The virus was playing with her, trying out different things, exercising its control over her motor functions. It toyed with her synapses causing random jerking limb movements and caused fleeting feelings to travel over he central nervous system, they came from nowhere and left abruptly. Rosie felt ever closer to having a complete nervous breakdown.

Cleaned and changed, with Morton top and scarf on, John returned to the living room to say goodbye to his wife. "I'll come straight home after the game, Rosie. Ok?" he said hesitantly.

Startled out of her anatomical scrutiny Rosie looked at him in confusion. She loved him with all her heart, but her instincts cried out to her that he should go now, and that he should stay away for as long as possible. "No, no, no. No rush John. You go to the pub as usual sweetheart. I'll be right as rain after a wee rest."

"Ok my love. I'll see you after the pub then. We'll get a fish supper tonight, eh? Save you cooking." John kissed his wife goodbye. "You have a good rest then Rosie love," he shouted through the house as he closed the front door behind him.

Once alone Rosie relaxed and relinquished any pretence of strength and control. She tramped wearily up the stairs and gazed at herself in the bathroom mirror. Her skin was grey, and her eyes bloodshot. Her head throbbed with a pulsing, throbbing pain and she felt deeply fatigued, tired, drained, beaten. She stumbled, with a ripping pain coursing through her stomach, into the bedroom she had shared with her husband for the last 40 years. Fully clad, Rosie flopped face down onto the bed and plummeted deeply into a black, dreamless sleep; one from which she would never return. She lay prone, her slow shallow breathing counting out hours that, for her, now had no meaning. She fell, after a while, into a fit of involuntary tossing and turning, her legs and arms twitching uncontrollably. Moaning sounds rolled from her foaming mouth to fly around the bedroom like fat droning bluebottles. Suddenly, Rosie Deacon stopped twitching, and stopped breathing. She had gone, the virus had complete control of her body and mind, and it was time for it to play.

From its twisted position on the bed the complex collection of body parts that used to be Rosie Deacon emitted a deep, guttural moan. It rose and crouched on its arms and legs on the bed. Its head bent back unnaturally and started to jerk from side to side like a broken metronome. It opened its eyes, they had drained of colour, leaving them only a misty, cloudy, grey colour; with pinprick pupils that stared maniacally out at its' exciting, new world. The creature stretched its head back and emitted a deep guttural growl.

The thing that used to be Rosie attempted to move, but it struggled to coordinate. It managed, ungainly, to change from crouching on all fours to assume a seated position. Its' legs splayed out in front of it, and its arms jerked and flopped, like they were being fried by electricity, its hands and fingers twitched and curled spasmodically. Flopping about like a haddock on dry land it bounced to the edge of the bed and slid off, landing clumsily on the floor in a crumpled heap.

The zombie lay on its back on the floor, with its head thrashing from side to side, its tongue flicked out its' gurning mouth depositing grey, glutenous drool flecks over its face and neck. It eventually managed to sit up mostly straight. Grasping the bedpost it started to understand how to move, and it pulled itself to standing. It was ravenously hungry for human flesh.

Taking a deep breath it roared a raging, guttural, howl, which duly announced its triumphant presence on the worlds stage. It puffed its chest out; proud, and angry. It innately knew exactly what it was looking for and it was impatient to hunt. The door proved to be a barrier, it grappled and thumped and pulled at the handle, frustration and luck combined to eventually open it.

The zombie paused at the top stairs and frowned, it stuck out an experimental leg. It didn't quite know how to coordinate movement between both legs, while going downstairs at the same time, so it just lent forward into the first stair. It clattered down the whole flight of stairs, breaking an arm on the way. It landed in a pile at the bottom, its right arm sticking out at an unnatural angle, the zombie registered no pain. It had achieved, after a fashion, what it needed to do, and that was all that mattered.

The zombie scrabbled at the wall with its unbroken arm, breaking most of its nails in the process. It pushed with its legs and made it back up into a vertical posture again. Growling deeply as it staggered around the house, its flailing limbs crashed recklessly into Rosie's various beloved ornaments and pictures. The zombie left a trail of wanton destruction in its wake.

The zombie lurched over to stand at the front window, it stared out with deeply craving eyes. It sensed something, and hungrily sniffed the air. There was something interesting, and tasty smelling approaching. A neighbour was strolling past the house. The zombie's olfactory senses shot its craving into overload, it pounded frantically on the window. This was what it wanted, this was its aim, its mission, its reason for being.

As he strolled heedlessly past, the neighbour heard the commotion. Frowning with alarm he gazed askance at the spectacle of Rosie Deacon pounding on her window. One of her arms was bent and obviously badly broken; and thick gloopy blood was dripping from her broken nailed fingers smearing the window. "Are you all right, Rosie?" the neighbour cried, shocked concern furrowing his brow deeply.

Inside the house the zombie's desperation reached fever pitch, on a table beside the window it found a heavy trophy John had won in a bowling competition. The zombie grabbed it and hurled it through the window.

"What the fuck," the neighbour exclaimed rushing towards the house.

The zombie ignored the broken glass lacerating its hands and legs, and climbed ungainly out of the window, its broken arm flapping about at a weird angle.

The peaceful, sunny Saturday environment was such a juxtaposition to what he was seeing coming out of the Deacons' window, that the neighbour froze. With his eyes almost popping out of his head his brain simply refused to accept what he was seeing. Unfortunately for him his mind couldn't comprehend the mortal danger he was in. Fear and self-preservation kicked in too late. As soon as the zombie was out, it pounced on its prey.

It was ruthlessly vicious in attack. It bit at the poor neighbour's face, gnawing huge lumps out of his cheek, he screamed in pain and shock. The zombie's dripping saliva contained high concentrations of virus. Salivatic transmission of the virus was swift and efficient. The first bite of his face transmitted massive levels of toxic virus straight into his bloodstream. This did not prevent the zombie from viciously assaulting its first victim. It ripped at his stomach and tore great strips of flesh from his face with its teeth. The levels of violence meted out, and the powerful strength of the zombie belied its age, physical condition, and diminutive stature. The hapless, unfortunate neighbour was left lifeless within seconds.

The corpse of Rosie Deacons' neighbour lay bleeding on the ground outside the Deacons' house. Rosie zombie, with blood smeared over its face and torn flesh hanging from its mouth, finally lost interest in its first victim, but its hunger was far from sated, it was inflamed, it craved more. The zombie dragged itself to its feet and staggered of in search of more victims.

The corpse of Rosie Deacon's neighbour twitched as the virus reanimated death. The corpse opened its eyes, the colour was drained from its irises, its pupils were just pinpricks swimming in a drab grey sea. The zombie neighbour dragged itself to its feet and set off on the same quest as the Rosie zombie.

The air on this warm peaceful Scottish summer day was rent with scream after scream as Rosie zombie and its neighbour claimed victim after victim. The cycle was vicious, effective, and appalling. Greenock and the surrounding area had changed dramatically, forever. The impact on the entire nation and indeed the world would be profound.

Chapter 10

John Deacon parked up his Volvo and joined the rest of the fans, habitually making their way towards Cappielow Park where Morton played their football. The atmosphere was strangely subdued. Today was the highlight of the season, this fixture was the single most important match in Morton's recent history, but there was no singing, no chanting, no excited banter. People were just quietly, and slowly trudging their way towards the stadium.

There was nowhere near the amount of people that would have been expected at a match off such importance. Those that were there did not look well at all. John sipped from his plastic water bottle, stroked his chin thoughtfully, raised his eyebrows, huffed, and blew out a long breath. He shrugged off his creeping doubts, and carried on striding past sick looking people towards the stadium. John was also distracted by thoughts of Rosie; he was worried about her being home alone.

Inside the stadium both sets of players were ensconced in their respective changing rooms. Inside the Morton changing room the atmosphere was also curiously subdued. Players were milling around the locker room, reluctantly changing into their white shorts and blue and white striped tops. Their manager, Benny Banks, was wandering around, frantically whispering to his small support team. "You can't tell me they are all sick, not today. How the fuck can they all be sick on the same fucking day?"

Though clearly exasperated, Benny also did not look well.

Adam Gillespie, head coach and physiotherapist bustled about preparing. Adam wasn't a qualified physiotherapist, a club of the lowly stature of Morton couldn't afford a qualified physiotherapist. But it fell to him to run onto the pitch, in the occurrence of an injury; with his bucket and sponge to 'treat' the players. This was not a particularly clinical approach to dealing with an injury, but it was all they had. "Boss, every-fucking-body is sick, yourself included." Adam said in a voice infused with his habitual stoicism. Benny had a grey pallor, and stomach cramps were causing regular painful spasms to starburst throughout his body.

Inside the Queens Park dressing room the mood could not have been more different. Their manager, Ewan Norwood, was thundering around their dressing room, shouting, and bawling and geeing up his players. The prize of a place in the semi-finals of the Scottish cup was equally as sought after for the Queens Park players as it was for Morton.

The Queens Park players largely ignored their ranting manager. They had spent the last week listening to the same rant repeatedly. They knew theoretically what they were supposed to be doing. But they also knew that the reality of football at their level was, that even though you might try to implement some kind of tactic, an underlying lack of ability often meant it was difficult to maintain any kind of strategy.

Some of the Queens Park players were ready, most were nearly ready, but one was no-where near ready at all. "You actually gonnie fucking get ready Natty?" one of the players berated the somewhat lackadaisical Natty St Louis in scattergun Scottish.

"Wha?" Natty looked nonplussed. "Wha dat?" Natty claimed Jamaican heritage and was one of the few black players to be playing in the Scottish leagues. Natty knew not what his teammates were saying to him most of the time, and they were equally confused by his sparse articulations, delivered in perfect Jamaican Patois. But Natty was fast, and he was by far the most skilful player at Queens Park, albeit only when the notion took him.

Ewan tentatively approached Natty and managed to lock eye contact with him. He spoke slowly, and just a little bit louder than usual. "He is asking if you are going to get changed into your strip at any point in the not-too-distant future St Louis?" Ewan lifted his eyebrows in question, and held up Natty's strip to emphasise the point.

Natty kissed his teeth and replied, "Mi wi dweet inna minute".

Ewan stood non-plussed, his eyes wide and vacant, trying desperately to process the communication just imparted by his player. Ewan sighed and turned to face the rest of his team, "I think he's going to get changed in a minute," he concluded.

With a great show of dignity, managing to communicate through his body language that this was his choice, Natty took his strip from his manager and started to finally get changed.

Due to his speed and skill, Natty's position was on the wing. His main striking partner was the centre forward Mark Hickey. Mark was changed and ready to go, he approached Natty. "Ye awright Nat?"

Natty raised his languid eyes and muttered a non-committal grunt.

"You're gonnie tear them apart today, Natty." Mark was aching to get on the pitch. "They're aw fat fuckers, and they're slow as fuck. Their defence is aw wee cunts too. Get the baw intae the box as much as you can Natty, and I'll be on a hat trick afore half time." Mark emphasised his point by demonstrating with a leap and a nod of his head.

Natty mostly got the gist of what Mark was saying. "What will be, will be, blood," he replied as he continued to get changed, at his own languid pace.

This was a greatly anticipated day for both sets of fans, and Cappielow had been slowly but surely filling up from early on. A Cappielow staff member walked up and down the tunnel outside the two respective changing rooms clanging a large bell to announce that the time for the teams to take to the pitch was imminent. Natty tied his last boot lace just in time, he was, of course, the last to finish getting ready.

Ewan took a deep contemplative breath as he studied his players readying themselves to face their opponents before battle commenced. The players jumped up and down taking deep breaths, adrenaline and nerves were well and truly pumping through their bloodstreams. Natty just stood, looking well and truly bemused.

In the Morton changing room Benny Banks was also reviewing his players as they lined up prior to accessing the tunnel. They looked like a strong puff of wind would bowl them over. Rubbing his stomach in an attempt to ease the mounting pain, Benny looked at his players and internally admitted defeat there and then. He knew in his heart that his players, in their current condition, couldn't beat their way out of a paper bag. "Just go out there and do your best lads, eh? Enjoy the day as best you can boys," Benny finally said, resigned.

Some of the players attempted to straighten their wilted postures, to try and summon some energy to play in the single most important game of their careers. Others just groaned and anticipated the moment when the match would be over so they could plunge into the oblivion of sleep.

The bell rang again, and the managers opened their respective doors, the players met in the tunnel. The opponents eyed each other, some of the Morton players stood tall and eyed their opponents with as much aggression as they could muster, but most of them just lowered their eyes and stared at their shuffling boots. They knew they were beaten before they walked onto the pitch, and sadly most of them didn't care.

The referee, who was standing at the head of the players turned to his linesmen, "Ready?" he asked. They nodded in affirmation. He turned to the captains standing at the head of their teams. "Ready?". Both captains surveyed their teams, the Queens Park captain made sure Natty was there. The Morton captain thought his team only looked ready for the knackers yard. Both captains nodded their assent to the referee.

The referee turned and ran out onto the pitch, followed immediately by the two teams.

As the teams ran on the pitch there was a massive, anticipatory roar from one section of the crowd, and a feeble half-hearted attempt at a welcome from the rest. The Queens Park section was full and pumped up, loud cheers and chanting songs rang out. The Queens Park players responded. They ran over to their enthused fans clapping, pumping fists, and howling with aggression. Natty strolled over to his wing and squinted at the bright warm sun in the clear blue sky.

The Morton section was only partially filled, even though they were the home team. Individual shouts could be heard among the general silence that greeted the Morton players. The Morton players mostly ignored their fans and chose to stand alone in their respective positions.

As a seasoned season ticket holder, John Deacon sat in the same seat he had been occupying for many, many years. The crowd around him was sparse and extremely sick looking, none of his friends had turned up. John sat stroking his chin and pondered what was going on, he examined the Morton players. They also looked sick. John's worrying presentiment grew; things were just not right, and he was unable to fathom how he should respond to it all. Phlegmatic stoicism was his habitual default attitude. "*What will be, will be*" he thought.

The two captains met in the middle of the pitch. They shook hands with each other and the match officials. The coin was tossed, Morton won the right to kick off. The players stayed in the halves of the pitch that they had initially occupied during the warm-up.

Two Morton forwards trudged up to the centre circle, waiting motionlessly for the referee to blow the whistle. The referee duly obliged, and the match was started.

The Queens Park players were pumped, and they sprang with speed into action. They dispossessed the two Morton forwards easily. The Queens Park midfield pushed up immediately, Natty broke into an explosive sprint, and flew up the right wing, a cross field ball from midfield found him easily. Natty flew past the Morton left back like he wasn't there and flighted a flawless cross into the box. Natty's cross was met head on by Mark Hickey, who guided the ball perfectly past the static Morton goalkeeper. The Queens Park fans went wild, not even a minute played, and they were one up already. This was the perfect start.

Lethargic, sick, and resigned to a bad day the Morton keeper picked the ball listlessly out of his net. He drop-kicked the ball apathetically towards the centre circle, the ball sliced out the pitch, one of the Morton players slouched slowly off to retrieve it.

Morton restarted the match, and the Queens Park players repeated their aggressive pounce. Once again, they were far too quick and forceful for the beleaguered Morton players, and inevitably the ball was swiftly and easily dispatched into the back of their net; again.

Slumped on the Morton bench, Benny Bank's head sank heavily into his hands. This was humiliating, and it looked like the situation was unlikely to improve. Benny looked round at his substitute goalkeeper; he looked green and was lying back in his chair with his eyes closed. Benny buried his head back into his hands.

Morton kicked off again. This time they passed it straight back to their defence to try to buy themselves some time before the Queens Park players pounced. Morton managed to string a few passes together, and this time the Queens Park players took it easy on them. There was a collective question going through the Queens Park players' minds. "*This is way too easy. What the fuck is going on?*" This question translated into physical hesitancy, they wanted to win the match, but not like this. There was obviously something deeply wrong, and it was making all but one of the Queens Park players nervous.

Natty ignored the collective anxiety and took the ball, without a fight, from the Morton midfield. Natty looked up and saw a direct path in front of him to the goal. He set off at breakneck speed and curled the ball beautifully past the once again static Morton keeper. Three nil. The game as a competition was effectively over and there was not even 10 minutes on the clock.

For the already ailing Morton players, watching the ball hit the back of their net repeatedly had a completely demoralising effect. They half-heartedly kicked off again passed it back to their defence who sliced the ball weakly out for a shy. John Deacon looked on askance. He stared around to seek some solace from fellow fans, his team were woeful, and the fans didn't even seem to care. There were no torrents of abuse, or howls of anguish, John was mysteriously surrounded by mute indifference.

In the stand opposite he saw fans actually sitting down in the terracing, some of them even appeared to be asleep. One of the Morton players collapsed on the pitch with no one even near him. The referee noticed. The referee was also acutely aware that this was not the game he was expecting to be officiating today. With an internal sigh of relief at the temporary reprieve from the sheer weirdness of the game, he blew his whistle to allow the fallen player to be attended to. Everyone in the stadium took the chance to internally reflect and attempt to process what exactly was going on.

Adam ran onto the pitch with his sponge and bucket of water. Due to the poor physical state of the players prior to kick-off Adam was worried, but not surprised, at the collapse. Examining the crumpled player Adam felt his concern soar dramatically, the player was ashen faced, and did not look like he was breathing, with panic rising in his chest Adam felt fruitlessly for a pulse.

Adam stood and turned to face the bench, waving his arms he shouted to call an ambulance, the bench was collectively absorbed in their own deteriorating physical conditions, so took no notice of Adam's frantic pleas. The referee in attendance saw Adam's panic, and the condition of the stricken player, and started to feel that he was perhaps far out of his depth, this was so not the day he was expecting at all. He feebly shouted to the bench to call for medical help too.

The raised hackles on the back of his neck caused Adam to become aware that the previously prostrate player, with no pulse, had now risen to his feet behind him. Adam turned, as his eyes needed proof that a formerly clinically dead person, was now standing upright. A guttural growl confirmed to him that the person who was, just a moment ago, depicting all the signs of death, was now animate. The referee stood dumbfounded thinking of all the many places he would now much rather be than here, officiating the creepiest match of his career.

The eyes of the previously dead player opened in his greenish, grey face. The colour of his irises had gone, pinprick pupils stared out piercingly from drab grey orbs. The virus had better mastery of motor functions by now, due to viral communications received from the zombies caused by Rosie. The player zombie pounced on Adam and started to gnaw great gouts out of his face, Adam screamed in horror and agony.

Adam's scream pierced the eerie silence that had descended on Cappielow. Every eye was turned disbelievingly towards the gruesome scene being played out in front of them. The referee's brain shut down completely, and his arms dropped by his sides. The zombie player turned from Adam, his job there was done, the virus was transmitted. The zombies' hungry eyes fixed on the referee momentarily before launching itself to feast on his face.

The whole stadium seemed in caught in a collective inertia. Mass miscomprehension caused individual paralysis. More screams ripped apart the bizarre, hushed torpor; one of the Morton fans had quietly died unnoticed in the stands, only to reanimate as a zombie. This zombie was now chewing his way through random spectators. The deadly fracas quickly spread throughout the fans.

Zombie Adam Gillespie, the zombie referee and the first Morton zombie sped across the pitch in search of more victims. The enticing smell of fresh flesh was more potent from the healthy Queens Park players and fans. The zombie craving quest headed in their direction.

Self-preservation kicked in strong with Natty St Louis, he glanced over at his strike partner Mark Hickey. Mark was paralysed by shock, Natty permitted himself an effort at a potentially life-saving intervention. "Bomboclaat! Dat a duppy Mark. Come make we lef ya so," Natty tried to motivate Mark to no avail. Natty resorted to shouting, "Mark, fucking do one," in broad cockney. Natty then sprinted off at top speed towards the dressing rooms. Mark, shaken from his petrification, took off as fast as he could to join Natty in a life-or-death sprint for the dressing rooms.

All over the pitch various players from both teams were being taken down by various zombies only to reanimate. The reanimation process happened quicker and more efficiently every time, the virus was rapidly perfecting its transmission process. The same process was mirrored in the terraces and stands as on the pitch. The chaos spread more quickly in the crowd due to the proximity of potential victims.

John looked around him completely stupefied by what he was seeing. He had a murky realisation, he connected what he was seeing with the condition Rosie was in when he left. John now knew what his wife's fate was. A wave of chaotic consumption undulated towards him. John faced the wave with tears streaming down his face, and capitulated, without a fight to the first attack. John went down with the weight of the zombie body that had attached itself to his neck. The virus raced around his blood stream and fulfilled its cold function, John Deacon joined the exponentially growing zombie race.

Natty evaded various lunging zombies by sheer fear fuelled speed. Mark was not as quick as Natty, but he was large and strong, and he had a powerful punch. Mark whacked zombies clean out of the air as they lunged towards him.

Natty was the first of the fleeing Queens Park forward line to make it to the entrance of the tunnel, Mark was not far behind him. Hot in pursuit of them was a hoard of howling zombies, their curling snarling lips baring gnashing grey teeth, snapping in anticipation of a feast of fresh flesh. Their zombie pinprick eyes focused hungrily on their targets as they barrelled towards Natty and Mark.

"Get a fucking shiff on Markie," Natty yelled standing in the open door of the dressing room.

An extra spike of life preserving adrenaline flooded his system, providing Mark with a burst of speed he had never had in his whole career as a footballer. He desperately leapt the last couple yards away from the zombies grasping claws and flew past Natty into the dressing room.

Mark tumbled to the ground and rolled over on the floor as Natty swiftly slammed the door closed on the pursuing zombies. The full frenzy of the zombies slammed hard against the door, clawing, and pounding and howling in a desperate, hungry rage. Natty locked the door, turned to check if Mark was ok, and then forced his panic to flee in an attempt to restore some of his natural poise.

Inexplicably, a persistent thought pervaded Mark's consciousness. This thought gained traction and Mark's fried brain was unable to focus on anything else, he turned to look at Natty incredulously. "You can speak normal?"

"Wha name normal? Mi naw no whey you ah chat bout," Natty shrugged.

"What the fuck is going on out there Natty?" Mark's concerns reverted to a more pertinent subject.

Natty swaggered across the dressing room and turned to face the dressing room door, his hands on his hips. The zombies continued to howl and scrape desperately at the door. The noise that reached them from the stadium outside was truly terrifying; a cacophony of screaming mixed with a throb of underlying moaning and growling.

Natty sighed, his body language changed from nonchalant to beaten, he dropped into cockney. "Fuck. I don't fucking know Mark." He pointed at the door, "That, is, fucking, mental!"

"What the fuck are we gonnie do?" Mark asked the obvious question.

Natty shrugged and walked to a nearby bench. "Sit tight in here I suppose. Someone's gotta come and sort this out for sure, innit?" Nattys statement dripped with doubt and blind hope.

Screams penetrated the door. "Who the fuck is gonna sort that shite out?" Mark spluttered, his panic peaking in hopelessness. "The Greenock Police? Are you fucking kidding me?"

Natty thought of his already extensive experience of the Scottish Police Force. "Shit, we are fucked!"

Outside the door the zombies intensified their efforts to break in and eat Mark and Natty. They scrabbled and pounded on the door which, for the moment, remained impervious to their attacks. The zombies could hear the bedlam coming from the stadium. Their primitive instincts informed them that the best opportunity to satiate their cravings was currently to be found elsewhere. They slouched off back up the tunnel following the sounds of their fellow zombies indulging in a fleshy feast.

Natty sat. Mark paced the floor. Mark's brain was firing a mass of desperate synaptic messages, which fused his mind and prevented any attempt at calm, cohesive reasoning. "Fuck, fuck, fuck. What the fuck was that?" Mark was on the verge of hyperventilating. "They were fucking eating each other!" Mark verbalised the main issue that his mind refused to comprehend.

Natty sat. Natty's brain was also struggling to process what he had just witnessed. However, Natty also had a philosophical outlook on life that assisted him to maintain a dignified approach to most situations. Though he would have to admit this current predicament was indeed the biggest test of this philosophy yet. Natty approached the dressing room door.

"What the fuck you doing Natty?" Mark shouted, panic rising. He was naturally a little apprehensive about Natty's intentions.

"Calm the fuck down Mark. And shut the fuck up." Natty brooked no disagreement. He pressed his ear to the door and held a finger to his lips. Natty needed Mark to be quiet. Mark stood shaking, adrenaline coursing through his system.

"I think they've gone," Natty concluded.

"They? What the fuck are they? They were people trying to fucking eat us! What the fuck was that all about?" Mark was still far from calm.

The sounds of carnage coming from the stadium intensified. Natty slumped down on one of the benches. "Mark, dude, I know just as much as you do about what that was. But I can tell you one thing. I am not stepping foot outside that door until I hear the rosy sound of silence coming from that pitch."

"So, we're fucking trapped here?" Mark's desperate, angry fear was unconstrained.

Natty had had enough, and he got angry. "You can fucking do what you fucking want Mark. If you fancy heading out there," Natty pointed at the door, from behind which, dreadful agonising screams were penetrating, "You are more than welcome, best of fucking luck to you. But I am going fucking no-where, yet."

There were bottles of water and Mars bars stacked up waiting for the players at half time. Natty helped himself to a Mars bar and a bottle of water. He chucked a bottle and a Mars bar at Mark. "You'll need water and energy Mark. Drink and eat, eh?"

Mark managed to catch them both. He stared at the refreshments. It was a normal thing to do, eat and drink, normal was appealing and wrong, but there was also nothing else to really do. Mark slumped to a bench and stared open eyed at the confectionary in his hands. Sighing he opened the bottle of water and took a deep draught of the cold water. It dawned on Mark the gist of Natty's thinking.

Mark stopped drinking and listened to the sounds of carnage coming from the pitch, he gulped, his mouth dried up. "Are you saying we are going to have to outrun that?"

"Mi no know," Natty replied.

"Oh, for fuck's sake Natty, drop the Jamaican. I know you're a fucking cockney now."

"You don't get to tell me what I am and what I'm not Mark." Natty carried on consuming. "What I'm fucking saying Mark, is, I don't know what we are going to do."

Natty's superior vehemence silenced Mark.

The screaming from the stadium continued to assault them.

Natty and Mark looked at each other, scared beyond scared. Their systems had cleared from their respective spikes of adrenaline. "Way I see it Mark", Natty summed things up from his unique perspective. "No one is going to be coming to check if anyone has survived that." Natty waved his hand in the general direction of the pitch. "We can't stay here forever." It was stating the obvious, but Natty had to say it to make it real. "So, at some point, we are going to have to leave. And I reckon once we do leave, at some point, we are going to have to run like fuck." Natty resumed eating and drinking.

Dumbfounded, Mark sat blinking. His imagination was unwilling and unable to begin to contemplate what would be out there once they emerged from the relative safety of their changing room. Mark silently started to nibble on a Mars bar.

Part 3

Chapter 11

The sun sat majestically in the middle of a cloudless Scottish sky baking Greenock in sumptuous heat. The small animals, that had made the hills surrounding Greenock their home, were busy. Breeding was a primary preoccupation for most animals at this time of year. They courted, begged, and fought with each other for the privilege of reproducing their unique genetics. Plants blossomed spectacularly; majestically displaying their natural beauty purely to celebrate the magnificence of existence. The flora and fauna surrounding Greenock were content and thriving. The local Homo Sapiens were enduring a distinctly more challenging experience.

Normally the denizens of Greenock would also be revelling in this rare blessing being bestowed on them by their frequently yearned for plasma giant. But circumstances in this Scottish town had become entirely abnormal. A unique and malevolent virus had succeeded in entering the bloodstreams of the majority of the town's inhabitants. The virus had achieved its initial aim and was now proliferating with aggressive and impressive proficiency.

There were isolated cases where, either due to superstition or suspicion, people had not consumed the tap water, and had therefore not ingested the virus. Some people had inadvertently made their water safe by boiling it, others were fortuitously kept virus free by drinking bottled water instead. There were even a small number of isolated cases where individual immune systems prevented the virus from taking hold via oral consumption.

But the virus was designed well, its weaknesses were compensated for. The virus had other ways to spread its toxins. Transmission via the bloodstream, bypassing the digestive system, was quicker, more efficient, and more likely to result in infection. Accessing an organism's bloodstream was simple, one bite from an infected host and the conveyance of contamination was accomplished. The virus was designed to multiply voraciously and to spread as rapidly and ruthlessly as possible. In the event that the virus was unable to convert a host for whatever reason, it was designed to kill it. The virus was devised to be mercilessly violent.

Initially when the virus converted its first few hosts it explored their physiology to assess the organism's functionality, and how to control and manipulate it. The virus was designed to transform its hosts, it was designed to utilise its hosts in order to achieve ongoing, optimum transmission. The virus was sophisticated, complicated, and brutally efficient.

A key asset of the virus was its ability to communicate across hosts. It could communicate basic information, regarding motor functions for example, to other hosts. The scope of this ability to communicate was large but not infinite. Once the multiplication process was underway the more hosts there were the more effective was its ability to communicate. The virus learned, evolved, and communicated this learning to other hosts in its immediate vicinity. This communication would be passed on rapidly until all the hosts evolved.

Viral violence was now spreading incrementally throughout the streets and housing estates of Greenock, Gourock and Port Glasgow. No part of the area remained unaffected by this brutal carnage.

Chapter 12

Sunlight blazed through unclosed curtains into a bedroom on the second floor of a flat on Emerald Crescent, nestled in the heart of the Stones estate. The rays from the sun had been inching across the floor since dawn, they were now fast approaching the firmly closed eyes of a loudly snoring Innes McDonald. Sunlight, his bladder, and alcohol cravings fought hard against the liquid anaesthesia liberally administered the previous evening to provoke consciousness in him.

In the end, the need to evacuate his bladder tipped the balance, and Innes struggled toward some semblance of sense. He experimented with opening his eyes, which was a bad idea, pain shot through his brain, and he swiftly pulled them closed again. His body felt clammy, sweaty, and shivery despite the heat. Unfiltered sunlight was too much for him to cope with. Wrenching himself from the bed he dived for the curtains and closed them; regretting his inability to perform this simple task before passing out the night before.

Innes flopped back in bed and attempted to return to sleep. His efforts were futile, his bladder demanded immediate attention. This time opening his eyes was a little less painful, and he swivelled to perch upright on the edge of the bed. He rubbed his eyes and head, then peered at the bedside table to see if he had any cigarettes nearby. He didn't.

Grumping with discontent he ventured out of the bedroom and slouched his way towards the bathroom. Standing up to urinate seemed like too much of an effort, his head was spinning badly, so, sitting down, he unleashed a massive jet of foul-smelling urine. Innes's stomach lurched, he burped and tasted curry. Successfully resisting the urge to vomit he flushed the toilet and vacated the bathroom to bounce painfully down the stairs in search of nicotine.

Scanning the living room as he entered, Innes ignored the hideous mess he had made the night before. He was fixated on finding a cigarette. A closed pack of 10 Club sat on the table beside a box of Bluebell matches. Opening the box, he was relieved to see a couple of cigarettes nestled perfectly there. His hand shook slightly as he lit one.

Next, he paid attention to his other insatiable craving, alcohol. Snuggled amongst the mess on the living room table sat a lone can of Breaker. It taunted him with its golden shininess. It had clearly been opened, but he couldn't remember if he had finished it. Reaching out a quaking arm he grabbed the can. The weight informed him that this particular can was half full. He tugged again on his cigarette and put the can to his lips to drain it. As soon as he started drinking, he became aware that lager was not the only constituent of this particular can, a gentle rattle informed him that there was a cigarette butt bobbing about in his beer.

Innes and his alcohol cravings were not about to be put off by a mere cigarette butt, he almost finished the can. He had just enough self-respect to not drink the part that would certainly contain flaky, wet tobacco, and a vile tasting, spongy fag-end. Picking sodden tobacco off his tongue he retched but didn't vomit. It was imperative that the alcohol, newly introduced into his system, remain there long enough to enter his bloodstream and brain.

There were numerous possibilities to source another can. His wife, Mary, was good at finding, and disposing of his stashes, but he was more devious and determined than she was. He visited one of his favourite places, the back of Mary's jumper drawer. Innes had given up hiding booze in his own clothes drawers years ago, it was too obvious. But she never thought to check her own drawers, ever. Nestled there at the back, under an old jumper, sat a most welcomed can of Breaker.

Springing contentedly down the stairs back to the living room with his can, he turned on the radio. Radio Clyde were reporting about the impending kick off between Morton and Queens Park. He cracked the can and savoured the taste of cigarette butt free beer.

Innes had made it a principle never to eat on an empty stomach, that was now not an issue, so he ambled into the kitchen to see what it could produce. There was nothing instantly edible in the fridge but fortunately the breadbasket yielded an unopened Swiss roll. He tore the package opened and devoured the contents. He was now ready to participate more actively in life as he knew it.

Bouncing back up the stairs to the bathroom, Innes checked out his attire (he hadn't managed to de-clothe the night before). The white t-shirt he was wearing had all sorts of stains on it, curry, booze, and other unidentifiable contaminations. His t-shirt would need changing, but his jeans passed muster, they would do for another day. At the top of the stairs, he deposited his stained t-shirt in the laundry basket and headed into the bathroom.

There was no point indulging in prolonged ablutions, so he just splashed some water on his face and gargled mouthwash. His stomach burbled to remind him he had consumed a curry last night, and that the time to pay the price was nigh. He took this opportunity to inspect his y-fronts. There were some dubious looking stains on them, but they were fresh on yesterday, so he felt they would hold for one more day. Mary wasn't due back for another couple of days, so it wouldn't really matter. Understandably, it had been a long time since Mary had any interest in his y-fronts, or their contents, anyway.

On the way back to the bedroom he checked the time on the wall clock. 1:05. The Diamond would be open. Innes pulled on a black t-shirt and a fresh pair of socks. Donning a battered pair of trainers and his trusty denim jacket, he considered himself well and truly ready for the pub.

The Diamond public house was a small, run-down establishment, located in the middle of the Stones estate. The Stones was not the worst housing estate in Greenock, but it was also far from the best. The walk to the Diamond took him past a little parade of shops where bookmakers, an off licence, and a general store sought to profit from providing the estate residents with their daily requirements.

Inevitably there was a small gathering of local kids hanging about at the shops. The boys were acting up for the girls, and there was lots of general mucking around. Innes spotted his niece, Fiona, who also spotted him. She proceeded to beg him, non-verbally, to please not embarrass her in front of her peers. Innes grunted her a curt welcome. This seemed to be deemed acceptable by Fiona, who sullenly grunted her appreciation, and salutations, back.

Innes reached the Diamond and pushed open the full-length swing doors. The pub interior matched the exterior perfectly, it was functional. The darkness and cool of the interior was in stark contrast to the bright, warm day outside. Inside, the pub smelt of a mix of cigarette smoke, body odour, and stale alcohol.

Innes strode across the sticky carpet to the bar. "How do Cammy," Innes announced his presence to the barman, manager, and owner of the Diamond, who was polishing and stacking wine glasses. There were numerous optic spots behind the bar dedicated to dispensing Eldorado wine, the favourite tipple of Diamond clientele.

"Fine and dandy Inny," replied Campbell Williamson, as he continued to polish the wine glasses. "Usual Inny?" he enquired arching his eyebrows expectantly.

"Aye, Cammy, a half and a half please mate," Innes replied taking a seat at the bar. Sitting a couple of seats down from him was Bobby Thompson from the water refinery. Bobby also lived on the Stones estate.

As Campbell sorted out his order, Innes scanned the room to see who else was there. The Diamond was relatively busy, considering the weather was nice, and the football was on. Conn O'Mara and Peter

Clarke, also from the refinery, were ensconced at the fruit machine at the back of the bar next to the toilet. *The* singular toilet was a male toilet. There were no female toilets in the Diamond. This pub didn't get many female customers, and they weren't particularly encouraged. If a female was brave, stupid, or desperate enough to desire a drink in the Diamond, she either had to have a strong bladder, or live nearby.

There were various groups, and lone drinkers, sitting at tables quietly consuming their alcohol. No one except for Conn, Peter or Bobby looked particularly well. Even for Diamond customers these people looked particularly grey and sickly.

All the people drinking in the Diamond were Stones estate residents. The Diamond was not a pub you went out of your way to visit, and the Stones estate was not an estate anyone ever travelled through to get anywhere, so all the drinkers knew each other in one way or another. Drinkers in the Diamond largely kept themselves to themselves, unless they were drunk, seeking attention, or both.

Innes took a large gulp of his wine, the sweet, vile taste caused his stomach to involuntarily judder, though vomiting was never going to be an option. He chased his wine down with a gulp of lager. He caught Bobby's eye, "Awright Bobby, how'd the night shift go?"

Bobby had adopted keeping himself to himself as a motto for life. If Joe Dunlop led, he would follow, but other than golf and the occasional drink, Bobby didn't really care about anything else. "Was awright I suppose Inny. Were you out last night?" Bobby was prepared to indulge in a small amount of polite conversation, it helped keep people from bothering him too much, it helped not draw attention to himself for being antisocial.

"Aye. I was out wi Vanie. Just managed to avoid spending any time wi that fuckin loon Fergie and his sidekick Dave Anderson." Innes had topped up with enough alcohol to feel vaguely sociable. "They kicked the crap out of some Celtic lads, who thought it was a good idea to pop into the Hole in the Wall for a pint."

"Celtic boys in the Hole in the Wall!" Bobby was incredulous at this news. "They cannie be local then." Bobby observed. "They got what was coming to them then. Don't know what they were thinking of going into in the Hole in the Wall."

"No one deserved what Ian Ferguson and Dave Anderson did to them poor boys, Bobby. They were a mess after them two bampots had a go at them." Innes shook his head, which released some residual pain. Innes changed the subject, "You no going to the Morton today then Bobby?"

"Naw, I've not been to Cappielow for years Inny." Bobby's body language informed Innes it was time for him to be left alone.

Innes felt the need to urinate. He nodded hello to Conn and Peter on his way into the toilet.

"Awright Inny," they chorused to the back of his head.

On the way back out from the toilet Conn sought Innes's attention. "Hey Inny. Huv you heard about Mac the Sack?" There was a gleeful glint in Conn's eye, he had a juicy story, and he was going to enjoy its telling.

"Naw," replied Innes wiping his hands dry on his jeans.

"You know Joe? Joe Dunlop? He's on the back shift wi Bobby." Conn nodded over in the general direction of Bobby, who studiously ignored him but kept an ear wide open. "And Mac the Sack. Everyone knows him." Peter was grinning, he knew what was coming and he knew it was gossip gold.

"Aye, I know Joe well. And every cunt knows Mac. Weaselly cunt." Innes eyed his alcohol on the bar poignantly. "What's that bald prick done now?" Innes was keen for Conn to get to the point.

Conn obliged. "Joe's only gone and caught Mac the fuckin' Sack knocking one out in the fucking storeroom."

Peter let rip a huge guffaw of pent-up laughter. "Dirty old bastard has been spanking the fucking monkey every night in the storeroom." Going cross eyed and miming the aforementioned act Peter caused Innes to temporarily forget about his booze.

Innes didn't particularly like, or respect, either Conn or Peter, but this news was class A gossip, and just had to be enjoyed. Innes sincerely joined in with the merry indulgences being relished by Conn and Peter, "No fucking way. Dirty old bastard. Fuck. I bet Joe is fucking rubbing his hands now. He's got Mac right where he wants him. Joe and his mates are untouchable now." Innes spotted the angle immediately.

"Aye," Conn replied. "It's a pity it's gonnie go to waste on that prick McGregor though. I'm fucked if I know why Joe bothers wi that cunt."

Sat at the bar Bobby stiffened at this statement. Innes bristled, he had been duly reminded why he didn't like Conn or Peter. His enjoyment of Mac the Sack's sexual peccadillos turned to fake. Innes didn't know Kenny that well, but he was a kindred spirit, and they had shared a drink or two in the past. "Och, Kenny is awright when you get to know him," Innes countered.

"Total fuckwit that boy if you ask me," Conn was not to be diverted.

Carrying on with his wanking mime, Peter Clarke literally milked the story for all it was worth. The rest of the Diamond drinkers paid the scene scant attention. At first it had mildly diverted them from how sick they were feeling, but their interest quickly waned.

"Dirty old bastard," Innes repeated. He was keen to get away from them, and even more keen now to return to his alcohol.

The swing doors of the pub clattered loudly open, "Utterly preposterous," Robert McKillvany heralded his arrival. He was largely ignored.

Innes seized the opportunity to break away from Conn and Peter, "Awright Vanie, how's yir arse for love-bites?" he returned to his perch.

"Clear as a peach Inn. Clear as a peach," Robert said as he joined Innes at the bar. "Half and a half please

Cammy my good man," Robert said straddling the empty stool next to Innes.

Innes drained both his drinks. "Same again for me too, Cammy."

Campbell deposited lager and wine for Innes and Robert and returned to tidying up behind bar.

Innes observed the obviously congenial disposition of Robert and correctly concluded that he had obviously had a similar 'breakfast' to himself. "How you doing Vanie? You remember getting home last night?"

"Nada Inn. Not a spark of a memory from the old grey matter. Care to enlighten me?" Swallowing half of his wine Robert turned to face Innes with a cheesy grin on his face. That he woke up in his house was enough for Robert, he considered how he got there to be superfluous information.

Innes started on his second wine. "Got any fags Rab?" Innes chanced his luck before informing his friend, "I got you in a taxi after Patel's. You missed John McClelland knocking the fuck out of some poor cunt at the boxing booth. And, by the way, if it wisnie for that poor cunt it was probably going to be you getting a dooin' from him. He fucking hates you Vanie."

Robert produced a battered packet of Regal small from his denim jacket. "The feeling is most definitely mutual Inn. John McClelland is nothing but an old has been." This comment, though true, was also interpreted as foolish, John McClelland was still considered as being a person to keep on the right side of. "He's well past it, fat prick. I'd've taken him." Robert pointed the open packet of Regal at Innes.

Innes took one. "Robert McKillvany, last night you couldn't have taken a shit my friend." Innes pointed out. "You were fucking blootered mate."

Robert refused to acknowledge his friends attempt at injecting reality into the conversation. "He's never been the same wi me ever since I pissed on him." Robert drained his wine with a thoughtful look on his face.

"Who's that Vanie?" Campbell had been eavesdropping on their conversation. Robert urinating on someone was enough to pique his active involvement.

"That fucking waste of space John McClelland fae the Homerton. I pissed on him by accident one night in the Rangers club. I was a wee bit pissed and missed my aim in the urinals, John was next to me, and he got a bit of a soaking. It was pure accident."

Refilling Robert and Innes's lager glasses gratis, Campbell launched into a refrain familiar to all Diamond regulars." That man's never been the same since they closed the yards. Fucking Tories. How's a working man, a welder, supposed to cope wi working in a fucking computer firm? It's just not going to work. A man needs a proper job, and McClelland is no different. Capitalists just don't give a crap about the working man." Cameron had seen a high horse approaching and he willingly took the opportunity to mount it.

Innes, as with most of the Diamond regulars, was familiar with Campbell Williamson's political rantings. Swivelling round on his bar stool he scanned the bar again. A few more people had trickled in. Frowning, he studied the various people that were sitting down. They didn't look well at all. This was not unusual for the Diamond, but it just didn't look right to him. One of the people he was watching slumped forward, his head hitting the table in front of him, hard. Again, this was not unusual in the Diamond, even at this early hour, but the way this person slumped was different. It didn't look like it was caused by an overindulgence of alcohol.

Innes had an uncomfortable feeling in his stomach, and he didn't think it was related to the previous evenings curry. He drank more wine. His default solution to any uncomfortable feelings was to drink more alcohol. Another person slumped forward, whacking his head on the table, only to remain like that, motionless. Innes's disquiet increased exponentially.

The discussion between Robert and Campbell continued behind him. "I'm telling you Vanie, Westminster don't give a fuck about what happens on the streets of Greenock. They'll flush us all down the crapper for a couple of bob, you mark my words." Robert was staring vacantly into space, contributing just enough for Campbell to feel listened to. Robert was always careful never to openly insult any man who provided him with alcohol.

One of the bodies who had slumped to the table groaned. Once again this was indeed a happenstance that had occurred many times in the Diamond, but the sound prickled the hair at the back of Innes's neck. He finished his drinks. He looked at Robert and Campbell, he looked at Bobby, Peter, and Conn. No one else way paying any of this any mind. That situation was about to change.

Two more drinkers similarly slumped forward onto the tables in front of them. The first two that had collapsed raised themselves, their heads jerked about like they were having a fit. They opened their eyes and stared round the room. Innes blinked furiously; his mind grappled to comprehend what he was seeing. These people looked grey, their skin looked flaky, but it was their eye's that caused Innes to question what he was beholding.

Innes had experienced hallucinations before, alcohol withdrawals had caused him to see many weird and not so wonderful things. But he had never seen anything like this. Their eyes had no colour to their irises, they had pin prick pupils swimming in muddy grey sclera, and these people all looked utterly insane. They did not look human. The way they moved was erratic and bizarre.

Peter and Conn continued to pour their hard-earned wages into the fruit machine, oblivious to what was going on behind them. Just as the last drum dropped into place, rewarding them with a jackpot score, two zombies launched themselves from their seats and pounced on them from behind. The zombies bit furiously on Conn and Peters' faces, they gouged at their eyes and clawed at their heads pushing their facial flesh further into their gaping maws. Peter and Conn screamed from excruciating pain and abject horror. Their howls pierced the air alongside the sound of coins falling from their pay-out.

At the first scream Campbell sprang from behind the bar. Violence was unfortunately commonplace in the Diamond, and Campbell was well practiced in dealing with it. But the levels of violence being meted out to Conn and Peter were beyond anything he had ever seen. It was way beyond anything anyone in the Diamond had ever seen.

Robert gawped, mouth open, eyes wide, truly horrified.

When the zombie's turned their attention from Conn to Campbell, Innes knew it was time to leave. "We've got to get the fuck out of here, Vanie," Innes stated but still he hesitated. Robert was frozen. Two of the zombies turned from their feasting and stared with mad, hungry eyes directly at Innes and Robert. Bits of gore dribbled from their mouths. This was enough to galvanise Robert and Innes. They flew out the doors like their lives depended on it, which they did.

The hungry zombies turned their attention to other customers of the Diamond who were not as quick as Innes and Robert. More of the collapsed came back to join the gore festival, their need to consume was overpowering. As they were flying out the door Innes saw Bobby being taken down as he attempted to flee.

Innes and Robert stood for a moment on the street outside the pub. They were breathing heavily, and both were as white as freshly cleaned sheets. Shaking hard, each asked themselves if what had just happened, had actually just happened. And if it had indeed actually just happened, what exactly should they do about it now? The horrendous sounds coming from the interior of the Diamond informed them that what they had just seen had occurred. Without a word, they turned and fled. The noise of the pub carnage receded as they ran for their lives.

As they sprinted past the shops Innes grabbed Fiona, his niece, shouting as he did, "You're fucking coming with me." Innes then shouted at Fiona's friends, "You lot run like fuck. Get the fuck out of here. NOW."

Fiona's friends goggled in disbelief at the fast-retreating figures dragging their mortally embarrassed friend behind them. What they failed to see was what was tearing up the road behind them.

The hoard of zombies from the Diamond crashed into the backs of the unfortunate youngsters just as Innes, Robert and Fiona reached the front door of Innes's house. Robert and Innes dragged Fiona in and slammed the door closed. "What the fuck you doing uncle Inny." Fiona had not seen anything that had happened, either in the pub or on the street, and she was righteously angry. The sheer look of panic and horror on Robert and Innes's faces informed her that whatever was happening, it was something way beyond normal. Fiona's outrage died in a burn of anxiety.

Innes and Robert fell over each other into the front room to hurriedly pull the curtains closed. They were breathing hard, and they pled for absolute silence from Fiona. They listened keenly to what was happening outside and watched the door nervously. They heard the hoard of zombies rampaging down the street. They heard the screams of Stone's estate residents being eaten, then turning into more zombies. Fiona's anxiety peaked; she could contain her silence no more. "What the fuck is going on out there uncle Inny," she whispered.

Standing by the curtains Innes motioned her to come quietly. Standing all together Innes parted the curtains, just a crack, so they could see what was going on. Outside the window former friends and neighbours were rampaging up and down Emerald Crescent eating each other. Fiona saw her friends being chewed and turning. She turned white and threw up. Innes solemnly closed the curtains.

Fiona wiped foamy vomit from her lips. "Uncle Inny, what's going on?"

Innes shook like a leaf in a hurricane. "Fiona I just don't know, I've never seen, or heard of anything like this, ever. Not in real life anyway."

"Are they fucking zombies?" Robert was shaking just as much as Innes and was just as white as Fiona.

"Rab, zombies are for movies, they're not real." Innes wasn't ready to accept there were zombies on the Stones estate.

"They looked fucking real to me Inn. And they looked like fucking zombies. And they were eating each other. What do you think they are?" Robert challenged Innes for an alternative theory.

He didn't have one. He walked over to the sofa and sank down, looking lost.

Fiona came to sit beside him. "Ma mates were eating our neighbours. Uncle Inny, what are we supposed to do?"

Innes put his arms around his niece and hugged her tight. "I dunno Fiona. But I'll look after you, I promise."

This statement caused a flood of thoughts for Fiona. "What about my mam and dad? What about my brothers? Uncle Inny what are we going to do?"

Robert came over to sit in the seat beside the sofa. He didn't intrude on the intimate family dynamic.

"I dunno Fiona. I need to think." Innes's mind was racing, but it was racing in circles and always ended up back at the part where he couldn't work out what had caused people to turn mad and eat each other.

"Would this be a bad time to ask if you had any booze in the house Inn?" Robert had decided what he thought the immediate course of action should be.

Fiona's anxiety exploded into anger. "Are you fucking kidding Vanie? At a time like this all you can think about is fucking bevvy! My mates are eating each other!"

Having a drink seemed to Innes as none too bad an idea either. "Don't be too harsh Fiona," Innes said, giving her shoulder a gentle squeeze. "A wee can or two will help us think. And I think we need to not rush into anything Fi." Innes turned to Robert, "To be honest Vanie, I don't know. I have to stash ma bevvy away from Mary, and I cannie really remember exactly where I've stashed stuff." Innes scratched his head.

"I'll give you a hand to look Inny." Robert was on his feet and ready to go on a quest for alcohol.

"What am I supposed to do while you two hunt for drink?" Fiona's anxiety creeped back.

"You can get the kettle on Fi. A hot, sweet tea will calm you down a treat. Come with me, I'm going to start hunting in the kitchen anyways," said Innes. He put his arms round his niece as he guided her toward the kitchen. "Vanie, go have a poke about the weans bedrooms, there's more of a chance in there than in oor bedroom."

Robert bounced up the stairs determined to sniff out any available alcohol. Innes and Fiona headed into the kitchen.

Robert found the boys bedroom by the Rangers posters on the walls. He stood back and thought like an alcoholic, which was not difficult for him. He checked among the detritus chucked on top of the wardrobe, feeling around as far back as he could, he touched cold tin. Bingo: it was a can of Breaker. He continued to search for more.

In the kitchen Innes was undertaking a similar hunting exercise. Fiona stood by the kettle sipping hot sweet tea. "What happened Uncle Inny? Why are people eating each other?"

Rooting about in the back of cupboards, Innes paused. He eyed a dusty, greasy Breville grill, discarded on top of a cupboard, the sight sparked a memory. "They just started slumping forward in the Diamond Fi. To be honest love, it looked like they died." Innes opened the Breville grill triumphantly producing a half bottle of Eldorado from within. "It was freaky, Fiona. Never seen anything like it. Their eyes freaked me out." Innes had the word zombie bouncing uncomfortably around his brain. He didn't wait till Vanie returned, he cracked open the half bottle of wine and took a long slug. Fiona finished her tea.

Fiona could still taste vomit; she filled a glass with tap water. She was just bringing the glass to her lips when an intuitive thought flashed forcefully through Innes's brain. Fuelled by the numerous times he had witnessed colleagues urinating in the water tanks, Innes's distrust of tap water made the connection with the zombie outbreak. "DON'T DRINK THE WATER FI," Innes barked at Fiona.

With her nerves already frayed, Innes's bark caused Fiona to launch the glass; water and all, into the air. It crashed and smashed against the kitchen wall. Innes stared with fearful distrust as the water slid down the wall. Instinctively he just knew he was right.

"VANIE, DON'T FUCKING DRINK THE WATER," Innes shouted running to the bottom of the stairs.

"Wouldn't dream of it Innes my good man. Utterly preposterous," Robert said smiling as he bounced down the stairs with two cans of Breaker in his hands. "Never much liked the stuff anyway." Robert noted the urgency in Innes's face. "What's wrong Inn?"

"I think it's in the water Vanie. In fact, I know it's in the water. We need to not drink the water, brush our teeth. Or even wash." Innes thought of all possible contacts you could have with water.

"Don't reckon that'll be too much of a hardship Inn," Robert said cracking a can of Breaker as he sat on a chair at the kitchen table.

Innes and Fiona thought about the ramifications of consuming contaminated water. They both looked at Fiona's empty cup of tea. They looked at each other. Fiona started to shake, and tears started streaming down her face. "Uncle Inny, am I going to turn into one of them things?"

Innes and Robert looked at each other, fear was written all over Innes's face. Robert looked away. "I don't know Fi. The water was boiled though." Innes sought to reassure his niece. "Boiling will kill off most, if not all, bacteria Fiona. You'll be alright sweetheart, honest." Going over to his niece Innes hugged her hard, she held on tight. Looking at Robert over Fiona's shoulder Innes filled him in. "Fiona's had a cup of tea made with infected water." Innes watched his friend as it dawned on him that the implications for them all were massive.

Innes held his niece for as long as he could. Breaking from the hug Innes went over to her empty cup, guilt gnawed at his gut, hot sweet tea, as it turned out. was not going to calm his niece down. Innes flung the cup in the bin. "Let's go sit in the living room, see if there's anything about all this on the radio," Innes said, worry and guilt dripped from his words.

Fiona seemed to regress in age, she looked smaller, her teenage bravado had vanished. Robert looked grim as they all trouped into the living room. For the second time that day Innes flicked the switch to bring his radio to life. Radio Clyde were covering the Morton match live. "I need to repeat," said the commentator, excitement booming from his voice. "There are only 5 minutes gone and Queens Park are two goals up. Morton are struggling, they have just not gotten out the traps yet. The Queens Park fans are going wild. The Morton fans are as quiet as the grave. Morton look beaten already. This is one of the strangest games this commentator has ever seen."

Innes was not in the slightest bit interested in the match, so he tried a few other stations. He managed to find a station in the middle of a news broadcast. "Like many other countries Russia is leaving Afghanistan with their tails between their legs," a war correspondent pontificated about the Russian occupation of Afghanistan. Innes let the station move on to the next story, which was about Margaret Thatcher getting a cat. He decided that the news of a zombie outbreak in Greenock would probably have been given more coverage than Margaret Thatcher's cat, probably. Obviously, what was happening in Greenock had not hit the news yet. He turned the radio back to the football, if nothing else, he thought it would bring some much-needed normality to their horrendous situation.

Robert looked at Fiona, she was sitting quiet and withdrawn. "I reckon I need something to eat Inny," Robert said looking over at Innes. "Gonnie gie us a hand in the kitchen, eh? We'll be back in a tick hen," Robert said trying to sound re-assuring.

With a somewhat quizzical look on his face, Robert was generally not known for eating, Innes followed him into the kitchen. Robert closed the kitchen door gently. "Inny, she might turn." He got straight to the point that was troubling him.

Innes sank into a kitchen chair; the weight of responsibility was too much for him. He noticed the wine bottle in his hands, he took long drink and passed the remains to Robert. "She's ma sister's wean, Rab," was all he could say.

Robert noticed the broken glass and the remnants of Fiona's water trickling down the wall. He went to inspect it. From a safe distance he tried to smell the water. "Do you really think there's something in the water, Inny?" Innes occupation seemed to make everyone think he was an expert in all water related issues.

"I dunno for sure Rab, I really don't. But I just don't trust it. There's something making people mad. People eating each other is not normal."

"Uncle Inny, Vanie. Quick," Fiona shouted from the living room.

Robert and Innes looked at each other, fear in their eyes. Without Innes noticing, Robert reached over and picked up a large knife as they left the kitchen.

"Listen to that," Fiona said pointing to the radio.

The commentator sounded completely different; his voice was strained with fear. "The Morton physio is getting back up! I don't know what is happening folks, ttttthis is mad," the commentator stammered, "There is blood everywhere and, oh my God the physio is back up and the two of them are attacking other players. Fucking hell, the crowd are turning on each other 'n all." The commentator had lost all semblance of professionality.

Robert, Innes, and Fiona all looked from one to another. Robert still hid the knife behind his back.

"Naw, naw, naw, fuck off you," the commentator said, though his voice was now distant, he had obviously dropped the microphone. "Get to fuck away from me." Raw fear exuded from his voice. Innes, Fiona, and Robert all heard the growling zombie advancing on the commentator. The poor man let out a petrified scream as the zombie bit and ripped his flesh.

The commentary ended abruptly. The station reverted to a panicked person in the studio. "We seem to be having some technical issues here folks I'm afraid," the voice said, though he was obviously aware he was convincing no one. "Here's some music while we see if we can sort the situation out." Bohemian Rhapsody sang out from the speakers.

Innes turned down the volume, "Shit," he said. "It's not just the Stones estate then." All three looked at each other in silence as a sotto voce Freddie Mercury provided a bizarre soundtrack to a most strange situation.

"Uncle Inny, I don't want to turn into one of them things." Fiona sobbed uncontrollably.

Innes turned the radio off and held his niece tight.

"I never much like Queen anyways," said Robert as he sat carefully on a seat as far away from Fiona as he could get. He carefully positioned the knife, unseen, between the cushions of the seat.

"Huv you had any water today Fiona. Other than that tea?" Innes asked holding Fiona by her shoulders.

She couldn't think straight. "I dunno uncle Inny, I suppose so. I cannie remember really. I mostly drink tea at home."

"You'd've probably turned by now if you were gonnie." Innes tried and failed to sound convincing.

"I reckon we just need to wait and see," said Robert.

Innes and Fiona turned to look at Robert who sat innocently sipping from a can of Breaker.

"I take it neither of you two have had any water today?" Fiona asked Robert and Innes.

"Naw," they chorused, credibly.

Innes and Fiona sat on the sofa facing Robert.

They began the wait.

Chapter 13

For some unknown reason Kenny dreamt about naked ladies running about eating peanuts and throwing loaves of bread at each other. He drifted closer to consciousness, becoming dimly aware he could hear a weird groaning noise. It sounded low and growling, it sounded nasty. Kenny's brain swam through a thick treacle of drug fuelled somnolence towards cognisance.

Lifting his head with a mammoth effort, he finally managed to persuade his eyes to open. It took some time for the blurry shapes in front of his eyes to coalesce into solid recognisable forms, he peered round the room. The groaning sound came from Angus Gaffney, still slumped beside him. Kenny heard a similar groaning sound coming from outside the house. He could also hear disturbing crashing and banging noises coming from the kitchen.

Kenny glanced back at the sleeping, groaning Angus, did a double check that there was no one else around, then gently reached for his tobacco tin. He felt the flatness of his pocket and panic hit him like a truck. He always kept his tobacco tin in the same pocket. It was gone. Kenny shot straight up, causing Angus to collapse on the floor.

Angus groaned again and opened his bleary eyes. "Fuck," he just managed say.

Kenny searched his every pocket, repeatedly. Again, and again he searched, refusing to believe he had lost his stash. His badly fried mind couldn't accept that his drugs had actually gone. After another full round of pocket searching, he had no option but to accept reality. "I've fucking lost my stash," Kenny exclaimed exasperated.

"I knew you were holding out on me, ya prick," Angus retorted.

Angus's comment didn't register with Kenny. There was only one thing he was concerned about. "I've no drugs!" He was horrified.

"Welcome to my world, ya cunt." Angus stood up. He stretched, his dirty cream t-shirt rode up over his flabby belly, exposing the rim of a dirty pair of y-fronts that looked like they were only being held together by stains. Angus's ripped jeans were sliding down, he hoicked them up and ambled into the kitchen to investigate the cause of the continuous clattering noises emanating from within.

The noises were being produced by Lennie. "What you doing Len?" Angus asked as he ventured into the kitchen.

"Mind your own fuckin' business," Lennie responded in his customary style. When he noticed it was Angus, he softened his tone, slightly. "I'm just looking for something, Gaff." He looked confused. "To be honest, I cannie really remember what I'm looking for. But when I find it, I'll know."

A despondent Kenny joined Angus and Lennie in the kitchen.

"Poor Kenny's had his drugs nicked." Angus indulged joyfully in some shadenfreude, he relished sharing Kenny's bad news.

"Is that his fucking name. Cunt's been coming round here for weeks now. Never told me his fucking name once." Lennie carried on rummaging in his kitchen cupboards, but with noticeably less enthusiasm than before.

At first Kenny was surprised at Lennie's requirement for formal introductions, then he processed what Angus had said. "Wait! You think my stash has been nicked, Gaff?" Kenny's despondency flipped into anger.

"Will be them two cunts McAdam and Curry. Fucking pair of weasels, them two." Lennie imparted his considered opinion.

"I'll fucking kill them." Kenny was raging.

"Jack Curry would fucking eat you for breakfast son." Angus sought to instil some reality in Kenny. He turned to look at Lennie. "So would Jenny 'n'all right enough," he added.

Angus and Lennie broke into loud raucous laughter. "I don't take any shite from either of them two goons," Lennie said. "But Gaff is right son, you're no match for either of them. They're always tooled up, and they're nasty bastards. You tooled up son?" Lennie asked, though he knew fine well what the answer would be.

This was the most Lennie had ever said to him. It was the most Kenny had ever heard him say to anyone without cursing them out. "No, Lennie I'm not tooled up, and never will be," he responded, quietly seething, though also secretly pleased that Lennie had chosen to converse with him. Lennie managed to maintain a certain standing among the local drug using community, even though they all thought him clearly mad.

Lennie gave up on searching for whatever it was he was searching for and stomped off to the living room. Angus and Kenny followed, for want of anything better to do.

Kenny still had money. "Do you know if Ed's coming back today, Lennie?"

Lennie reverted to type. "Do I look like Ed McDonald's fucking secretary." Flopping on his threadbare sofa he closed his eyes.

Angus replied to the question. "Ed won't be back till later. He won't come back until the grafters have rinsed the shops." Angus noted that Kenny's question implied he still had available resources. "I could probably get you a score from my mates if you wanted, Kenny? The gear's naw bad n'all you know?"

"Cheers Gaff, but I reckon I'll wait till Ed comes back. I'm gonnie get some jellies off him as well." Kenny bowed to the inevitable, "I'll sort you out Gaff, don't worry."

Angus took and treasured the offer; he was now closer to his next score, he just needed to stick close to Kenny to seal the deal.

Kenny heard more groaning noises coming from the street, he decided to investigate. There was nothing else happening anyway, Lennie's house was completely devoid of any external entertainment. There was no radio or television set, as these were sellable items. There were piles of tatty second-hand books, but Kenny wasn't that desperate yet.

Wandering over to the window he pulled back the greasy, grey net curtains. On the street outside he saw the receding back of a figure as it stumbling jerkily down the street, moaning loudly. "Fuck, you should see this guy lads. He is so fucked."

Angus and Lennie joined him at the window. The figure wore ripped clothes, and his shoes were untied. Eventually the stumbling, moaning figure dragged its legs so much that both its shoes fell off. Angus and Lennie exploded in loud, raucous laughter. Lennie shouted at the window, "Hey mate you've lost your shoes, ya dumb fuck." The stumbling figure didn't acknowledge hearing anything, Lennie's windows were thick and solid. The figure carried on slouching and moaning down the street.

"Fuck, I wouldnae mind a wee bit of what he's had." Angus voiced his envy.

"Aye, but maybe he's had a wee bit too much," Kenny expressed his reservations.

"Fuck," Lennie loudly exclaimed. "Food." His crinkly face lit up. "That's what I was looking for in the kitchen. Food. I'm fucking starving."

Angus thought about it. "Come to think of it, I don't think I've eaten anything for days. Lennie, what's the chances of finding anything to eat in your kitchen?"

"Pretty low, Gaff." Lennie knew what scraps to be found in his kitchen would be way beyond edible.

Kenny saw a chance to augment his newly accepted status. "I'll stand youse both a poke of chips then eh?" he announced with a smile on his face.

"Gonnie get us a pickled onion." Lennie leapt at the chance.

"Gonnie get us gravy, and a pickled onion." Angus pushed the boat further.

"Aye Kenny boy, gravy for me'n all mate, eh?" Lennie liked the sound of chips and gravy.

"Three chips and gravy with a pickled onion it is then." Kenny headed for the door.

"Get us a bottle of scoosh 'n' all son, eh?" Lennie put in one last request before Kenny left for the chip shop.

"Aye, awright, Lennie." Kenny's tone let them know they had pushed him as far as he was willing to be pushed.

"Get Cream Soda." Angus honed the order specifications.

The chip shop was located further down the road from Lennie's house, the same road that the shambling figure had just stumbled down. Kenny could see the figure in the distance, he picked up speed.

When he was just a few yards behind him, he hailed the unknown person. "Oi mate! You awright?" Kenny shouted, as he pondered the potential of cadging a bit of whatever drug this wreck of a human being had recently consumed.

The figure turned round slowly. With the sun blazing behind its back, its eyes were obscured in shadow. Kenny noticed its face was a very pale grey, and his skin looked to be flaking. A klaxon warning bell sounded loud in Kenny's instincts. "You awright mate?" he ventured hesitantly. Kenny's nose wrinkled, he smelt the overpowering stench of fresh excrement.

The zombie growled a low, hungry warning, then sprang for Kenny, swinging its grasping hands to claw at him. The virus was still getting used to operating the motor functions of its new hosts, it missed, and the momentum of its effort caused it to fall ungainly at Kenny's feet. Just for a moment the zombie was unable to move, and Kenny got a clear look at its face, and eyes. The sight chilled him to the bone and a massive shiver snaked up his spine. The zombies' face was grey and flaky, and its eyes were just pin-prick pupils swimming in a dirty, grey, dead sea.

Time froze for Kenny, and his vision tunnelled, until the hungry zombie sprang for him again. Self-preservation kicked in, and Kenny turned and sprinted back where he had come from. The zombie clambered to its feet and chased after him, but Kenny's system was fuelled by fear pumped adrenaline, he was quick. Racing back into the house he slammed the door behind himself. Kenny remembered the front door didn't lock, so he sat with his back to the door and pushed with all his might.

Lennie and Angus heard him return. "That was fucking quick," Lennie shouted from the living room.

"Too fucking quick," Angus said rushing into the hallway to see what was happening. "What the fuck are you doing?" he said looking at the sight of a very scared looking Kenny holding the door fast with his back. Angus was non-plussed. "What the fuck are you doing, Kenny?" He repeated with rising worry, his primary concern was that a Police raid was imminent.

"There's a fucking…….." Kenny couldn't think what to call the creature that was chasing after him, but he knew that whatever it was, it was most definitely not human. "There's a fucking thing chasing me." Just as Kenny finished talking the zombie hit the door. It was stronger than it looked, and the door bucked against Kenny's back. "Help me out, Gaff. There's no way we can let that fucking thing get in here."

Lennie had been listening, the commotion had piqued his curiosity, he had to investigate. "Have you fucking lost it son? What the fuck is going on?" Lennie looked askance as his door was battered hard by the zombie. The creature groaned and moaned loudly. "What the fuck are you doing to my door ya fucking cunt?" Even though his door was not very functional, it was still *his* door and Lennie was very much perturbed at the violence being meted out against it.

Lennie motioned for Kenny to stand back so he could confront whoever was wrecking his already admittedly rather ropey front door. This prospect horrified Kenny. "No Lennie, please just trust me. You really do not want to see that fucking thing out there."

"What the fuck are you going on about, son? Why do you keep on calling it a thing? What the fuck is out there, Kenny?" Lennie was getting as mad and deranged as the zombie. "Is it the fucking Polis, Kenny?"

Kenny shook his head.

"Then get the fuck out the way. No cunt does fucking *that* to my fucking door." Lennie shouted, pointing at the door as the zombie continued to try smashing its' way through. Lennie's' rage was more persuasive to Kenny than the thought of the thing behind the door. He stood up and back just as the zombie hurled itself at the door again. This time, meeting no resistance, the door flew wide open, and the zombie sailed into the house. It fell flat on its face and sprawled spreadeagled on the floor.

Lennie had a heavy wooden leg of a previously dismantled chair sitting beside the entrance to the living room. It was commonly known as the equaliser, and was there to be utilised in exceptional circumstances, where violence, or at least the threat of violence was required. Lennie and Angus stared into the face of the zombie thrashing about on the hallway floor and knew that this qualified as exceptional circumstances. Angus, being closest to the equaliser grabbed it promptly proceeded to beat the zombie mercilessly. He battered its ribs, its back, its arms, and its legs, he beat it repeatedly everywhere. The zombie didn't even flinch, it clearly felt no pain.

With hungry determination the zombie flew at Lennie, who kicked out and punched it hard. The zombie turned and flew at Kenny as potentially easier target. As the zombie was in mid-air Angus swung the chair leg and connected full force on the side of its head. There was a sickening crunch as the equaliser smashed its skull into its brains. The zombie fell to the floor and twitched out the last thread of what passed for its life. The virus couldn't re-animate when the brain was so assaulted. Death died again.

The three lads stood around breathing hard, staring at the zombie lying prostrate on the floor.

"What in the fuck was that?" Angus was first to break the silence.

Lennie looked askance at Kenny. "Why the fuck did you let that…….." He pointed to the zombie, his finger twitching like a pendulum on speed. "………In my fucking house for?"

Kenny stared at them both.

"And I take it you didnae get the chips," said Lennie, as he stomped over the corpse of the zombie back into his living room.

Angus silently followed him; red faced, shocked, and gripping the equaliser tightly. Kenny followed them into the living room, flinching as he stepped gingerly over the corpse of the zombie. Lennie flopped onto his sofa. Angus returned to the spot he was in previously. Kenny slid down beside Angus.

"That was a fucking zombie, is what that was," Kenny said, his face pale and his voice shaking.

"Fuck it. As if the Homerton wisnae fucked enough as it is. It's crawling with fucking zombies now, is it?" Lennie slumped back into his sofa and exhaled loudly.

Angus turned to face Kenny. His face was just as pale. "Are you being fucking serious? Zombies?"

Kenny shrugged. "What would you call it?"

Angus and Lennie looked at the corpse lying in the hall. The three lapsed into a heavy silence as they contemplated the ramifications of their new discovery.

"Does that mean there's going to be more of them?" Lennie sat forward on the edge of the sofa, gripped by an idea he did not at all like.

Angus and Kenny didn't particularly like that idea either. The three of them leapt to the front window. They tentatively lifted the net curtains and stared out at an empty street. The Homerton estate was never empty. Even in the small hours of the morning there was always someone out and about, doing whatever it was they were doing. It was now ominously empty.

"I could really do with a fucking hit." Angus's mind retreated to the only place he really felt safe.

"I could use a boot 'n'all," Lennie concurred.

"Me too." Kenny agreed.

They lapsed into silence again as they contemplated the street.

"Do you think Ed will still come here?" Kenny ventured.

"Ed might be a zombie." Angus posited an unthinkable proposition.

"Do you think we could go to his house?" Kenny asked, though he knew what the response would be.

Angus and Lennie were horrified. "Ed would fucking kill us if we went to his house looking for a score," Lennie killed that idea.

"Should we go see if Bobby is at the shops?" His recent violent outburst caused Angus to desperately seek some anaesthesia. "We could check and see if there are any more of them." He looked at the corpse of the zombie. "We need to know one way or the other really," Angus pleaded, he desperately wanted more heroin.

Kenny and Lennie contemplated his idea. Both of them knew that eventually they would have to give way to their chemical compulsions, though the prospect that there might be more zombies out there horrified them all. "We'll need to get tooled up." Lennie made the decision.

Angus was still grasping the chair leg tightly, he looked at it, then looked at Lennie. "You keep the equaliser, Gaff. 'Mon son I've got something else we can use." Lennie took Kenny up the stairs. Kenny had never been up the stairs in Lennie's' house, not many people had. Lennie didn't care what anyone did in the ground floor, but he liked to keep the top floor as much to himself as he could.

He led Kenny to a bedroom bare of furniture except a filthy mattress on the floor, again there were books everywhere. Opening a built-in cupboard, he revealed a large pile of various sized metal pipes. "I've been collecting these for the scrappy. Worth a couple of bob these," Lennie said as he rummaged about, hefting and trial swinging pipes of various lengths. He settled on a couple, passed one to Kenny and kept the other for himself.

Kenny held his iron bar and felt his inadequacy rise. He had never even been in a fight before, apart from silly schoolboy brawls. He had never had to contemplate having to actually use a weapon on anyone. Kenny took a couple of practise swings to get used to the weight. He looked at Lennie and saw grim determination in his eyes. He felt a little less scared as he followed Lennie back down the stairs.

They found Angus standing at the window scanning the street. "You ready for this lads?" he asked. Angus whacked his hand with the leg chair, checked out the other two with their metal pipes and seemed satisfied enough with what he saw.

"Aim for the head," Kenny said whacking his hand lightly with his iron pipe.

"What?" Lennie looked at him, his brow furrowed.

"It's in all the zombie movies. It's how you kill them. Everybody knows that!" Kenny said.

"I fucking didn't." Lennie looked angry. "Did you know that Gaff?"

"No Len." Angus gestured to the zombie corpse with the equaliser. "When I papped that on the head it was just a fluke I guess. It worked though." Angus stared at Lennie and Kenny, "We ready?"

Climbing over the zombie corpse, they stood at the threshold of the front door. "Fuck it. Let's go," Lennie said. They all looked at each other, took a collective breath and stepped out into the front garden.

Lennie's house was halfway down the road that led to the shops. Bobby would be found at the shops if he were dealing. Standing on the path in the middle of the front garden they looked up and down the road. All was quiet, they ventured cautiously out of the garden and started to walk down the road; checking all around them as they went.

"Are you sure about this zombie thing Ken?" Angus asked, the normality of the street was causing him to doubt his recent run in with a zombie.

Kenny was having a similar experience; he was starting to feel foolish walking through the Homerton estate, in the middle of the day, wielding an iron bar.

"Bobby's there." Lennie pointed to a gathering hanging about outside the newsagents, next door to the chip shop. They all felt their hopes surge, precious heroin could be all but a few yards away.

Jenny and Jack were part of the gathering. Remembering his stolen drugs, his iron bar started to feel potentially useful again to Kenny. Angus shoved the equaliser into the band of his trousers. Lennie and Kenny remained holding theirs, ready. They reached the shops without any zombie related incidents.

"Awright Bobby?" Angus broke the ice.

All of the addicts gathered at the shops stared quizzically at the three of them walking about tooled up.

"Awright Gaff. You guys going to war?" Bobby had been starting to get worried, his estate was too quiet and seeing these three carrying heavy weapons shot his paranoia into overdrive. Jenny and Jack sneered and sniggered at Kenny.

Angus thought quickly. "I heard there wis a mob fae the Stones out robbing addicts Bobby. Didnae want to take any chances, eh?"

This response satisfied Bobby somewhat, though he was still far from convinced. "I'd fucking love to see any of them pricks try anything like that wi me around Gaff. I'd fuck up anyone that tried that on my patch." Bobby stood arrogant and defiant, determined to make a show of protecting his customers.

Kenny was still extremely nervous about zombies, though everything seemed bizarrely normal. He got quickly down to business. "Three bags Bobby, eh?"

Bobby had a quick look around for anything suspicious, rummaged in his jacket pocket and held out his hand. Kenny slipped him three £20 notes and received three small packages of heroin.

Happy, relieved, and now keen to return to safety Kenny turned to go. "Eh, what about the chips, Kenny?" Lennie asked hopefully.

Kenny was incredulous, "Really?"

"I'm still fucking hungry, son," Lennie pleaded.

Kenny looked around. On one side a lone lurching figure stumbled down the hill, it looked like a teenage girl. On the other side, past Lennie's house, another figure lurched their way, this one looked like Danny Cameron; the McDonalds look out. Danny also didn't look like he was walking normally. Kenny looked at both figures and looked back at Lennie and Angus, his eyebrows raised in a question.

I'm really fucking starving, Kenny boy," was Lennie's' begging response.

"Bit of chips and gravy would be the business, Kenny," Angus agreed. "We'll be awright if we are quick."

Sighing, Kenny ceded to the inevitable. He shot into the chip shop and barked his order to the man behind the counter.

Outside, Jenny sparked up a conversation with Bobby. "You'd fuck up any cunt that came from the Stones, eh Bobby?"

"Jenny sweetheart, I would be all over them cunts like a rash." Bobby was incredulous, his ego refused to accept that anyone could have any other reaction to him other than fear. Jenny had played on his ego perfectly. "No Stones prick would set foot on the Homerton once they saw me here."

In the shop Kenny harassed the counter assistant, pleading with him to hurry up. Kenny shuffled quickly from the counter to the window and back repeatedly pleading for speed. His breath caught in his throat when he spotted the teenage girl breaking into a loping run.

Outside, Jack had identified the lurching figure. "Is that wee Aggie? What the fuck is she doing coming doon here? She's no on the gear, is she?" Jack started laughing at her. "What the fuck is wrong wi her, she's running like a spaz."

Bobby and Jenny turned to look at the figure stumbling down the road, it was un-coordinated and ungainly, it fell in a crumpled heap. They all laughed, except Angus and Lennie who just looked imploringly into the chip shop. Kenny finally pestered the counter assistant enough for him to get his chips.

Bobby saw Danny Camron loping down the other side of the road. "Is that that wee cunt Cameron? He's supposed to be keeping a fucking look out."

Bobby was extremely displeased; at the back of his mind, he was worried now about potential incursions by the Stones gang. "Oi Cameron ya wee cunt, get the fuck back up there," he shouted at the approaching figure. The figure ignored him and kept on coming.

Kenny, Angus, and Lennie all retreated to the other side of the road. The approaching figures were heading directly for the gathering outside the shops. Jenny and Jack were laughing nervously, they were starting to become uncertain about what was going on. Bobby was apoplectically angry, he couldn't countenance anyone, least of all a 14-year-old boy, disrespecting him.

Bobby, Jenny, and Jack could now see what the approaching figures looked like, they all froze with their mouths open, their brains desperately tried, and failed to process what their eyes were seeing. Wee Aggie leapt onto Jenny McAdam just as Danny Cameron jumped on Bobby. "Let's fucking go," shouted Angus. Kenny needed no second bidding, but Lennie was unable to not gape incredulously at the horror happening right in front of his eyes.

As Kenny and Angus sprinted up the road towards his house, Lennie stood and watched as wee Aggie ripped into Jenny McAdam's face. Danny Cameron was battered around the face by Bobby, but his efforts had absolutely no effect on it, it clamped its teeth onto his nose. With one wrench of its neck Danny ripped off Bobby's' nose, blood spurted everywhere. Bobby emitted a blood curdling scream. Jack Curry tried to run, but Wee Aggie grabbed his legs and brought him down, it jumped on his back and started chewing at his neck. This was enough for Lennie, he turned and fled.

Angus and Kenny reached Lennie's house, they watched as Lennie sprinted up the hill away from the zombies now chasing him.

"Run Lennie," shouted Kenny.

"What do you fucking think I'm doing," he shouted back, as he ran as fast as he could. He made it to his front garden and up the path, just as the zombies approached the entrance to the garden. Lennie flew into his house, Angus managed to slam the door on the advancing zombies. The zombies flung themselves desperately at the door tearing at it and pounding it ferociously.

"We're going to need to dub up this fucking door," Angus stated the obvious.

"I'm on it," said Lennie recovering his breath. "Gaff can you hold the door for a bit?"

Angus nodded, wedging himself against the door and the stairs. "I think so. But whatever your thinking about doing, do it fucking quick will you?"

"We need to move that," Lennie said pointing at the corpse of the zombie lying in the hall floor, it was in the way. Kenny looked at it and his stomach lurched. "Grab the legs," Lennie directed. Kenny dry heaved and reluctantly picked up the legs. They half dragged; half carried the corpse out of the way of the door and dumped it unceremoniously on the living room floor. The zombie hadn't quite gone into rigor mortis yet, so it's bashed-in head lolled about like a nodding dog, dripping gloopy blood and brains out on the floor.

"Follow me." Lennie led Kenny out to the back garden. "Grab them," he pointed at the pile of internal doors resting against the wall. Lennie picked up a door and ran back inside. Kenny did as he was directed.

Lennie wedged his door against the front door and the bottom of the stairs. Kenny did the same. They repeated the process until all the doors were wedged against the front door.

Angus gingerly let go of the front door. The zombies outside continued to pound but the front door remained resolutely closed.

"I knew they would come in handy one day," Lennie said. Angus and Kenny looked at him.

Lennie looked at the poly bag full of wrapped up chips. "Did you forget the scoosh?" he said looking angry.

Kenny's mouth hung open, the zombies continued to pound and scrape at the front door. "Well, I'm not going back," he said.

"Well, I'm fucking starving," Lennie announced. Kenny's mouth continued to hang open. He silently pointed at where a hoard of zombies were crashing against the front door.

"Aye well life goes on Kenny boy, eh?" said Angus. "Gonnie gie us my bag, I'm scanting for a hit." Angus stood in front of Kenny with his hand open. Kenny dumbly handed over a bag of heroin.

Angus went into the kitchen to get a glass of water to use for cooking up his heroin. Returning to his habitual slumping spot he cooked up a hit of heroin and injected it. This time he only took half of a bag. Due to the current situation, he was unsure where his next hit would come from.

"Gie's a poke of chips then son." While Angus was busy cooking up and enjoying his hit, Lennie wanted to eat. Kenny sighed and handed over a poke of chips. He placed the other beside Angus and took his own chips over to the sofa. Kenny gave Lennie his bag of heroin, who nodded his thanks.

Kenny and Lennie ate their chips and Angus injected himself to the sound of zombies crashing repeatedly, and consistently against the front door. Elsewhere on The Homerton estate they could now hear more and more screams as the zombie apocalypse took hold and started to ravage the area.

Lennie finished his chips and disappeared into the kitchen; he came back with a roll of tinfoil. "You got a pen Kenny?" he asked. Kenny passed him his pen. Lennie made himself a tube, passed the pen back and took a large chase of heroin. Kenny did the same.

Lennie looked over at the corpse of the zombie. "That......," he pointed at the body, "………needs to be out of my fucking house, now."

Kenny and Angus looked at each other.

"Who's gonnie help me?" Lennie asked.

"I've bought youse chips and smack," Kenny said, hands in the air. "I've done my bit."

Angus accepted his argument was pretty unassailable. He sighed, stood up, and stared with disgust at the gruesome zombie corpse. "What we going to do with it then Len?"

"Fling it oot the fucking window is what we're going to do with it. Grab its legs." Lennie once again went to stand at the head of the zombie corpse. He grabbed the arms, and Angus, with his face displaying extreme distaste, grabbed the legs. With Lennie leading they dragged the zombie corpse up the stairs. Kenny followed them. At the top Lennie dragged the corpse to the window at the front of the house. The zombies underneath heard the noise and turned their attention to what was happening above them.

A strong smell of excrement wafted up to them from the zombies below. Lennie hoisted the zombie's top half out of the window, his lips curled in distaste. "Them fucking things smell like shit," he noted as he got ready to dispatch the zombie corpse from his house. "Ready?" he asked. Angus nodded his head silently, scared that if he opened his mouth, he would be sick. They heaved the corpse out of the window. As the zombies were howling at the window above them, the corpse landed with a crunch right on top of them.

The zombies were enraged at having a zombie corpse thrown on top of them, they tore at the corpse with their hands and teeth, pulling and kicking and chewing at it. They dismembered and gutted the zombie corpse. Human innards, limbs, and congealed blood were now spread out in the garden. Kenny looked out and thought, "*I didn't think anything could make Lennie's front garden look worse, but there you go.*"

"I'm thirsty," Lennie announced. He tramped down the stairs and into the kitchen dusting his hands on his jeans. Angus and Kenny followed. Lennie grabbed an empty jam jar from the sink and filled it with water.

Kenny stared at the water as it gurgled out of the tap. The voice of Mack the Sack rang loud in his mind, "*Before the end of the shift you need to let out 100 units from Brimmington.*" Kenny's mind made an intuitive connection. He had seen workers discharging bodily fluids into the water tanks many times. As he watched Lennie raise the glass to his lips his instincts hollered clearly to him, and he became one hundred percent convinced. Kenny flew across the room and slapped the make-shift glass from Lennie's hand.

"What the fuck," Lennie was aghast at this intervention.

"It's in the water," Kenny spluttered.

"What's in the fucking water?" Lennie demanded.

"It's what's causing the zombies. There's something in the water." Kenny was animated and convinced, "I'm fucking sure of it, Lennie, don't drink the fucking water."

"How?" Angus started to look worried. "I mean how could you know that Kenny?"

"I don't know Angus, but it makes sense. The whole place has gone to shit. You can hear it. It's all over the place." Kenny motioned with his arms. Kenny looked at the track marks on Angus's hands and arms. "Where did you get your water for your hit, Gaff?" Kenny asked, concern rising.

Angus went red. "You know where I got the water. The fucking taps ya prick." He stomped off into the living room.

Lennie and Kenny followed.

"He boiled the water though, Kenny." Lennie was worried. "That'll kill whatever it is, won't it?"

"I don't know Lennie, I'm not an expert." Kenny looked over at Angus who now looked as scared as anyone had ever looked. "But I reckon you're right." Kenny was aware Angus badly needed re-assurance. "Yes, it should kill whatever it is." Lennie and Kenny sat on the sofa opposite Angus, who had reverted to his slumping spot.

"Should've chased it like youse," Angus said holding his head in his hands. He slumped further.

One of the zombies outside had wandered over to the window and was now bashing at it monotonously with his arms. The windows on Lennie's house were thick, solid, and very well made, they wouldn't break easily. The zombie bashing the window was a noseless zombie Bobby McDonald.

"He always was an ugly cunt," Lennie commented.

Angus laughed but looked despondent. "Well, I guess I just need to wait and see if I'm joining them."

Lennie and Kenny looked at each other. Lennie looked at the iron bars nearby. Kenny sighed.

The zombie Bobby McDonald continued pounding monotonously at the window.

The three lads began the wait.

Chapter 14

The zombie that used to be Jim (Mac the Sack) Mackenzie opened its eyes. It was lying fully clothed on top of Jim's bed. There was no waking up process, it was unnecessary, the virus was instantly alert, it had converted the host fully. The virus had learned from zombie Rosie, and the others, the ability to compel the host to perform basic motor skills.

Zombie Mac sat up straight in bed and looked around the room. It took in sensory information garnered from the host. It could feel through its fingers, it had no interest in touch, it ignored it. It could taste stale beer and the remnants of peanuts eaten by Jim in the morning, it had no interest in human food. It could smell stale body odour coming from the host, it didn't care. It could hear people walking and talking outside the window. This was an invitation to feed, to infect, to propagate. The zombie was extremely interested.

Zombie Mac growled hungrily. It jerkily pushed itself up from lying down on the bed to achieve a sitting position, it looked around the room. Looking round the room it spotted a window and a door; it was dimly aware that these represented potential exit routes. Zombie Mac crawled to the edge of the bed and clumsily flung its legs over the side, it stood and flung itself from the bed and staggered to the door. It knew that this would be the way out, but it was just not sure how to make the door work. Zombie Mac growled loudly and deeply and started grappling with the door. It pulled and pushed violently in an attempt to get the door opened.

"That you up Jim?" Jim's mother, Isobel, shouted up the stairs, she had heard the commotion coming from the bedroom. Isobel had returned from the shops; she knew her son was on a night shift; she had returned to make him something to eat for when he woke up. Isobel was baffled and worried about the noises coming from her son's room.

At the sound of a live host nearby zombie Mac became frenzied, it howled and growled in frustration and anger. It started to pound frenetically at the door. It attacked the door handle furiously and eventually succeeded, by luck rather than ability, in making the handle turn and the door open.

Isobel was now exceedingly disturbed by the noises coming from up the stairs. She came out from the kitchen to stand, with a certain degree of trepidation, at the bottom of the stairs. "Are you ok Jim? I've made you a wee corned beef sandwich to eat," she ventured as she saw the figure of her son come lurching down the stairs towards her.

The zombies were still not particularly good at coordinating the complex procedure required to walk downstairs. It fell and crumpled down to the bottom of the stairs. Isobel shrieked and rushed to her son. "Oh my God," she cried as she rushed to help him. "Jim are you ok?" Ina turned him round.

As she turned what she thought was her son round, zombie Mac grabbed her by the head and bit hard into her neck. It's jaws clamped shut and it shook its head like a dog devouring a lump of meat. Jim's mother gargled blood and screamed loudly. Zombie Mac continued to chew. Driven by her ailing heart, blood spurted out of her torn jugular spraying zombie Mac in the face. Zombie Mac drank in Isobel's blood, as his saliva transmitted the virus.

The virus flew through Isobel's bloodstream in a heartbeat. It entered her brain and shut it down instantly. Isobel flopped to the floor and zombie Mac accordingly lost interest. Zombie Mac licked its lips, the metallic tang of blood tasted good, but it wasn't enough, the taste only increased the intense craving for more flesh. It stood, swaying, with blood dripping down its chin, it listened. When Isobel had screamed it had been heard by a couple of passers-by walking down the road. Zombie Mac could hear them talking outside as they approached the house.

"I'm telling you Josie I heard a scream coming from this house."

Josie replied, "There's nothing now though, Calum, it's all gone quiet. We should just leave well alone," Josie sounded both embarrassed and scared.

They walked slowly up the stairs that led to the path leading to the Mackenzie's front door. "Josie, it sounded like someone was getting murdered in there. Did you not hear it?" Calum asked, he couldn't believe Josie wanted to blatantly ignore their civic duty.

Zombie Mac could hear them talking, he could smell their warm bodies, his cravings caused him to frenzy. Isobel rose behind him, she popped her neck and opened her eyes, she growled; she was seized with the same intense craving as her zombie son. She joined zombie Mac in growling and pounding frenetically at their door.

Josie and Calum stopped half-way up the path. The noises emanating from the house ahead caused Calum to question the value of civic duty. He turned to speak to Josie just as the combined force of two frenzied zombies pounding on the old wooden door caused the old door jambs to shatter. The door flew open, and the two hungry zombies were released.

It took time for the sight that was bearing down on them to register with Calum and Josie. By the time it did it was too late to do anything about it. Zombie Mac jumped on Calum, and zombie Isobel jumped on Josie. The four of them crumpled down the steps, broke open the gate at the bottom, and tumbled out onto the street. There were a few people out on the street, quietly going about their normal business. They all stopped to silently gape at the completely abnormal sight that was now rolling about on the street in front of them.

Josie was bitten and turned instantly but Calum, unbeknownst to him, had a unique and powerful immune system. His immune system resisted the virus being pumped around his bloodstream. Zombie Mac sensed the futility of his bites. This enraged him. Zombie Mac and zombie Isobel started to rip Calum's' body to bits. They chewed and ate his body parts. Josie turned zombie and joined in. Calum was dismembered and had his guts ripped open, the zombies relished eating his internal organs. Calum's head became detached from his body due to multiple neck bites, and the violence of the zombie attack. Calum's decapitated head rolled down the hill dripping a trail of torn flesh, blood, and bits of brain behind it. The horrified bystanders vomited and retched at the most disgusting sight any of them had ever seen. As one, they fled.

Zombie Mac stood in the middle of the road; blood and gore dripping from him; in his hand he gripped a string of steaming entrails, freshly ripped from Calum's body. Zombie Mac howled at the street, at the town, at the world. Curtains nervously twitched, and numerous people rushed frantically to their phones. The police were called, multiple times.

A brave, and unbelievably foolish, neighbour decided to confront the brazen perpetrator of such gratuitous violence. He came stomping angrily out of his house brandishing a crowbar. "Jim Mackenzie, I don't know what you think you're doing, but I'm just not having it pal." The neighbour advanced towards zombie Mac waving the crowbar threateningly. "I'm not afraid to use this you know, Jim," the neighbour threatened, just as zombie Mac flew at him.

The unwise neighbour didn't stand a chance. Zombie Mac feasted on his face, and the neighbour fell in seconds, the virus had claimed another victim. The neighbour had left his front door open, as a potential escape route back to safety. His most unfortunate family cowered in the corner of their living room, petrified with shock. His two young children cried uncontrollably, and his wife screamed hysterically. They were helpless, and completely vulnerable. Zombie Mac and the newly turned neighbour stalked into the house and fell on them to feast. They capitulated without a fight. They were all turned.

Zombie Mac, and the newly turned zombies returned to the street and went on the hunt for more victims.

Mac led the growing hoard. The virus had mastered how to make the host do anything it wanted physically, but there were numerous parts of the brain that the virus was uncertain about. The virus had accessed the Hippocampus of Mac the Sack and it was confused, but intrigued with the images and powerful feelings it found there.

The virus accessed scenes there that seemed mysteriously significant. Deep in the brain of Mac the Sack the virus explored events that seemed to be connected and prominent. Without particularly knowing why it was doing it the virus made the hosts bowels move. The event had such prominence in Jim Mackenzie's mind the virus assumed it was important. The virus then communicated this ability to the rest of the zombies. All the zombies currently rampaging all over Greenock, Gourock and Port Glasgow released the contents of their bowels, all at the same time.

Zombie Mac and his hoard of zombies marauded down the street picking off any unfortunate individuals they came across. They approached the bottom of the street, at the junction with the main road into town was located. As the hoard of zombies reached the bottom of the street, they heard the wail of sirens heralding a fleet of police vehicles that were speeding towards them.

Mac and his hoard stood swaying at the bottom of the hill as the police cars turned the corner and came into view. There were so many police cars and vans streaming up the road that all the cars on the same side of the road had pulled over to let them pass. The cars on the opposite side had slowed to a crawl to better view the emerging situation. The occupants of the cars had never seen anything like Mac and his hoard of zombies, no one knew what was going on, but it was obviously something well worth gawping at, especially from the confines of a nice safe, locked car.

The police cars and vans stopped, and the officers disembarked. Mac and his zombies, covered in blood, torn flesh, and decorated with the occasional entrail, stood swaying, and drooling at the fresh, new meat. The police nervously stood huddled close to each other as they attempted to process the sight of Mac and his hoard of zombies. None of them knew what they were supposed to be doing about the abominable creatures standing before them. The police waited for some kind of instruction, or order from their lead officer.

The lead officer was acutely aware that his officers were waiting for commands. They needed leadership. The lead officer was also very much aware that he had never before seen anything like Mac and his zombies, ever. He was aware that his training had been woefully inadequate in preparing him for this current situation. He looked at his officers, and he looked at Mac and his zombies, the magnitude of his situation hit him. He was way out of his depth, and he knew it. He didn't know what to do, so he prevaricated.

All Mac, and his zombies, perceived was fresh meat. They howled like loons and sprinted en masse at the police. The police braced themselves for impact, some of them turned and fled, others sneaked back into their cars and vans. But much to their credit, the majority stayed to fulfil their duty of protection. They pulled out their truncheons, to prepare for the impending impact.

The police were dressed in normal cloth uniforms. They were not kitted out in riot gear, and they had no other means of protection other than their truncheons. Mac and his zombies hit them hard and viciously. They were frenzied in their attack. The zombies bit, ripped, grappled, and gored. The police managed, by accident rather than design, to fell a couple of the zombies by landing some lucky head shots. But the zombies were too vicious and unrestrained. The police were outnumbered, and they had no knowledge about how to subdue these inhuman adversaries. The zombies felt no pain. The police were overpowered and beaten in all but a few gore filled seconds.

The police all turned to zombies, and stood swaying with Mac and his hoard. As soon as the result of this battle became obvious to the occupants of the nearby cars; there was an urgent dash to be somewhere else, anywhere else. It was now obvious that this was not a good place to be. Unfortunately, the conditions on the road meant that a quick getaway was now impossible. In the ensuing panic there were a lot of crashes and only a few outlying cars managed to escape.

The zombie police battered the windows out of the cars and piled in to maul the occupants. There was no way out. The road was closed on both sides, and any new cars that approached were quickly overpowered by zombies. Anyone who tried to make a run for it was pounced on. The recently turned zombies all piled out of their cars and set out to convert more hosts.

The main road had become like a zombie beehive with zombies spinning off on all directions. They ran off down nearby side roads and up and down the main road, the zombies scatter-gunned to seek, devour and convert any and all victims they could find.

Mac stood proud in the middle of this carnage as his slow zombie brain accessed more memories. Zombie Mac visualised two faces. It understood that these people were furiously hated by the host. Zombie Mac was dimly aware that these faces belonged to the names of Kenny McGregor and Joe Dunlop, though the concept of names didn't make much sense to it. The residual anger felt by the host to these people caused the zombie to desire nothing more than to be able to eat these faces. Zombie Mac decided it would go on a hunt for them.

Zombie Mac accessed another of the hosts enduring memories. He awkwardly pursed his zombie lips and blew hard. Eventually, with a bit of practice, from out of zombie Macs mouth there emitted a raspy tuneless, badly whistled version of Elvis Presley's Can't Help Falling in Love. Whistling Elvis, zombie Mac slouched off on a personal quest to find Kenny McGregor and Joe Dunlop.

Chapter 15

Joe Dunlop woke up to the sound of his wife shouting at their children to keep quite so as not to wake their dad. He yawned and looked at the bedside clock. It was 1:00 pm. He had been asleep for about five hours after his night shift. Joe's body communicated to him that he was not getting any younger, and that he required more sleep. Joe's Scotsman's brain communicated to him that five hours was enough for any man, and that there would be plenty of time to sleep when he dies. He slowly raised himself from his matrimonial bed.

On his way to the bathroom he heard his wife shout again at their children that she told them to be quite, and that they should be ashamed of themselves for waking up their hard-working father. Joe's wife went on to inform their children that they should show him more respect due to him working hard to support them all. Joe could imagine the sour look on his children's faces.

After urinating and splashing cold water on his face he ran his wet hands through his thinning grey hair, and flattened out some spirally, unruly curls. He now felt ready to face the day.

Joe stomped heavily down the stairs and popped his head into the living room. His son was slouched on the sofa engrossed in a hand-held video game; his daughter was perched on the floor in front of the TV. "Morning people," Joe announced his arrival.

"It's afternoon dad," said his daughter, without taking her eyes off the TV.

"Hrrmp," grunted his son, also without making eye contact.

"Well, it's morning to me," Joe said. "And it's wonderful to get such a warm welcome from my loving family." Joe's voice was dripping with sarcasm.

Barbara, Joe's wife, came bustling out of the kitchen. "So, so sorry Joe. I tried to tell them to be quiet but……" She slid past Joe into the living room and pointedly stared at her children. "……. they just don't listen, do you?" Barbara stood in the middle of the living room with her fists bunched at her waist, she looked fierce.

"Ach, don't worry about it love. They're just young and daft," said Joe as he wandered over to ruffle his son's hair, prior to plopping down beside him on the sofa. "Ain't that right son?"

Dennis registered his extreme ire at having his hair ruffled, and he ignored his father.

"Eh Chrissie? Daft as a brush teenagers ain't they?" Joe stared into the back of his daughter's head, as she deliberately focused harder on the television. Christine also ignored her father.

"Cup of tea Joe?" Barbara asked.

"Aye, cheers Babs, and a bit of toast and all if it's going eh?" Joe replied. "I'm starving." he rubbed his stomach.

"You guys want tea and toast?" Barbara asked her children.

"Aye," grunted Dennis.

"Yes please mum," Joe suggested a more appropriate response.

"Naw," replied Christine.

"No thanks mum," Joe again furnished his daughter with a more suitable phrase. "Good manners cost nothing," he added. His children continued to ignore him. "Have I gone invisible all of a sudden or something?"

"Och, give it a rest dad will you," Christine sounded vaguely frustrated. "I'm trying to watch telly." Madonna was dancing on the television screen, singing about being a material girl.

"Load of old rubbish if you ask me." Joe turned to face his son, though his son continued to focus on his computer game. "You sure you don't want to go to Cappielow today Dennis?" Joe asked hopefully. "There's a lad I know fae work has a couple of spare tickets. We could still make it if you wanted?" Joe was keen to go as he knew what he would have to do if he didn't get to go to the football.

"Naw, dad, I grew out of going to see Morton years ago." Dennis didn't look up from his computer game.

"Ach, you're joking Dennis, you never grow out of football." Joe was horrified, and ever so slightly offended.

"I'm naw saying I've grown out of footie dad." Dennis finally looked up from his computer game. "What I'm saying is, that I have grown fed up watching that useless lot being crap every week."

"Oi, watch your language." Joe admonished his son, though he was well aware Dennis used much worse language when he was out of earshot of his parents. Joe didn't really mind Dennis swearing, but he knew his wife would expect him to administer an admonishment. "They're in with a shout of making the semi-finals you know Dennis? I know they're not all that. But they're in with a real chance this time."

"They'll mess it up for sure dad, they always do." Dennis returned to his game.

Barbara bustled back into the living room carrying a large tray of tea and toast. She silently dispensed the tea and toast and sat down on the armchair next to her husband. The family all sat facing the television, Chrissie Hynde and UB40 were on now.

"Did I hear you two talking about going to the footie this afternoon?" Barbara asked the room without making eye contact with either her husband or son.

"Aye, but our son and heir thinks he is too mature now for the Morton," Joe said as he gave his sons head a gentle shove.

"Hey, watch my tea," Dennis complained.

"That's good. You'll be able to help me with the shopping after all then Joe. Won't you?" Barbara looked ever so slightly smug.

Dennis snorted. "So that's what all that was about. Looking for a way out of going to the shops dad?"

"I don't know what you're so smug about. You two will be coming with us 'n all." Joe dropped the bombshell.

"No way," chimed Dennis and Christine in rare, perfect unison.

"I'm 15 years old, mam," complained Christine. "I'm too old to be dragged round the shops with my mum and dad for God's sake." Christine stared bug eyed at her mother.

"Another one with delusions of grandeur Babs," said Joe, immensely pleased at the reaction his bomb had caused.

"Can I not just go over to Duncan's mam?" Dennis pleaded to be allowed to visit his best friend.

"No ye cannie Dennis. You see Duncan every day at school, and most nights during the week." After dealing with her son, Barbara turned to her daughter. "And you young madam, when you're old enough to get a job and pay rent on your own house, then you can 'not come to the shops' with your family. But until then you need to do exactly what me or you dad tell you to do. Alright?"

Barbara was done, and now wanted to change the subject. "How was work Joe?"

The question caused Joe to recall discovering Mac the Sack masturbating in the storeroom, he smiled. "Not bad Babs. Not a bad night's work at all."

"You gonnie pop down the Diamond before shopping Joe?"

"Naw sweetheart, I reckon we should probably just get going. I want to water the garden first, then I reckon we should head." Joe finished his tea and toast and went back up to the bedroom. He changed into a pair of jeans and a t-shirt and bounced back down the stairs. By-passing the living room, where his wife and children were sitting in a frosty silence, he stopped off in the kitchen to get a bottle of water from the fridge. It was a hot day.

Stepping into the back-garden, the heat of the day caused his good mood to rise even further, he took a long drink of water. Walking over to where the garden hose was coiled up next to the outdoor tap, Joe peered over the three fences that demarcated his garden. He was the only one out. Frowning, he attached the hose to the tap and turned the water on. He started watering his crab apple bushes and rhododendrons, drenching them with water. Much to his surprise numerous voles scurried quickly out as the water hit, they scampered straight out of the garden. He watered the nasturtiums and rhubarb next. The same thing happened. As soon as the water hit the wildlife within bolted away, as quickly as they could. Joe had performed this simple procedure numerous times, and he had never seen anything like it.

Turning off the tap he looked around again at the neighbourhood. There was still not a soul out. This struck him as most unusual, with weather like this he would have expected more people to be out. He shrugged, shook his head and, after finishing of his bottle of water, he went back indoors. Locking the back door, he shouted through the house, "You guys ready?"

"Sure am," his wife shouted back. Barbara, trailed by two sullen teenagers, emerged from the living room, ready for a trip into town.

The Dunlop family left their home and walked silently along the road to the bus stop. The street was very quiet, they were the only ones on it. "There wasn't a soul out when I was in the garden earlier," Joe commented.

"I know, it's quiet out." Barbara replied, looking puzzled. "Maybes they've all gone to the game?" she ventured.

Joe looked at his watch. "Naw. It's too early. They're maybes all in the town, or in the boozer tanking up before they go." The Dunlop family stood on their own at the bus stop. Joe was thinking about the way the garden creatures behaved. He was aware of how strange this would sound to his family, so he kept his thoughts to himself. The bus arrived; there was no one on it apart from the driver. They boarded in silence, the bus driver looked pasty faced and distracted, he did not look well.

Joe sat silently beside his wife, just behind the bus driver. Christine and Dennis sat silently staring out the window directly behind their parents. The bus driver drove badly, nearly missing a couple of red lights. Joe winced at every stop the driver nearly missed. Joe muttered to Barbara, "If he's that sick he shouldnae huv gone to work. He shouldnae be on the road I reckon."

"This is weird," Christine vocalised the thoughts that were present in all of their minds.

"It's maybes too hot for everybody. They're probably all in-doors keeping out the heat." Barbara tried to rationalise the bizarre.

"Mam. This is Greenock. It's never hot." Dennis exposed the obvious flaw in his mother's argument.

"At the first sign of sun everybody and his dog is out." Dennis resumed staring at the empty streets.

The closer they got to the town centre the more people they saw. "See," said a desperately defiant Barbara, "There's people out enjoying the sun." They all studied the obviously sick looking people slowly wandering listlessly towards the town centre. Their presence there looked more like habit rather than design, or indeed desire.

Christine and Dennis exchanged worried looks. Joe's mind searched fruitlessly for a rational explanation. Barbara silently chewed her cheek; she could feel her anxiety rising.

Their bus arrived at the town centre terminus. The driver opened the passenger doors and then immediately opened and climbed out of the driver's door. He stretched and hunched over. Placing his hands on his thighs for support, he retched. The Dunlop family left the bus, Barbara called a nervous, "Thank you," to the oblivious driver.

"Let's just get what we came for, and get out of here quick eh?" Grim faced, Joe voiced his plan.

There were people present in the town centre, but mostly they looked listless, tired, and their faces were grey. They looked drawn and haggard. Joe couldn't stop thinking about the voles running away as he was watering the garden.

They walked tightly and quietly, as a unit, up the steps by the bus terminus, to the supermarket. Entering the supermarket all four noted that the shop was not nearly as busy as it usually was. Though there were people there shopping, it all looked far from normal. Most of the shoppers looked ill, and as if they would all rather be at home, in bed. Others looked well enough and were proceeding with their normal Saturday routine, though, similar to the Dunlops, they were also casting anxious glances at the condition of those around them. The staffing levels of the supermarket looked sparse, and those that had bothered to turn up for work mostly looked ill.

Christine and Dennis looked anxiously at each other again. Christine spoke for them both, "This just looks weird. Can we not just go home mum?"

Barbara refused to give in. "Don't be silly, there's probably just a bug going around the town. If we don't get the food in we'll have nothing to eat next week," she pleaded. Barbara wanted support from her husband. No one looked convinced.

Joe reiterated his only plan. "We'll get what we need quick, and get a taxi home." He was getting increasingly concerned about how sick and grey everyone looked. Joe didn't have any logical explanations for what he was seeing, and he couldn't process what he was feeling, but his protective instincts were going into overdrive. He was getting the message that they all really needed not to be where they were.

Going round the supermarket aisles, Joe pushed the trolley, and Barbara filled it quickly. Barbara shouted orders to get items to Christine and Dennis, who were being uncharacteristically obedient, and briskly efficient. During their passage through the supermarket the Dunlops happened upon numerous people just standing around staring into space. Going down the freezer aisle they came across someone who had completely given up and had resorted to sitting against one of the freezers holding his head in his hands. "Do you think that'll do us?" Joe asked his wife with more than a hint of urgency in his voice.

"Yeah, I reckon so." Barbara knew the shopping expedition was over, and she was relieved at being given the opportunity to end it. The family went to the nearest checkout with their trolley. There was no queue. Their checkout lady looked healthy enough, but she was obviously worried about the condition of most of the people around her. "Funny old day eh?" she ventured to the Dunlop family in general.

"Aye, it looks like there might be a bug going about town." Barbara tested her idea out loud once again. The checkout lady looked as unconvinced as Barbara and her family were.

The checkout lady quickly processed the Dunlops purchases, and they made their way hastily to the exit. They passed by a middle-aged woman who had given up trying to be vertical, and had resorted to lying on the floor, she looked asleep. No one intervened or checked if she was ok. As the Dunlops approached the exit the woman started twitching violently, her arms and legs jerking about uncontrollably.

"She's having a fit," Barbara shouted as their checkout lady ran to assist.

"Are you ok, hen?" the checkout lady asked as the woman stopped jerking and twitching. The previously twitching, jerking woman slumped grey faced and lifeless on the floor; she looked dead. The checkout lady looked panicked, she looked around for help. Looking directly at Barbara she cried out, "Help."

As Barbara automatically started to move towards the scene, Joe instinctively put his hand out to stop her. The formerly fitting lady flicked open her eyes. Her skin had gone completely grey and flaky, and her eyes were now grey and devoid of corona. The fitting lady had turned. The checkout lady was bent over her, which presented the zombie with easy pickings. The zombie grabbed the checkout lady and started chewing her face. The checkout lady let out a loud blood curdling scream.

Joe grabbed Barbara tighter, in order to prevent her from intervening. He needn't have worried, Barbara, like the rest of her family was utterly repelled by what she was witnessing. Joe looked at his shocked children. "We need to get out of here," he said. No one heard him. His family were paralysed by the sight of their checkout lady being eaten alive by another human being.

The zombie customer looked directly at Joe and his family as she dug into, and ripped open, the checkout ladies stomach. Blood, entrails, and the contents of the checkout girl's stomach, spilled out onto the floor, the zombie stuffed the entrails into its mouth. "We need to get the fuck out of here, NOW," Joe screamed at his family as he dragged his wife towards the exit. At the sound of their father swearing Christine and Dennis snapped out of their petrification. The Dunlops fled the supermarket.

A few people in the supermarket, who were still virus free, tried to run towards the exit. They were cut off by the zombie customer. This allowed the Dunlops vital seconds to run to the nearest taxi. There was no queue. Joe jumped into the front seat, his wife and children piled into the back. "Stones estate please pal. Ruby Road," Joe barked, urgency bled from his words.

Joe turned to the taxi driver, the driver looked grey and sick. "Was that a scream I heard in there? It sounded like someone was being murdered." The taxi driver sounded only marginally interested.

Joe registered the driver's pallor, but he also knew that he and his family desperately needed to escape from the area. "It was nothing pal. Just some burd slipped and fell is all. We're in a bit of a rush here pal if you don't mind?" Joe endeavoured to be as courteous as possible, though his entire being wanted to scream at the driver to get a move on. Joe kept glancing nervously at the supermarket door, muffled screaming could distinctly be heard coming from within the shop.

The taxi driver shrugged his shoulders. "He who pays the piper calls the tune, eh pal?" the driver managed to say, though even speaking was an obvious struggle for him. Sighing heavily, the driver slowly started to pull away from the supermarket.

Joes mind raced in multiple directions. He tried to think about how bad the taxi driver looked, and what, if anything, he should do about it. He tried to process the horrors he had just seen, and what could possibly have caused it. He thought about the weirdness of the town and the state of the people in it. Finally he thought about his family sitting in the back seat of the taxi. Joe turned to look at them, they were ashen faced and stunned into silence. He made eye contact with them all and was marginally assured that at least they were not physically harmed, though they all looked extremely traumatised.

Christine was sitting in the middle seat, she noticed the colour of the drivers face, she looked at her father, her eyes wide with fear. "I know," said Joe quietly as he turned back to look out of the front window. Again, in his mind's eye, he saw the voles running away from the water when he was in his garden. Joe shook his head; he couldn't believe he had just see one human being eating another. Another glance at his pale faced family rammed it home to him that he had.

Joe looked directly at the taxi driver as the car was pulling out of the car park and onto the empty road. His eyes were rolling back in his head. Anxiety, fear, and helplessness flooded Joe's system. "Are you alright pal," Joe asked nervously.

The drivers eyelids sank closed, and his head flopped onto the steering wheel. He was out cold, unconscious. The car veered onto the pavement and crashed into a streetlamp. The engine stalled. Adrenaline flooded Joe's system, he reached slowly over to shake the taxi driver gently, Joe feared what he expected to come next. The taxi driver was unresponsive, and not breathing. The taxi driver was dead.

"Dad?" asked Christine, her voice trembling. "Is he gonnie go mental?"

"Joe?" asked Barbara. "Are we gonnie be alright?"

"Dad?" asked Dennis, scared out of his wits. "What's happening?"

Joe stared at the taxi driver, glancing briefly at his family. Imperceptibly the dead taxi driver started to twitch. When the driver started to twitch and jerk more pronounceably Joe frantically searched the car for a weapon. There was nothing. The driver started to flay around violently. Christine and Barbara screamed, Dennis whimpered and cried. The taxi driver slumped back against the steering wheel, then threw himself back against the seat. It moaned, and opened its grey, pin-prick pupiled eyes.

The burst into violence was brutal and quick. Growling deeply the zombie taxi driver flew at Joe. Joe had nothing but his fists and a system full of adrenaline to fight with. Joe's desperation to protect his family was paramount. He grabbed the zombie taxi driver by the neck with both hands as the zombie flew at him, its lips were pulled back in a growling snarl. Joe was strong, he was full of adrenaline, he battered the head of the taxi driver repeatedly against the steering wheel, and against the driver's side window. The window smashed. Joe pounded the zombie's head mercilessly against the rim of the broken window. Shattered glass shredded the zombies head and neck. Thick, congealed blood oozed out of the wounds. The zombie howled and fought back angrily, biting out and flaying at Joe with its clawed hands. Joe felt his arm being bitten, this enraged him, his fury redoubled his violence. He heard the zombies head crack open after a particularly furious blow against the metal rim of the window. The zombie went limp and inanimate.

Joe stared wide eyed at his hands; they were smeared with congealed blood. Joe stared at his family sitting in stunned silence, except for a slight whimpering sound coming from Dennis. Christine put her arm around her brother and squeezed him. "It's alright Dennis, it's dead. Dad killed it." Christine said, "It's dead dad, in't it?" Christine sought confirmation and reassurance from Joe.

"Aye," Joe said, his voice hoarse from adrenaline now spent. He looked back at his bloody hands that were now starting to shake.

"Get that fucking thing out of this car."

Dennis stopped crying. Christine and Joe stared at Barbara. No one, not even Joe, had ever heard Barbara swear before.

Joe snapped out of his post violence stupor. Checking all around the car he opened the door and got out. Standing up straight, Joe looked back at the supermarket, it was still far too close, but so far nothing was coming. Joe checked the nearby roads, there were a few people still trudging their way slowly towards the town, and a couple of others who had given up and were just sitting by the side of the road.

Joe quickly ran round to the driver's door. He checked the damage caused by the crash, it seemed to be minimal, he prayed the car would still function. Grabbing the door handle, Joe ignored the congealed blood dripping down the door. The door opened easily despite the damaged window. The corpse of the zombie flopped halfway out when Joe opened the door, he pulled the rest of it out, it flopped on the pavement. Joe wiped his blood smeared, shaking hands on the shirt of the twice dead taxi driver, and climbed into the driver's seat.

"What you doing, Joe?" Barbara asked, her voice still shaking with fear.

"We need to get the fuck out of here Barbara. I need to get this thing going."

"You don't know how to drive Joe!"

"I know Barbara. But we need to get the fuck out of here." Joe turned in his seat to look at his wife. "And we need to get out of here, quickly. I sort of know, theoretically, how to drive. I've just never done it before." He turned back nervously to look at the panel in front of him. The steering wheel was dripping with congealed blood, he cleaned the wheel with his cloth hanky, and tossed the hanky out the broken window.

He turned the key and the engine spluttered to life. The car was still in gear, so it stalled, and the engine died again. "Fuck," said Joe.

"And would you please stop swearing in front of the kids, Joe."

Joe breathed in deeply through his nose. He thought that the fact that the kids had just seen a customer eat a checkout lady, they would not be so focused on his bad language, but he also knew better than to argue with his wife, at any time. His wife's intervention actually helped clear his mind from the panic that was close to overwhelming him.

Joe noticed the gear stick was in second gear, he gingerly pushed in the pedal he knew was the clutch, and took the car out of gear. He started the car again, the engine spluttered to life and remained ticking over. Joe looked at the gear stick, he would have to reverse the car, as it was stuck against the lamppost. He found the letter R on the gear stick and tried to get the gear stick to stay in the R section. It kept jumping out, he couldn't get it to stick.

Joe looked out of the back window to see a hoard of zombies come spilling out the supermarket door. The zombies were unaware that Joe and his family were nearby, and they wandered around aimlessly. A few were sniffing the air, and a couple of them started to wander in the vague direction of the taxi. Joe felt panic rise in his throat.

With the clutch still depressed, he put the car into first, then second, then third, then fourth gear. But when he tried again to get the car into reverse, he still couldn't get it to engage. Barbara looked out the back window, she saw the zombies wandering in their direction. "Joe, we need to get out of here."

"I know, I cannie get it into reverse."

Dennis and Christine looked out the back window. Dennis started to cry loudly again.

Joe couldn't understand why he couldn't get the car into reverse, his eyes darted from the rear-view mirror to the gear stick. He watched the zombie's getting closer and closer. Dennis's crying got louder, and more intense, Christine started to whimper.

"Joe, what we going to do?" Barbara was feeling increasingly desperate.

"I don't know Babs. I don't understand it." Joe tried to force the gear stick over, it didn't work.

As they approached the taxi, the closest zombie became aware there was live flesh inside. It let out a gurgling growl and howled, satisfied that it had found what it craved. Other nearby zombies responded to the call, and started to make their way to the taxi. As the zombies reached the back of the car Joe became aware of a round lever under the knob of the gear stick. He lifted the lever and pushed; relief flooded his system when the gear stick slid easily into reverse.

Joe lifted the clutch and pressed the accelerator, the taxi lurched back crushing the nearby zombies under the wheels. The zombies howled, not out of pain but out of anger and frustration at being denied their catch. Joe cleared the taxi from the lamppost and managed to get it into first gear. Lifting the clutch, Joe pressed the accelerator, the taxi shot forward and away from the supermarket, and the chasing hoard of zombies.

The relief in the taxi was palpable, Dennis stopped crying, and Christine and her mother sat more comfortably in their seats, though Barbara was still nervous about her husband driving. Joe managed to get the taxi into second, and then third gear. The Dunlop family sped swiftly away from the supermarket. Joe gripped the steering wheel tightly, his body hunched with tense concentration. He managed to keep the taxi on the correct side of the road, without hitting anything, and travelling at a reasonable but safe speed.

"We going home dad?" Christine asked her dad.

"Aye sweetheart," Joe replied with a relived sigh. "We are".

Driving up the main road, heading towards the Stones estate, they saw various people collapsing, and hordes of marauding zombies. Coming towards the tail end of a bad traffic jam Joe applied the brakes, the car stalled. There were zombies everywhere. There were zombie police smashing car windows and eating people. Then Joe saw someone he thought he recognised. "I think that's Mac the Sack." Joe struggled to understand what or who he was seeing, but he was sure he recognised the water refinery manager.

Barbara looked out the window at the figure covered in gore wandering down the street towards them. "I don't know about that Joe, and to be honest I don't really care." Barbara looked out the window as their car started to be surrounded by zombies. "We need to get out of here now, Joe".

A couple of the zombie police spotted the fresh meat sitting in the taxi. Mac the Sack saw him and his slow zombie brain connected the face with the name Joe Dunlop. Zombie Mac howled; this was one of the people he wanted to eat.

Zombie Mac, and a few of the zombie police, loped towards the Dunlops taxi; they were on the car before Joe managed to re-start it. He managed to start the car as zombie Mac tried to grab him through the broken driver's window. This time Joe made no mistake, he flung the car straight into reverse. Joe felt zombie Mac's nails drag across his skin as the car sped backwards and away. He felt blood trickle down his arm as he span the car backwards and round to face the other way. In the rear-view mirror he watched the angry, gore covered, zombie face of his former manager howling as the taxi sped away.

"That was definitely Mac the Sack," said Joe as he turned off the main road to navigate the back roads to the Stones estate. "Whatever this thing is. It couldn't have happened to a better person."

"I don't care if it was the bloody Queen of Sheba. What the hell is going on Joe?" Barbara was deeply shaken.

"How am I supposed to know that?" Joe looked at the wounds on his arm, he had been bitten and clawed and he was extremely worried about what that might mean.

"Give it a rest you two. Dennis are you alright?" Christine looked at her brother. He was silently crying and rocking in his seat.

Joe and Barbara snapped out of their bickering. "You alright son?" They asked in unison.

Barbara lent over Christine to reach for her son. "Don't worry Dennis. We'll be alright." Barbara rubbed her son's quivering leg. "Your dad and me will make sure you're alright son."

Dennis let go of his pent-up feelings, burying his head in his hands he howled uncontrollably. Christine put her arm back round him, and held her brother tight. Joe looked at his wounded arm. "Aye son don't worry. We'll get home and hole up there till….," Joe thought about his recent sighting of the Greenock Police. "…..the Government, or someone, sends somebody to help us." He was acutely aware of how lame this sounded.

The back roads were empty. The houses looked oppressively quiet. Driving down the main road of the Stones Estate, past the Diamond pub, Joe saw Innes McDonald, from the water refinery, fleeing from a hoard of zombie's, with his friend and a teenage girl in tow. Joe drove past. He needed to get his family into a place of safety.

Joe turned into Ruby Road, there was no one on the road. He parked the taxi right outside his house and turned the engine off. The family piled out of the car with great haste and sprinted to their house.

Briefly, Joe stood in the doorway of their house. He thought again of the animals running away from the water. He thought about Mac the Sack and the look of venomous hate on his grey zombie face as he clawed at his arm. He thought about the sight of Innes running down the road being chased by zombies, and he wished him well. Turning his back on the street, Joe entered his house and locked and bolted the front door.

Christine, Barbara, and Dennis had all gathered in the kitchen. Barbara was tightly holding both her very scared looking children when Joe strode in. "Don't anybody drink the tap water." The tone of Joe's voice brooked no argument, or further comment.

Joe filled a kettle and switched it on. He watched it in silence until it boiled. He poured the boiling water into the sink and waited until it cooled a little. Barbara started to calm her children with comforting words, and reassurance, that everything was alright now they were home and safe. Barbara kept looking at her husband's arm.

Once the water was cool enough Joe scrubbed his hands and arms clean with washing up liquid. The wounds on his arm were livid purple.

"Joe, do you think this thing is in the water?" Barbara couldn't stop glancing at Joe's injuries while she was talking.

"Aye, I do love." Joe dried his arms and hands on a kitchen towel. Traces of blood transferred to the towel. "I just know it is Barbara. It was the voles. Why would they run from water?" Joe threw the bloodied towel in the bin. "And how come there's so many people affected? Everyone who doesn't work at the water refinery drinks the water."

Barbara didn't know what her husband was talking about voles for, but this was the least of her concerns. "And what about your arm?" Trepidation laced Barbara's words; her eyes desperately sought solace from her husband.

Joe knew what his wife was asking, he broke eye contact and looked at the ground, his mind was racing, and he didn't like where it was heading. "I don't know Barbara, love. I just don't know."

Christine and Dennis both caught the gravity, the reality, and the subtext of their parents communications. Dennis started to cry again; Christine comforted him and looked anxiously from Joe to Barbara. "You're gonnie be alright dad, in't it?"

"I suppose we will just need to wait and see love," Joe said. He sighed and walked slowly into the living room. His family followed.

Joe turned on the television and flicked from one channel to the next. There was nothing but normal Saturday afternoon programmes on, horse racing and sport. He turned it off and sat down with a sigh, his family sat with him. He didn't know what the right thing to do was.

"Wait here," Joe eventually said.

Joe went to his toolbox in the kitchen and came back with a hammer. Tears were in his eyes, and he swallowed as he handed the hammer to his wife. "If it happens," he said with his voice quivering. "Hit me on the head as hard as you can."

With tears streaming down her face Barbara silently reached for the hammer. Christine and Dennis howled with anguish.

Joe sat back down. The Dunlops began the wait.

Chapter 16

Stella tried desperately to return to sleep, unconsciousness was her preferred state of being. Unfortunately, facing away from her partner in bed did not prevent his presence from permeating her awareness. She felt a dull ache between her legs, and her arm was tender. But the most pernicious injury manifested itself in Stella's sub-conscious reflections.

"He's probably right, I probably did deserve what I got. I don't mean to do it, but I probably do wind him up about working while he can't get a job. It's not even his fault, it is his bad back. My dad always said I wouldn't amount to anything, that I was too dumb. I really am a worthless piece of shit."

Somewhere in Stella's core, defiant rebellion sought to rebalance the patent injustice being played out in her mind. *"I have got to be worth more than this. I can do so much better than him. Bad back my arse. What would Jean do? What would Jean say? Why have I never spoken to her about this?"*

Her warped thinking had an answer for everything. *"Jean Gourley is probably a dried-up old virgin who would swap her right arm to have a man like John Reid."*

Internally recoiling at thinking such a vicious thought about one of her few remaining friends; she wondered if Jean knew about her domestic violence situation? Curling tighter into a ball she fought the urge to move. If she indulged in gratuitous restlessness he might wake up.

Feeling a soft shift in pressure at the bottom of the bed, Stella became aware of four light little paws making their way surreptitiously up the bed. Rolling gently over on her back, Stella's legs straddled Fluffy, as her cat made her way up to see her. Stella glared at the recumbent lump in the bed beside her, John was lying on his back snoring and dribbling, she grimaced in disgust.

Fluffy started to climb up Stella's body, causing her to wince as her cat trod on her tender stomach. She reached out to gently stroke her. John grunted and turned round causing her to catch her breath. If he were to wake up now and find Fluffy on the bed it would be a very bad start to her day.

It was 9:23, she decided it would be best for everyone if she just got up. The blissful oblivion of sleep was now firmly out of reach, and the less time she was aware of sharing a bed with John Reid the better.

Gently placing her cat on the floor she slid, first one leg, then the other out of the bed, without changing the angle of her body. This was done to reduce any change in pressure that might cause John to awaken. Using her sore arm for leverage, she slid out of bed and propelled herself to her feet in one smooth motion. Stella was well practiced at getting out of bed without waking her partner, who continued to snore and drool on the pillow.

Stella stepped into her slippers and draped her dressing gown over her shoulders. Fluffy knew the routine well, so she skipped happily out of the bedroom, and down the stairs to the kitchen, followed by her person, who, ever so gently, closed the bedroom door behind them.

When her cat's kitchen needs were dispensed with, Stella commenced meeting her own. She shuffled over to the sink to fill the kettle and stared vacantly out the window, her eyes alighted on the visual monstrosity that was Lennie Wilson's back garden, she sighed.

Wondering what caused Lennie to live that way, Stella thought about her own dysfunctional life. She pondered briefly if heroin would make life more bearable. Staring at the pile of doors propped up against the wall of his house, she concluded that whatever the benefits of heroin were, the price was probably not worth paying. Lennie was generally considered to be completely mad. Growing up on the Homerton she had seen him decline physically and mentally over the years. Being a few years older than Stella, he moved in different social circles, so she had never really ever spoken to Lennie. Besides, her mother had always warned her away from people like him. Stella wondered why her mother had never warned her away from people like John Reid.

Talking to her parents about how John beat her was pointless. Growing up she had heard her parents fighting, but had never actually seen any physical violence. Any time she tentatively broached the subject of how awful John was, her mother would launch into such a litany of praise about what a strong man he was, and what a pity he was so misunderstood by others, that further discussion was discouraged. Stella couldn't even begin to contemplate talking to her father about domestic violence. He would just tell her it was her own stupid fault and leave the room.

Taking her breakfast into the living room, she turned on the TV and flopped carefully down on the sofa, curling her legs underneath her. Fluffy finished eating her breakfast and plopped herself beside her. Curling herself against Stella's feet, Fluffy indulged joyfully in a vigorous post breakfast wash. Stella flicked through the channels and settled on a Channel 4 music programme. Music soothed her nerves and helped her switch off.

Stella zoned out, the music had stultified her thinking like a mild tranquiliser, until thudding footsteps coming from the bedroom snapped her fully alert. Fluffy dived off the sofa scampering quickly to hide behind it. Remembering his comment from the night before about sitting in silence Stella opted to turn the television down, not off.

Loud hacking, coughing, and spitting noises emanated from the bathroom as John's body came to terms with the damage caused by his previous evenings' indulgencies. Stella listened with disgust as he noisily emptied his bladder and unleashed a torrent of trumpeting farts. The eternal argument raged again in her mind: *"Why in the hell am I still here with that?"* Rising from the sofa she stared up the stairs, disdain writ plain on her face. Sighing she returned to the kitchen to prepare his breakfast.

The stairs thump, thump, thumped, heralding the imminent arrival of John Reid.

Standing at the sink Stella ensured she had her back to the door as John entered the kitchen. She sought what little control she could get. John sat at his customary chair at the kitchen table.

"Morning," John ventured.

Stella sucked in a large helping of air, as she fixed her face and turned. "Morning John," she smiled convincingly. "Fancy a wee cup of tea and a bacon roll?" Putting the kettle on to boil she played her part in their domestic façade to perfection.

Relieved that Stella wasn't going to cause a scene John relaxed. "Aye, perfect Stella love. I've got a hell of a drouth on this morning." John followed this announcement by getting up and grabbing a glass from the cupboard. Slouching over to the taps he filled the glass with tap water and drank deeply. Looking at him, Stella said not one word about him drinking from the tap.

"I reckon I might head into town to the shops after I make your breakfast, if that's ok with you?" Stella said lightly.

"Sounds fine to me pet. Bring me my breakfast in the living room eh?" John headed into the living room

"Will do John," Stella shouted at his back as he left the kitchen. She knew her duties were, for the time being, done. For now, she would be mostly left alone.

She cooked John's bacon as he liked it, placed it perfectly in a perfectly cut roll, and covered it with the correct amount of brown sauce. She made his tea as he liked it and brought it all to him in the living room on a clean plastic tray. John hadn't bothered to change the channel, so he was watching the end of the same music programme she was watching earlier. He moaned about how stupid everybody looked, and how awful the music was.

"I'll just go get ready and head into the town then?" Stella said in neutral monotone.

John grunted something that sounded vaguely consenting.

Stella was nearly free; she went upstairs to get ready.

Rapidly dressing, Stella was free from pervasive, detrimental thoughts. She thought only about the glorious couple of hours freedom she would enjoy being away from him. Dressed in jeans and a t-shirt she bounced back down the stairs and breezed into the living room; he was still grousing at the television. "That'll be me off then, John, I'll be back in time for lunch."

"I was thinking I might come give you a hand with the bags, love? What do you think?" John asked with a malicious glint in his eyes.

Even though she was well practiced at hiding her feelings, her face dropped, anxiety hit her stomach harder than any punch could have. Stella was thrown, John had never come to the shops with her. Confused, she started to stammer something, searching for the correct words, "Err, uhm, ahh."

He cut her off. "I'm only fucking joking ya daft cow. I wouldnae be caught fucking dead in a supermarket." John turned back to watching television. "Away ye go and fix yir face."

Aware that she had just been played, Stella slowly trod to the front door, catching the eyes of her little cat as she went. Fluffy silently pleaded with her not to leave her alone with him. Guilt added to the confusion clouding her mind. She closed the door on her precious cat, and closed her mind to her abhorrent partner. Determined to disregard her dysfunctional life for a couple of precious hours she set off for the bus stop. To get there she had to walk to the top of her street, then down past Lennie's house. As she passed the shops she noticed two obvious drug addicts examining the contents of a tobacco tin. They cast furtive glances around them, then, spotting Stella staring they glared defiantly back at her.

"Snooty bitch," Jenny McAdam muttered as Stella marched past.

"Junky scum," Stella replied as she walked quickly by.

Jenny pulled a fuck you face, and resumed her investigations. The two drug addicts seemed to be having a dispute.

The bus arrived and transported Stella into Greenock town centre. The town was quieter than usual, but Stella was oblivious, she was simply happy to be out and about and away from John. Strolling through the town centre, she saw, and self-consciously ignored, a few people she knew. John had gradually 'persuaded' her to stop having any contact with her friends.

Stella was enjoying the tranquillity of relative anonymity when someone behind her called her name. She turned to see the rambunctious figure of Jean Gourley bustling towards her.

"Morning Stella love. You up with the lark as well eh?"

"Morning Jean." Unconsciously Stella rubbed her sore arm. "Aye, Jean. I like to get into town early on a Saturday, beat the crowds."

Jean observed Stella rub her arm. "Your John not in with you?" Jean arched her eyebrows.

"No, Jean. My John's not much of a one for shopping." Outside of work Stella always felt rather uncomfortable and nervous. She was at her happiest in work where she knew the routine and the rules.

"I bet," Jean grunted, her chubby fists planted hard on her ample hips. "Typical man, pampered and ungrateful."

Stella shuffled and snorted a nervous discharge of a giggle. "Och, he's not that bad really." Stella didn't want to talk about John, and right now, all she really wanted was to be somewhere else, anywhere else, Stella sought the solitude of mundane behaviours. "I'd best be off then Jean. See you at the grind Monday morning eh?"

Jean sighed, resigned, "Aye, Stella love. See you Monday. You look after yourself Stella, cause there's nae one else will, eh?"

Stella smiled as they parted company and walked slowly off to the supermarket.

The Supermarket looked short staffed, and was much quieter than Stella would have expected. She took her time shopping but ensured she didn't spend more than her weekly allowance, which was predictably meagre. But she couldn't string out the pleasure indefinitely, John wouldn't take kindly to being left alone for too long. Walking back to the bus stop Stella became aware that the town seemed to be getting quieter instead of busier. She noticed most people on the bus home didn't look well at all.

Anxiety descended again on her, like a blanket made of nettles, as her front door loomed. Putting down the shopping bags, she dredged her shoulder bag for the front door keys. *"At least Fluffy will be glad to see me,"* she thought.

"I'm home love," she announced breezing past the living room to deposit the shopping in the kitchen. For her arrival to be met with stony silence was not particularly unusual. Fluffy scampered up to her, rubbing her head excitedly against her leg, pleased to have her person back. Plus, shopping often meant chicken roll, or a sliced ham treat for her.

Fluffy waited impatiently in the kitchen as Stella bit the subservient bullet and sought out unsolicited contact with John. She found him still asleep on the sofa with the television still on. The horse racing was on now, for John to sleep through horse racing was unheard of, a deep furrow of worry lined Stella's forehead. But she decided not to look this most welcomed gift horse in the mouth and left him to slaver more drool on his grubby looking vest.

Returning to the kitchen Stella turned the radio on, keeping the volume low so as not to wake John. Stella set to emptying out the shopping bags as she listened to a news report about the impending football match being played at Cappielow. Fluffy greeted the sight of familiar shaped packaging with urgent mewing. Stella didn't make her wait. As her cat ate, Stella made her own lunch, a frugal plate of beans on toast.

After lunch, Stella started to get uncomfortably concerned about the lack of attention coming from John. Her pleasure at the unusual amount peace she was enjoying was spoiled by a creeping anxiety seeping through her system that something was wrong. Treading gently, she tiptoed into the living room to check on him. He was still flopped out on the sofa, though he was not sleeping peacefully at all. White foam frothed at the corners of his mouth as he muttered and babbled an incoherent stream of garbled nonsense. Thrashing his arms and legs about; he twitched uncontrollably. Stella could see his bulging eyes rolling around behind closed lids. His pallor was a pasty grey.

Stella was deeply conflicted. John didn't look at all well, and he was most definitely not behaving normally. She desperately wanted to feel his brow, to see if he had a temperature. But she had been in this situation before, where her attentions to his health had resulted in the most horrendous of flare ups. He didn't like being fussed over. She was fearful about the potential consequences if she inadvertently woke him. Anxiously glancing at him, she left him alone and returned to the kitchen, though her mind was spinning in turmoil.

Stella had allowed herself the rare luxury of purchasing a copy of Celebrity Magazine from the supermarket. As soon as she sat back down at the kitchen table Fluffy jumped up on her lap. Abstractedly stroking her cat, she tried to divert her disturbed thoughts by reading about Bruce Springsteen's wedding, and Samantha Fox's top tips on how to handle being a page three model.

Her mind refused to be distracted from her internal discord. "*What if he's really ill. That did not look in any way normal.*" She tried to focus on a story about EastEnders. "*He hates it when I fuss over him. If I woke him up he would kill me. The last time I had to take a week off work until the bruises faded. I nearly ended up in hospital.*"

Stella's internal distress communicated itself to Fluffy, she jumped down. John start to moan and groan loudly. Stella bolted into the living room. John, still completely unconscious, was now writhing about on the sofa with his limbs flailing around like a puppet on methamphetamine.

Suddenly, he completely stopped moving and flopped on the sofa like a lead weight. Stella was petrified, rooted to the spot. It looked like he had stopped breathing. Her eyes blazed wide and she reached out a trembling hand just as his eyes shot open. Staring out of pin prick eyes zombie John growled at Stella. She was too petrified even to scream.

Stumbling backward, Stella was already moving when zombie John rose awkwardly to his feet. His grey eyes fixed on her, and he howled. Lurching forward he swung a clawed hand to grab her. His howl broke her trance and she bolted back into the kitchen. Slamming the door closed, she held it tight with both hands while her mind desperately tried to process what she had just seen.

Zombie John lurched to the door and started to pound on it. Stella stood firm behind it, pushing it closed with all her weight. Zombie John moaned loudly and shoved at the door; it was desperate to feed. Its ferocious attack started to break the flimsy kitchen door. A flailing fist broke through the door, it tore its arm open on the way back. Thick gelatinous zombie blood slid slowly down the now shredded door. Stella screamed; she was acutely aware now that her very life was threatened.

The door started to disintegrate further from the ferocious assault. Zombie John sensed victory. Stella knew she needed a new plan, she looked desperately around the kitchen for a weapon. Grabbing one of the wooden chairs she ran back as far into the kitchen as she could. Zombie John threw open the door and staggered towards her, arms out, hands grasping. Its foam flecked mouth broke into a maniacal grin. Screaming Stella threw the chair at it as hard as she could. It broke across his shoulder, the zombies' be-socked feet slid on the linoleum floor, and it crashed to the ground face first, broken teeth and zombie drool peppered the kitchen.

Zombie John clambered back onto its feet, the injuries it had sustained had no effect, it pounced at Stella. She grabbed it by the throat as it grabbed her. Its grip was like a vice on her arms; and its head twisted to try to bite her hands and arms. Stella was strong enough, just, to keep it at bay. They wrestled around the kitchen. Stella spotted a breadknife sticking up in the dish rack.

She pushed and wriggled her way to the dish rack. Zombie John frenetically, and unsuccessfully, tried to bite her anywhere. All the years of abuse and hate boiled up in Stella. She roared and pushed the zombie back as far as she could, she grabbed the breadknife and, as the zombie flew back at her she rammed the breadknife, hard, into its left eye. With the breadknife sticking out of its eye socket, as gelatinous blood and an eye snaked down its face, zombie John dropped to the floor, dead.

Gasping, Stella leant back against the kitchen worktop. She looked at the motionless body of her former partner and burst into tears. Mixed emotions whirled around inside her like a tornado. She felt fear, panic, horror, disbelief, relief, and somewhere deep inside her, Stella felt a small bubbling burst of pure joy. She was finally free from the tyranny of John Reid, though the circumstances of her release were beyond surreal.

Out of the corner of her eye she saw movement in Lennie's garden. Scared that someone had seen her murder her partner, Stella peered closer. She saw Kenny and Lennie picking up the doors from his garden and running back inside. They looked like they were on a serious mission. Stella had never seen either Lennie or Kenny looking serious in her life. They couldn't have seen what she had just done to John from there. No one had seen.

Stella looked at the drip, drip, dripping tap. She recalled watching John draining a glass of tap water that morning. Her mind firing with adrenaline made the leap; Stella was convinced she had finally been proven correct regarding her suspicions about the water.

Fluffy, who had ran behind the washing machine when the fracas started, crept back out when silence reigned in the kitchen once again. She trotted, cautiously, over to the corpse of John Reid, sniffed and wrinkled up her nose, her mouth hung open, she had smelt something rotten. She mewed and trotted over to Stella, purring, and rubbing against her leg. "Looks like it's just you and me now sweetheart," Stella said as she picked her up. Fluffy's warm, vibrating body caused unrestrained joy to flow through Stella. "Just you and me forever now wee love. That bastard has finally gone for good."

Strange sounds coming from the radio fought for her attention. There was something unbelievably disturbing taking place. She heard the football commentator screaming in terror for his life. He was shouting something about people eating each other. The football commentator sounded petrified. The hairs on Stella's neck stood up as he was attacked. The transmission was cut off to be replaced with a very confused radio producer who played covering music while they obviously tried to come to terms with what had just occurred.

Stella looked at Fluffy, and then at the corpse of John Reid. Stella's joy gently subsided and a gnawing anxiety started to creep around her system. Stella realised that something dreadful was happening in Greenock, and she was roundly and soundly caught up in the middle of it. She looked out again at the back garden of Lennie's now quiet house. She became aware of noises coming from the surrounding area, growling, moaning, windows breaking. The radio babbled inane music and the television next door droned on about horse racing.

Stella didn't know what to do. She turned off the radio and television and carried Fluffy upstairs to her bedroom. She lay down on her bed breathing deeply to calm her mind. Stella knew a seismic shift had happened in her life, she just didn't know what she should, or indeed could, do next. She wondered if the events unfolding would mean the police would miss her heinous criminal act. She wondered how bad things were going to get. From the sounds coming from outside Stella was, in truth, unsure even about how long the rest of her life would even be. But no matter how long it was, the rest of her life would now be free from John Reid.

Chapter 17

Ian Ferguson heard someone moaning. *"Wish that cunt would just shut the fuck up."* His head felt fuzzy and painful, and anything that exacerbated the ache was most unwelcome. A dawning awareness occurred to him that it might be himself that was moaning. Paranoia propelled him rapidly into complete consciousness. His eyes flew open to check where he was and who, if anyone, was within earshot. Ian feared humiliation more than anything else. Rising to his elbows he reconnoitred his situation. He was lying fully clothed and alone on Dave Anderson's old sofa. Ian realised the moaning was coming from the street below. He ignored it.

Bright rays of sunlight streaming through off-white net curtains caused the throbbing in his brain to intensify. Swiftly reclosing his bleary, bloodshot eyes he flopped back to a prone position on the stinky sofa. He was sweating profusely, he smelled bad, and his flesh was creeping. Ian felt like his body was coated with thick, slimy, cold sausage skin.

Feeling his knuckles tingling his mind endeavoured to recall the previous evening's debauches. Remembering twirling the pool cue in the Hole in the Wall, singing the sash, caused him to grin. Thinking about how cool it must have looked helped the throbbing in his head to subside, somewhat.

He decided it was time to get some of his more immediate needs met. Nicotine was first on the list. Swinging his legs round he sat up on the threadbare sofa. Hacking and coughing he spat a large, green gob on the floor. Looking round for his trainers, he found them and used the sole of one to grind his expectorate into the already manky looking carpet.

"Dave," Ian shouted, "We got any fags?" He looked round for any stray cigarette packets. There were none. He snorted and stood. Hitching up his jeans he plopped the top button back into place.

Ian barged through the small flat, ploughing straight into Dave's bedroom. "Dave, we got any fucking fags. I'm gasping for a smoke." Ian's nose wrinkled as he became aware of the noxious smell in the bedroom, stale alcohol, and flatulence, mixed with body odour and unwashed clothes created a close, cloying, repellent atmosphere.

Dave was stretched out, spread-eagled, and snoring loudly. His prone body was half covered with a dirty looking bare duvet. Dave had manged to get most of his clothes off the night before, and had passed out wearing only his y-fronts and socks. Ian kicked out at a foot dangling over the side of the bed. "Fucking hell Dave. Shift your fucking arse, eh." Dave started, shocked into consciousness. "I need a fucking smoke." Ian continued to demand his needs be met.

Dave rose rapidly to sit on his bed. With his hair sticking out at random angles his face betrayed no emotion as he stretched and scratched at his hairy, barrel chest.

"Dave. Fags. Eh?" Ian was getting impatient, and he could feel his brain filling with the hot, thick steam of anger, being ignored was an anathema to his ego.

"Doubt it," Dave replied as he stood, shrugged his shoulders, and shuffled into his bathroom. Ian was left frustrated, listening to the sound of a lengthy stream of urine pattering loudly into the lavatory water.

Ian watched as Dave returned to the bedroom to rummage in his denim jacket. He produced a tatty ripped up packet of cigarette papers. "We'll do the roaches," he announced as he shuffled past into the living room, Ian followed. Dave went to work dredging the overflowing ashtrays in the living room. After he had collected a pile of previously smoked joints he stuck three cigarette papers together and filled them with burnt tobacco from the pile.

In the end he manged to assemble a rather thin, mean looking, roach joint. Dave passed it to Ian who lit it from a ubiquitous packet of Bluebell matches, discovered amongst the debris on the living room table. Ian coughed violently, hacked, and, once again, spat on the carpet. Dave's face betrayed none of the anger he felt at having his home so disrespected. Ian smoked the joint until his lungs could take no more then passed it to Dave who puffed tentatively on the rough joint.

"You got any scoosh?" With his nicotine cravings sated, Ian moved on to the next need on his list, hydration.

Without speaking Dave wobbled unsteadily to his feet. He returned from his visit to his kitchen with a half-full bottle of Irn Bru, which he duly handed over. Ian drank his fill then handed the remains to Dave, who finished it.

"What about them fucking Celtic cunts last night, eh Dave?" Ian moved onto his next need, ego feeding.

"Did you see my head butt?" Ian's eyes sparkled. "I got him a fucking beauty. His nose burst all over his fucking, ugly, fenian face."

Dave quietly sighed. There was an inevitable familiarity about the scene currently being played out. Dave knew his place, and mostly he accepted his role in the Ian Ferguson show. Being a fighter was pretty much all that Dave had ever been good at. He had struggled academically at school, and he was not built for any sport that was popular (football). There were not many people he knew that were going to dedicate their lives to violence, so Ian was an obvious candidate for friendship. Ian was only ever going to be a dedicated lunatic. But every once in a while Dave wondered if there might have been other options open to him. There was a heavy price to pay by being Ian Ferguson's friend.

Subtly sighing, he forced a laugh. "Aye, I don't know what they were thinking coming into the Hole in the Wall wi fucking Celtic tops on. Mad, eh?"

"Aye, they'll no forget me in a hurry." Sitting up on the sofa Ian puffed his chest out slightly. "We got any money Dave? I reckon we should head oot, get a couple of cans and see who we can bump into. Eh?"

Dave sighed and scratched his head. "I reckon I might have a ten-spot stashed somewhere." Dave had learned long ago that it paid to be prepared in order to meet his friend's needs. "That should sort us out for starters, I reckon."

Ian was in no mood to remain in Dave's flat any longer than he had to. He needed to be on the move regularly just in case he was missing out on something happening somewhere. Ian pulled on his trainers and looked around for his jacket. Dave looked at his naked body. "Probably going to have to give me a minute to get ready, eh Fergie?"

"Get a shift on then ya lazy wee shite." Ian was ready. He could hear moaning coming from the street outside again, and it sounded like something he should investigate.

Dave shuffled quickly off to the bathroom. Shutting the door to ensure a modicum of privacy, he emptied his bowels. Looks stopped mattering to Dave a long time ago, so after splashing some water on his face and spraying his torso from a can of Old Spice, he felt his ablutions to be complete. In his bedroom he found a freshly laundered t-shirt and changed his underwear and socks. Sniffing at the crotch of yesterday's jeans he judged that they passed muster and pulled them on. After donning a pair of tatty white trainers Dave felt ready to face the outside world.

Dave lived on the top floor in a block of flats a 15-minute walk from Greenock town centre. When they opened his front door the screaming and moaning sounds coming from the street below became so much more pronounced. They looked at each other with questions lit on their faces. Ian shrugged his shoulders and led the way bouncing down the old, well-trodden, concrete stairs. Dave could feel his initial apprehension rise into full blown anxiety. In contrast, Ian was singularly excited to see what was causing such a furore.

As they descended the staircase the screams and moans got louder and louder. Ian's curiosity caused him to speed up. Dave's increasing anxiety caused him to slow down. But leaving Ian to his own devices was not an option. Dave felt he had no alternative other than to keep going, down and down.

Ian got to ground level first. The front door was made of heavy panels of solid wood, there was no glass for him to look through. The noises coming from beyond the door sounded horrendous. Dave caught up with him.

"What the fuck is going on out there?" Dave's face was white, and the hairs stood up on the back of his neck.

"I dunno, but it sounds like a proper fucking rammy." Ian was clearly impatient to see what happening outside, adrenaline was already coursing through his bloodstream, he was in his element. "We going oot to see what's what, eh Dave?" Ian was like a small child on Christmas day.

Dave was caught in two minds. He most definitely did not think it was a good idea to step outside. All his primal instincts were shouting at him to go straight back up the stairs, immediately. He desperately desired nothing more than to return to his flat and shut the door. But Dave had known Ian for many years, and he was uncomfortably aware that he would be constitutionally incapable of reticence when it related to matters pertaining to violence. Dave was also conscious that, despite his better instincts, he would indeed end up following Ian into the fire, as he had continually done since they had become friends. He sighed deeply. Obviously lacking any enthusiasm, he replied, "If we must."

"There's no fucking battling going on in Greenock without Fergie boy getting his bit." Anticipation caused his breathing to shorten as he pulled the door open to launch himself out. Cautiously, Dave followed, his fighting instincts prepared him to focus on whatever threat presented itself.

They both stopped in their tracks on the pavement outside as they attempted to comprehend what was happening. The air tasted metallic and there was a faint sulphurous smell. Their eyes popped wide, and their brains short-circuited trying to absorb the scene in front of them.

Dave's flat was situated on a wide road with expansive pavements. Multiple zombies roamed around searching for fresh flesh. People were in the process of being eaten, beaten or turned. The road and pavements were covered in blood, internal organs, and prostrate mutilated bodies. Blood flowed in rivulets down drains and formed into thick, gelatinous puddles.

"What the fuck," Dave spluttered.

"No fucking way," Ian shouted. Ian had always existed on the borderline of being completely psychotic. With the overt madness occurring on the streets in front of him, his brain gently gave up any attempt at control, his sanity finally snapped.

Dave looked into Ian's eye's and finally recognised the insanity that everyone in Greenock knew was there.

"I'm fucking having myself a bit of this." Ian screamed, laughing maniacally as the zombies lurched towards him. He didn't wait for them to come to him. "Come ahead ya fucking manky cunts." Ian's fists balled and flew with full force into the faces of any zombies within punching distance. Zombie jaws popped and broke, zombie cheek bones were shattered, and zombie noses were squashed against grey, flaky faces.

As a couple of zombies attempted to attack Ian from behind Dave had a moment of clarity. He knew that he had made a bad choice many years ago when he chose to associate himself with Ian. He also knew that it was too late and that, here and now, his choices were extremely limited. He knew he was stuck with Ian and his lunacy, whatever this might cost him. His only choice now was how he went. Dave looked at the people getting eaten, he looked into the inhuman eyes of the zombies, and he chose to go down how he had lived, fighting.

Ian and Dave fought ferociously back-to-back. Many zombies were brutalised severely, some were finished completely by the pounding their heads were given by the duo. But it was not long before both were bitten. From the first bites they received the virus coursed victoriously through their bloodstreams.

Ian went down first. Dave watched him die as his own body started to shut down. He stopped fighting, his eyes closed, and the virus took over. His brain and his heart stopped.

Their eyes flashed open. Grey pinpricks stared out at the world. Zombie Ian stood and filled its lungs, it howled a vicious challenge to the world. Zombie Dave stood solidly beside zombie Ian; ready to do in death what he had done in life.

Part 4

Chapter 18

The sun slid slowly off to sleep, again, as night rose to cloak its surroundings in a dark grey shroud. Within the encroaching darkness, madness and mayhem held sway over a small part of central belt Scotland. Greenock, Gourock and Port Glasgow had become a writhing pit of zombie carnage. Screams shredded up the surrounding hills and echoed through the Clyde valley as the conurbation was indiscriminately decimated.

Dotted throughout the area, some properties had caught fire due to cookers being left on as the occupants were either turned or eaten. Thick black smoke drifted across the area. There were no Fire Brigade left alive to douse the engorging flames.

Streetlamps lit up the unfolding scene in a sinister orange glow, reflecting off the thick smoke burgeoning from burning dwellings. Zombies roamed randomly around completing this picture of perfect pandemonium. Zombies dismembered and devoured individuals who were incapable of becoming infected. Body parts and internal organs were strewn across roads, pavements, cars, and gardens. Crashed cars had been left abandoned on most roads and the main streets had become completely impassable by car.

Hordes of zombies gathered in large numbers at various houses where petrified survivors cowered. The zombies smelt fresh flesh and they were obsessively driven to consume it, convert it, or destroy it. The zombies communicated with each other and were gradually learning how to access the houses. They started by aimlessly hurling various objects at windows, where nought but a pane of glass and some flimsy curtains served to protect the trembling inhabitants. Breaking windows provided the zombies with the occasional success at houses that were fitted with cheap, poor-quality windows. Older houses with thicker windows were proving more difficult for the zombies to access.

The knowledge that windows were a weak point was communicated to every zombie, which started a frenzy of attacks on windows. All doors, including basement doors, were tried, tested, and battered upon repeatedly. Some residents, appalled at being targeted in their homes, tried to escape through the attending hordes. All the people trying to escape this way made the same fatal error. They tried to push through the zombies, barging past or tentatively pushing them out of the way. They were understandably reticent to touch these stinking, rotting creatures. Those trying to escape this way didn't make it far, all were attacked, bitten, and either infected within seconds, or ripped apart and consumed.

So far, there was no sign that anyone in authority either knew about the situation, or knew what to do about it. All local protection was lost when the Police were attacked, turned, or consumed. The local Police force were annihilated in minutes, and their calls for support were either ignored, or received a very confused, non-committal response.

The night ahead for the denizens of Greenock, Gourock and Port Glasgow, would be unprecedented in history. The night ahead would have local, national, and indeed world consequences that would never have been credited had it been a movie plot or a work of fiction.

Chapter 19

Lennie's bedroom was up the stairs at the back of his house. The three lads sat in pensive silence, trying to ignore the sound of zombies moaning and banging relentlessly on the front door and downstairs windows.

The furnishings in Lennie's bedroom reflected the rest of his house, it was sparse. On the floor was an old mattress, leaking stuffing and springs. The mattress was covered with a rather unclean duvet and a naked pillow at the top. Inside one built in cupboard was a pile of what few clothes he possessed, in the other was his collection of scrap metal. Lennie also had a large collection of second-hand books, some were stacked in towers against the walls, others were scattered haphazardly around the room.

Lennie stood with his back to the room, staring out the window into the back gardens. Angus sat slouched on the floor picking his scabs. Sitting gingerly on the edge of Lennie's mattress Kenny felt restless, looking around him he picked up and started to read a large tome from Lennie's collection.

"You read this one Lennie?" Kenny broke the silence.

Without turning around Lennie replied, "I've read all the books in here, so yes I've read it."

"What's it about?"

Lennie glanced at the book Kenny was flicking through.

"That's mostly about some Russian bint shagging around." Lennie glanced at Angus; visually located his iron bar (which was within easy reaching distance), and then returned to staring intently out the window.

Kenny looked at the size of the book Lennie had just somewhat succinctly summed up. "Dragged that out a bit then didn't he?"

"It's awright though. It's about right and wrong 'n stuff like that. You know human needs and hypocrisy and that."

Kenny rapidly revised his previous judgements regarding Lennie.

"I need a hit." Angus had not spoken since they had tramped up the stairs to get away from the zombies at the front window.

"Probably best off having a boot." Kenny alluded to the elephant galumphing around the room.

Angus sighed, "You got any Jimmy Boyle up here Len?"

Lennie tore himself away from the window. "Naw. You'll need to get it from the kitchen." As Angus roused himself from the floor Lennie scrutinised him closely. "Stick yir heid oot the window at the front on yir way doon eh? Let me know how many of them there is out there."

"Why?" Angus asked as he slouched, shoulders slumped, on his way out of the back bedroom.

"It's just something I'm thinking about. Bring enough foil up for me too eh?" Lennie waited until he heard Angus's footsteps going down the stairs, he turned to

Kenny. "How long do you think it would take?" he asked.

Kenny didn't need him to extrapolate. "How am I meant to know that Len?"

"It's fucking Lennie to you son." He paced the room. "I don't know either, but we need to know when he's safe." Lennie stared at the closed door and then stomped back to stand near his iron bar, he resumed staring out the window.

"Why did you ask Gaff to check how may Zombies there is out front?"

"We cannie stay in here forever. There's fuck all here." Lennie turned and slumped down beside the window. He picked up and hefted his iron bar. "I don't think there's as many of them out the back as there is at the front. The back gardens are all sealed off from the street by houses. It'll be safer."

"Where we gonnie go?"

Lennie slumped further. "I've not really thought that far ahead to be honest. But I know we cannie just sit here. We've got to do something."

Angus returned from the kitchen. "Anyone got a pen?" he asked.

Kenny rummaged in his pockets and produced a small red bookies pen; he threw it to Angus who made himself a tube then threw the pen and foil to, Lennie. He made himself a tube, then threw the equipment to Kenny. They all busied themselves chasing heroin.

Angus finished first. "Well that was just a wind up." He registered his frustration at not being able to inject. "When do you think we'll know?" Angus looked at Kenny and Lennie; a pleading vulnerability bled from his eyes.

Lennie looked to Kenny to answer. Kenny looked at his wrist, he didn't have a watch, none of them did. "How long do you reckon it's been?" Kenny asked.

"Fuck knows. I reckon it's been a good few hours though," Lennie replied.

Kenny made up his mind. "Do you know what? I reckon you're going to be alright. By the looks of them things out there, this is some fuck-off powerful virus. I reckon if you had it you would've known about it by now."

"How many of them were out front?" Lennie resumed staring out the back window.

Kenny had provided Angus with a bright, shining ray of hope. Angus took an internal inventory of how his body felt, and decided it felt no worse than usual, he took this to be good news. "Fuck knows. There's a fuck of a lot of them, so it was hard to tell. I'd guess there's probably about 20 or 30. Fucking minging too."

"Lennie thinks we should make a break for it out the back way." Kenny filled Angus in about the plan.

"And go where?" Angus asked the same question as Kenny.

"I've been thinking about that, Lennie," Kenny stepped in. "If it's in the water. And I just KNOW it is in the water. I'm going to need to go to the refinery to shut off the water supply."

"Bit fucking late for that." Lennie looked completely astonished; his forehead wrinkled worse than a Shar Pei.

"I know, but I feel responsible. If there's a virus flooding the Greenock water supply then I, as a worker at the refinery, need to step up, take responsibility, and stop it." Kenny had never taken responsibility for anything in his life, this was a new experience for him, it felt strange.

Lennie and Angus looked at each other, Lennie smiled and raised his eyebrows. Angus started to laugh first; Lennie followed. They both lost control and laughed so hard they cried. Lennie tried to speak, "Responsible? You?" was all he could manage. Angus and Lennie savoured the release laughing provided them with.

Kenny bristled. "At least I've actually got a job," he mumbled. This comment only served to increase their laughter.

"There'll be plenty food in the canteen!" Kenny offered up a more practical reason for going to the water refinery.

Angus brought himself back to matters he considered more pressing. "I'm more worried about where my next hit is coming from. That last boot was just a wind up. That'll no hold me for long." The reality of their situation killed the last of the laughter.

"Has anybody got anything?" Lennie asked. "This isn't the time to hold out lads."

"Them fucking zombies out the front nicked my stash." Kenny held his hands out and shrugged his shoulders.

"I've never been able to hold on to any gear." Angus spoke his truth. "How about you Len? You must have something stashed for an emergency?" Angus looked hopeful.

Lennie hesitated, just for a millisecond. Angus's eyes lit up, he pounced, "What you got Lennie?"

"I might just have a couple of bottles of meth stashed somewhere." Lennie knew he would have to share. For the first time in his life Lennie knew that he would have to exist as a part of a team. For better or for worse he was aware he was in this with the other two lads. This meant certain levels of honesty were indispensable.

"Show!" Angus wanted physical reassurance.

Retrieving a thin strip of metal from his scrap metal cupboard Lennie used it to pull up a loose floorboard, from which he produced two full, brown 50ml bottles of methadone.

"Anything else in there Lennie? Any jellies?" Angus checked it out for himself.

"Naw. That's it lads. That's yir lot." Lennie said holding up the two brown bottles.

"Better than nothing I suppose." Angus played something over in his mind. "He'll no need as much as me though," Angus said pointing at Kenny.

"That's not fucking fair ya prick." Kenny was up on his feet remonstrating, his arms waving about. "I bought youse a bag of smack each." Kenny was apoplectic.

Lennie spoke, "I don't think any of that matters Kenny. The only thing that matters lads is that we are in this together." He looked seriously at Angus and Kenny. "And the only way we are going to get through this," he waved a hand in the direction of the outside world. "Is by sticking together." He paused. Angus sat back down, cowed. Kenny remaining standing, he stomped over to glare out of the window. "From now on in, we are a team I'm afraid lads, and besides," Lennie continued, holding up the bottles of methadone. "These are mine, so I get to say who gets what, and I say we all get the same. Fair is fair."

Kenny scanned the blackness out the back window. "There's a couple of other lights on back here." He stared up and down the row of houses opposite. "Two to be exact."

"I saw that earlier," Lennie said as he walked over to stand at the window.

Joining them Angus glanced at Kenny. "You know anyone over there, Len?"

Lennie puffed out his cheeks. "Don't think so Gaff. I'll know their faces for sure. Everyone knows everyone on the fucking Homerton. But I just keep myself to myself here." Lennie turned his back on the window and started rummaging in his scrap iron cupboard. "It's another reason why I reckon we should go out the back." Lennie started pulling out differing lengths of metal bars. "I reckon the more mob handed we are the better when we have to start fighting them fucking things. We should go check out who's in them houses with the lights on."

Angus and Kenny looked at each other. Angus saw a rather scared looking skinny drug addict. Kenny saw an older, fat, unfit drug ravaged addict. They both looked at Lennie and saw an unstable, drug addled lunatic.

"We're fucked." Angus sank onto the mattress and closed his eyes.

"Are we not just gonnie run away?" Kenny said hopefully to Lennie.

"Aye. I mean we're gonnie try to just run away from them, obviously. But we're not gonnie be able to get anywhere without coming face to face with them at some point. And I really don't like the looks of their faces." Lennie piled up various different metal bars. "You saw what they did to them at the shops, we're gonnie have to be ready to fight. It's going to come down to fight or become one of them eventually. And I know what I'm gonnie fucking do." Lennie whacked an iron bar into his hand. "We need more people. We need a small army."

Lennie started rummaging in the other cupboard containing his clothes.

"What you looking for now?" Angus had raised himself by his elbows to see what Lennie was doing.

Lennie pulled out a battered old army rucksack. "I knew I still had this." He shoved the metal bars into the bag. Then, carefully wrapping them in a sock each for increased protection, he put the methadone bottles carefully in the rucksack. "I'm ready to go I reckon," he announced.

"WHAT?" Angus and Kenny responded in unison.

"We've just had the last of our smack. There's nothing else to do or say." Lennie pointed towards Angus with his iron bar. "He's probably not going to turn. So we might as well head off, check out them houses, and see who else is normal out there."

Kenny briefly wondered if, by implication, Lennie classified himself and Angus as "Normal". Kenny also had enough self-awareness to know that the word "normal," was rarely used to describe himself.

"Who made you the leader then?" Angus swung himself up off the mattress, defensive.

Lennie responded, "You got any better ideas?"

He had no answer. Muttering to himself Angus strafed the floor with his trainer and searched vainly for another option that did not entail leaving Lennie's house. "I'm just saying maybe's we need to talk about it for a bit, is all."

Lennie looked non-plussed. "What the fuck is there to talk about, Gaff? We have fuck all here. No food, no drugs. And there is absolutely no chance that anything is just gonnie waltz in the front door. And anyway, if it did, currently the front door is crammed full of rabid fuckin' zombies." Lennie strode over to the back window. "We've got to go lads. So we might as well go now. We need to go see who's over there." Lennie stared at the lights.

Angus and Kenny shuffled over to stand beside him. They both stared at the houses displaying dimly twinkling lights behind closed curtains.

"They might all be empty." Kenny voiced his thoughts; he really didn't want to set foot outside.

"Only one way to find out," Lennie responded. "And besides, if they're empty, we'll raid them for supplies." Donning the rucksack he challenged Kenny and Angus, again. "Youse coming or what?"

They looked at each other. Angus turned back to stare out the window, the thought of what 'supplies' might mean started a particular train of thought for him. Kenny stared hard at the stained, cracked ceiling and tried in vain to think of a way to avoid all zombie contact.

"I'm going downstairs to see if I can find anything else that might come in handy. When youse two make up your minds, you can come join me." Lennie stomped out and down the stairs into his kitchen.

Kenny mulled the issue over in his head. "He's right Gaff. We cannie just sit here. We're going to have to leave at some point."

Angus sighed, "I know. But there's something I don't think you know about Lennie." Angus went back to the mattress and flopped on it again. "A few years back Lennie was in Fraggle Rock." Angus emphasised the point he was making by twirling a finger at the side of his head.

Kenny blinked; he wasn't particularly surprised.

"It's bad enough the world's gone to shite without following a madman into a pile of zombies." Angus got back up and went to the window to check out the lights opposite. "But he's also right about getting us more mob handed to survive this."

Kenny bowed to the inevitable, he picked up his metal bar. "Fuck it. Let's go then Gaff." Angus sighed and grabbed the equaliser, they both trudged reluctantly down the stairs.

They heard Lennie banging about in his kitchen as they entered. "You find anything useful? Any knives?" Angus asked.

"No really. It's all a pile of shite in here really." Any sharp knives that there were in Lennie's kitchen had long since disappeared to be used for nefarious reasons.

"We reckon we're ready to go then, Lennie," Kenny announced, trying to sound sprightly.

Lennie stopped rummaging, he turned to look at them. "Right. I'll take point and you……..," Lennie pointed at Kenny, "…..take my right flank. You……..," here he pointed at Angus, "……take my left flank."

Angus and Kenny looked at each other, astonished. "What the fuck are you talking about Lennie?" Angus voiced their shared bemusement.

"I was trained in the TA once." Lennie hefted his rucksack on his back and grabbed his iron bar from the kitchen worktop. "Youse ready then?" Lennie marched over to the back door.

"Naw really. But I'm mightily relieved to know we've got an ex-serviceman in our ranks." Angus's sarcasm sailed right over Lennie's head.

Lennie opened the kitchen door. The light from the kitchen reached out in a small arc, leaving a dense wall of shadows beyond. The imagination of the three lads filled in the visual void with gruesome projections of horror. What was illuminated only served to remind them what a mess the back garden was in. "We could do with a torch," Kenny pleaded without much hope.

"That'll be first on the list once we get into them other houses." Lennie set his jaw, and stepped out. Kenny and Angus followed in the formation previously ordered by Lennie.

The sky contained nought but a blanket of stars, it was a new moon night. The milky way could clearly be seen seemingly flowing alongside wisps of smoke coming from nearby burning buildings. There was little light penetrating the blackness of the back gardens the three lads were about to traverse. Screams of people being eaten pierced the darkness only too well. Zombies howled and moaned; the lads knew not where the vocalisations were coming from.

"Right, let's get going then." Lennie's throat was dry, he was, and sounded, nervous.

Slowly, Lennie led them through the slew of debris that had gathered in his garden. Every creak of a gate or swish of a tree caused them to flinch. There was no aural respite from the screaming and howling. They made it to the fence at the bottom of the garden, they peered over and around. "Ah cannie see shite," Angus succinctly summed up their situation.

"We're gonnie be vulnerable to attack when we're climbing the fences and walls." Lennie peered blindly into the darkness.

"I feel like we're being watched." Kenny had tremors trampling up and down his spine, his skin felt like it was crawling with cockroaches.

"You first then squadron leader." Angus tried to gulp down his fear.

Holding his iron bar tight, Lennie started to climb over the fence. When he was halfway over they heard a low growling sound that rose in volume as a zombie came rampaging out of the darkness. Kenny and Angus instinctively leapt backwards as the zombie crashed into the fence. Lennie and the zombie tumbled into the next-door garden; the zombie went straight into attack. Lennie swung his iron bar hard at the zombies' jaw as at it stretched out its head to chew him. The bar connected perfectly and shattered the zombies' jaw. Broken teeth flew out of its battered mouth. The zombie continued to grapple and claw as it tried to force some of Lennie's flesh into its bloodied, broken, gaping maw.

Angus remembered the methadone in Lennie's bag, and vaulted the fence in one leap. Not wanting to be left alone, Kenny jumped after him.

Pushing desperately back Lennie upended the zombie onto the grass. He slipped and fell hard on top of the zombie. He brought the base of the iron bar, gripped with both hands, down hard, slap bang in the middle of the zombie's forehead. The blow crushed it's skull and it's brains oozed out. The zombie lay lifeless.

Breathing hard Lennie stared down at the motionless corpse. In the darkness they heard more zombies growling and moaning. The zombies knew now there was fresh flesh nearby, and they desperately desired to consume it. The lads could hear fences being broken down. They stood back-to-back in the garden that backed onto Lennie's and waited. Nothing happened, the zombies didn't have unfettered access; yet.

The lads were starting to see clearer, as their eyes became accustomed to the darkness. The house next to the garden they were in had a light on and there was clearly a zombie in the garden. The zombie was desperately trying to get over the large wall that separated it from the fresh flesh newly presented to it.

"We're gonnie need to kill that." Lennie pointed at the zombie with his iron bar. Thick gore dripped from the base of his bar.

"Your turn Kenny boy," Angus said. "Me and Lennie have done one each."

Kenny's face dropped, he looked from Lennie and Angus to the zombie who was growling and grappling at the top of the wall as it attempted to get at the lads.

"Got to lose your zombie virginity sometime son," Lennie backed Angus up.

Kenny looked up at the window with the light on just in time to see the curtains twitch. There was someone inside. Someone who was probably extremely scared to have a rabid zombie roaming about in their back garden. Kenny looked back at the zombie grappling at the wall growling and moaning as it tried to climb over. Tentatively, he started to inch his way towards to the wall.

"We'll back you up son, don't worry." Lennie nodded towards the zombie, directing Kenny to get on with it.

Kenny took a deep breath and quickened his pace; marginally. As he crept forward the zombie intensified its efforts to get at him, it was getting frenetic. It moaned and groaned, desperately grappling at the wall, trying awkwardly, and unsuccessfully, to climb over it. As Kenny approached the zombie managed to fluke it's frantic, uncoordinated efforts to scale the wall. By luck rather than design it managed to get a foothold that propelled it up and over the wall. It flopped on the ground in front of Kenny, who let out a rather high-pitched scream. Kenny swung his metal bar and missed the zombie by a mile.

"You'll need to get much closer," shouted Angus.

The zombie scrambled to its feet and lunged for Kenny. Kenny swung his bar again, but again he was far too hesitant. The blow connected with the zombie's face this time, but all it managed to achieved was to flick the zombie's head to one side.

"Batter it Kenny, you need to give it some welly." shouted Lennie.

The zombie recovered quickly and grabbed for Kenny. The zombie attempted to sink its teeth into his neck. Self-preservation kicked in and adrenaline flowed through Kenny's system as he faced the all too real prospect of a gruesome death. He bent, and buckled, and broke free from the zombie. Kenny battered it's legs as he slipped past it, he heard bones break. This didn't deter the zombie one iota, it continued to hobble menacingly towards him grasping, growling, and gnashing its teeth.

Kenny swung his bar with full force, it smashed the zombie's nose, thick blood glooped out, but the zombie kept advancing, thick blood clung to its teeth as it growled. Kenny roared in rage and swung the bar hard again, this time it connected with the vulnerable spot right at the temple on the side of the zombie's head. The zombie dropped instantly, poleaxed, it remained immobile.

They could see now, that at one point, this zombie was just a little old man. Possibly a father and grandfather.

"Good work," Lennie marched past and jumped over the wall.

Angus patted Kenny on the back as he walked past. "Well done Kenny boy. That was not an easy thing to do." Angus followed Lennie (and the methadone) over the wall.

Breathing heavily Kenny stared down at the mangled body of the old man that had turned into a zombie.

Kenny had killed.

He was acutely aware that in these very strange circumstances life was now about kill or be killed, but he had still just killed what was once a human being. Kenny felt a huge wave of guilt, his stomach lurched, and he threw up.

Kenny turned to see Angus looking at him from over the wall. "'Mon Kenny, we need to get inside eh. Need to get into a safe place."

With numbness spreading through him, Kenny climbed the wall and jumped down. "I'm awright Angus. I reckon I'm going to have to get used to this."

"I only hope none of us get used to this Kenny. This is not something I ever want to get used to." Angus put his arms around Kenny and led him over to where Lennie was now knocking furiously at the back door of the house with the light on.

"Let us in will you," Lennie shouted as he banged repeatedly on the back door. He was keen to be indoors again.

"Perhaps three loonies with iron bars shouting, 'let us in,' is not the best approach to take Leonard my good man." Angus stood back to stare up at the window. "Keep an eye out for them fucking things would you Kenny," Angus asked.

Glad to not have to look at anyone, nor have anyone look at him, Kenny was relieved to just stare into the void of darkness.

Angus leaned his head back to stare at the lit window. "Gonnie let us in, please." Angus spread his arms wide. "We're normal. We just want to get in somewhere safe."

Angus's statement was met with no response.

Lennie started banging the door again. "Let us in for God's sake, we could get fucking eaten out here." He banged repeatedly at the door.

Angus lost his temper. "Fuck sake Lennie, I've just told you. Fucking take it easy will you mate."

Kenny briefly forgot his troubled conscience, and his lookout duties, he turned to Lennie and Angus. "Whoever is in there is not going to have anything to do with you two shouting and swearing all over the place." Kenny walked over to stand under the window. Looking up, in his most polite voice, he gently shouted, "Hey. Can you hear me? Listen. We came from the other side of the road. We don't think we can just stay indoors, alone. We all need to get together and help each other out. We have weapons and we'll help you survive all this." Kenny swung his arm in the direction of the gruesome noises coming from the street. "The zombie in your garden is dead. I killed it." He felt his gorge rise again, but swallowed it back down. "If you don't want to let us in; no worries, we'll leave. But we won't come back, we have other houses we need to go to. And we need to go to the source of this and shut it down."

Kenny paused. Lennie put his ear to the door. "I think someone's coming. Nice one Kenny boy".

The door opened, just, there was a security chain on the door. Through the small crack in the door an old eye peered out. "Is he really dead?" a voice asked.

"Aye," Lennie answered. "Can we come in please. There lots of zombies out here." Lennie stared around him to emphasise the point.

The door closed again. They could hear the sound of the chain being taken off. The door reopened fully to reveal a slim, elderly lady, dressed in a pink frilly nightgown and tartan slippers. The three lads piled into the house and the door was closed again. The elderly lady put the chain back on.

The three lads shuffled their feet and looked around the house, it was very old-fashioned looking and smelled of moth balls. "Bastard tried to eat me," the elderly lady announced angrily as she strode off towards her kitchen. "Do you boys want a cup of tea?" she asked.

Her words caused the lads to snap out of their communal daze, the juxtaposition between the zombie filled darkness and the flowery wallpapered house had temporarily fried their brains. They followed the elderly lady into the kitchen. "We think what's causing all the zombies is in the water. It might be best not to have tea," Kenny informed the lady. "Though we do know boiling the water kills it." Kenny looked at Angus. Angus shot Kenny a look telling him it would probably not be a good idea to go into specific details.

"I've been drinking tea all day and I'm alright," the elderly lady informed them. "My Jim was drinking the water with his Barley water earlier. Reckon that's probably what made him to try to eat me," this was said as a matter of fact, there was no emotion exhibited.

The penny dropped with the three lads simultaneously. "So him out there was your husband?" Angus needed definite confirmation. Kenny went as white as a ghost.

"Aye, that was my Jim."

"How did you get him out the house?" Lennie was looking at the elderly lady trying to understand how she could have gotten a rabid zombie out of the house.

"No-body messes with me son," the elderly lady bristled. "Do you boys want a cup of tea or no?" she asked again.

"Eh, aye. I suppose it wouldnae do any harm," Angus replied for them all, "Three sugars for me please," Angus added and went to sit at a formica topped table set against one of the walls.

"Same for me," Lennie said.

Kenny still looked very pale. "I'm sorry. I killed your husband," his voice wobbled, and he sounded on the verge of tears.

"What you killed out there wisnae my Jim son. You wanting a cup of tea?" she asked Kenny gently.

Colour started to return to his face. "Aye, I suppose. Black. No sugar for me please." Kenny went to sit with Lennie and Angus around the kitchen table.

Silence reigned as the elderly lady busied herself making four cups of tea.

"So, what's your name?" Angus asked.

"Ina," she replied, as she brought over four steaming cups of tea and a plate of digestive biscuits. The lads fell on the biscuits like they hadn't eaten in a month.

"I'm Angus," Angus sprayed through a dust of digestive crumbs. "That's Kenny, and that's Lennie," he pointed a biscuit at them as he spoke.

"Everyone knows Lennie," Ina spoke with a frown. "Your garden is a bloody mess son."

Lennie frowned and ignored her.

Kenny looked at Ina's nightdress. "Were you just going to go to bed?"

"Aye son."

"Even though your husband was wandering about your back garden as a zombie?" Kenny was incredulous.

"Nothing I could do about that son. I'm usually in bed for nine."

"Even though the whole town is in the middle of a zombie apocalypse?" Kenny struggled to understand.

"What are zombies?"

Kenny didn't really know how to answer this. "Eh, we think there is a virus in the water and it's killing people, then bringing them back to life, and then they eat people. I think is pretty much it." Kenny was acutely aware of how ridiculous this sounded, especially when it was contrasted with having tea and biscuits with someone dressed in a pink nighty who was old enough to be his grandmother.

"You said outside that you had weapons. What do you have?" Ina dunked a digestive in her tea and ate it.

Lennie pulled a couple of lengths of pipe out of his rucksack. "We've got a few of these. We could probably do with some knives if you have any?" Lennie looked at Ina hopefully.

Ina held out her hand. "Let's see one." As Lennie passed it she didn't flinch with the weight.

"We know head shots work," Angus informed her. "But you've got to hit them really, really hard," Angus looked at Kenny.

"I reckon I could do that," Ina informed them, matter of factly.

"How old are you?" Lennie asked.

"Old enough to know my manners." Ina closed down Lennie's line of questioning. "So is this going on all over the town then?" Ina asked Kenny. "There's nothing on telly or radio about it. I checked."

"If we're right, and it is in the water, then yes, it'll be going on in Gourock, Greenock and the Port. Either way, from the way them things are going, it will have spread through the whole area by now anyways. We've got another house to check here, just up a bit." Kenny helped himself to another biscuit, there were not many left, Angus and Lennie finished them but one, which they left for their host.

Ina dunked the last biscuit in her tea. "I guess I won't be going to bed after all then eh? I suppose I better go and get dressed." Ina looked hard at the three lads. "You wait in here for me. And don't touch anything. Don't think I don't know about you Lennie Wilson!"

Lennie's eyes bulged and he spluttered a bit, but he said nothing. Ina closed the kitchen door as she left.

Angus waited until he was sure she was out of earshot. "Are we really gonnie take her with us? She's fucking ancient."

"And she's a fucking daft old bat and all," Lennie made his feelings about Ina crystal clear.

"And she is a living, breathing, human being." Kenny couldn't believe what he was hearing. "I made her a promise outside that we would look after her, so she is most definitely coming with us."

Ina came bustling back into the kitchen dressed in a pair of flared jeans, a jumper, a light jacket, and a pair of trainers. "So you boys said you were going to the source. What do you mean, the source?"

"This one here….." Angus nodded at Kenny, "……works at the water refinery, and wants to go back to shut off the water. He wants to stop the virus from spreading."

"It's a bit late for that is it not?" Ina replied.

"That's what we said," Lennie agreed. "You don't happen to have a torch do you Ina?" he asked. "And I guess we should take some food with us in case we need it."

Perusing her cupboards Ina produced a couple of cans of Campbells soup and some Heinz baked beans. "I reckon my Jim will have had a torch in his tool cupboard. I'll go and have a look."

Lennie piled the food into his rucksack with the metal bars. Ina returned with a large, heavy, rubber torch, she handed it to Lennie.

Lennie looked her in the eye and saw a steely determination there. "Are you sure you're ready for this Ina?"

"What else am I going to do son. Wait here to die? I don't think so." Ina looked at Angus and Kenny, turning back to Lennie she said, "Lead the way then son," she nodded at the back door.

Kenny was more assured that he would now be able to fight for himself, he felt ready. Angus and Lennie were ready. Ina was clearly ready. They headed to the back door.

"I'm sixty-five by the way," Ina said looking at Lennie as they stepped through the back door together into the murky madness.

Chapter 20

For the umpteenth time Innes picked up the telephone handset, listened to the unrelenting silence on the line, pap-pap-papped the clear switches, growled at the phone, and then replaced it gently back on the base. He fought the urge to pick it back up (just in case), turned, and crept quietly back up the stairs to the bedroom. The zombies outside continued to pound on his front door.

Sitting on the floor Robert stared vacantly up at him as he returned. "Still nothing Inn?"

"Zip," Innes perched on the bed where Fiona sat looking morose.

"I'm worried about my mum, and brothers uncle Inny." Fiona's teenage bravado was long gone.

"I know Fi. Me too. Wish I could get a hold of my Mary," Innes sighed.

"Where's her sister live?" Robert asked.

"She's doon near Ayr." Innes was agitated, restless. He stood back up and tried the radio again, searching the stations for any scrap of information about the situation. There was nothing. The radio blared normal at them, and it jarred them. Innes turned it off, again.

On the chest of drawers a black and white portable television was broadcasting a banal game show. They were waiting for the newsflash that would surely inform them about what was happening, and what the authorities were going to do about rescuing the survivors. Occasionally Robert would shout out an answer to a question, other than that the TV was ignored, the TV was also foisting nothing but denial at them.

"The radio and TV are shite. I need to know how far this fucking thing has gone?" Innes couldn't understand why his communications devices were communicating only nonsense.

"Is it worth doing another trawl for bevvy Inny?" Robert asked hopefully, he was fast approaching the most sober he had been for a long while.

Innes was also becoming uncomfortably sober. "I doubt it Vanie. I think we've hit all my usual spots."

Robert had been mulling over the concerning lack of accessible alcohol, he had an idea about a possible opportunity to get some. "I've been thinking things over Inn." Robert felt the time was right to posit his proposal. "You and me Inny. We work better with a wee drink in us." Robert stood up and started to pace the room. "I reckon all that madness out there will have left the offie….." Robert searched for a suitable word. "……vulnerable."

Fiona was staring quizzically at the space where Robert had been sitting.

Robert continued. "I don't reckon anyone would blame us if we……..," again Robert searched for an acceptable word, "………liberated a few cans, and perhaps a bottle of wine or two."

Fiona snapped straight out of her funk. "Vanie, if I set foot outside this house I'm going straight to my mam's. I'm not going to no fucking off licence."

Fiona's eyes were again, inexplicably drawn back to the spot on the floor Robert had recently vacated. There was something there that looked out of place, it bothered her.

Robert looked over at Innes with his eyebrows raised. He suspected Innes would be a reliable ally for his scheme.

"Are you allowed to swear?" Innes was dimly aware that maybe he had some kind of responsibility over Fiona in the absence of her parents. He was also aware that the recent dramatic change in local circumstances would also mean that certain societal rules would have changed, including the rules Robert was alluding to. Innes thought that a visit to the off-licence for some free booze sounded like not too bad an idea. It was a distraction, it was doing something, it was probably better that sitting around listening to game shows and zombies trying to break into his house. He was, however, cognizant that venturing outside would incur obvious challenges.

Fiona's curiosity had become too much to bear. "What is that?", she asked as she jumped off the bed to inspect the object she had been staring at since Robert had started pacing the room.

She pulled a massive kitchen knife out from behind the chest of drawers and jumped to an accurate conclusion. Turning to stare incredulously at Robert she brandished the knife. "Were you gonnie use this on me?"

Robert turned red and stammered, "Well, if you turned, we were gonnie need to do something to protect ourselves wuren't we Fi?" Robert looked to Innes for support.

Innes decided the best course of action was to change the subject. "How do you feel Fiona? Are you alright?" the tone of his voice made it clear what he was referring to. "I'm thinking that you're probably not going to turn," Innes decided. He turned to Robert in an attempt to unite them. "Don't you think she would have turned by now, Vanie?"

Robert jumped at the chance to change the subject away from the somewhat contentious subject of him stabbing Fiona. "Definitely Inny, definitely. By the sounds things out there I reckon most of Greenock has turned. She'd've gone by now if she was going to, for sure."

"Just as fucking well too, Vanie. Or you'd have stabbed me up." Fiona slammed the knife on the chest of drawers. She strode over to stare out of the window.

Innes had been processing Robert's idea. "I reckon we could do both things you know folks. I reckon we could do your house first, Fi, then hit the offie." Innes had been coming to terms with their new reality and decided action was needed. "But we need to think about something. We're gonnie need to fight them things." He was still uncomfortable with using the word zombie.

"Aye, Inny. I've been thinking about that too. We need to pap them on their heids. In all the zombie films you kill them by papping them on the heid." Robert had, at least theoretically, thought about how to deal with zombies. "We'll need heavy things. You got any hammers or anything like that?"

"Reckon I've got a few bits and pieces in my toolbox we could use." Innes looked at Fiona with concern. "You can stick between me and Vanie, Fi. We'll protect you out there."

Fiona seemed to shrink, her recently resurrected bravado faded once again. The reality of their situation was too much for her. She loved her uncle Innes, but she was also acutely aware of his obvious failings. Her trust in Robert McKillvany had diminished since she had discovered his intention to stab her, her faith in him wasn't particularly high to start off with.

"Do you two want to stay up here or come with me? My toolbox is in the kitchen." Innes looked at Robert and Fiona. They clearly planned on going with him. They had all arrived at the same conclusion, that they needed each other, and that unity was now key to their personal survival. Individual shortcomings would just have to be tolerated and compensated for.

With Innes in the lead they sneaked down the stairs. The cacophony caused by the zombies was clearer, and scarier, at ground level. Innes led them into the kitchen, he got his toolbox out of a kitchen cupboard. Innes's 'toolbox' was a cardboard box full of tools and random bits and pieces. He pulled out a hammer and crowbar and, after rummaging further, he pulled out a wrench. "I reckon these will do the job folks. What do you think?"

Robert and Fiona looked vacant. They were both coming to terms with what they were going to have to do with the tools lying on the kitchen floor.

As he was rummaging Innes came across a torch, he tried it, it worked. He trawled further; a memory was triggered. Pulling out a battered tin, Innes quickly pulled open the lid and triumphantly produced a quarter bottle of whisky. Robert whooped quietly with delight.

Fiona sighed, "You two better not be pished when we have to fight them things."

Innes replied, "Vanie was right Fi. Me and him work better when we've had a wee drink or two."

"Does that mean we can go to my mam's first then?"

Innes looked to Robert, he shrugged. Innes replied, "I suppose so Fi."

Innes's mouth starting filling with saliva as he uncorked the whisky bottle, he swallowed half and passed the rest to Robert. As Robert swallowed the last of the dregs the lights snapped off. He dropped the bottle. Fiona screamed, and Innes let out an involuntary yelp. Innes grabbed and flicked on the torch. "What the fuck," Robert spluttered. "Is that the fuses?"

"Doubt it. I reckon the electrics huv been turned off." Firing on the torch, Innes looked around him for threats. The kitchen was empty save for the current occupants. He looked out the kitchen window, there were no other lights on anywhere. "Fuck. That's all we need."

"What we gonnie do now, uncle Inny?"

Exasperated, Innes started to get angry. "I reckon we don't change our plans. We go look for your mam Fi. And then we fucking go to the offie. If I'm gonnie die, I'm fucking well gonnie go pished."

"Fucking right Inny. I'm with you." Robert didn't have any difficulty getting on board with the whole getting drunk thing, but he wasn't so certain about the dying bit.

"How we gonnie do it?" Fiona was more concerned about practicalities.

"Any suggestions?" Innes looked at Robert and Fiona.

"I reckon we just burst out the front door and run like fuck," Robert proposed.

"You gonnie go first?" Fiona asked.

Robert's exuberance faded. His body language answered the question.

Innes knew who would have to go first. "I'll go first. Then Fiona comes out. Then you at the back Vanie. If we get split up for any reason, Vanie, our Sharon is at number 42, just passed the Diamond."

"So we need to go *past* the offie, *and* the Diamond then?" Robert sought clarity.

"Aye Vanie. Do you think you can manage that?" Fiona sought assurance.

"Aye, aye, aye. No probs. I'm just asking." Robert backed off, holding his hands up.

"Are we ready then?" Innes asked. "We're gonnie need to fight our way out. There's a whole load of them at the door."

The reality of what they were about to do was enough to sober even Robert up.

In the dim glow of the torch Robert and Fiona imperceptibly nodded their heads. Innes sighed heavily. He located the tools lying on the floor. Solemnly he handed Robert the hammer, Fiona the wrench, and took the crowbar for himself. "That ok for you?" Innes asked them both.

They stared vacantly at the heavy tools in their hands, and once again nodded their assent.

"Fuck it, let's go." Innes turned off the torch and rammed it into his trouser belt. He started to march towards the front door.

Fiona stopped, "Vanie, you were doing the right thing earlier. If I turn into one of them things, finish me off would you?"

Robert's eyes filled with tears; his voice broke as he spoke. "Will do Fi. But we're not gonnie get caught. We're gonnie make it, love. Me and your uncle wouldnae let a few fucking zombies get in the way of a bevvy now would we?"

Fiona and Innes laughed; the tension was released. Innes hugged his niece, "Remember, fight our way through, then run like fuck. And you stick between me and Vanie. We'll protect you. Won't we Vanie?"

"Utterly fucking preposterous. We sure fucking will Inn. Let's go see your mam Fi." In their own individual ways they fired themselves up for what they were about to do. They marched to the front door wielding their tools. The zombies outside smelt their approach and increased their efforts to breach the door.

"Remember," Innes said, as much to himself as it was to Fiona and Robert. "These fucking things aren't our friends or neighbours. They're vermin. Our friends and neighbours would want the same as you Fiona, they wouldn't want to live like that."

Innes reached out to the door handle. "We ready?"

"Fucking do it," shouted Fiona, adrenaline had restored her bravado.

Innes took a deep breath, for a split second he had a moment of clarity, he knew he would do all he could to survive and protect his niece and his friend. He was ready to fight like a demon. He opened the door. The zombies were unprepared to gain access to their goal so easily. They fell on the floor in a snarling, crumpled heap of thrashing limbs and craning heads, stretching to gnaw on the now accessible flesh.

Innes went to work the moment they hit the floor, battering their heads viciously with his crowbar. A split-second later Robert and Fiona joined him in dealing with the first flush of zombies. They were the easy ones, they were prone.

Innes saw everything in slow motion, while his movements went at double speed. He understood that Fiona and Robert were managing the first flush, so he turned his attention to the zombies that were now fighting to get into the house. He recognised all these people, though their features were now twisted and demented by the virus. Innes had no hesitation in going at these zombies in the same violently clinical way that he went at the first flush. Using his crowbar he pushed his way through the front door. He stood on the threshold and swung his crowbar like a bat, connecting with zombie heads at every swing. Innes gradually inched forward. As he cleared the threshold he became aware of Robert fighting on one side and Fiona on the other. They were both wielding their tools with the same deadly efficiency that he was. Innes managed, in the heat of the battle, to acknowledge his deep pride regarding their efforts, especially those of his young niece.

As they advanced down the garden path, the number of Zombies started to thin out. They picked them off with precision. A pathway to the front gate presented itself. "Let's fucking go," Innes shouted and took off for the street, Fiona followed, and Robert ran directly behind her. Robert checked over his shoulder and saw no threat, there were just a pile of zombie corpses lying in puddles of thick, gloopy blood, his nose wrinkled in disgust.

Innes ran hard, checking that Fiona and Robert were with him. There were zombies milling about on the road. As soon as they became aware there was fresh flesh available they changed, they charged, they hunted the fleeing trio as they sprinted down the road.

All the years of debauchery had taken its toll on Innes and Robert, they couldn't keep up their blistering pace. Robert saw that the zombies behind them were gaining on them. "Inny, they're catching us," he managed to yell, though his lungs were now burning. Innes was battering any zombies that came for them head on, but his lungs were also burning, and he knew they were slowing. "Fuck it. Let's stand and fight," he shouted.

"We can't," Fiona shouted. "There's too many of them. We need to get back inside somewhere."

Innes looked around and couldn't help but agree. The zombies were not slowing down, and they were all attracted to the three human beings racing down the street. There were a lot of zombies coming their way.

"Right," Innes puffed, he was badly out of breath, but he had formed a plan. "Form a triangle. Keep moving. And batter the crap out of anything that comes your way."

Fiona stepped to one side of Innes; Robert stepped up at the other. With Innes at the front they kept trotting down the road. They passed the shops and were approaching the Diamond. Robert looked longingly at the pub as he battered zombies, though it currently looked dark, empty, and foreboding.

"We're making it," Robert shouted, sweat pouring down his face. "Keep on going. We're gonnie make it to your mam's, Fi".

Zombie faces loomed out of the dark at them. Then, from the gloom, a face they recognised only too well moaned out to attack them. It was Fiona's mother, Innes's sister. She attacked on the side defended by Innes and Fiona; Robert was helpless to intervene. Fiona howled in anguish. Innes cried as shock set in his core. "It's not her," he screamed as he swung his crowbar to crash into the temple of his sister. She crumpled as her zombie brains spilled out onto the street.

Fiona stopped and dropped her wrench. She howled, "Mum, mum, mum," over and over and over again.

"We've got to keep going Fi," Innes shouted with tears streaming down his face.

Robert positioned Fiona between himself and Innes. Innes pulled her along, they were very nearly at the gate of number 42. The garden was empty of zombies, and the front door was open.

Puffing heavily Robert shouted, "One last sprint. We can make this." He checked out Fiona and Innes. Innes was clearly struggling, and Fiona was distraught and defenceless. Even if she did have a weapon, the shock of seeing her zombie mother being killed by her uncle had completely taken the fight out of her.

"We are so not fucking dying today. You cunts are UTTERLY FUCKING PREPOSTEROUS," Robert hollered as he hit a frenzy of violence. He managed to slay all the nearby Zombies. "You two. Fucking run, run, run," he shouted. Innes and Fiona were completely compliant with his command, they ran. Robert followed.

Once they were in, Robert slammed the door shut. The lock was undamaged. He threw the bolt at the top of the door across. The street zombies gathered once again at the door howling and pounding in their relentless pursuit of prey.

Fiona collapsed on the floor. She was inconsolable. Innes knelt down beside her, out of breath and sobbing he held her and cradled her in his arms.

Robert still had adrenaline pumping round his bloodstream from the battle. His instincts were primed, he grabbed the torch from the back of Innes's trousers, firing it up he scanned their surroundings for any immediate threats. The house was dark and quiet. He looked back at Fiona and Innes, Innes was crying, while gently rocking Fiona. Behind them the zombies continued to moan and pound at the door. The door looked solid. "I'm gonnie go check the rest of the house. Make sure it's clear." Robert announced, Innes vaguely acknowledged he had heard, and that Robert should go.

He started with the ground floor. The living room looked like it had been ransacked by burglars. Vases, pictures, and ornaments were broken and strewn over the floor. The sofa was ripped, and shredded cushions were thrown over the floor. Robert spotted a drink cabinet and made a mental note to explore this later.

The kitchen at the back of the house was empty and clear. It didn't look like whomever or whatever had damaged the living room had bothered even going into the kitchen. Robert went over to the back door and listened. All was quiet. He peered out the kitchen windows. All was dark.

Robert checked out the contents of the fridge. There were 4 cans of lager, he smiled, perhaps they wouldn't need to go to the off licence after all.

Passing Innes and Fiona as he went up the stairs Robert sought to get Innes's attention. "Probably best bypassing the living room and going straight to the kitchen, Inny. The living room is a bit of a mess."

Innes nodded. Robert trudged up the stairs.

Standing on the top floor landing Robert listened. All was quiet. He was sure that there was nobody in, and that there were no zombies around, but he had to make sure. The first room he came to was obviously Fiona's parents' room. It was empty, and untouched. The next room looked like it was Fiona's room, it was also empty and untouched, as was the toilet. There was only one room to go.

With an empty mind, and expecting nothing, Robert casually opened the door and shone the torch in. His stomach lurched. Shock caused him to instantaneously vomit. This was Fiona's younger brothers' room. Both younger brothers were probably still there, there were so many dismembered body parts scattered around he couldn't tell, blood and innards were splattered everywhere. Robert pulled the door closed quickly, but the torchlit vision of the massacre remained scorched in his mind. With his hands on his thighs Robert was violently sick again.

He stood straight and took a massive deep breath, he smelt death, and retched again. With his head spinning he tripped back down the stairs. Fiona and Innes had obviously gone into the kitchen. Robert went straight to the drinks cabinet where he found various bottles of spirits. He reached for a half full bottle of vodka and took a big slug. It burnt down his throat and the fumes pacified his racing mind.

Robert turned to see Innes standing in the doorway of the kitchen. Robert was shaking and his face was as white as a freshly bleached sheet. He raised his fingers to his lips and mouthed, "Shhhhh."

Innes preferred whisky, walking over to stand beside Robert he uncorked the whisky bottle and took a drink. Quietly he asked, "What's up?"

Robert puffed his cheeks and pointed to the kitchen. "We need to get *her* out of here." Robert didn't know how to tell Innes his nephews had been brutally slaughtered. "*We* need to get out of here, Inny."

"Why? What's going on Vanie? I need to know." Innes took a bigger drink of whisky. He knew by the state of Robert that something very wrong had happened.

Robert took a large drink of vodka; he took a deep breath. "There's something up the stairs that neither of you need to see." Tears filled his eyes and rolled down his stubble covered cheeks. "Your nephews are dead Innes. What's left of them is up the stairs mate. I'm so sorry," Robert sobbed.

Innes felt numb. In the space of a few minutes he had killed his zombie sister and had now been told his nephews had died, horrifically. He took one last long slug from the whisky bottle then hurled it against the living room wall.

The noise of the bottle smashing brought Fiona out from the kitchen.

"We need to get out of here," Innes's voice sounded grim and determined.

Fiona was pale, and her eyes were red from crying, "Why uncle Inny? What's happened? What's wrong?"

"Your brothers are gone Fi," Robert answered for his friend as he glanced at the stairs.

Fiona looked at the state Robert was in and knew it was bad. "I need to see it." Something was crystalising in Fiona. "Are they in their room?"

Robert was horrified, he still felt sick. He knew that he never wanted to see anything like that ever again, so the thought of a teenage girl looking at that gruesome carnage appalled him. "No, no, no Fiona. You so *don't* need to see that." Robert motioned with his head at the room above.

Without speaking Fiona marched towards the stairs. Innes intervened and stood in front of her. Fiona's eyes contained dark menace. "Get out my way uncle Inny. I'm going to see my brothers."

Innes didn't know what to say, but he saw the grim determination in Fiona and knew that there was nothing he could say or do that would prevent her from doing what she wanted to do. She took the torch from Robert and, leaving him and her uncle silently standing in the gloomy living room, she trod steadily up the steps.

She didn't draw breath, or hesitate as she marched to her brothers' bedroom and flung open the door. She sprayed the light from the torch around the horrendous scene of murderous carnage. She spotted the decapitated heads of her brothers. Hate, anger, and the need to revenge her family's deaths crystallised hard in a kernel at the centre of her being. She closed the door gently, and slowly descended the stairs; she was not the same person going down as the one that went up. All of her sadness, grief and fear were subsumed and consumed in the kernel of revenge and anger that would from now on be central to her existence.

As she strode back into the living room Innes and Robert studied her closely, they looked at each other quizzically, this was not how either of them expected her to react. "You ok Fi?" Innes asked.

"I'm fine uncle Inny." Detached, Fiona gazed around the wrecked living room.

"I need a new weapon." Fiona stated as a matter of fact. She thought about it for a few seconds, then turned and stomped back up the stairs. Shining the torch ahead of her she barrelled straight into her brothers' room. Ignoring their body parts strewn around the floor Fiona rummaged in a cupboard. From there she produced and wielded a baseball bat. It felt good, solid, heavy, and it carried with it a degree of righteousness. Her brothers beloved baseball bat would now be used to reap revenge on the zombies for her family's untimely, violent demise.

Next, Fiona visited her own bedroom. Standing in the middle of her room she stared coldly at the posters on the walls. Internally Fiona bade farewell to her former life. From her cupboard she grabbed her old school satchel, put a change of clothes in it, and grabbed a denim jacket. She was ready. Fiona didn't look back; she closed the door to her old bedroom, and to her old life.

Fiona thudded back down the stairs, and into the living room, her eyes were blazing. "We heading back out? We still need to go to the Diamond right?"

Innes and Robert looked at each other. Innes's head was spinning. He could clearly see something fundamental had changed within Fiona. He could feel his family disintegrating in front of him and he felt powerless to do anything about it. Innes was struck dumb.

Robert took another slug of Vodka, he stammered, "I'm not sure we need to go to the Diamond now Fiona. I guess we could just find another house to plot up in. Plan things maybe?" Robert was aware this sounded lame, but he really didn't have a clue about what was going on or what they should do next.

Fiona stared hard at them both. "I'm fucking killing as many of them bastard things that fucked my family Vanie. Awright? Uncle Inny, I don't care where it is you want to go, I'm going with you. And on the way I'm going to take as many of them fucking things down as I can. Go to the Diamond. Go look for aunt Mary if you want. I don't care. You're all I have left. So it's me and you now, ok?" Fiona stood resolute and ready. "Vanie, you should come with us as well, if you want to? We all stand a better chance if we stick together."

Innes and Robert looked at each other. Fiona had grown up quickly, and she had hardened fast.

"Aye, I'm with you Fiona," Robert stared at her with a newfound respect. He reckoned she looked more than capable of taking on any number of zombies now.

Robert and Fiona turned to look at Innes.

"Fuck," Innes sighed. He walked over to the battered sofa and perched on the edge. He buried his head in his hands for an eternity, perhaps hoping when he faced the world again it would all look quite different.

Innes raised his head. "What about your dad Fiona?" Innes asked this though he knew her relationship with her father wasn't good.

"Fuck him. He was a shit dad, and a shit husband. You know it too uncle Inny." For Fiona, the discussion about her father was over.

"Diamond it is then folks." Innes didn't know what to do, so he reverted to what he knew best.

"I've got everything I need." Fiona patted her satchel and hefted her baseball bat. "Get your tools then lads. Time we were off." Fiona was keen to leave her former home. It was home for her no more.

Robert and Innes retrieved their tools from the kitchen then joined Fiona in the hall.

This time Fiona stood at the door. "Same as last time, but this time I'll take the front." Innes and Robert just nodded. Fiona was fired up and determined. Shoving the torch in her satchel Fiona opened the front door of her home for the last time, and led her uncle and his friend out into the zombie filled night.

Chapter 21

Stella started into consciousness again, she had been drifting in and out of sleep since her traumatic, but liberating, afternoon. Though she was enjoying the tranquillity of the darkness she tried to turn the bedside table lamp on. It didn't work. Rousing herself she tried the overhead light. Still nothing, no light. Sourcing the torch she kept in her beside cabinet she sprayed a beam around the room to check all was safe, Fluffy's eyes flashed bright at her. Outside, Stella could hear the ongoing disturbance of the zombie onslaught, it was a discordant symphony of death, destruction, and pain.

Though the kitchen was the last place she wanted to go, her rumbling stomach told her a trip there was long overdue. Fluffy also informed her that it was high time some food was produced.

Closing the bedroom behind her she told Fluffy to stay while she went to fetch food. Fluffy looked happy to stay in the bedroom, she could still smell what was festering in the kitchen. Shining the torch light in front of her, Stella crept quietly down the stairs. Standing outside her trashed kitchen door she stole herself for the sight she knew she was waiting for her.

The busted kitchen door creaked as it swung unsteadily open. The room smelt bad, metallic, cloying, thick. There was little light coming in from the moonless night, so she sprayed the torch light over the floor. The body of John Reid lay in a puddle of dense congealed blood, staring at it she felt nothing but nausea. Skirting blood splatter, and bits of broken teeth, she filled a polythene bag with food for her and her cat. A wave of revulsion swept over her as she dodged the corpse again on her way out, she shook it off and bounced back up the stairs to her cat.

After a cheese and pickle sandwich, as Fluffy was munching her cat food, Stella wandered over to stare out the bedroom window. The whole neighbourhood was in complete darkness, except for the lone light of a torch that was clearly making its way towards her house. Feeling safe in her judgment that the zombies hadn't mastered torches she assumed she was about to be visited. This of course didn't necessarily mean that the people would be friendly, this was the Homerton estate after all.

As they made their way over the wall into her garden Stella counted four people, but she couldn't make who they were, and there was no way to interpret the nature of their visit. Grabbing her torch Stella crept back down the stairs. She grabbed a knife, traversed the corpse again and carefully, and quietly, opened the door leading into her kitchen porch. Tiptoeing over to the back door she listened for indications about the intentions of the people now approaching her house.

She heard a voice she recognised asking someone else about why all the lights had gone out. Stella was assured that the owner of the voice most definitely posed no threat to her, she quietly eased open the back door. "Kenny McGregor. Am I pleased to see you?" Stella whispered as she shone her torch in their direction. She didn't know Angus, but she knew Ina and Lennie, she knew they posed no threat.

"How you doing, Stella?" Kenny smiled at his water refinery colleague.

With the door open, the noises howling round the estate were more acute. "Doing ok I suppose Kenny." Stella stepped gingerly out into her back garden and shone her torch around searching for any threats. "What's going on? Any of you got a clue?"

"Do you reckon we could talk about this inside, Stella?" Lennie started towards the door.

She stopped him and blocked the entrance to the house. "There's something you need to know before I let you in." She was very much aware that normal no longer applied to the current situation in Greenock. But she didn't know how these four would react to an act that would ordinarily have been considered murder.

She took a deep breath and said, "My John went mad, with whatever is doing all that." She indicated the estate in general. "He attacked me." Stella felt vulnerable to judgement. Then a defiance rose within her, and she stood proud. "It was either going to be me or him that survived. And I made damn sure it was me." Stella looked them all in the eye, though she couldn't read any of their reactions due to the bad light.

There was no mistaking what Stella was telling them. Lennie motioned to be let in. "Good riddance to bad rubbish if you ask me Stella hen," he said. "He was a fucking prick if you want my opinion."

Silently she stood back to let them in. Lennie had the torch, so he went first. He shone the torch over the carnage and destruction that was wrought in Stella's kitchen. Angus, Kenny, and Ina joined him; they all silently surveyed the scene.

Ina wasn't fazed. "Let me introduce myself love," she stood in front of Stella with her hand out. "I'm Ina. I've seen you around for years. But we've never been properly introduced."

"Stella," she simply said as she shook Ina's hand.

"I'm Angus," Angus introduced himself, "I'm a mate of Lennie's." He was aware of how this would be interpreted by Stella. Being a friend of Lennie's had unavoidable connotations. "But call me Gaff. It's what people call me. My second name is Gaffney," he explained.

"Pleased to meet you, Angus," Stella chose to be polite.

Kenny tore his stare away from the carnage on the kitchen floor. "You ok Stella?" Kenny thought a more sympathetic approach was required to balance out Lennie's somewhat unorthodox approach to bereavement counselling.

Stella sighed, she didn't know where to start, or how to communicate her feelings regarding the death of her partner. "I'm awright Kenny. Me and John's relationship was somewhat turbulent." Stella snapped out of her thoughts. "We should go into the living room. Get away from that," she said pointing at the corpse, she led the way.

Angus and Lennie sat gingerly down on the sofa, they felt out of place in such a well-cared for home. Ina looked round the living room, evaluating everything, subtle communications indicated that she approved of Stella's efforts. Kenny looked like he was bursting to speak, but he didn't quite know where to start.

"Anyone want a cup of tea?" Stella slipped into hostess in the only way she knew how.

Everyone leapt at the chance to indulge in a familiar social norm. Instructions were provided as to how everyone took their tea.

"So, how do you know Stella?" Ina asked of Kenny once Stella had left the room.

"We work together at the refinery. She's in the gatehouse."

Subconsciously Angus's social awkwardness triggered a train of thought started earlier about what 'supplies' he might find in someone else's house. "Does anyone know where the toilet is?" he asked innocently.

Everyone looked blank.

Angus rose and shouted into the kitchen, "Stella, can I use your toilet please?"

"Sure Angus, it's the first room on the right at the top of the stairs."

"Call me Gaff, Stella, everybody does," he said as he slouched up to the toilet.

Stella watched his back disappear up the stairs as she passed by on her way back to the living room. She knew Angus would be a heroin addict, but she welcomed having people in her house. The ordinariness of making tea for guests was comforting. People never came to her house. She wondered why it took such an abnormal situation as a zombie apocalypse for her to achieve something akin to a normal life.

Angus relieved himself in the toilet, though this was not his primary purpose for visiting the bathroom. He scoped the room for possibilities, and after he finished urinating, he went straight to the cupboard/mirror situated above the wash hand basin. It contained exactly what he was hoping to find. He picked up pill bottle after pill bottle, read and rejected them, until he came across a bottle that informed him it contained DF118 tablets. "Bingo," he said quietly, as a triumphant smile lit up his face.

Angus rattled the bottle to gauge how full it was, opened it, and poured out a handful. He threw them all in his mouth and swallowed, remembering not to wash them down with tap water. He stuffed the remaining pills in his pocket, flushed the toilet, and bounced happily back down the stairs.

The others were chatting about the current situation when he returned. Angus picked up the one cup of tea left on the tray and sat back down next to Lennie, who was sitting silently looking awkward on the sofa.

"I thought it was in the water," Stella was saying when Angus returned.

"You too?" Kenny was animated. "I knew it was in the water. And I think I know how it got there too." Kenny sighed and stared into his tea. But he knew he needed to get this off his chest, he knew he needed to start getting honest with people. "I think it was me. It's the only thing I really remember about last night. Mac told me to pull some water down from

Brimmington. I reckon that's where the poison, or whatever it was that's caused all this, came from." Kenny looked worried and ashamed; he didn't know how Stella and Ina would take this news.

"It's not your fault," Stella leaned over from the sofa to pat him on the leg. "You were just following orders Kenny.

"That's what the Nazis said," Lennie blurted out.

"How was he supposed to know," Ina turned to Kenny. "Never you mind him son. He doesn't even know what planet he's on most of the time."

Lennie bristled again at Ina commenting on his defective character. "That's why we're going to the refinery," Lennie ignored her slight. "This one here wants to make good his fuck up and turn the water off."

Stella contemplated their idea. She had a strong desire to leave her house, and to never come back. "The refinery's not a bad idea you know. It'll have electricity at least; it's got a back-up generator. There's food in the canteen as well. And the building is solid." Stella turned to look in the direction of the kitchen, "Besides, I need to get out of here. I don't belong here anymore, and I need to get away from him." Stella retreated once more into her own thoughts.

Ina understood, "Sounds like not too bad an idea to me." She agreed with the idea but wanted to know more about how they were going to execute the plan. "How are we going to get there though? The roads are pretty full of those zombie things." Ina hefted her metal bar. "I'm up for a fight, but I reckon avoidance is probably the best policy."

"There's a path over the hills that eventually takes you to the refinery," said Stella returning to the here and now. "I've taken it back from work a few times when, you know, when I needed a bit of time to myself."

Angus was starting to feel the effects of the pills. "Be a bit dark will it no?" he joined the discussion from his place of newfound internal warmth.

"We've got two torches, and as long as we stick together I reckon we should be all right," Stella looked round the room to gauge support for the plan.

"Oh aye, and I forget. Our Lennie is TA trained, so he'll get us there. Won't you Len?" Angus laughed at his joke. Lennie didn't.

Fluffy had been watching proceedings from the doorway. Once she realised these people were not going to shout at her, or abuse her, she made her entrance. She jumped straight onto Lennie's lap. "Back way would be better," Lennie said as he patted Fluffy and scratched behind her ear. Fluffy purred. "Pass us up my rucksack would you Gaff?" Lennie asked. Angus snapped out of the dream he was slipping into and passed him the rucksack. Lennie started to root about. He checked the methadone bottles were still there, and that they remained intact. Rummaging past the food he produced an iron bar, which he passed to Stella. "You need to pap them on the head hard". Lennie didn't make eye contact with Stella but continued to make friends with her cat.

"They don't feel pain, and hitting them anywhere else doesn't have any effect," he added.

"Thanks Lennie," Stella looked askance at the bar in her hand. "I stabbed my John in the eye. I guess I got lucky."

"I reckon their brains can't take trauma. Knife in the eye would do it." Lennie went back to rummaging in his bag, though he had absolutely no reason to do so.

Stella looked at her cat curled up comfortably on the lap of the unstable addict. "I'll need to take her with me."

Everyone except Angus stared at Fluffy. "How we gonnie do that?" Kenny asked, he looked at Stella. "How you gonnie fight zombies carrying a cat?"

"She's family Kenny, she's coming with me or I'm staying here with her, end of." No one was in any doubt as to the force and sincerity of Stella's statement. "I've got a carrying case. She can go in that. If I need to fight, I'll drop the case. If I go down, it's up to you what you do. All I'd ask is that, if you don't want to save her, let her out her case, and let her go." Tears filled her eyes, she stared at the others. Angus didn't look like he was listening.

"You're going to need to be able to run with it as well, Stella. We'll need to move fast to get away from them." Lennie had accepted the cat as part of the team.

"She's my responsibility Lennie. I'll do my best and accept whatever the consequences be."

"We'll protect you as much as we can Stella. We're a team. Ain't we? Zombie killers." Kenny looked round at the others as he spoke.

Angus realised he was being addressed and gleaned that the conversation was something to do with killing zombies. "We've killed one each," Angus spoke up. "It's your turn next Ina."

"I don't think that's how this is going to work Angus." Lennie said. "When they come for us, they're going to go for the weakest member," Lennie glanced at Ina as he said this. "They'll be like all other predators; they'll be looking for weak spots. We all need to be prepared to be as vicious as they are, and our greatest strength is each other. We need to work as a team and support each other. And we'll need to take the fight to them. If it looks like one of us can't outrun them, we stop and fight as a unit. Ok? When we fight, stick tight in a circle, and defend your bit. And if one of us is in trouble we all pitch in, ok?"

Lennie's speech caused a sombre tone to seep into the room. They became aware of the reality they faced, and no amount of tea was about to make their future palatable.

"Have you heard anything from your mam, Kenny?" Stella knew Kenny's mother well.

Kenny was ashamed, he had not thought once about his poor mother. "No way to contact her Stella. We've not had access to a phone. Can I use yours?"

"I tried it earlier Kenny, it's not working. Do you want to try to get to her's first?"

"Don't think so Stella. The water refinery was always the plan. I think we probably need to stick to that." Kenny looked to Lennie for confirmation. He nodded.

"I need to get out of here," Stella announced flatly. "I need to get away from him," she nodded with her head towards the kitchen.

Lennie turned to face her. "You should have done it years ago. That prick was a fucking waste of space."

Kenny spluttered and tried to cover for his friends' indiscretions. "I'm sure Stella just wants to grieve the passing of her partner, Lennie."

Stella interjected, "Naw Kenny, Lennie's right. I should have got shot of him years ago. Should never have gone with him in the first place, truth be told."

There was a lull in the conversation, this allowed the outdoor sounds to gain dominance. Lennie looked around the room. Everyone had disengaged and had disappeared into their own worlds to contemplate what the next few hours held for them. Lennie let the silence hang for a bit then he stood up. Fluffy plopped to the floor. Lennie looked at every scared face in the room and felt a strong desire to protect every one of them.

"Listen up folks," all the faces looked up as Lennie spoke. "Stella. Is there a way straight to the hills from the front of your house?"

"Aye, near enough Lennie. There's an alley just down the road. It takes you in-between two houses then straight onto the hills."

"You'll need to lead us then Stella. We don't want to miss it. I'll come right behind you. I'll get any of them that come near you. You just get us onto the path. Ok?" Stella nodded.

Lennie continued, "Gaff, Kenny, Ina, youse three trot in a line just behind me and Stella. Youse need to scan constantly round, 360 degrees, ok? Shout if there's contact and then we can huddle and fight them off. Ok?" Lennie didn't need to explain what he meant by contact.

Sitting near Gaff, Kenny leaned over and whispered, "Not bad for a madman though, eh?"

Gaff shrugged, he had not exactly heard all that Lennie said, he was drifting in and out a bit, but he could see Lennie had managed to provide some assurance, and he was reluctantly impressed. Ina and Stella nodded their heads seriously.

"Ina," Lennie continued. "If we're going too fast for you, just shout, ok?"

Ina looked at Angus, Kenny, and then back to Lennie, raising her eyebrows she said, "I don't think it's me you need to worry about young man."

Lennie looked at Angus and wondered quite why he looked so out of it. He shook the thought from his mind and dismissed it as probably not the most important thing to think about at the moment.

"Fuck it. Are we heading to this refinery or what then?" hearing Ina swear was unexpected. It galvanised the group and they all started to look as if they were ready to fight for survival.

"I'll get the cat case then," Stella said as she rose to rummage in a cupboard in the hall.

"What? Are we taking the fucking cat?" Angus quietly asked Kenny.

"Where have you fucking been, Gaff? We just talked about it just now?"

Angus shrugged off any need for a response and busied himself getting ready to face the outside world again, which largely meant making sure he had the equaliser.

Returning to the group with the cat case, Stella called her cat over. "Now, you need to know my little love that we're all going to look after you." Fluffy purred and rubbed her face against Stella as she was placed in the cat case. Tears streamed down Stella's face.

"Ready?" Lennie asked the group. They nodded and quietly made their way to the front door.

As she opened the door Stella turned to Lennie. "My cat is called Fluffy by the way."

"Good name for a cat," he said smiling at Stella. Lennie was glad there was limited light so no one could see him blush.

Chapter 22

The Dunlop's front door creaked ominously under yet another zombie onslaught.

"Turns out that even though the new front door might look nice, unfortunately it doesn't really cut the mustard as an actual door," Joe said, looking pointedly at his wife.

Barbara arched her eyebrows. "Aye, so when I was buying a front door, I should have asked the salesman if the door was zombie proof? Really?" she responded.

Irate, Joe stood and started pacing the floor. "What I'm saying is that there was nothing wrong with the old door. At least it was solid."

Barbara stood and planted her fists firmly on her hips, "And how exactly does that help us now?"

Christine had had enough. "Will youse two stop it." She looked with concern at her little brother as she pleaded with her parents, "Youse two need to stop bickering. We need some kind of plan." Christine stared at the front door, where every bombardment brought closer the stark reality that their house was about to be breached by zombies.

"Fuck," Joe puffed as he slumped back into his seat, his mind deeply troubled.

"Mind your language, Joe. We don't need to let our standards slip just cause the world outside has gone to pot," Barbara said.

Dennis stared at their fragile front door; the zombie assault was relentless. "We're going to need to get out of here." Dennis looked petrified, but he had the courage to verbalise the unpalatable idea that the rest of his family were desperately trying to avoid.

"I know, Dennis," Joe forced a smile. He looked at his family as the reality of their situation was rammed home with every bang on the door. "We'll be awright family, we'll fight our way out. No one messes with the Dunlops right?" Joe's heart ached, his love for his family was deep, and his need to look after them boundless, being forced out to face a hoard of rabid zombies caused him unimaginable torment. But the issue was being forced.

Barbara contemplated her family, their faces warmed by the soft glow of candles, lit when the electricity failed. Tears started to stream down her cheeks, "At least it doesn't look like your turning, Joe," she managed to say.

Joe hugged his wife, and held her tight. Christine put her arm round her brother who responded by resting his head on her shoulder.

"We'll need weapons," Joe said as he released his wife. Barbara stopped crying. Drying her eyes she sat in-between her children and held them tight. Joe trod gently over to the drawn curtains. He peeled them back slightly and recoiled at the mad zombie eyes that sought his, and his family's flesh. He ignored the zombies and took a longer look out the window. "The taxi is still there, and it looks clear." Joe knew he needed a plan. "We'll fight our way out. Pile in the car. And go. Ok?"

"Go where?" asked Barbara.

"We could go to my work to start with? It's out of the way. There'll be light from the generators. And there's food in the canteen." Joe looked round at his family for approval. They all nodded quietly back. No-one had any better ideas. "We'll be alright there for a bit. Then we can wait till help comes." He closed the curtains.

An ominous cracking sound came from the front door. It spurred Joe into action. Dashing into the kitchen he found, and flung open his toolbox. Grabbing hammers and spanners quickly he hurried back to the living room to hand them out to his petrified family. The front door groaned again in complaint from the weight of zombie's piling up against it.

"Fuck it family. They'll be in here soon. We've just got to go." Barbara didn't correct Joe's swearing this time. He looked all of his family directly in the eye, willing them to glean just a bit of his strength. "Barbara, me and you are gonnie have to fight hard. Kids, you just do your best, and please, just do what we say ok?"

Dennis looked petrified but he trusted his father implicitly.

"Come," Joe said, his gut a storm of anxiety. He marched over to the door and grabbed the car keys. "The taxi doors will still be unlocked. Get to it as soon as you can and just pile in ok?" They all nodded.

The door didn't wait to be opened. The hinges gave out and it crashed to the floor. The zombies now had unfettered access to the flesh they craved, a pile of them sprawled into the house. Joe and Barbara were fast, furious, and frenzied. They rained down hammer blows on the heads of all the zombies that invaded their home, and threatened the lives of their family.

Joe was aware now that he wasn't going to be infected. The fact that he hadn't turned from the injuries sustained from the taxi driver, and Mac the Sack, provided him with an extra weapon. Immunity. He howled and pushed all the oncoming zombies out of the door. Barbara and Christine joined him, and they all fought their way up their garden path, beating zombie heads to a pulp.

Hanging back, Dennis noticed a clear path forming, he took his chance and sprinted to the taxi. He flung open the doors and turned to fight to keep the pathway clear. "Dad quick," he shouted. "It's clear."

Nearby zombies were enticed by the melee, Dennis met them face to face. "You're not fucking getting me or my family," he roared as he took down zombie after zombie.

Joe saw the pathway. "Go Chrissie. Go Babs. Get in the car," he shouted as he continued to fell zombies.

Diving for the car, Barbara and Christine piled into the back seat. Dennis was still dropping Zombies. "Dad, get in the driver's seat," he shouted to his father. "I'll be right behind you."

Joe looked with pride at his son as he felled their enemy, and he dived into the driver's seat. He shoved the key into the ignition just as Dennis jumped into the car and slammed the door. The car burst to life. Desperation supplied Joe with more confidence about driving this time. He slammed the car into first, and shot off up the road. The Dunlops lived on a crescent. As they drove round they saw nothing but zombies and carnage. Joe moved up the gears and sped up.

At the end of the crescent he stopped and turned to check out his family. "Are we all ok?", he asked, he was breathing hard.

Their eyes were blazing. They had survived victorious from their first zombie battle. "We're ok I think dad," Christine said. She was proud, surprised, and a little exhilarated.

"I'm fine," said Dennis laughing.

"We are fucking brilliant," roared Barbara, her eyes alive with pride.

"Language, Barbara," Joe laughed as he set the car rolling again to take them out of the Stones estate.

The main road heading out of the Stones estate was littered with abandoned cars. There were zombies everywhere, sludging about, moaning and looking for victims. Joe was just able to navigate round the cars, and he wasn't worried about hitting zombies. Up ahead he saw a massive, unsurpassable blockage. A whole pile of zombies were going hell for leather at a small group of survivors who were battling to remain so.

"Up ahead folks," Joe pointed it out. "There's someone in big trouble." He peered but couldn't make out who it was. The survivors were battling frantically, but it looked like they were tiring under a massive zombie onslaught.

"We've got to stop and help," Christine was in no doubt about what was the right thing to do.

"I don't think we've really got much of a choice folks. The road is blocked," Joe said. All the Dunlops were still fired up from their previous battle, they had confidence in their abilities.

Joe parked the car. He turned to check his wife and daughter in the back seat, "Are you all ok?"

Barbara nodded grimly. "I'd rather not go out there again, but you're right," she looked at her daughter with pride. "We can't just leave them."

"I'm fine dad," Christine said, strength oozing from her.

Joe turned to Dennis, "You alright son?"

Dennis looked bright eyed and alive. "I'm with mam. I'd rather not go out there, but I know we have to. We'll be awright though. We're the Dunlops, we'll fight as a team."

Joe tousled his hair, this time Dennis only expressed deep satisfaction. "Aye son, we'll fight as a team." Joe turned again to look at his whole family. "We'll form a diamond shape. I'll lead. Barbara and Christine you come either side of me. And Dennis, you make sure we are not attacked from the back. Got it?"

They all nodded.

"Fuck it, let's go." Joe opened the driver's door. His family followed.

They formed the diamond shape Joe suggested and started to march determinedly towards the fight. As they approached, peripheral zombies from the battle smelt them and turned to attack. Joe spotted who it was in the middle of the hoard, he shouted over. "Hey Innes. Cavalry to the rescue."

Innes, Fiona, and Robert had been starting to feel the fight slipping away from them, they were being overwhelmed. At the welcome sight of Joe and his family pitching in, their energies were restored; they had just been presented with the precious gift of hope. Fiona took a deep breath and redoubled her efforts; more adrenaline flooded into her system; her eyes were ablaze with fury as she meted out punishment to the zombie's responsible for her family's demise.

The Dunlop diamond carved through the densely packed zombies, and joined Innes and his crew in the middle. They all formed a fighting circle. "What's the plan Innes?" Joe shouted to his water refinery colleague as they furiously felled zombies.

"Finish these fuckers off, then head to the Diamond for a bevvy was our plan," Innes hollered, smiling as he cracked zombie heads open with his crowbar.

"Sounds like a good enough plan to me mate," Joe shouted back as he pulped zombie brains with his ball peen hammer. "Make mine a lager tops."

The zombies started to thin out, and the fighting circle expanded, picking off the remaining zombies with ease. Fiona put down the last zombie with a grim smile. "That's for my family ya prick," she said as the zombie fell.

The fighters were jubilant and exuberant in their victory, until they saw Joe make his way hesitantly over to the last felled zombie. "Bobby?"

Joe plummeted from the heights of adrenaline fuelled victory, to a dark pit of gut-wrenching pain. The reality of what had happened hit him like a punch to the solar plexus. Tears trickled down his cheeks as he sank beside the corpse of his friend, Bobby Thompson. These creatures they were killing used to be friends and family.

Joe picked up the corpse of Bobby and cradled his broken head in his arms. "Bobby. I'm so, so sorry mate," he cried.

"Bobby was his mate." Innes said quietly to Fiona.

Fiona's face was impassive, "We're all going to have to get used to losing people." She turned and marched toward the Diamond. "Come with me Vanie, we need to make sure the pub's clear." Robert did as he was told.

Pulling the torch out of her satchel Fiona carefully pushed open the door of the Diamond, she sprayed the torch round the pub and listened carefully for any sound heralding an imminent attack. The floor and furnishing were covered with blood, and there had been at least one poor person who had been taken to bits and partially consumed. Robert paled and looked to Fiona who remained expressionless.

Treading slowly, and carefully, avoiding the gore, Fiona undertook a thorough investigation of the pub interior. She checked the back door was locked and that the cellar was clear. Robert followed her.

Outside, Barbara approached her husband. She spotted more zombies making their way down the road. Gently touching his shoulder she said to him, "Joe, we really need to go now."

Innes helped Joe to his feet, and Christine and Barbara put their arms round him and led him to the pub. Dennis followed, keeping an eye open for danger. Innes held the door for everyone and bolted it shut when everyone was safe inside. "Serve them up then, Vanie," he shouted over to Robert.

The Dunlops sat at the bar. Innes joined Robert behind the bar, both of them were like kids in a candy shop. In the midst of a nightmare they had realised one of their dreams. Fiona lent against one of the pillars by the front door and listened to the zombies congregating, and pounding on the door. The Diamond door, by force of necessity, was installed with security in mind, once bolted it was solid and unyielding.

Innes sorted out various alcoholic beverages for the adults, he looked over at his niece, "Fiona. You want a coke?"

Fiona silently shook her head.

"You should take on some liquid, Fiona. You know we can't drink the water." Innes was concerned about how his niece had changed, and wanted to do what little he could to look after her.

Joe gulped down the hurt he felt at Bobby's fate, and washed it down with some whisky. "You reckon it's in the water too then Inny?"

Innes and Robert had poured themselves a large wine each. "Aye. I don't know why, but my gut tells me that's where it's come from. This is everywhere by the way. We heard it all kick off at the Morton match on the radio."

"We saw it in the toon as well Inny." Barbara shook as she remembered how close they came to being eaten by the taxi driver.

Christine took a coke over to Fiona. "You awright Fi?"

Fiona nodded and took the offered drink. "Thanks."

Christine was a year younger than Fiona. But they were in the same school. They knew each other to see.

"This is mad eh?" Christine tried again.

"Aye," Fiona said taking a drink of her coke. She didn't extrapolate.

Christine listened to her parents discussing their plan to go to the water refinery with Robert and Innes.

"We'd need to take some bevvy with us," she heard Robert say.

Robert went on a scouting mission, looking for something, he came across a battered looking Rucanor bag. He emptied out the contents, which was an unworn, pristine gym kit. He disappeared back behind the bar and Fiona could hear the clanking of bottles and tinging of tin cans being loaded into the bag.

"I saw a checkout wummin being eaten in the supermarket," Christine stared off into space as she recalled the traumatic sight. When she returned to the here and now she realised Fiona had slipped away to perch on her own at the bar. Christine returned to sit with her parents. Fiona kept her eyes on the door.

Barbara eyed her husband sipping his whisky. "You boys better watch it with the drinking. We've got to go back out there you know?"

"Bit of Dutch courage never did anyone any harm," Innes replied.

"Mrs Dunlop is right uncle Inny. Youse have been drinking pretty much all day." Fiona stood, "We ready to go then?"

Joe threw back the remains of his whisky. "Reckon we can dispense with the Mr and Mrs. I'm Joe and this is Barbara."

Innes introduced his niece.

"But yes, I reckon you are right Fiona. We should get going again. The sooner we get somewhere safe the better." Joe grabbed his hammer; his family followed his lead. "How do you want to do this Fiona? It's going to be a tight fit in the car you know?"

"I reckon you and me should take the first flush when we open the doors, Joe. Once we get out it's a case of make it to the car as soon as we can. Us young one's will just need to sit on your knees." Fiona looked at the adults. They nodded their heads mutely.

"I've been scratched and bit before. I reckon I'm immune. So yes, I should face first flush." Joe looked at Fiona and saw past her young years recognising only steely determination. "Will you be ok?"

"Aye," Fiona turned to face the door. "We ready then?"

Joe stepped up beside her and spoke for his family, "We're ready."

Fiona opened the door and once again they faced the stramash of flailing limbs and biting teeth that was hell bent on their destruction.

Part 5

Chapter 23

The moonless night was marble dark. Cloudless skies would have been displaying the infinite, stellar beauty of the cosmos were it not for the numerous plumes of dense, acrid, smoke that billowed from numerous burning buildings. A gentle wayward breeze swirled the smoke into hungry clouds with grey flumes and wispy black fronds. All the area needed was a wandering Dante and Virgil and the scene would have been complete.

Habitually nocturnal animals attempted to maintain their normal routines, but they were disturbed by an instinctive awareness that the delicate balance of nature had been unduly disrupted by a cataclysmic event.

On such a stupendously beautiful Saturday night the streets of Greenock should have been humming with the sounds of revelry, drunkenness, and petty violence. But Homo Sapiens were now confronting an existential crisis, the consequences of which were incomprehensible. The magnitude of the circumstances humanity faced was unparalleled.

The British Government were, predictably, wholly unprepared. The zombie onslaught had but only an exceedingly small window of opportunity where a successful outcome could have been achieved. The only effective solution would have been unpalatable and completely unacceptable to even the most ruthless of dictatorships. The British Government understandably hesitated, and in that hesitation all was lost.

Half a dozen military helicopters hovered high in the air over the apocalyptic scene, spraying the ground below pointlessly with powerful spotlights. They were mostly unable to penetrate the dense smoke. There was no army presence on the ground yet, the risks being, at this stage, unquantifiable. The citizens of Greenock, Gourock and Port Glasgow were left isolated to face the first flush of the zombie assault alone.

The virus had been swift, efficient, and deadly. There were only small pockets of resistance left clinging on for dear life. The collective visceral intelligence of the virus was contemplating the next move. It was designed to permanently hunt for as many hosts as possible, but it also needed to complete its local job. A split was formed, the majority of the zombies started to move out of the area, some went east heading towards Glasgow, some went south to pick up all the small towns on the way to Largs and onwards. A smaller, but still substantial, gathering stayed behind locally to pick off the few remaining uninfected human beings in the area.

Once Glasgow fell to the zombie assault the overall result would be a forgone conclusion, the virus would be wholly uncontainable. The only solution would have created so much collateral damage that no

Government would have been courageous enough to sanction its use.

The window of opportunity incrementally and inexorably started to close.

The river Clyde flowed serenely by.

Chapter 24

Stella's front door was free from zombies, her road backed onto the countryside, so there were fewer zombies in the area. Stella set off with her cat case cradled under one arm, and the iron bar Lennie had given her in her other hand. Lennie trotted behind her as close as he could get without causing her to trip. Lennie's already confused mind was further bewildered by strange, but not unpleasant, feelings coursing through his system. Lennie was unused to feelings of any kind, other than feeling high or junk sick.

Ina, Angus, and Kenny jogged together, with Ina in the middle. They ran behind Lennie, scanning the road with serious faces searching for zombies. Spotlights spraying the ground, and a recognisable sound, informed them that helicopters were now buzzing about above them. "Hey Len, do you think we can get them to come down and get us? Do you reckon they're coming to the rescue?" Angus shouted to the back of Lennie's head.

Scanning the sky Lennie couldn't see the helicopters properly through the smoke, but the sound was faint. "They're too high to see us Gaff. I'd reckon they're just surveying the area." Lennie had not initially noticed the helicopters; his mind was elsewhere.

"Contact," Stella shouted as she gently placed the cat case on the ground. There were three zombies running down the road towards them. Ina didn't wait for them to reach them. With a speed that surprised them all, Ina sped down the road heading straight for the zombies. The zombies were uncoordinated, and predictably they lunged for Ina once she was within striking distance. Ina nimbly leapt to one side while bringing her iron bar down, with force, slap bang in the middle of the right-hand zombies' head. Ina pirouetted, as light as a ballerina, and from behind did the same to the middle zombie. The remaining zombie turned and lunged. Ina ducked and rolled under its outstretched body, as she twisted out and up she leapt and swung hard to connect with the zombies' temple. All three lay motionless on the street within a split second.

Ina picked herself up, dusted herself down and strolled back to Stella, Kenny, Lennie, and Angus. They all stood staring at her with their eyes wide, and mouths hanging open.

"I trained in Taekwondo years ago son. Black belt," she said looking at Lennie. "You never lose it. Not bad for the weakest member, eh?"

Angus roared with laughter. "Fuck it Ina. I'm sticking close to you. You're our secret weapon."

Kenny hugged Ina, "Fucking hell Ina, you're brilliant."

A shocked Lennie said, "Well, isn't life just full of surprises. Thank you Ina."

There were more zombies approaching from a distance. "Reckon we need to get going," Stella said as she picked up Fluffy to set off again.

"Come with me you two," Ina said to Kenny and Angus. "We'll take them out." She indicated the handful of zombies making their way up the street towards them. "I know the wee alley into the hills

Stella. Wait there with Lennie and we'll meet you there, once we've finished with this lot." Ina started to trot towards the zombies, then shouted, "NOW," to Kenny and Angus who were standing about looking vacant. Startled, they responded as directed, and trotted respectfully after Ina.

Lennie and Stella strolled together towards the alley that would take them into the hills.

"Do you reckon there will be any of them in the hills Lennie?" Stella asked as they walked.

"Fucked if I know," Lennie reacted, then coughed. "I mean," he stammered, "I don't really know Stella. I'll go first with the torch and make sure the path is clear. As long as you keep me right about where we're going?"

"Will do. You can't go wrong really. There's only one path, you just follow it round 'till you see the refinery."

Stella and Lennie watched from a distance as Ina, Angus, and Kenny dealt with the zombies heading their way. It was mostly Ina that dealt with the zombies, though Kenny and Angus whacking at them provided a useful distraction that made her job easier. Kenny and Angus had fun whacking zombies.

"You have to swing your weapon from your core." Ina patted her stomach in demonstration as they walked back towards Lennie and Stella. Ina demonstrated a few controlled swings. "It helps you maintain your balance. And helps for your next move. Make sure you keep breathing deeply. It helps keep your head clear." Angus and Kenny nodded their heads attentively. "You need to keep a clear head when you're fighting so you can anticipate your enemy's next move. It's handy that our current enemies seem to be incredibly stupid."

"Wee Ina is going to come in handy, I reckon," Stella remarked.

Lennie nodded enthusiastically. "Looks like she's giving my lads some training as well." He kept scanning the street for threats.

"Shall we head for the hills then folks?" Ina said smiling as they approached.

Lennie led; Ina took the rear-guard. She was given Stella's torch. Zombies were instinctively drawn to masses of humanity, so there were none wandering around the hills. But every snap of a twig, or rustle of a bush, caused taught nerves to jangle as the group trekked through the dark hills.

Rounding a corner on the path Lennie came across the banks of loch Mintern. The becalmed, quiet waters reflected the black of the night. The group joined Lennie to stare into the dark loch. There was no obvious sign of contamination, but the water seemed to exude a vile hostility. The group had no doubt that this was where the current situation originated from. Kenny gazed up at the banks of loch Brimmington, further up the hill. He felt the dead weight of his responsibility. Ina stood beside him. "It's not your fault son. There was no way you could have known."

Kenny knew the refinery was just down the hill from Mintern. "I just need to do what I can now Ina. I need to turn the water off." He trudged off in the direction of the refinery.

Chilled to the bone despite the warmth of the night, the group silently followed Kenny. At the prow of the hill they could make out the silhouette of the refinery sitting like a dark pantheon to pandemonium, silent and brooding.

As they crunched across the car park they saw clear evidence that the water refinery had not escaped the ravages of the zombie attack. Various body parts, internal organs, and gore spattered the gravel surface though, at the moment, there were no zombies in sight.

The gatehouse door lay open. Lennie cautiously approached and lit up the inside with his torch. "Stella, you know the place best. Come with me and let's see if you can get the lights on."

Stella gently placed her cat case on the ground. Fluffy had been quiet and still on the journey. Now that she sensed the journey's end she emitted a gentle mew, as Stella placed her on terra firma. Letting her know she was there and that everything would be fine Stella whispered, "I'll be right back my wee love. Rest easy."

Ina handed Stella her torch and held her arm in reassurance. "We've got your back love."

Knowing that Ina was watching over her provided Stella with enough courage to enter the dark but familiar gatehouse. With Lennie at her side Stella tried the light switches. Nothing, no light. "We'll need to switch on the emergency generator manually."

"Go for it. I'm with you," Lennie nodded.

Slowly, shining the torch in front of her, Stella entered the back office of the gatehouse. It was empty. She opened the electric panel and scanned the switches. "I've never had to do this," she said, as much to herself as to Lennie.

Shrugging, she located the emergency generator switch, said a quick prayer, then flicked the switch. Deep in the bowels of the refinery the emergency generator lit up, purred to life, and efficiently pumped electricity instantly all around the refinery. One by one the lights flickered on; the gatehouse lit up. The group piled into the gatehouse. The radio 'entertainment' emitted nothing but crackly static. Stella did a quick search on the radio in case there was someone, anyone, broadcasting any information about the situation. There was nothing but hiss.

"Right, we need to split up and make sure the refinery is clear." Lennie focused their attention. "Ina. You take Kenny and Gaff. Kenny knows the refinery." Ina nodded, Kenny and Angus just looked vacant. Lennie turned to Stella, "Does the front door lock?" She nodded, and locked the door. "You come with me." Lennie turned back to Ina, "If there's any issues, shout contact, and keep on shouting until we arrive. We'll do the same. Priority is to make sure any doors that lead to the outside are secured."

"Aye, aye captain," Angus said as he pulled a salute.

They stepped out of the gatehouse and onto the refinery floor. Kenny gazed ruefully at his workstation, the pipes, where all this madness had originated from.

"Ina, Gaff, I need to do something first before we check the refinery." Kenny walked over to his workstation. He woke up the sleeping computer and, by simply clicking on a few switches, he turned off the water supply for the whole area. He closed the pipes from Brimmington to Mintern and ensured no more infected water was being pumped out from the refinery. He sighed, "Right. Let's go check the place out." He led Ina and Angus down the corridor towards the loading bays and the storeroom.

"Feel better now son?" Ina asked as they walked down the corridor.

"Not really, Ina," he replied. "It doesn't really change anything. But I suppose it was the least I could do."

"Shhhhh," Angus said. "What's that?"

A rattling noise was coming from further down the corridor.

"That's the disabled toilets." Kenny knew exactly where the noise was coming from.

The rattling noise continued. As they carefully, and quietly approached they could see the doorhandle of the toilet being spasmodically twisted as the door was tried. Someone, or something was trying, and failing, to get out.

"Can one of you kick the door open," Ina whispered. "I'll take whatever comes out ok?"

"I've done a few doors in my time, Ina," Angus said with some pride. "I'll do it."

"After three then son," Ina said and held up three fingers. She mouthed the numbers as she lowered one finger at a time. As the last digit sank Angus gave the door a solid, ferocious kick with the heel of his boot, directly beside the lock. The door burst open. Ina prepared to attack.

A dazed looking young man emerged from the broken toilet door, rubbing his eyes, and staring aghast as a fierce looking elderly lady threatened to hit him with an iron bar. He cowered back into the toilet. "Don't hit me," he pleaded.

"I reckon he's alright Ina. I don't reckon Zombies can speak," Kenny said as he stared at the frightened creature stood before him. "Don't hit him."

"What on earth were you doing in there, son?" Ina lowered her iron bar.

"I've been locked in here for ages. I pure shat myself when the lights went out." Wide eyed and grinning foolishly, the young man exited the lavatory again.

Kenny squinted at him, "Do I know you?"

"I'm Calum Jones. I was in the same school as you, but I was in the year behind yours. I started here a couple of weeks back."

Angus struggled to get his head round what was going on. "Wait a minute," he said. "What do you mean you were locked in there? It's a toilet. It's supposed to lock. And you were inside, where the lock is!"

Calum snorted a self-deprecating laugh, "I know. I don't know what happened. But I just couldnae get the door to open. I think it might be broke."

Angus still battled hard to comprehend, "Do you know what's been happening out there son?"

Calum looked as baffled as Angus. "What do you mean? Where's the back shift?"

Angus turned to Kenny, "He's not got a fucking clue what's going on."

Ina drew Calum aside. "You need to brace yourself son. This is going to come as a bit of a shock." Ina explained in broad brush strokes what had being going on in the area for the last few hours.

Calum's eyes grew wider and wider, they looked like they were about to leave their sockets. He looked at the three of them. "Are youse bamming me up?" was all he could come up with.

"What have you been doing in there, Calum?" asked Kenny softly.

"To be honest, since the lights went out I just crashed out until they went back on again, just now." Calum looked vacant, his mind desperately trying, but failing to understand what had happened to the world while he had been asleep.

"I reckon I'll take a wee hit'n a miss while we're here folks if you don't mind," Angus announced as he breezed past Calum into the toilet. He closed the door, studied the lock, and tried to fathom out how someone could be so dumb as to not know how a lock worked. Angus popped into the cubicle and rapidly swallowed some more DF118. He had a perfunctory pish, then joined the others back in the corridor.

"So we need to make sure the building is safe," Ina explained to Calum as they prepared to continue their tour of the premises.

Calum didn't look like he was any closer to accepting, or understanding what he had been told. They checked the storeroom and the loading bays, all was quiet, empty, and secure. Calum walked beside Kenny. "So," Calum searched for something to say. "You planning to go see any good bands? I went to see The Alarm last week at Barrowlands. They were brilliant."

Kenny stared hard at Calum; his brow furrowed worse than Lennie's on a bad day. "The world has gone to shit Calum. I'm not going to see any bands. No one is."

Kenny dropped back to walk with Angus who looked mean enough to put Calum off walking with them. "He's fucking mad," Kenny said.

"He'll get on with Lennie then," was Angus's reply.

"Doubt that very much indeed," said Kenny as they emerged once again onto the refinery floor. They could hear Stella talking to Lennie in the gatehouse. They had clearly finished their recce.

"I reckon they've all headed into town looking for people to eat," they heard Lennie say as they reached the gatehouse.

"We've found someone," Ina announced their return.

Lennie and Stella popped their heads out the gatehouse hatch, (Stella had let Fluffy start to get used to her new surroundings). "Meet Calum Jones," Ina introduced him. "This is Stella and Lennie. Lennie is our leader. Aren't you Lennie?" Ina blinked at Lennie with her eyebrows raised.

"Aye, like fuck," Angus murmured in an aside to Kenny.

Lennie blustered, "I don't know about that Ina. I've been trained in the TA is all. You awright Calum? Have you drank any water from the taps recently?" Lennie scrutinised the new arrival.

"Naw, I was warned when I started here about………..," Calum searched for an appropriate way to communicate what he was told about people pissing and wanking off in the water tanks. "………..you know, not drinking tap water and that," he settled on simple.

"We think the thing that's causing all the zombies is in the water," Kenny filled Calum in on their thinking.

Being careful not to let Fluffy escape, Stella and Lennie stepped out of the gatehouse.

"Where have you been? What happened to all the zombies? Did you see where they went? Did you fight them off?" Lennie had many questions for Calum.

"He's been locked in the toilets Len," Angus said with a smile.

"What? The whole time? How the fuck do you get locked *IN* a toilet?" Lennie looked like he might explode.

Calum looked embarrassed. "That kind of thing just seems to happen to me a lot." He smiled sheepishly and scratched his head, as if trying to find a more acceptable answer there.

"Leave him alone Lennie," Stella intervened. "You must be starving poor lad." Stella gave Calum a shoulder hug. "I reckon we should all head to the canteen, get us something to eat. What do we think?" Stella looked round for approval, which was obviously unanimous.

"Are all the doors dubbed up?" Lennie asked.

"Aye, all safe and secure," Kenny replied.

"Having something to eat is not too a bad idea then, Stella," Lennie's face did it's best to smile.

The canteen was located at the bottom of the other corridor, opposite the one that led to the storeroom and the disabled toilets. Stella walked with Calum and Ina; Lennie, Angus and Kenny walked together.

"What do you think of Calum then Len?" Angus asked.

"Seems," Lennie searched for the word. "To be honest he seems as thick as shite."

Angus laughed, "He was locked *IN* the toilet. He doesn't have a fucking clue."

"So he lives up to his name then? He's a proper Mr Jones." Lennie replied.

"Eh?" Angus didn't get the reference.

"You know. Bob Dylan? He's not got a clue what's happening. Lennie said.

"Never of heard it," Angus replied. "The only one I liked of his was the one about getting stoned."

"Rainy Day Women," Lennie informed him. A nagging thought reoccurred to Lennie. He studied Angus closely and made a mental note to check his methadone bottles at the first opportunity. "I reckon when we get to the canteen we should have the first bottle of meth," Lennie said, looking at Angus for a reaction.

"Gets my backing," he replied innocently.

"Me too," Kenny was oblivious to the undercurrent at play between Lennie and Angus.

When they reached the canteen, the males naturally took their places around one of the tables where the refinery workers normally sat.

"We'll do the cooking then?" Stella said pointedly.

"You cannie trust them to do it," Ina replied nodding her head in the direction of the motley crew of males sat round the table.

Stella looked at them and ceded that Ina was indeed correct in her assessment regarding the capabilities of the four gentlemen. Ina rolled up her sleeves, checked out the contents of the fridge and cupboards and shouted out, "Slice, tottie scones, fried eggs, and beans. That sound ok for you all?"

Enthusiastic approval was unanimously vocalised.

Stella and Ina set about preparing the food with a practised efficiency. "He likes you; you know?" Ina said to Stella as an aside as the lads told Calum in detail what was happening on the streets of Greenock. Calum still did not look like he was any closer to grasping the severity of the situation.

Stella only uttered a non-committal grunt.

"He's as crazy as a loon. But I reckon he's got a good heart," Ina continued as she cooked.

"I don't think I can really think about things like that at the moment Ina," Stella set about making cups of tea.

"Probably right." Ina finished off cooking and started plating up food.

Everyone fell to the food like it was their last supper. As they ate they contemplated their chances of survival and what ongoing risks there might be to longer-term existence. There were various seismic psychological shifts taking place in many of their minds. Ina watched them all eat.

"I reckon we should base ourselves in the gatehouse for the time being," Ina announced as they were drinking their tea.

"Not a bad idea Ina," Lennie approved. "Me, Kenny and Gaff just have to sort a wee bit of business, then we'll meet you back there awright?" Lennie made it clear that the nature of their 'business' was private.

"I'll just get Fluff something to eat," Stella said, searching the fridge for cold meat. She picked up a few bottles of water, glasses, and a couple of bowls for her cat. "See you at the gatehouse then eh?" Stella left with Ina and Calum. Calum looked like he was quite happy just being told what to do.

Lennie found three glasses. With his suspicions confirmed, Lennie noted that his two bottles of methadone were untouched. Being extremely careful he poured out three equal measures of methadone.

Angus watched closely and grabbed for the one he thought looked like it might contain the most.

"Cheers," Angus toasted as he swallowed his methadone, he rimmed the glass with a finger and sucked it to ensure not a drop of the precious liquid was wasted. Lennie and Kenny did the same.

Lennie glanced quizzically from time to time at Angus as they strolled back down the corridor to the gatehouse.

Chapter 25

Zombie Mac with its zombie police, and a whole other load of zombie Greenockians, marauded towards the town centre. They were drawn there by deep-rooted instincts, and the enticing smell of untainted meat. On the way into town they smelt sporadic invitations to feed wafting deliciously out from various dwellings. En mass they would descend on these houses like a pack of starving hyenas. By now they had learnt that sheer weight of numbers and constant, coordinated battering was enough to breach most places. They relentlessly fed and increased their numbers exponentially.

As they swamped into the town centre the zombies became aware that the scent of untouched flesh was getting stronger. Mac started baying angrily and its hoard followed suit. This cacophony of primal howling brought frightened faces to the windows of the tower block that was producing the compelling odour.

The oft complained about broken door entry system of the tower block proved no barrier to hungry Mac and its hoard of gore besplattered zombies. Piling into the building they howled their way up the stairs to the first floor; the acoustics of the stairwell caused their untempered hollering to reverberate throughout the entire building. The huddled, terrified, people; now trapped in this towering mortuary, exuded such a stench of fear that the crazed zombies were propelled to even greater heights of violent desperation.

The stairwell was cited at the centre of the block, there was only one way up and down. One frantic family grew desperate enough to attempt an escape using the lift. When the lift doors opened on the ground floor they were greeted by a thick baying mass of zombies that promptly tore them to bits.

Zombies piled up the stairwell, branching off at every floor to ransack the flats there, turning or eating the wretched, screaming occupants. Those on the higher floors could do naught but cower and cry as they listened to their inevitable death inexorably approach.

Once they reached the top of the tower the zombies piled out onto the roof. All the residents had been taken or eaten, there were no more victims, the tower block had been rinsed. A few Zombies fell over the edge smashing their bodies to bits on impact with the ground. The zombies on the roof heralded their victory by howling out over the rooftops of Greenock town centre.

Even though the town centre had been well and truly ravaged, the zombies still needed more flesh, they piled back down the stairs and scoured the town centre for more. But Mac and his entourage were not the only zombie hoard in town hunting. Led by Ian (Fergie) Ferguson with Dave Anderson ubiquitously in tow, their smaller, but still sizable hoard of zombies, were also in town feverishly seeking flesh. Being a Zombie had not blunted Ian's ferocity any.

The two hoards met in the middle of the desolate town centre. The two forces melded seamlessly into one massive, ugly, destructive force. As the majority of the zombie presence started to leave the area to continue their mission to infect the world, this massive, combined hoard stayed behind. Zombie Mac had unfinished business to attend to. This unfinished business went by the names of Joe Dunlop and Kenny McGregor.

Chapter 26

Dealing with the small amount of zombies outside the pub was a relatively simple matter for the Diamond crew. Fitting seven people inside a taxi was not so easy. Innes sat in the front passenger seat with Fiona on his lap. Barbara, Robert, Christine, and Dennis all squeezed into the back seat.

Joe fired the ignition and they set off.

"Better hope the police don't stop us eh?" Robert said, "I reckon this car would most definitely qualify as overcrowded."

"We saw the police earlier Rab," Joe said as he negotiated a gathering of zombies. "The police are all zombies." Joe remembered seeing Mac the Sack. "Inny. I saw Mac the Sack earlier by the way. He's a zombie."

Innes remembered the story he had heard in the Diamond. "I heard you caught him in a rather embarrassing situation at work, Joe." Innes left out the graphic details in deference to the woman and children in the car.

Joe laughed, "That was just last night and all Inny. What a difference a day makes eh? Don't reckon old Mac will be worrying too much about that anymore." He felt a twinge of pity for his old boss.

"Joe, how are we going to get to the refinery? The main road is blocked, remember?" Barbara reminded her husband.

"Well, there's a couple of ways we can go. I was going to try the direct way first. It still avoids the main road. We'll see how it goes eh."

Joe drove out of the Stones estate using the back route, as before. They drove past various burning buildings and feasting zombies. The car attracted unwanted attention from a few zombies, but Joe was able to drive fast enough that they never got close. He mowed down a few just out of mercy for who they used to be.

Taking the side streets, Joe wove through Greenock. He drove round the dams on the edge of the town and started to head for the refinery. There were no other cars driving on the road, and he had to slow down many times to navigate abandoned vehicles. As he slowly negotiated a particularly tricky crossroad, Robert raised the alarm. "Fucking hell. Look at that."

In the distance, makings its way up the hill, was a massive hoard of zombies. Innes could make out the figure of Mac the Sack slouching majestically at the front. "That's fucking Mac alright Joe. Turning into a zombie doesn't seem to have improved him any," Innes noted.

Squinting at the hoard Robert spotted two faces well known to him, "Inny, is that not Fergie and Dave Anderson?"

Innes scanned the hoard and spotted them. "Fuck. It is n'all. They were fucking mad enough as people. Fuck knows what they're going to be like as zombies." Innes shuddered.

Mac and his zombies smelt and spotted the car, they knew this meant humans. En masse they emitted a loud, blood curdling roar and, resembling a writhing sea of flailing limbs, they broke into a loping run. Joe didn't wait for an invitation, he floored the accelerator and sped off up the hill towards the refinery.

Joe and his passengers were deeply chilled by the sight. "Fuck, I really hope they don't follow us," Robert articulated their collective fear.

An atmosphere of deep solemnity descended in the car as Joe drove past the Homerton estate. There were many buildings burning on the estate. Joe's sense of foreboding increased as he turned the corner to see the refinery all lit up. This was not what he was expecting. "Someone must have beaten us to it folks. They've turned on the emergency generator."

He parked at the far end of the car park and killed the engine. The Diamond crew disembarked from the car. With their recent brush with the massive zombie hoard still fresh in their minds, their nerves were very much on edge. They all had their weapons ready. Joe motioned for the group to be silent as they tiptoed quietly up to the gatehouse door, the gravel car park crunched gently beneath their feet. Joe listened at the thick door of the gatehouse; he could hear indistinct mumbling.

"Well, they're not zombies anyway," he whispered. "I'm going to knock. Get ready," Joe took a deep breath and knocked hard on the gatehouse door.

Joe's knock killed the murmuring in the gatehouse stone dead. They could hear the shuffling of furniture and feet; and eventually the door was pulled swiftly open. In the doorway stood a defiant craggy faced lunatic and a sweet looking elderly lady. Both were armed with metal bars.

Joe wasn't quite sure who he was expecting to open the door, but the sight of the two who did was enough to completely throw him off his track. "Errrr," he stammered, "Is there any chance we could come in? We're not going to do you any harm." He spoke loudly and clearly as he knew there were more people inside.

"Joe?"

Joe recognised the voice that spoke from within, "Kenny?"

"Bugger me, Joe Dunlop, am I pleased to see you." Kenny rushed out of the gatehouse. "It's alright Lennie, Joe's ok." Kenny gave Joe a huge hug. Joe wasn't used to being hugged by a man, but he hugged Kenny back, awkwardly.

Stella came bursting out of the gatehouse past Lennie and Ina. "Joe!" Stella was also overjoyed to see Innes there too." Innes, you've survived. You didnae get the jail then?" she laughed.

"You know my uncle well then," Fiona said as she breezed past the crowded doorway. "I should like to remind you all, there might just be a massive zombie army making their way here right now."

"What?" Lennie reacted as the Diamond crew shuffled past into the gatehouse. Barbara and Robert nodded polite hello's to Ina, Stella, and Lennie as they passed. Christine and Dennis mutely followed.

"What army of Zombies?" Lennie wanted the information quickly, he was worried.

Joe explained about the grim discovery they came across on their way to the refinery. He tried to emphasise the point that they weren't sure the zombies would follow them, or if they were even capable of following anything.

Everybody introduced themselves, and the gatehouse became a babble of voices indulging in the pleasure of big, small talk.

The small room was now obviously completely overcrowded. Lennie stepped out onto the car park; Ina followed.

Pensively, Lennie walked over to the gate of the refinery and stared out at the still empty road leading to the Homerton estate, and Greenock town.

"Do you reckon they'll come here?" Ina asked.

Lennie shrugged, "Fucked if I know Ina. But I think we'll have to start thinking about what we're going to do if they do."

Ina and Lennie stood contemplating the night and what it might bring. Ina looked at Lennie, "We've got some good people in there, son. We'll think of something." She lapsed into silence. "C'mon, let's get back inside, enjoy some company while we can."

Ina patted Lennie on the back as they were walking back towards the gatehouse, "You'll do fine," she said.

Lennie flinched from the contact and, frowning deeply he looked at Ina trying to work out what she was talking about.

They walked back into the brightly lit gatehouse, the lively chatter within broke over their heads like a wave on a warm beach. Ina stood for a few seconds watching humanity at its most banal, and yet at the same time most profound. Eventually she clapped her hands loudly, the chatting ebbed to silence. "I reckon we should all head back down to the canteen," she said. "There's more room there, and we can all sit and have a nice cup of tea." Ina looked to Joe and Fiona. "Have you eaten? There's plenty food. And Stella and I are not bad cooks, even if I do say so myself. Eh lads?" Ina looked to Angus, Calum, and Kenny.

"Aye," Kenny answered, "They make a mean slice breakfast." Angus and Calum nodded in agreement.

Ina walked in silence beside Lennie as they watched the backs of the others bobbing down the corridor chatting to each other on their way towards the canteen.

Chapter 27

Zombie Mac revelled in the power it felt coursing through its system as it ran at the head of its huge hoard chasing the taxi containing the much sought-after human flesh. Being surrounded by its army of zombies, Mac had started to become aware of certain things. It noted that the zombies all followed its lead when he brayed angrily. It noted that the hoard appeared to be following it.

As Mac and its hoard tracked the route of the taxi Mac saw the Homerton estate. There would be pickings to be had there, it could smell them. Mac experimented, it tried to communicate with its army of zombies. It directed them to enter the estate. It didn't need to direct them what to do once they were in the estate, it knew they would infect, or consume, everyone they came across.

Without exception the zombies did exactly what Mac directed, they flooded into the estate, howling their arrival. Directed by their acute sense of smell they systematically sought out houses that contained uncontaminated human beings. The zombies had gained a certain amount of cunning from their previous experiences. They were able to coordinate their attacks. They had learned to recognise when doors were beginning to weaken and to then to intensify their efforts. They had learned that by coordinated perseverance they could penetrate even the most solid door. It didn't take long for the remaining surviving residents of the Homerton estate to be either killed and eaten, or infected, Mac's army continued to grow.

Ian Ferguson had taken to being a zombie as an addict takes to crack, it was ferocious, and it wielded its ferocity as a treasured lethal weapon. Dave zombie was systematic, clinical, and brutal. Zombie Ian seemed to prefer it when its victim had immunity. When it detected an unfortunate individual with immunity it frenzied. It became a tornado of clawing, biting, punching, kicking, and it always ended up ripping their poor, defeated bodies completely to bits. Zombie Ian then relished its victory by stuffing its mouth with bloody hearts, entrails, and livers. Zombie Ian looked like a crazed, demented butcher let loose in an abattoir.

Zombie Mac marched ungainly down Homerton High Street, watching its zombies decimating the estate. It grinned like an insane despotic General, relishing the most heinous war crime. Zombie Mac brayed loudly into the darkness of the night, its army followed its example and, as one, they unleashed the loudest most insane howl that echoed eerily up and down the valley.

Chapter 28

The Diamond crew demolished the food that was presented to them. Most of others, having recently eating, just enjoyed another cup of tea. Angus made repeated visits to the toilet, and completely zoned out from any form of sociability, his DF118's were disappearing fast. Innes and Robert enthusiastically partook of the alcohol they had liberated from the Diamond.

Finishing her food, Fiona sipped at her tea, she looked around at the others, most of whom seemed to be behaving like this was a social event. Coughing to clear her throat she spoke up loud and clear. "We should start getting ready for a fight. If those things….," her face spoke of her disgust, "…..make it up here, then we'll need to be ready for them."

Fiona's succinct speech caused instant silence, various faces assumed expressions of gravity as reality dawned, (Angus, Kenny, and Robert were exceptions to the rule). Christine felt surprised and awed that a girl Fiona's age could be so forthright with a group of adults. Lennie noticed Ina looking pointedly at him, he cleared his throat and spoke up, "She's right. I reckon we need to do a recce of the building; find some weapons and stuff that we can use in a fight."

Ina followed his lead, "Yes indeed. We could do with a lot more weapons, solid but easy to wield would be good. Protective suits and gloves would be excellent too if there are any."

Joe piped up, "I know the place well. I used to do portering. I know the stores and where all the tools are." Joe looked at Kenny. "You should come with me. You know the place as well."

Kenny was feeling nice after his small glass of methadone, he had missed what Joe said but he pulled a serious face, and nodded his head, as that seemed like it would be an appropriate response.

Lennie asked if Joe needed any more help.

"Naw, it's awright. I'll find my trolley and pile everything onto it, Lennie. Thanks."

Kenny picked up the gist of what was happening.

Kenny and Joe went to find the trolley. Joe waited until they were out of earshot of the others. "So how do you know Lennie and Angus then Kenny?"

"Call him Gaff Joe, everybody does."

"Well, Gaff looks completely out of it if you ask me." Joe studied Kenny closely.

Kenny didn't really know how to answer this. So he ignored him.

"You know Kenny, it's really none of my business if you experiment with drugs. I don't know why you would, but it's none of my business. But them two look like they are on the hard stuff Kenny. You're not on the hard stuff as well are you?"

Kenny thought about what Joe was saying. "So why is it "experimenting with drugs," but drinking is just drinking? And 'just drinking' is alright. Innit? Inny and that other one. What's his name again?" Kenny didn't wait for a name to be supplied. "Them two are fucking blootered. But you're not giving them a hard time are you?"

Joe thought about it, Kenny had a point. Innes and Robert were indeed busy getting drunk, and had been most of the night. The wisdom of which was, of course, questionable. Joe wasn't prepared to let things go though. "But drugs are just wrong Kenny. You know that son? Right?"

"So how is it you're supposed to tell what's "Right" and what's "Wrong" then Joe? Who decides that? You? Society? The Church? The way I see it there's a lot of things that used to be wrong are right now, and vice versa. And who's to say that won't change again in the future." Kenny thought about what the future might be. "And in case you hadn't noticed Joe, the world has completely gone to shite. How are you supposed to know what's right and wrong when you have to bash in the head of a wee old man that's turned into a zombie? I killed Ina's husband you know? That was "right" but it was still murder Joe. Should I be arrested? Stella killed her waste of space partner. Was that wrong?"

Joe thought about the zombie police, and in his mind he saw the wasted face of Bobby Thompson as his zombie corpse lay lifeless in his arms. They walked on in silence. "I just worry about you Kenny. I worry about my kids." He paused, "At least, I used to worry about the world my kids were growing up in." He laughed hard. "I don't suppose I need to worry about that anymore. Do I?"

Kenny laughed with him.

Joe sighed, "Bobby Thompson's dead by the way. He was a zombie. Fiona finished him off."

"Sorry to hear that Joe. But it's best they don't carry on living as zombies."

Joe thought about all the zombies he had gleefully killed and mown down with the taxi.

They walked on each absorbed in their own thoughts.

In the canteen, Lennie looked round the room at the expectant faces, his mind was going into overdrive, in truth he had never felt more alive, engaged. Ina had told him that now was the time to plan, and he had numerous ideas about what needed doing. "Fiona, take Calum……..," (Lennie had forgotten their names, so he just pointed at Dennis and Christine), "………and them two. Youse need to keep guard at the front gate. At the first sign of any zombies send a runner to raise the alarm. Ok?"

Fiona just nodded. Christine silently fumed as she knew Lennie had forgotten her and her brothers' names. She noted that he hadn't forgotten Fiona's name.

"Barbara, Stella, don't shout at me for this, But can youse two tidy up in here?"

Without complaint about his blatant sexism Barbara and Stella set about their task.

This left Innes, Robert, and Angus. "Ina, could you take………," (again Lennie's memory failed him, and he just pointed at Innes and Robert, who either didn't notice, or didn't care), "……..them two and see if there's anything in the offices that might come in handy." Lennie thought again, "Maybe you can take a look outside, see where our weak points are, and strengths, you know in terms of security and the building and stuff."

Lennie looked hard at Angus; he had completely zoned out. "You can come with me, Gaff," was all he said. Angus didn't look like he had heard.

Ina nodded her head slowly. "Good thinking, Lennie. We're right on it." Ina rose and gestured to Innes and Robert. "Coming lads?" she said.

"Be right with you Ina," Robert said. "Just got to finish my can first," he took a drink.

Ina's mouth smiled at Innes and Robert. Her eyes communicated something completely different. "Now lads," she said quietly.

Innes and Robert stared vacantly at Ina. They realised that the immoveable object of their latent alcoholism had just met an unstoppable force. Robert sneaked a last drink as they rose to do Ina's bidding.

With Robert and Innes following meekly behind her, Ina watched as Kenny and Joe disappeared round the corner heading towards the storeroom. "We'll have a look in the offices I think gentlemen. See what we can see, eh?"

Innes and Robert feigned enthusiasm, and eagerly nodded their assent.

In the canteen, Calum walked awkwardly over to Fiona, who stood ready with her baseball bat. Christine followed suit, with spanner in hand, Dennis copied his sister. They trooped out in the same direction as Ina, Robert, and Innes.

Lennie marched over to Angus. "Coming?" was all he said.

Angus snapped out of his dream. He wasn't sure what Lennie was asking of him, but he realised he was going somewhere. Angus rose unsteadily to his feet and followed Lennie. Lennie followed Fiona and her team towards the gatehouse.

On the way to the gatehouse Christine tried to connect with Fiona again, she got just as snubbed in the refinery as she did in the Diamond. Fiona was monosyllabic.

Following them into the gatehouse, Lennie closed the front door behind Fiona and her team as they ventured out into the car park. "Remember, as soon as you see them let us know," Lennie shouted after them.

"I think we'll remember that ok, Lennie," Fiona said under her breath as they strode out into the car park.

Angus stood swaying, staring vacantly at Lennie through hooded eyes.

"What have you got, Gaff?" Lennie asked directly.

"Don't know what you're talking about Len," Angus felt the hostility coming from Lennie and he was ready to meet it with his habitual, stubborn defiance.

Lennie sighed and flopped onto one of the seats in the gatehouse, Fluffy welcomed the company and leapt onto his lap, purring gently. He absently patted her.

"I can't be bothered with this Gaff." Lennie rubbed his face, "Look Gaff. Me and you have been around long enough. Let's just cut the bullshit. I know you've got something." Lennie began to comprehend the magnitude of the psychological changes that had been taking place within him. "And to be perfectly honest with you. I don't even think I care anymore." Lennie gently placed Fluffy on the floor and stood. He opened the gatehouse front door and looked out. A breeze blew in carrying with it the smell of Greenock as it burned. Lennie turned to face Angus. "All this is way bigger than us Gaff. We need to drop all this petty, druggie shite, and we just need to start getting real."

This wasn't what Angus was expecting at all. He would have been much more comfortable with angry confrontation. Guilt and shame creeped out to twist up his gut, and ruin his buzz. Meekly he sat down.

Lennie continued, "This is probably going to get fucking messy, Gaff. And some of us, maybe all of us, won't make it. And you know something? I always thought if I was going to die, I would want to go as fucked out of my head as possible." Lennie paused, "Thing is Gaff, dying's a very real possibility now. And I don't want to die fucked." Lennie looked at the door leading into the refinery. "There's real people here Gaff, real, dysfunctional, beautiful people. And they need me, they need us Gaff. I reckon this is the first time in my life where anyone has actually needed me, and I think I like it."

Lennie tried to make eye contact with Angus, who kept his head hung. "You know where my meth is, Gaff," Lennie continued. "If you want it that bad, it's yours. But give half to Kenny eh?" Lennie passed Angus as he walked slowly over to the door leading to the refinery. On the threshold he turned to face Angus. "I'm off it Gaff," he said as he closed the door behind him.

Angus sat dumbfounded. He could feel the weight of his near empty pill bottle sitting heavy in his pocket. Angus felt tears come to his eyes. He swallowed his shame down. Angrily he snatched the pill bottle out of his pocket, swallowed the last few remaining pills, and slammed the bottle into a nearby bin. He could feel reality hammering hard at the door of his mind, and he desperately wanted to escape, but there was nowhere to go. Tears threatened his eyes again. Angus left the gatehouse and saw Ina, Innes, and Robert searching nearby offices, they looked like they were nearly done.

As Angus stomped past searching for an empty office Ina noticed the redness in his eyes and face. "I think we're done with the offices," she said to Innes and Robert. "You two should go back to the canteen. Have a well-deserved drink why don't you. I'll check the security situation myself." Of course they needed not a second invitation, they legged it back to the canteen.

Knocking gently on the door, Ina entered the office Angus had gone into. "You ok son?" she asked.

From his prone position, lying on the floor, Angus grunted that he just wanted some rest.

Crouching down beside him, Ina rested a hand gently on his shoulder. "You just remember son. We're all a team now. A team of equals. We need you, just as you need us. None of us will survive this if we don't all stick together. And we'll just take you as you are.

You as you is good enough for us, Angus. Rest easy now, son." Ina patted his shoulder, and left the office.

Angus couldn't hold back the tears anymore, he curled up on the floor and cried quietly. The drugs still in his system, and his emotional distress, lulled him into unconsciousness.

Ina left the refinery, via the gatehouse, to scope out the grounds.

Joe and Kenny rifled through cupboards and bins in the storeroom. Joe had found part of what he was looking for, and was piling his trolley with protective overalls, he had also found gloves with handy grips on them. "I found Mac the Sack knocking one out in here last night, Ken." Joe had come across Jim's stash of pornography. "That's how I got you out last night without being sacked."

Kenny looked at Joe as he rifled through bottles of various chemicals, Kenny briefly wondered why these chemicals had not killed the virus. "You're a rock Joe, you always have been. I know you've been looking out for me since I started here." Like many of the refinery refugees Kenny had also been thinking about his life, his behaviour, and what, if anything, he should do now.

"Thing is Joe," Kenny continued. "Like I said, you're a rock. But I'm not. Way I see it Joe some folks are rocks, and some folks are like water, you know they just go with the flow. I'm like water, Joe."

"What the fuck are you talking about Kenny?"

Kenny continued, "Thing is Joe. It might take time, but water will always destroy rocks. It just wears it down, turns it into sand." Kenny sat. "I need to not wear you, or anyone else, down Joe. It's not fair on anyone."

Joe sat beside Kenny and put an arm around his shoulder. "Sand still is still useful though, Kenny." Joe stood, "And it's pretty." Joe pulled a pose like a ballerina. Kenny smiled. "'Mon son," Joe said, giving Kenny a playful whack on the shoulder. "We need to go get some serious tools."

Kenny sighed and stood, "I reckon this whole zombie thing is just messing with my head."

"Your head was always a fucking mess anyway, Kenny. Let's get some tools."

Outside, at the refinery gate, Christine watched Fiona as she stared intently into the distance looking for the first sign of any zombies. Christine desperately wanted to connect with this person, who clearly had the respect of the grown-ups. Christine wanted what Fiona had.

"So, have you actually seen these things?" Calum asked Dennis.

"Aye, me and my family have been fighting them all day. How come you've not seen them? They're everywhere."

Calum was embarrassed, "I got stuck in a toilet."

Dennis frowned.

"Bad business all this ain't it?" Christine tried again with Fiona.

Fiona grunted.

"You heard anything about your family, Fi? Are they alright?"

In the darkness Fiona's face turned crimson. Burning, she turned to Christine. "My family are all fucking dead ok? That's why I'm here with my uncle Inny and that fucking waste of space Vanie. If my family were still alive I'd be with them. Just like you are, ok?"

Christine shrank back from Fiona's anger and inched away from her. Dennis and Calum gaped silently. Fiona turned back to stare at the road, her breathing shallow and quick.

Then, like a harbinger of doom, they heard the most horrendous, inhuman howling coming from down the road. Their spines tingled. "Calum go raise the alert. That's them. It sounded like it came from the Homerton." Fiona turned to Calum who was rooted to the spot, he had never heard anything so terrifying. "NOW CALUM," Fiona shouted.

Calum snapped out of his fear induced inertia, and sprinted, fast, back to the refinery.

Chapter 29

After he talked with Angus, Lennie sought out other company. He was in the canteen helping Barbara and Stella when they heard the zombies howl. A couple of seconds later Calum's voice rang out through the silent refinery. "IT'S THEM. THEY'RE HERE," he shouted out, terror causing his taut voice to pitch high.

Lennie, Barbara, and Stella dropped what they were doing, Innes and Robert placed their cans carefully on the table. As they ran down the corridor, they saw Kenny and Joe sprinting across the refinery floor to the gatehouse.

Ina was already at the front gate.

Lennie and the others ran to them. "Where are they?" Lennie asked.

"Can't see them yet Lennie," Fiona answered, "But they just let loose a huge roar."

"I think we all heard it," Ina said.

"I reckon it came from the Homerton. So they're near," Fiona said peering into the distance.

"How long do you reckon we've got?" Lennie asked.

"Hard to say," Stella replied, "It would probably be about an hour and a half walk if you followed the road. Do they run?"

"Aye, they run," Joe said remembering them at the crossroads. "But they're not very fast. I reckon they'd probably walk. It looks to me like they only run when they're chasing someone."

"But we don't know for sure that they're going to come here, right?" Calum asked hopefully.

"They're coming," Fiona killed his hope.

"We've got to get ready then." Lennie looked round at the group. "Where's Gaff?" he asked.

"He's having a wee lay down in one of the offices," Ina said, "He looked worn out poor boy."

"Me and Kenny will get the weapons," Joe said. "'Mon Ken." They jogged back to the refinery.

"Right, everybody back in," Lennie said. "Ina, are you sure all the doors are secure."

"Aye Lennie, I checked them all. They're as safe as houses." Ina replied.

"Unfortunately, most of the houses we've seen have proved to be anything but safe from them things," Barbara warned.

They all trooped back into the gatehouse. "Youse head on down to the canteen, I'll go check on Gaff," Lennie said.

Lennie watched as they all trooped down to the canteen. He was struck by how such a strange group of people had been thrown together in such unlikely circumstances. Lennie was well aware that he would most definitely qualify as strange. He felt scared and, since the ferocious howl of the zombies, self-doubt had started to manifest itself in his mind. He feared for their very survival, and doubted his ability to adopt the mantle of leader, that appeared to have been thrust upon him. Shaking his head to try to clear the clouds, he turned and found the office Angus was asleep in. It was the only one that was in darkness.

Lennie left the lights off. He crouched down beside Angus and gently shook him, "Gaff. They're coming."

Angus mumbled something incoherent.

Lennie shook him harder. "Gaff you need to get up pal. You're needed."

Angus turned over, sat up and ruefully rubbed his face. "I'm not so sure about that Len. I'm not that sure I'm that much use to anyone right now."

Lennie sat back and crossed his legs. "Gaff, things out there are fucked up. And by the sounds of things they're going to get a whole heap worse. And the reality is, we might not make it pal. But I can tell you one thing Gaff. If we're going down, we're sure as fuck going to go down fighting. I'm not for giving up. And even though you might be a complete cunt, I'm not for giving up on you either. Now get the fuck up and let's get ready to kill some fucking zombies." Lennie kicked Gaff on the foot.

Angus laughed, "Lennie you're as mad as a fucking loon." He stood and stretched; his belly hung over the waist of his trousers. "Fuck it, let's go do this then Len."

Lennie's craggy face broke into a broad smile. He walked with Angus out of the office, and down the corridor to the canteen. Ina was in the middle of reorganising the canteen furniture when they entered.

"We just need one big square table with thirteen seats round it. From now on we are one team folks ok?" She was directing the men to do the lifting and shifting. Angus joined them to help. Lennie stood beside Ina.

"Is he ok?" Ina asked quietly.

"Aye, he'll be fine," Lennie replied.

Joe and Kenny appeared with a trolley full of solid looking tools and protective clothing. Lennie went over to inspect the tools. "We need to gaffer tape the handles, so they don't slip."

"No worries, I know where the gaffer tape is," Joe jogged off to get it.

Stella and Barbara were busy making tea, and plating up piles of biscuits.

As Joe returned the rearrangement of the furniture was done. "Inny, Rab, give us a hand taping these handles eh?" Joe asked. Innes and Robert joined him, and they set about the job. Everybody else sat round the table as tea and biscuits were dispensed. A silence descended. Eventually all eyes ended up looking at Lennie. Lennie looked incredibly uncomfortable. He took a deep breath, "So where do we want to meet them? Do we go out to meet them on the streets? At the gate? What do we think?"

Joe stopped in the middle of taping a wrench. "Meeting on the streets is a bad idea. They could outflank us there, and we'd end up surrounded."

"That happened to us at the Diamond, and if it wasn't for Joe we'd have been fucked," said Innes.

"I don't fancy meeting them at the gate either," said Fiona. "They'd break down that fence in minutes. Then it's the same deal. We'd be surrounded."

"The way the refinery is set up at the back is probably the best," Ina piped up. There's a wall just beyond the loading bays so they can't surround us. We could fight them from the loading bay closest to the back wall."

"Loading bays it is then," Lennie decided. "Stella, can we light up the car park?"

"Aye, there's floodlights. You can turn them on from the gatehouse." Stella thought about how to protect the refinery from incursions. "There's metal shutters you can pull down at the gatehouse door too. Should stop them getting in at the front, for a while at least."

"Right," Lennie lapsed into silence, he had been thinking of a strategy. Eventually he continued, "I reckon what we'll do is this. We'll take them on at the loading bays. We'll have nine out fighting in a line. We'll have two of us guarding the loading bays in case any strays break through the fighting line, they need to *not* get into this refinery. And, if we can, we should have two people indoors resting. We can rotate the guards and resters." Lennie looked around at the raggle taggle bunch. "I reckon we'll all need to take rests."

Calum raised his hand.

"You don't need to raise your hand Calum, just speak up," Lennie told him.

"Err, can we not just sit it out in here? Maybe they'll just go away?" Calum smiled nervously, hopefully.

Kenny piped up, "Ahm afraid not Calum. They'll get in somehow. And they're not going to go away. They'll just keep at it till either they get in, or we go mad. There's no getting away from it, we need to fight it out."

"Can we not just run now?" understandably Calum desperately wanted to avoid fighting zombies.

"I'm not running," Fiona said. "I'm fighting."

"It's a good plan Lennie." Ina wanted to move on from the conversation of avoidance, she was proud of Lennie. "Now if you lot don't mind. I'm going to follow Gaff's lead and go and get some rest before it all kicks off. I suggest you all do the same. Now would be a good time to conserve some energy, we're going to need it."

Christine had a thought, "We should have some bottles of water and some kind of snacks in the loading bay, at the resting bit."

"Excellent idea, errrrr........," Lennie said.

"Christine," she informed him of her name. "And my brother is called Dennis."

"Errr, excellent idea Christine." Lennie smiled at her, unfortunately Lennie's smile did not make him look any less mad. "Can you and Dennis sort that out now then?" he asked.

Even though Lennie was clearly mad, Christine bristled with pride. "No probs Lennie."

"I'll give you a hand." Barbara was also proud of her daughter. "Do we all need to fight Lennie? Or can the little ones just stay indoors?" Barbara put in a last pitch effort to protect her children.

"We're fighting mam, no arguments," Dennis let her know this was not negotiable.

Christine, Dennis, and Barbara piled snacks and water onto the trolley alongside the protective equipment.

"We should make sure there are spare weapons in the resting area as well," Fiona said, remembering how she dropped her spanner when she came face to face with the zombie of her mother. Fiona's eyes were fire.

"We'll sort that out Fi." Innes nodded to Joe who nodded back. They continued to gaffer tape the tools.

"Me and Stella will sit in the gatehouse," Lennie announced. Stella nodded. "We'll let you all know when they get here. Ina's right go and rest," Lennie said as he stood up. The meeting was over, the plan was set. They had done all they could to prepare, the outcome was now in the lap of whatever Gods there were.

Innes and Joe finished gaffer taping a pile of solid tools, they piled them onto the trolley.

They filed out of the canteen chatting amongst themselves, calm, determined, and completely petrified. Joe took his trolley to deposit it in the loading bay chosen for their last stand. Stella grabbed another packet of cold meat from the fridge and followed Lennie and the others down the corridor towards the gatehouse.

Chapter 30

Fluffy greeted Stella with a mew of affection as she and Lennie walked into the gatehouse together.

"I'm going to go have a look outside," Lennie said. "See if there is any sign of them. You coming with me?" Lennie felt like a schoolboy, his skin was crawling with embarrassment as he talked to Stella.

Stella attended to her cat who was purring and rubbing her face against her leg. "Aye. Will do Lennie. Just let me feed wee one first eh?"

Fluffy welcomed her food as always. Stella and Lennie stepped outside into the warm night. They walked over to the gate and stared out at the empty street. There was no sign of the zombies, for the moment the night was silent and peaceful.

Despite the heat of the night Stella shivered, she looked back at the refinery. "We're back where this all started then. What do you think happened Lennie?"

Lennie hadn't really thought about this, up until now his life had always been about his immediate needs, he'd never really had any reason to think about things like consequences, actions, reactions, cause, and effect. "Was probably the Government trying to poison us," was the best he could come up with. Paranoid thinking had become second nature to Lennie.

"Why would they do that though?"

"They've never liked the Scots much. We're too arsy."

"Nah. Government are a bunch of wankers. But this is just pure evil. God knows who could be responsible for something like this."

"All I'm really thinking about is getting through it all, to be honest with you Stella." Lennie stared down the street, but his mind was elsewhere. Lennie was trying to catch up with thoughts, feelings, ideas, and circumstances that were all previously completely unthinkable. "I think for the first time in my life I am realising just how precious life is, to be honest. And that all I have really done is take it all very much for granted."

Stella looked at Lennie, she was surprised by his candour. "Wee Ina has decided you're our leader."

"Aye, I know. I made the mistake of telling Gaff and Kenny I was in the TA once."

"This'll be a test of your training then. This is a test for us all I reckon. I suppose I was doing the same thing as you. Taking things for granted. You know, not taking responsibility for my life, my choices." Stella remembered all the abuse she suffered at the hands of John Reid. "I never, ever got to do just what I wanted to do. I've never really had the chance to just be me." Stella felt all the years of impotent anger rise. "I just accepted shite as my lot, and never once tried to do something about it." Stella laughed, "And it took an outbreak of zombies to finally set me free. How mad is that?"

Lennie smiled, "My life, before all this stuff. It wasn't living, it was just existing day to day, hour to hour. It's taken all this to make me think that I am actually in charge of how my life is going to be. It's just that, as it happens, the rest of my life just might be incredibly short. But I'm going to be in charge of it. And I think that's all that really matters just now."

"Aye, it's a sair fecht right enough Lennie. But it's a fight that's worth having I reckon." Stella sighed, "Should I go get the lights on now then?"

Lennie brought himself back to the here and now, there was still many things that needed to be done. "Naw, I reckon we should dub up the gatehouse now though. But we'll leave the lights off for the moment. Don't want to guide them here. With a bit of luck they might not come after all. Who knows?"

"I don't think you're as mad as people make out you know, Lennie Wilson," Stella said as she took his arm to walk slowly back to the refinery gatehouse. Lennie hoped the night was dark enough to hide his blush.

Fluffy was happily grooming herself on top of one of the desks when they returned. Stella went to the electrics panel and flicked the switch to bring down the metal shutters of the gatehouse. "All these switches are clearly labelled if you need them and I'm not here, Lennie. Stella patted her cat on the head, "What am I going to do with you now wee madam?" Stella asked Fluffy.

"What do you mean?" Lennie asked. Lennie had assumed that the question was just as much for him as it was for Fluffy.

Stella felt a lump rise in her throat, her voice cracked as she answered. "Well I don't want to leave her locked up in here in case……you know," Stella left the details of the 'in case' unspoken. She opened the door that led into the refinery, and wedged it open with a fire extinguisher. "You go explore the factory my wee love. If anything happens, and I don't come back, find a way out and get yourself a nice place where you can live and be happy." By the end of this speech tears were flowing down her cheeks. Lennie was also filling up. Lennie had not cried for a long time.

Lennie reached for Stella and held her tight. She cried into his chest. He waited until her crying started to subside. "I've got to go do something Stella." He held her by the shoulders and looked directly in the eyes, "Will you be alright?"

Stella wiped away her tears. "Yeah, I'm probably going to follow Fluffy around make sure she's alright until, you know......" again Stella left the rest unsaid.

Fluffy sniffed her way around the refinery, heading in the direction of the canteen.

Lennie located his rucksack and took out the sock containing the last bottle of methadone. In the first darkened office he saw Innes and Robert drinking wine, Fiona was stretched out on the floor beside them with her eyes closed. In the next one the Dunlops all lay holding each other, eyes closed. In the next one Ina was sat on a chair with her eyes closed, she looked peaceful. Calum sat on the floor next to her with his eyes wide open, he looked nervous.

Angus and Kenny were in the next one, they lay side by side and looked like they were drifting away.

Lennie knocked at the door and entered. "Lads," he announced himself. "Are youse awake?"

"Aye, aye captain. Bright eyed and bushy tailed Lennie," Angus replied as he sat up, he still looked very stoned.

"Just resting my eyes, Lennie," Kenny said as he raised himself to his elbows.

Lennie sat between them; he passed the sock containing the methadone bottle to Gaff. He turned to face Kenny. "I've told Gaff this already Kenny, but I'm aff it. I've told Gaff he needs to share the rest of my meth with you though."

Angus coughed, "I've been thinking about this. Kenny, I've kinda been holding out on you."

Kenny just blinked.

Angus continued, "I found a bottle of DF118's in Stella's. I've been necking them all night." Angus passed the methadone to Kenny, "You have it all." As he was making this gesture the howling beast of his addiction was berating him for this needless act of generosity.

Kenny took the bottle, "What do you mean you're off it, Lennie?"

Lennie stared off into space, "I don't really know why to be honest. I've just been, I don't know, I've been woken up I suppose. All this has just made me think about things, and how I really want things to be. I just don't want to be so fucking numb all the time now. Even if it is only for the next however long."

"I know what you mean Lennie," Kenny replied, "I was just saying to Joe that this whole thing is making me think about stuff." Kenny plopped the methadone bottle out of the sock. "But there's no way in the world I'm going out there to meet them things without something in my system." Kenny necked half of the methadone and passed the other half to Angus. "Here Gaff, I appreciate the gesture 'n all but you were right back in the flat. I don't need as much as you. But next time you come across something I want in ok?"

Angus laughed, "Deal, Kenny. You're alright you know Ken." Angus offered the other half of the methadone bottle to Lennie, "You sure Len? It's yours if you want it?"

The desperate demon of his addiction begged him to grab the bottle and finish it, but he pushed it away. "It's all yours Gaff." Lennie stood and smiled, "I'll leave you two love birds to your dreams. I'll give you a shout when it's time, eh?"

Lennie went back to the gatehouse, dwelling on the battle within, and the battle soon to come. He could hear Stella in the canteen, her voice echoing down the empty corridor as she chatted to her cat.

Wandering into the gatehouse Lennie grabbed the first thing he could find to read as a distraction. He sat at a desk scanning the handover notes. Putting down the clipboard he closed his eyes and breathed deeply. He could feel the first warning signs that opiate withdrawals were on their way. His skin felt tingly, and he felt cold and shivery. He decided that his strategy would be to just observe what was happening in his body, to detach, or remove his core being from the symptoms he would soon be suffering. Lennie had never experienced withdrawals before. His heroin habit had never been huge, and he had always managed to get by on scraps, but he had heard all the graphic horror stories. He decided he would just ignore all those stories and observe the happenings in his body as they arrived. He made a safe place for himself at his core, his decision to stop would be his inviolable centre. He knew that as long as his core remained intact, as long as his decision to stop remained sacrosanct, he would be alright. He remembered how good it felt to hold Stella, he decided that Stella would be in his core. He would build his core from principles, and fill it with things other than the all-consuming narcissism of addiction. He thought about Ina and her obvious faith in him, even though she clearly thought him mad. He placed Ina gratefully in his core. Lennie thought about his friends, old and new, and how he would now only be honest in his dealings with them, those that survived. He thought about Fiona, and how he would treat her, and the others only with the greatest respect. Lennie decided he would fight like a bastard to protect every one of the refinery refugees.

Lennie's heart sank, he could hear the zombies coming. The faint sound of their inhuman grunting and moaning grew louder, and louder as they slouched their way inevitably towards the refinery. Lennie waited, he wanted to give his people as long he could to enjoy their peaceful reposes. He waited until he could hear the creatures crunching the gravel in the car park. He took a deep breath, stood in the gatehouse refinery doorway, and shouted, "THEY'RE

HERE." His voice reverberated round the empty refinery.

The office doors flew open. Stella came running from the canteen. Fluffy stayed where she was.

They gathered in silence in the gatehouse listening to the sound of their nemeses gathering. The first zombie reached the gatehouse shutters and commenced its predictable pounding. It was soon joined by a plethora of others.

"Can you get onto the roof here?" Lennie asked quietly. "I want to see how many there are."

"Aye, there's a staircase in the last loading bay takes you up there," Joe replied, he gulped down his fear.

"Time to hit the lights Stella, please," Lennie requested.

Stella flicked the switch and light from the spotlights seeped through chinks in the gatehouse shutters. Lennie took a deep breath, "Let's go see them. Lead the way Joe, eh?"

Stella got the roof keys from a cupboard in the gatehouse and lobbed them to Joe.

They jogged to the loading bay, each lost in their own thoughts and feelings. Barbara ran close to her children. They tramped up the steps, and, after fumbling with the keys, Joe eventually managed to open the roof door. They trod carefully up to the edge of the flat roof and stood at the wall at the edge, they looked out at the vision of hell that was marching their way towards them.

Calum had never seen the zombies. Until now it had only been a story for him, a scary story, but a story no less. The story was now a reality and it shocked him badly. Kenny stood beside him and put his arm round his shoulders. "They go down with a good head shot, Calum. They're not people, they're cunts. They're cunts that have stolen our friends and neighbours. We can provide our friends with peace. Just do what you can and stay safe alright?" Kenny stared out at the zombies, wondering where in the hell his words had just come from. Calum stood a little taller.

The end of the stream of zombies that was trudging their way towards them could not be seen. The zombie river seemed endless. The refinery refugees were rocked to the core, none more so than Lennie. The fight had, until now, been largely theoretical, now it was real, fear and self-doubt completely overwhelmed him. He started to slowly step back, to detach himself from the group. Ina noticed his retreat. She inched her way towards him. "You ok, Lennie?" she asked.

"Err. Aye, Ina. I'm ok. I mean it's not great is it, but I'm alright," he stammered. Lennie did not sound ok.

"It's scary son. Of course it is. But we'll all do what we can do. If our best is not good enough, then so be it. You'll be alright though son. You're TA trained remember?" Ina laughed a little.

"Ina, my 'TA training' was marching round the Battery Park wi a plank of wood instead of a gun. How the fuck is that supposed to prepare me for this." Lennie felt naked panic start to overwhelm him.

"Cometh the hour, cometh the man, Lennie Wilson. And at this moment son, you are the man." Ina looked Lennie in the eye. "I for one believe in you Lennie. And I suspect I'm not the only one. We'll be alright. You'll be alright. You just need to believe it son." Ina gave Lennie a hug then left him to think.

"We need to get out there now and face them," Robert spoke. "We need to get out the back before they start to pile up too much." Robert looked at Ina, "And let me tell you Ina, I'm fucking having a swally before I head out there."

Ina laughed and hugged Robert and Innes. "You go for it chaps." Ina looked at them all. "Robert is right though. We just need to go do this."

They took one last look at the madness marauding towards them and turned to tramp down the steps to the loading bays that were to be their last location of sanctuary.

Chapter 31

Joe silently handed out the protective overalls and gloves. As he handed the equipment out to his family, he made eye contact with them, sickening dread gripped his throat.

Focused, Fiona was dressed and ready before anyone else.

Innes and Robert passed a bottle of wine between them as they dressed. The sight of the zombies had such a sobering effect on them that the wine they drank did little but provide them with a modicum of Dutch courage.

Kenny and Angus looked determined, and managed a few silly jokes, mostly about how mad they looked with their white overalls and gloves.

Calum trembled badly as he dressed, he fumbled putting on his gloves, and dropped them repeatedly, his jangling nerves had fried his mind.

Lennie and Stella silently watched the others as they got ready themselves.

Ina dressed quickly, and went to help Calum. "Just take lots of deep breaths. You'll be fine, son. Just hang back and watch us first and join in when you feel ready. Ok?" she smiled warmly.

"Right, grab yourself a weapon when you're ready people, "Lennie barked. He and Stella went to the weapon pile and grabbed a couple of solid looking spanners. Innes decided to retain his crowbar. Robert and the Dunlops grabbed new weapons, and piled spares near the loading bay doors. Fiona chose to keep her baseball bat as her weapon of choice.

Christine and Dennis strategically placed water and snacks near the door. They made sure the refreshments were well away from the weapons. They didn't want someone grabbing the wrong thing and ending up running out to attack a zombie with a mars bar or a bottle of water.

Ina guided Calum to the pile of weapons. "Try a few out, and pick one that just feels right." Ina proceeded to do exactly what she had just told Calum to do, she found one that suited her. Calum picked up and waved a few about before settling on a hammer.

"Now, when you swing make sure you're balanced, bend your knees a bit and lower your centre of gravity. "Ina demonstrated; her spanner swung in graceful arc's as she moved with ease through each swing. Calum tried a few swings. All eyes were on Ina, and a few of the others practiced swinging their weapons the way she suggested. "Keep breathing deeply, and try not to panic. They are stupid and will behave stupidly. Keep your mind clear and focus on the next swing. Always try for a head shot, but don't forget about defence. Always keep your eyes on their mouths and make sure you use your weapon for defence, not your arms." Ina picked up another weapon, so she had one in each hand. "I'm going to go for two weapons, but you should do whatever you are comfortable with." Though she was essentially talking to Calum, she was aware that everyone was paying close attention to her. Lennie, Stella, and Joe tried out two weapons and, after a few trial swings, decided they would give it a go.

The initial flush of zombies made it round the corner, they announced their unwelcome presence by banging predictably on the first loading bay door. The racket they made rolled like thunder through the empty refinery.

The refinery refugees stook in a circle, their fate was literally just round the corner. "Any last words, Lennie?" Ina asked, she exuded calm. Her obvious ease helped everyone else maintain at least some level of composure.

Lennie stammered, "Errrr, I suppose we just need to go out and fucking bash some zombie heads." Lennie struggled to think straight. Just standing next to Stella was causing him to get an erection. Lennie was completely baffled as to why his body should behave in such an inopportune way. It had been many years since Lennie had had an erection, and unfortunately his state of tumescence had fried his already somewhat fragile mind.

Ina looked at Stella. "Stella love, have you got anything you'd like to say?"

Similar to the others, Stella had been lost in her own thoughts, contemplating her own mortality and what her life meant to her. She looked round at the circle of expectant, anxious faces.

Stella just opened her mouth and let what was there come out. "You know, before tonight, to be honest, my life had been nothing but misery." She looked at Lennie. "You were right, Lennie. My partner was a prick. He used to beat me senseless." Stella felt no shame in admitting this in front of all these people, some of whom she hardly knew. "This place," she looked round the loading bay. "This refinery, was the only place I ever got any respite away from him."

Stella stood tall. "And now, no matter what happens tonight, I know I am finally free. And I can honestly say, despite what's waiting for us outside there, I am, at this moment in time, truly happy." A few tears trickled down her face; she was not the only one shedding a tear. "If this is the end of it for me, for us, then I couldn't have picked better people to spend my last few hours with." Stella looked sideways at Lennie. "Now let's just go and bash some fucking zombie heads."

As the other twelve howled a resounding "*Ye-Ha*" cheer, and the zombies continued to moan and pound the doors, Lennie smiled. "Couldn't have put it better myself," he said.

They all turned and, standing in a row side by side, they faced the door. "We all go out fighting first," Lennie issued some last-minute instructions. "Then Christine and Dennis," Lennie looked at them to make sure they got the message. "You drop back and rest first. Calum and Gaff, you drop back and guard the refinery after we push the first flush far enough away. Not one of them fuckers is getting in here tonight," Lennie had fire in his eyes. "Joe, open the fucking doors."

Joe pressed the button to raise the roller doors. As they inched upwards, adrenaline flooded the fighters systems. As the doors slowly rose, so did the noise of the zombies. "Come ahead ya manky fuckers," Angus growled, he was ready for a fight.

The zombies smelt their targets; the smell set off a series of braying howls.

"*MANKY CUNTS. MANKY CUNTS.*" Angus started to chant loudly to counter the cries of the howling zombies. One by one the chant was taken up by the others. Eventually even Barbara joined in. Looking at her children chanting she laughed and chanted louder.

Finally the door reached a level that allowed the first zombies to duck under, but by ducking they left their heads vulnerable to attack. They were easily dispatched by the more experienced zombie battlers in the group.

Realising there were victims to be had, more and more zombies piled round the side of the refinery, sludging their way towards the loading bays.

Inching inexorably upwards, the doors reached head hight. Ina flew at the front few zombies swinging both arms like a ninja warrior. The zombies dropped; pole axed. Side by side, Stella and Lennie swung rhythmically and picked off the few zombies Ina missed.

The door reached the top, no one noticed. The zombies tried desperately to flood into the loading bay, but they were met by an impenetrable wall of focused fighters. Joe and Barbara wore ferociously angry faces as they protected their children. Dennis and Christine picked off any zombies that their parents missed. Angus and Kenny marched forward slaying zombies, prodding, and pushing them back. Slowly but surely the line of fighters established themselves just outside the loading bay. They pushed and prodded and killed their way further and further away from the refinery. The integrity of the refinery remained inviolable.

As Ina had told him to do, Calum held back. The thought of killing something, anything, especially something that was humanoid had horrified him. When he saw how nakedly aggressive and evil looking the zombies were, his scruples soon vanished. He saw how successful the fighting force were, and it gave him the confidence he needed to start doing his bit. He tentatively started to take down zombies.

Calum spotted what they needed to do, strategically. He saw that, to preserve the integrity of the refinery, they would need to fight along the wall that led out from the refinery to the perimeter fence. By fighting along the wall and curving round at an angle they could block the zombies from gaining access to the refinery. Then they could start to move down the length of the building pushing the zombies back. He saw that faint heart was going to be of no use to either him, or these people, who were fighting fiercely for their lives. Zombies clearly didn't care about rules or propriety, he owed them no respect. Calum raised his ferocity level to match the other battlers.

Slowly but surely they managed to swing round and clear their loading bay entrance; the refinery had still not been breached. Christine and Dennis fell back as per their instructions. Panting hard they stood level with the refinery door and watched the fighting progress. Christine looked at her brother and laughed hysterically, "That was fucking mental."

Infected by her laughter, as he watched his parents mow down zombies, Dennis giggled. "Manky cunts," he shouted, they both roared with laughter.

Angus and Calum dropped back. "We'll follow the line," Angus shouted to Calum. "We'll pick off any that get through."

Calum nodded. They watched for any potential breaches, and pounced in to assist when a weakness threatened the integrity of the fighting line. No zombies managed to get past this fearsome, fighting force. The line marched slowly onwards. The fighters had found a killing rhythm and the zombie bodies were piling up.

Ina's weapons seemed to whirl with the minimum of effort, her energies were thus conserved, and not a single movement was wasted, with every swing she scored a kill. Ina was breathing hard, but she was proving to be incredibly fit. A few of the others started to look like they were flagging. Angus stepped up and shouted at Robert to rest. Calum did the same for Kenny. Christine and Dennis stepped up to take the place of the guards.

Robert and Kenny staggered back into the refinery, they grabbed as many bottles of water as they could and piled them as near the fighting line as they dared. The fighting line remained unyielding, inching forward steadily.

As they caught their breath, Robert and Kenny drank deeply. Robert laughed hysterically as he looked at the water bottle. "Water? And it tastes good! Who knew?"

Kenny laughed, drank, and watched the battle intently. Some zombies seemed to be more fired up, more vicious that others, but they were easily spotted and more often than not Ina dispatched them easily.

Stepping carefully over their kills the fighting line eventually reached the far wall of the refinery. They had made it past all the loading bays. Lennie and Barbara swapped for Christine and Dennis.

Panting heavily as she swapped places with her children, Barbara shouted to them, "Stay safe please children." It broke her heart to watch her children face up to the relentless zombie attack, but she was reconciled that the only way they would survive this was if they all played their part.

As Lennie lurched past, Kenny waved his bottle of water at him. "Make sure you get some water, Len," he shouted.

"It's still fucking Lennie to you, ya prick," Lennie shouted and laughed as he flopped to the ground, grabbing a bottle on his way down.

Barbara never took her eyes off her children as they matched the other fighters in ferocity and accuracy, she was astounded, scared and incredibly proud.

"Hold the line," Ina shouted. They halted, held their line, and relaxed the pace a little. The stream of zombies was never ending, but the fighting line held firm. Innes and Stella dropped back to be replaced. They held the line until all fighters had had a chance to take a break, and replenish their energy with water and Mars Bars.

An ugly, growling face floated out of the melee of zombies, biting at Robert as he fought. "Fucking John McClelland ya prick. I should piss on you again," Robert shouted as he swung his weapon to release John from his viral invader.

Zombie Mac had been watching events unfold from the back of its hoard. Its primal brain informed it that things were not going well, it barged its way through the middle of the hoard. Its zombie army had been decimated. As it got nearer the front-line, zombie Mac had clear line of sight of the people who were beating its army. It recognised Joe and Kenny instantly. Fury exploded in Mac; this fury spread like another virus throughout the remains of the zombie army. Mac let loose a vengeful howl and fought frantically to get to its mortal enemies. With pure rage flowing through it, the zombie hoard frenzied. For the first time the zombies started to push back the fighting line.

"ALL HANDS. ALL HANDS. ALL HANDS." Lennie shouted desperately as the zombie assault threatened to swamp them. The two guards and resters were already on their way. The zombie frenzy had sparked the atmosphere like lightning. You could almost smell the anger.

"THIS IS IT PEOPLE," Ina shouted, as she moved up a gear. Her whirling weapons unleashed a torrent of zombie death. "IT'S DO OR DIE TIME," she yelled.

The fighting line naturally adopted a V shape that led Ina, at the front, closer to zombie Mac, as it desperately tried to get to Joe and Kenny. Ina spotted Mac as the focal point of this wave of fury, she whirled through the zombies like a vengeful tornado. Zombie Mac brought the remnants of its hoard to bear down on this elderly dispenser of zombie death. The fighting line wobbled and started to break up as Mac tried to isolate Ina, Innes and Robert stuck to her side defending her from attacks as she crept closer to Mac. Ina tripped, stumbled, and started to go down. Mac roared in triumph as he leapt to grab at her crumpling body. At the last minute, as Mac was about to land its prize, Ina curled and rolled between the zombies legs. Overbalancing, Mac fell face first on the ground; Ina was up and stable in a shot. She jumped and landed on Macs back and brought both her weapons down hard on the balding crown of zombie Mac. It's head smashed to bits as its brains spewed out of its caved in skull.

The reduction in the zombies' fury was instant. Without their leader their frenzy fizzled and died, except for two other zombies who held onto their frenzied state and intensified their violent efforts. Zombie Ian and zombie Dave leapt at Ina. With a brute force that would have destroyed concrete, zombie Ian head butted Ina, her nose exploded, and she dropped, cold. Calum leapt into the fray and grabbed her. He dragged her out as Innes and Robert turned to attack Fergie and Dave. Innes and Robert, like the rest of the fighters were completely exhausted by now. Zombies don't feel fatigue. Kenny and Angus joined Innes and Robert to batter weakly at Dave and Ian. They still didn't go down.

The fighting line had finally been broken. Tired fighters were all getting isolated in their own separate battles. Calum ran back to the refinery with the unconscious body of Ina slung over his shoulders. He placed her safely just inside the loading bay and washed the blood off her face. Calum remembered the recovery position from his health awareness training, and managed to get her into a rough approximation of it. Picking his weapon back up Calum guarded her prone body. Stray zombies tried to get at them due to the fighting line breaking down. Calum dealt with them easily and protected both Ina and the refinery.

Innes, Robert, Kenny, and Angus were being beaten back by zombie Ian and zombie Dave. "You are so not fucking getting another member of my family you fucking manky bastards," Fiona hollered, as like a whirling dervish as she brought her baseball bat down so hard on zombie Ian's head that both his head, and her baseball bat broke in a stramash of wood and brains. Zombie Dave paused just long enough for Innes to recover some strength; he swung his crowbar to connect perfectly with Dave's temple. Dave went down, finally finished.

Dennis looked round at the battlefield. The refinery refugees were clearly winning. The zombie army had dwindled dramatically. The remaining zombies were being picked off easily. Dennis scanned the battlefield and broke into a wild, joyful laughter. He started to dance and sing, "*We beat the manky cunts. We beat the manky cunts.*" Dennis didn't notice the last remaining zombie lurch towards him. Joe did, "DENNIS," he shouted at the top of his voice, just as the zombie pounced. The zombie clamped its teeth around his throat. Dennis gargled a muted scream as his blood flooded into his thorax.

Christine screamed, "NOOOOO." as she sprinted towards the zombie chewing her little brothers throat. With a mighty swing she nearly took the zombies' head clean off.

The fighting was over, the last zombie had been killed. No one cheered. The only noise was the sound of Joe wailing his pain. Joe had dropped to his knees as his son had been taken. Barbara stood breathing heavily and weaving, her brain refused to accept what was happening. Barbara fainted. Innes ran to help her, he held her tight. Panting, the other fighters watched on transfixed, frozen.

Though tears blurred her vision, Christine never took her gaze off her brother. She knew what was about to happen. Christine stumbled back as Dennis started to twitch. His face turned pale and grey, and its eye's flicked open to reveal the grey eyes of a zombie. Zombie Dennis growled as it rose.

"YOU'RE NOT TAKING MY WEE FUCKING BROTHER," Christine bellowed as she swung her weapon to connect perfectly with zombie Dennis's head. Christine dropped her weapon as the now lifeless zombie corpse of her brother fell.

Fiona sprinted to her and held her upright and close, as Christine cried hysterically into her shoulder. Fiona cried with her, and finally mourned the passing of her own family. "That was probably the bravest thing I have ever seen, Christine. You did what you had to do." Fiona managed to say through her pain. Christine wrapped her arms round Fiona and held on tight.

Robert sat with Joe and rubbed his back, there was nothing he could do or say, and he knew it.

Lennie motioned to Angus and Kenny to step away. They wandered round to the front of the refinery and stared down the hill towards Greenock town, which still burned in the night.

"So what now," a subdued Angus asked. "What do we do? Where do we go now?"

A tremor ran through Lennie's body as it reminded him he was currently on the road heading directly towards withdrawal city. He wiped his streaming nose and thought about Angus's question. "They say that the answer is blowing in the wind, my friend." Lennie licked his finger and held it up, a breeze blowing in the direction of the refinery gave Lennie his answer. "I reckon we stay here," he said pointing his moist finger at the refinery.

Angus managed a short laugh, "You are fucking mad, Lennie Wilson."

"Aye, but you're still going to follow him, Gaff." Kenny said as he looked round the battlefield at the survivors slowly making their way off the car park, and into the safety of the successfully protected refinery. Stella carried the body of Dennis.

Angus stared at his burning town, nodded, and turned back to see what he could do for those in need. Lennie and Kenny followed.

Chapter 32

The sun rose, and brought light to a new day. Dark plumes of rolling clouds rode in from the sea on a rising wind. The fickle Scottish weather was reverting to type after the recent spate of clear, dry, warm conditions. Long grasses and reeds surrounding the refinery swayed in the burgeoning wind as the small mammal population avoided the area completely. An overpowering stench of zombie death hung in the air.

Inside the refinery Calum sat facing the radio as he intently searched, once more, for something other than static. Calum had not been able to sleep, and had decided to search the radio for something, anything that would help explain the rapid descent into chaos that had occurred in Greenock. He couldn't believe that a zombie apocalypse was producing precisely zero communications from anyone, anywhere.

Flicking back to FM he started systematically turning the dial slowly once again, from left to right. Static, static, static. Then something buzzed, and a faint voice surfaced from the electric noise. It was garbled and weak, but it was indubitably a human voice. Making minute movements of the dial Calum sought greater clarity, but the voice vanished. Turning up the volume Calum filled the empty gatehouse with the sound of radio fuzz, he had switched off the speakers to the wider refinery so the others, resting in the offices, wouldn't be disturbed.

A voice crackled tantalisingly out of the speakers again, Calum strained his ears. With the increased volume level he could make out fractionally more content. Calum distinctly heard the words "zombie," and "Glasgow." And even though the quality of the transmission was awful, you could clearly hear terror in the voice of the person broadcasting as he described what he had obviously just witnessed.

Calum tried hard to hear more but he had heard all he was going to. He decided what he had heard was clear enough and that he should probably go tell someone, he decided to seek out Lennie.

Lennie was lying awake in a darkened office listening to Angus and Kenny snore and babble in their sleep. Calum quietly opened the door a crack and poked his head in, "Lennie, you awake?" he whispered.

Lennie's nerves were jangling, Calum's muted, urgent attempt to grab his attention caused him to jerk fully upright. A little too loudly Lennie barked, "Aye. What's up?"

Angus and Kenny surfaced into relative consciousness.

"I've just picked up something from the radio." Calum stepped into the office and closed the door. "I couldnae hear much. But I heard enough to know that the zombies have hit Glasgow."

"That's pretty much the whole of Scotland fucked then. There's no one will stop them now." Lennie's limbs were aching, but he struggled to his feet.

"I dunno, I reckon the Possil boys could give them a run for their money," Angus said yawning. Angus's first thought was about his drug habit. There were no drugs left and his immediate vicinity was now presumably devoid of drug dealers. Angus then remembered how he felt as he watched Stella carry the brutalised corpse of Dennis into the refinery. "Has anyone checked on Joe and his family?" he asked. Thinking about others was new to Angus, he liked it. He vowed to himself do it more often.

Kenny stretched and stood up. "I'll go check on Joe. I'll see youse back in the canteen eh?"

"Aye, that sounds like a plan," Lennie said. "I'm gonnie head down there now," he looked at Angus and Calum. "Youse two coming?"

"You go. I'm gonnie go check on Ina," Calum said.

Kenny knew where he would find Joe and his family, so he parted ways with Lennie and Angus as they trudged off to the canteen. Kenny headed down the other corridor to the loading bays.

Innes and Robert had heard the voices, they popped out of their office to see what was happening. "The zombies have hit Glasgow," Calum told them as he walked past. "Lennie and Angus are heading to the canteen. Kenny's going to see if Joe and his family are alright."

"Cheers Calum. 'Mon Vanie, lets head to the canteen," Innes stretched out his aching limbs.

Robert grabbed the remains of their purloined alcohol, and they both followed Lennie and Angus towards the canteen.

Ina was up and had the office light on when Calum knocked at the door. "Och, don't be bothering to knock," she shouted through the glass window of the office at Calum as he knocked.

Sheepishly he entered the office. "How're you feeling Ina? How's your head?"

Livid, blue bruising had established itself firmly around Ina's badly bloodshot eyes, and her nose was a broken mess. "I've felt better son, I'll admit that." Pushing her hands into the small of her back, Ina leant back with pain etched clearly on her face. "I need to remind myself I'm sixty-five, and start acting my age I reckon."

"You were brilliant last night Ina," Calum's voiced oozed reverence. "We'd all be dead if it wasn't for you."

"I'm paying for it now son. But there was more than just me out there, you know. You were brilliant too, Calum. And I reckon I would be dead too if it wasn't for you. Thank you for helping me, son. There were a lot of brave people out there last night." Ina sighed, one of their number didn't make it, and that hurt her worse that her broken nose. "How's Barbara and her family?"

"Kenny's gone to see them now. The rest are heading for the canteen. It sounds like Glasgow has gone."

"Oh my lord. The whole country is in trouble then. It'll take more than a bunch of people with industrial tools to beat that lot." Ina tried to ease her back out with one last stretch. "Canteen sounds like an excellent idea. I could murder a cuppa." Ina held onto Calum's arm. "Let's go."

Kenny gently pushed his way through the opaque plastic curtains, and crept quietly into the loading bay. Dennis's body lay covered on the desk Kenny had sat at a lifetime ago, the pictures of the naked ladies had been removed. Joe sat upright and solid in a chair beside his son. His eyes were red, it didn't look like he had slept. Barbara and Christine were asleep on a makeshift bed, fashioned out of spare protective clothing, spread on a wooden pallet. Fiona sat on the floor beside the pallet quietly dosing. She hadn't left Christine's side since she had put her brother out of his misery.

Joe looked up as Kenny pushed his way into the loading bay, Fiona opened her eyes and closed them again once she registered there was no threat.

"You alright, Joe?" Kenny asked softly. He knew it was a stupid thing to say, but he also knew there was really nothing he could say that would make things any better for him.

Joe stared at Kenny for a few seconds. He brought his mind back from the pit of pain it was consumed with. Joe breathed heavily, he knew it was pointless trying to answer Kenny's question, but he also knew Kenny didn't really expect an answer. "We're going to bury him later." Practical detail seemed to be the safest place for him to be. Joe looked at the covered body of his son. "We're going to bury him up in the hills, under a tree probably."

Barbara woke up and, without uttering a word, tears resumed streaming down her puffy face. Christine woke up and held her mother, stroking her hair and mumbling soft words. Fiona watched and kept her distance.

"Morning all," Kenny averted his eyes from them all, and also sought safety in practical. "We're all meeting in the canteen if you want to come get something to eat. If not I'll bring something round to you all later."

"Cheers Kenny. I'll pop round in a bit," Joe said.

Kenny bowed out and trod slowly round to the canteen.

As Ina and Calum sauntered into the canteen, those that were present stopped what they were doing, stood up, and clapped. Robert tried to start an, *Ina, Ina, Ina*, chant but it wasn't really picked up by the others. Ina brushed off their admiration and requested a cup of tea. After helping her to a seat, Calum went to help Stella with breakfast.

When Kenny arrived in the canteen he was probed with questions regarding the wellbeing of the Dunlops. Stella provided Calum with platters of slice rolls, toast, and fried potato scones to distribute to the tables. Angus sat with Innes and Robert and helped them reduce their alcohol haul, he figured drink would take the edge off his cravings for opiates. Kenny joined them but refused the booze offered.

With his shoulders back and his head held proud, Joe strode into the canteen and announced, "We're going to bury my Dennis up the hill somewhere. You're all welcome to come, but we understand if you don't want to, or don't feel up to it." With his task completed Joe turned round to return to the loading bay.

"Joe Dunlop," Stella shouted. "Sit and have something to eat and a cup of tea." Stella looked to Calum. "We'll take something round to the others. We're a team now Joe. Sit." Stella's tone brooked no argument.

Joe did as he was instructed. Stella sent Calum round to the loading bay with breakfast for the others.

Fluffy was content to put up with the occasional judder that shook Lennie's body as she lay curled up in his lap.

Relishing the replenishing qualities of her tea, Ina sat back and looked at Lennie, "What's the plans then, Lennie?" she asked loudly as she munched on a slice of toast.

The question looked like it had pulled Lennie back from some distant land. Lennie was avoiding food, but was enjoying a hot sweet tea. "I reckon we need to sit tight here for a bit. But we'll need to clear away them bodies out there. Any ideas where we could dump them?" Lennie looked round the room, particularly at those that used to work in the refinery.

"We could empty the clarification tanks and dump them in there. It's going to be proper smelly round here though, Lennie?" Innes piped up.

"There's some here that need a few days rest to recover, Inny." Lennie was aware he would need at least 5 days to be past the worst of his withdrawal symptoms, Ina looked beaten and tired, and he had no idea how long Joe, and his family would need. Lennie knew that moving now was not an option. "I reckon we'll just need to put up with the smell for the moment, until we can think of somewhere better to go. We'll dump the bodies in the furthest away tank."

Innes looked at Joe. "Joe. Me and Kenny will get a couple of shovels and we'll come with you, send off your boy." The rest of the room let Joe know they would all be coming to bury Dennis.

Joe nodded.

In silence they finished their breakfast and followed Joe out of the canteen round to the loading bays.

Ina, Stella, Calum, Lennie, Angus, and Robert filed quietly into the loading bay as Kenny and Innes continued on down the corridor to the storeroom for shovels.

When Kenny and Innes returned to the loading bay, Barbara, Christine and Joe were standing in a row beside the still covered remains of Dennis. Fiona stood on her own, as close to the Dunlops as she could respectfully be. The rest were standing in a row behind Fiona, their heads bowed in silence. Kenny and Innes stood in the doorway of the loading bay with shovels slung over each shoulder.

Joe noted that all were present. The time had come to bury his son. With great dignity he lifted the remains of his son and turned to the crowd standing quietly behind him. "Let's go," was all he said.

Fiona went over to the outside doors and pressed the same button Joe had pressed just a few hours ago. The shutter rose presenting them with an obscene scene of zombie death.

Kenny threw a shovel to Angus, strode out, and started to shovel dead zombies out of the way. Angus joined him. Innes presented a shovel to Robert, and they too joined in to clear a path to the front gate.

Fiona thought about the security of the refinery. "Stella, wait behind with me will you? We'll close this door and go join them round the side. I'll need you to lock the gatehouse," she said. Lennie stayed behind with Stella and Fiona; he grabbed a handful of spare weapons; he had also thought about security. "Just in case," he said to Stella.

Kenny, Angus, Robert, and Innes waited at the front gate for Joe, Barbara, Christine, Ina, and Calum to pass, they followed them in pairs. Lennie, Stella, and Fiona caught up. Fiona took some weapons and, keeping one for herself, she distributed a couple silently to Ina and Calum.

Angus spoke quietly to Kenny on the way to the burial. "We'll need to go on a drug hunt when we get back Kenny. I'm rattling," he whispered. "We'll hit a few of the houses in the Homerton, see what we can come up with from the medicine cabinets."

"What if there's a whole bunch of zombies?" Kenny asked hoping Angus had already thought about this. Kenny was also keen to source some kind of substances to keep his withdrawals at bay.

"We'll run like fuck and get Ina," Angus laughed quietly.

"That's a plan then, Gaff," Kenny smiled.

Lennie and Stella walked behind them. "Can I ask you something, Stella," he asked.

"Fire away," she replied.

"You've never told me your second name?"

Stella thought about it. "Do you know what Lennie. I don't think I really want a second name. I reckon from now on in I'm just going to be Stella. I think that's good enough for me."

Joe skirted loch Mintern and branched off to head away from the Homerton. A lone Oak tree stood halfway up, near loch Brimmington. He stopped and placed Dennis gently on the ground.

Angus wasn't looking particularly well anyway, so he relinquished his shovel to Joe without a word. Joe started to dig. Kenny, Innes, and Robert joined him. Apart from Barbara and Ina everyone took turns and helped out. Joe never stopped digging until Dennis had a deep hole to dwell in safely for his eternity. Joe led the others out of the grave once it was ready. He dropped his shovel and sought out his wife and daughter. They embraced. Tears flowed from everyone. Joe picked up his son, laid him in his final resting place, then slowly started to cover him with earth. As with the digging he was assisted by the others.

The grave was quickly filled, then they all stood back. Joe looked up and around, his voice thin and croaky he asked, "Has anyone got any words?"

"As I'm the oldest, I guess it really should be me that says something," Ina walked to stand beside Joe at the foot of Dennis's makeshift grave. "Fourteen years is far too young to lose your life," Ina looked directly at where Dennis lay. Barbara's sobbing was, by this point, unrestrained. "And in your final days you saw and did things no fourteen-year-old boy should ever be confronted with. But I watched you fight, Dennis, I watched you fight for your life, and I watched you fight for your family. You were brave beyond compare Dennis." Ina looked up to catch Christine's eye, "And in your death your sister, with great courage, gave you dignity." Standing beside her

Fiona held Christine tight to prevent her from collapsing from the weight of her grief.

Ina looked round the rest of the grim looking faces, "By all rights people, we should all be in there with Dennis. We had no right to achieve what we did last night. We achieved it because we fought for each other." Ina looked at Fiona. "We will all have lost people we love last night. And many, many more will die before all this is over, if it ever is. But we should and will continue to fight, we'll fight for ourselves, and we'll fight to preserve, and honour the memories of those that have lost their lives." Ina breathed deeply. She looked back at where Dennis lay, "I salute and respect you for fighting, and giving your life for us Dennis. Thank you." Ina walked away with tears streaming down her face.

Kenny walked past the grave, stopped, stood, and looked at where Dennis lay. "Thank you Dennis," he said, then followed after Ina to help her back to the refinery.

One after another they followed suit, and thanked Dennis for their lives.

Joe, Barbara, and Christine just stood. After Fiona thanked Dennis, she stood away from the grave with a spanner in her hand and waited until the Dunlops had said their private farewells. Fiona walked behind them when they finally were ready to return to the refinery.

As they were walking back the storm that was threatening finally made good its promise. The sky opened up and a torrent of rain washed over them.

Lennie looked up at the rain pelting his face, it felt good. "At least it will put the fires out," he said.

"And wash away the blood," Stella replied.

Down in the valley the Clyde meandered it's way peacefully out to sea. Further down the coast, in the ravaged town of Largs, a zombie stepped out from the beach and into the Clyde estuary. Nearby zombies noticed and followed suit. Soon a whole hoard of hungry zombies sludged silently into the Firth of Clyde, only to resurface who knows where. Zombies have no need to breathe.

And thus began the beginning of the end.......

Epilogue

"Natty, I cannie eat another fucking Mars Bar," Mark Hickey looked sick as he tried to remove the sticky chocolate from the roof of his mouth. Mark took another long drink from a bottle of water and threw yet another empty Mars Bar wrapper onto the mountain piled in the middle of the dressing room floor.

Natty St Louis, and his Queens Park strike partner, had changed out of their football kits and into civilian clothes as soon as a relative peace had descended outside their dressing room.

Natty looked at his watch, they had been locked in the dressing room for over twenty-four hours now. Natty loved a Mars Bar, but even he was sick of the sight of them now, Natty hungered for real food. He stood and swaggered over to the door. "Time tuh lef, ya so."

Natty's obstinate refusal to ensure his communications were understood, even in a crisis, had resulted in a rudimentary increase in Mark's understanding of Patois. He ambled over to join Natty by the door, Mark was also desperate for something other than a Mars Bar to eat. "Do you reckon they're still out there on the pitch?"

"Di duppy, dem? Mi no care, fi be honest." Natty looked like he was ready to venture out. He looked round the dressing room for something he could use as a weapon, there was nothing. Natty was not about to leave the safety of his dressing room without something he could do some damage with. He started to assault the dressing room benches, kicking and wrenching at the wooden legs.

"What the fuck are you doing Natty?" Mark was worried his friend had lost his marbles.

"Mi naah guh out there widout a weapon, Mark." Natty succeeded in wrenching a couple of the legs from the bench. He handed one to Mark.

With his decision made, Natty didn't hesitate. Flinging the door wide open he stepped out into the tunnel. After he saw that Natty wasn't jumped on by a duppy, Mark hesitantly followed.

Mark followed Natty out of the tunnel and onto the edge of the football pitch. "Fuck...." Mark said as they surveyed the carnage left by the duppies in the stadium. There were detached limbs, heads, and ripped open torso's lying about everywhere breeding flies. They could make out Queens Park strips covered in blood. These were their friends.

It had clearly rained heavily while they were in the dressing room, which had washed away the worst of the gore, but the human remains strewn around the stadium disturbed them immensely.

"Let wi get outta here," Natty said grimly.

Mark didn't struggle to understand the intent behind his words.

Neither Mark nor Natty knew Greenock well, so they just followed the track of the river downstream. The streets were deserted.

As they got closer to the town centre they saw a figure swaying around in an ungainly manner. The creature sensed, or smelt them, as it turned round they noticed a Naan bread hanging from one of its ears. The duppy growled, and sprinted towards Natty and Mark.

Acknowledgements

Thanks to the real Natty St Louis, both for the use of his name, and for his assistance with Jamaican Patois.

Thank to my uncle Dougie for providing me with inspiration, humour, and stories.

Thanks of course to my mum and dad, I like being Scottish (and an extra special thanks to my mum for being my editor).

As previously stated, the characters in this book are fictional, all except Naan Bread man, though his thoughts on race relations are, to me, unknown. The real Naan Bread man is probably dead by now. Thanks to my uncle Dougie for introducing me to him.

The only real names I borrowed are, John Howie (my uncle), Natty St Louis, Dave Anderson, and I borrowed the Dunlops from my Aunt Janette, though these characters are still fictional. Natty was never a semi-professional football player, but he does like a Mars Bar. I made Dave a bigot, as I knew it would please the real Dave. All other names are made up, though I'm sure it won't stop speculation in Greenock circles, if anyone there ends up reading this.

Those in the know will also be very much aware that I have taken a lot of liberties regarding the geography of Greenock, the estates are fictional. And there is no water refinery in Greenock.

Thanks of course to my family who supported me throughout.

I'd like to thank Steve Jones (guitarist from The Sex Pistols). I read his autobiography, Lonely Boy, a few of years ago. In it he talks about how he is happier when he is involved in some kind of creative process. This statement struck a chord with me (pardon the pun). I relate to what he is saying, it spurred me on to start creating something again, this was why I started to write again.

Thanks Covid -19 for giving me the time and space to devote to writing. And thanks to Morag for kicking my arse to start writing again when I had stopped.

Thank you to anyone who has ever written a zombie book. I've probably read it and you have all inspired me.

Printed in Great Britain
by Amazon